SONS OF THE HYDRA

More Chaos Space Marines from Black Library

SHROUD OF NIGHT
by Andy Clark

• FABIUS BILE •
by Josh Reynolds
BOOK 1 – PRIMOGENITOR
BOOK 2 – CLONELORD

• BLACK LEGION •
by Aaron Dembski-Bowden
BOOK 1 – THE TALON OF HORUS
BOOK 2 – BLACK LEGION

• AHRIMAN •
by John French
BOOK 1 – AHRIMAN: EXILE
BOOK 2 – AHRIMAN: SORCERER
BOOK 3 – AHRIMAN: UNCHANGED

NIGHT LORDS: THE OMNIBUS
by Aaron Dembski-Bowden
(Contains the novels *Soul Hunter*, *Blood Reaver* and *Void Stalker*)

KHÂRN: THE RED PATH
by Chris Dows

WORD BEARERS: THE OMNIBUS
by Anthony Reynolds
(Contains the novels *Dark Apostle*, *Dark Disciple* and *Dark Creed*)

STORM OF IRON
An Iron Warriors novel by Graham McNeill

SPACE MARINE BATTLES: THE SIEGE OF CASTELLAX
An Iron Warriors novel by C L Werner

PERFECTION
An Emperor's Children audio drama by Nick Kyme

CHOSEN OF KHORNE
A World Eaters audio drama by Anthony Reynolds

SONS OF THE HYDRA

AN ALPHA LEGION NOVEL

ROB SANDERS

BLACK LIBRARY

A BLACK LIBRARY PUBLICATION

First published in 2018.
This edition published in Great Britain in 2018 by
Black Library,
Games Workshop Ltd.,
Willow Road,
Nottingham, NG7 2WS, UK.

10 9 8 7 6 5 4 3 2 1

Produced by Games Workshop in Nottingham.
Cover illustration by Johan Grenier.

A CIP record for this book is available from the British Library.

ISBN 13: 978-1-78496-731-4

See Black Library on the internet at

blacklibrary.com

Find out more about Games Workshop
and the world of Warhammer 40,000 at

games-workshop.com

Printed and bound by CPI Group (UK) Ltd, Croydon, CR0 4YY

It is the 41st millennium. For more than a hundred centuries the Emperor has sat immobile on the Golden Throne of Earth. He is the Master of Mankind by the will of the gods, and master of a million worlds by the might of His inexhaustible armies. He is a rotting carcass writhing invisibly with power from the Dark Age of Technology. He is the Carrion Lord of the Imperium for whom a thousand souls are sacrificed every day, so that He may never truly die.

Yet even in His deathless state, the Emperor continues His eternal vigilance. Mighty battlefleets cross the daemon-infested miasma of the warp, the only route between distant stars, their way lit by the Astronomican, the psychic manifestation of the Emperor's will. Vast armies give battle in His name on uncounted worlds. Greatest amongst His soldiers are the Adeptus Astartes, the Space Marines, bioengineered super-warriors. Their comrades in arms are legion: the Astra Militarum and countless planetary defence forces, the ever-vigilant Inquisition and the tech-priests of the Adeptus Mechanicus to name only a few. But for all their multitudes, they are barely enough to hold off the ever-present threat from aliens, heretics, mutants — and worse.

To be a man in such times is to be one amongst untold billions. It is to live in the cruellest and most bloody regime imaginable. These are the tales of those times. Forget the power of technology and science, for so much has been forgotten, never to be re-learned. Forget the promise of progress and understanding, for in the grim dark future there is only war. There is no peace amongst the stars, only an eternity of carnage and slaughter, and the laughter of thirsting gods.

Have you ever watched a serpent cross the burning sands? Watched one slither beneath the surface of the sea? They are creatures of lethal beauty. They move with a confident economy, caution and grace.

Of our path, I can only say this. We are the serpent that slides and winds, appearing to head this way and then that, all the while our movement taking us ever forward. While our brothers have fallen wholesale to stagnation and damnation, we have retained our identity and purpose.

▮▮▮▮▮ *Outsiders struggle to comprehend our motives. To the princes primordial we are allies uncertain. We are unmoved by the living lies of the xenos. To the ailing Imperium, with its myriad afflictions, we are both poison and antidote.*

We suffer them all, as they suffer us. redacted redacted redacted redacted *It is the way of our Legion. The way we have made it. The way it has to be. For we are the most necessary of evils and the destinies we craft for others, as well as our own, cannot be denied.* ▮▮▮▮▮▮▮▮

████████████████████████████████

████████████ '

– credited Alpharius Omegon,
Primarch of the XX Legion,
at ████████████
(circ. 9██123.M██)

PART I

'FOR THE EMPEROR!'

α

THE SERPENT'S EGG

'Initiate burn.'

The machine-spirit of the Dreadclaw *Serpent's Egg* registered the command and responded, the Alpha Legion drop pod breaking away from the main swarm of cultist vessels. Armoured assault boats, hump shuttles and orbital lighters were left behind as the Dreadclaw rocketed ahead of the flotilla of adapted boarding craft.

While the Dreadclaw streaked silently across the void, the roar of the ancient rocket engines could be felt through the pod's reinforced superstructure, through the troop compartment, the floor hatch and the descent cradles. Caged in one of these and surrounded by heavy-duty pneumatics, gravitic dampeners and inertials, was Lord Occam. Occam of the Alpha Legion. Occam the Untrue. Strike master and leader of the warband known as 'the Redacted'.

'Aft pictcaster,' Occam ordered, his voice a cold-blooded hiss. He could hear the evenness of his breathing feeding back across the vox of his serpent-head helm, along with that of his five power-plated companions.

Again, the craft's machine-spirit complied, with almost reptilian indifference. The runescreen mounted in front of Occam's command cradle sizzled before crystallising into a pict-feed of the craft left behind by the Dreadclaw's acceleration. He surveyed the scene with the confidence of a master tactician, the overlays of his plate optics flushed with identica and estimates of velocity and distance.

While the Dreadclaw carried the Redacted within its pitted, viridian hull, the freight compartments of the trailing cultships were packed with members of the Seventh Sons. Each a mask-wearing death cultist, the Seventh Sons and their disciples were devoted killers to a man. They were feverishly loyal to Occam the Untrue and his small band of merciless traitors. Faithful to the archenemy Alpha Legion. Devoted to an Imperium of chaos and confusion.

'Boarding harrow on target,' the Alpha Legion strike master announced. 'Cycle hull casters.'

One by one the hull exterior pictcasters gave Occam a three-hundred-and-sixty-degree view of the hazy void and the Absinthia system beyond. Half the void was dominated by the sunburst smear of the Maelstrom. The distant warp storm raged on in silence.

Within the Absinthia system itself, sun-hugging gas giants and rocky outliers were just visible through the dust. Planets, shattered by ancient, apocalyptic wars against long-dead xenos races, orbited their system star in crumbling stability. These dead worlds were crowded with a blizzard of haulage brigs and the baroque platforia of orbital mining operations. Their exposed, ore-rich cores were plundered by chartered hordes of environment-suited guild slaves. Also in wide orbit around the Absinthia star were system defence platforms and small void forts. With a small flotilla of system ships, patrolling monitors and adamanticlads, they provided security for the mining worlds and protection from the corsairs and pirates that prowled the sub-sectors bordering the warp storm. This proved hardly necessary, however, since the capital world of the Absinthia system, Vitrea Mundi, was the Adeptus Astartes home world of the Marines Mordant.

'Forward casters,' Occam said.

Ahead of the *Serpent's Egg* was Vitrea Mundi itself: a large, bleak planet of smoky white. The mining world had been home to the Ultramarines successor Chapter for six thousand years. The planet's landscape was dominated by giant salt crystals and systems of soda lakes. Amongst the scarring of open-cast craters, Vitrea Mundi boasted but one city. Visible from orbit, Salina City was settled like a dark polar smudge about the mighty 'Bas-Silica' – the fortress-monastery of the Marines Mordant.

High above the planet, Occam could see the wreck of the battle-barge *Assiduous*, freshly returned from coreward sectors where the Marines Mordant had lost two companies of battle-brothers to Hive Fleet Leviathan. Acid-splashed and battle-damaged, the venerable vessel had barely made it back to Vitrea Mundi. Caged in orbital scaffolding and surrounded by Adeptus Mechanicus forge tenders, the battle-barge was undergoing extensive repairs. It was here that the target of the Redacted lay.

In truth, the Redacted were but one of a number of Alpha Legion warbands operating within the Absinthia system. Like Occam's small band of renegades, they were gathered under the banner of Quetzel Carthach – Angelbane,

Master of Harrows and Arch-Lord of the Alpha Legion. The disparate warbands had come together under his leadership like a pack of opportunistic death world predators. While retaining their own character, leaders and motivations, the warbands joined Carthach and his own – the Sons of the Hydra – for mutual dark glory. Together, under the banner of the Sons of the Hydra, the Alpha Legion cells had secured victories that could not be achieved alone. Like the one they were currently trying to secure against the Marines Mordant.

'Scrambling augur returns,' Occam said, flicking switches. Addressing the machine-spirit of the *Serpent's Egg* once more, the strike master told it, 'Cut thrust and roll to port.'

Mina Perdita made her way through the cargo compartment of the bulk lighter. Instead of pallets of freight to be shuttled between sprint traders and a planetary surface, the craft was crammed with cultists. Recruited and liberated from the penal colonies of Korsino 421, where the Alpha Legion had already ensured that serpent cults, death cults and ritual sacrifice held sway, the Seventh Sons were devoted to the murderous needs of their legionary saviours. Dressed in dusty robes, scraps of armour and gorgonesque masks, the Sons still wore their explosive penitentiary collars about their necks. Decorated in the form of serpents, the collars were the ultimate sign of subservient loyalty to their Legion masters.

The cultists and their disciples stood in unwavering discipline, waiting for the signal to unleash their talents. They held their venom-slick blades and needle pistols close to their bodies, however, and moved aside for Mina Perdita. The Seventh Sons were ritual killers and serpent cultists to a man, but all respected the art of death as it was represented in Perdita's hallowed flesh. She came from the clandestine temples of the Officio Assassinorum.

Dressed like a Seventh Son, she carried a cult mask as she passed through the crowd. Her face was already not her own, however, the effects of polymorphine adapting her surgically modified flesh to become a living lie. One day she might be female, and the next, male. Dark-skinned and then light. Her face could assume the broken brutality of a hive world ganger or the clean patrician lines of spire nobility. She was everyone and no one.

Such was the Assassin's devotion to her calling that few could even remember – including Perdita – whether she had originally been man or woman. While retaining the name and pronoun, she was just at home in the semblance of one as the other. Sometimes, for perversity's sake, she made it deliberately difficult for others to tell.

Regardless of her lethal abilities and gift for deception, Mina Perdita knew that the criminals and cultists wouldn't lay a finger on her. For like the High Serpent – the leader of their death cult – Mina Perdita answered directly to Lord Occam. She was an agent and operative for their demigod overlords, and as such had the ear of the dread warriors of the Legion.

Pulling herself up the ladderwell with gymnastic ease, Perdita found herself in the cramped cockpit of the lighter. While a Seventh Son sat in the pilot's seat, the High Serpent lounged at the co-pilot's station. Portly and sporting a top-knot that draped down the back of his shaved head, the High Serpent had thrown his own mask casually upon the station console. Perdita grunted before allowing the flesh of her face to tremble and spasm into the semblance of one of the High Serpent's trusted disciples.

Freydor Blatch – leader of the Seventh Sons – did not look like the head of a death cult. Unlike his followers, Blatch lacked the physical prowess and sharp reflexes of a killer. The only sharp feature he boasted was his tongue and the wit that proceeded from his thin lips. His ears jangled with hoops and cult icons, while his chubby arms were entwined in serpentine bracelets. He had even had the rolls of belly fat protruding from his cult robes tattooed to appear like the coils of a great snake. Sitting at the station and staring out into the dust-stained void, the High Serpent looked positively bored.

'Perdita,' Blatch acknowledged, spinning lazily around in the co-pilot's chair and giving the disciple a casual look. 'Glad you could join us. The show is about to begin.'

The Assassin didn't bother to change, keeping the thick-necked appearance of the disciple. Perdita was unsurprised that Blatch had recognised her. Polymorphine, syn-skin and the practised skills of an actress were enough to fool most people. They were not nearly enough to fool Blatch, however, who had long been in the business of deceiving others. Most of the time the High Serpent recognised her, but even he had his blind spots.

A consummate charlatan, Freydor Blatch had made it his life's work to move between the ranks of the Ecclesiarchy and the cultish groups of heretics festering in the underbelly of various cardinal worlds. Perdita had heard that Blatch had grown up on Laurentia Secundus, a Schola Progenium prodigy. A wastrel, too impressed with himself to settle for the life his drill-abbots had planned for him, Blatch had moved about the Ecclesiarchical planets of the

Crozier Worlds like interstellar flotsam. Assuming the guise of pontiffs and cult figureheads with fraudulent ease, Blatch had garnered wealth and influence. That was before coming to the attention of the Alpha Legion and accepting an offer from Occam the Untrue that he could not afford to refuse.

Mina Perdita could neither have accepted nor refused such an offer. Her temple training and brutal Officio Assassinorum indoctrination made choice an illusion. The Holy Ordos of the Inquisition had despatched her to infiltrate the Sons of the Hydra and assassinate Quetzel Carthach, Arch-Lord of the Alpha Legion. She had failed, and death would have awaited her if it hadn't been for the intervention of Lord Occam.

Disguising her failure as that of another, Occam took her as his prisoner. Too valuable a tool to be allowed to rot in a cell, he broke her. He shattered Mina Perdita and reassembled what was left into something both lethal and loyal. Now she was his. Keeping knowledge of Perdita's infiltration and intended assassination from Carthach himself, Occam the Untrue engaged her lethal talents for the Redacted. And so, that was how a trained killer and a professional con artist came to work for the renegade Space Marines of the Alpha Legion.

'Aren't you watching it?' Blatch said to the pilot, getting out of his seat to slap the cultist across the back of his shaved head.

Perdita narrowed her eyes and peered through the cockpit canopy. The Dreadclaw drop pod carrying her masters had streaked off before shutting down its thrusters. Like a warped and blossoming flower, the rolling pod opened its landing claws, beneath which lurked the venomous threat of Alpha Legion infiltrators.

Blatch leant forward and depressed a vox stud on the co-pilot console, encoding an open channel: 'All craft – cut thrust.'

Like the Dreadclaw, the flotilla of cultist boarding craft killed their engines and drifted with inertial grace towards the *Assiduous*. The Assassin felt the deceleration through the deck and reached up to steady herself against the low ceiling of the cockpit. She watched the *Serpent's Egg* hurtle towards the Adeptus Astartes flagship, the battle-scarred behemoth seeming to grow before the silent advance of the lone pod. The launch bay of the battle-barge's hammerhead prow section gaped open before the spinning Dreadclaw, like the mouth of some great beast of the void.

Perdita looked between Freydor Blatch and the Seventh Son co-pilot.

'Scramblers?' she said, her adopted voice deep.

'Scramble augur returns,' Blatch blurted across the open channel, attempting to hide the fact that he had forgotten. 'All craft – engage scramblers.'

Minutes passed in heart-thumping silence as the cultist flotilla followed the *Serpent's Egg* in on its clandestine approach. Despite the acid burns running along its flank and scaffolded sections bearing bite damage caused by something like a colossal beak, the capital ship was an imposing sight. Perdita could see macrocannons, fusion beamers and hull-mounted plasma projectors, the monstrous barrels of which were all aimed forward at the approaching flotilla. With such weaponry, it would take nothing for such a craft to wipe the Redacted clean from the face of the void.

'Brothers,' Perdita heard the High Serpent say across the open channel, his voice echoing through the cargo holds of bulk lighters, modified haulage brigs, hump shuttles and assault boats. 'Serpents. Seventh Sons all. We make our final approach – our mighty lords, as they do in all things, leading the way. The Emperor's servants hide within the thick hulls of their battleships and behind the towering walls of their fortresses. In doing so, they prove themselves unworthy of Him. As the Master of Mankind sacrificed himself for humanity's continued survival, so we sacrifice the weak upon the altar of his efforts. For the Imperium deserves only the strong. The enduring of flesh. The certain of mind. Those resolved in body and spirit to do what must be done – no matter the cost – to realise the Emperor's true and manifest destiny...'

As the Dreadclaw sizzled through the atmospheric screens of the launch bay, the flotilla drifting in behind, its presence hidden from augur arrays and unnoticed by Adeptus Mechanicus constructs hard at work on exterior repairs, Blatch released the vox stud. 'Etcetera, etcetera...'

β

SPITTING VENOM

Occam the Untrue knew the *Assiduous* to have a glorious tradition of victory. It had fought broadside to broadside against the Despoiler-class battleship *Sacrilegionary* on the edge of the Maelstrom, destroying the Chaos flagship – long lost to Slaaneshi deviance and mutiny over five thousand years before. It had rammed aside greenskin space hulks of the Octarian Empire during the Volvox Wars. It had survived the tyranid hordes and great devouring bio-ships of Hive Fleet Leviathan. Not even the successor sons of Guilliman, with their ritual and stale strategies, saw the Alpha Legion coming.

'Stand by for high-speed insertion and impact,' Occam told the legionnaires of the Redacted. He heard the creak of tightening cradle supports and straps. He felt the *Serpent's Egg* buck and wobble as the wicked tips of the pod's outstretched landing claws made contact with the battle-scarred craft waiting on the polished flight deck. Cycling through the casters, Occam watched the

21

kaleidoscopic progress of the Dreadclaw. Like a bullet entering flesh and bouncing off bone, the pod ripped and ricocheted its way through the busy launch bay. The unchecked velocity of the *Serpent's Egg* battered Thunderhawks aside, toppling the venerable craft. Orbital transporters were hooked and torn from their landing gears and cable restraints, smashing into tracked trundles of munitions and equipment. Claws pierced the hull plating of Adeptus Astartes landers and lighters. The craft were catapulted across the bay into acid-splashed Land Raiders and armoured personnel carriers, newly chained down into their transport and diagnostic positions.

Occam felt the forces tear through his genetically engineered body. After the silky absence of gravity in the void, the sensation was unpleasant. The machine-spirit of his plate registered its protestations while the Dreadclaw clunked, screeched and thundered its way through the unfolding havoc of the launch bay. The warband were thrown violently this way and that by the impacts, directional changes and brutal deceleration. The cradle inertials and the hydraulics of their plate took the worst of the punishment. Each legionnaire had been blessed with the constitution of a demigod. Slabs of muscle and the resilience of black carapace and bone absorbed forces that would have torn an ordinary man apart.

'Retract landing claws,' the strike master told the machine-spirit of the *Serpent's Egg*. Through the cracked runescreen, Occam saw sparks shower after the drop pod like the tail of a comet as it made contact with the flight deck. The troop compartment was filled with the excruciating reverberation of metal scraping against metal.

Before long, the Dreadclaw left the pandemonium of

upturned gunships, smashed tanks and scattered supplies behind. Occam's gauntlet hovered by the manual ignition of the deceleration thrusters. Ordinarily, such systems would be used for atmospheric stability and landing. Occam found, however, that bone-jolting collisions and the friction created by the bay floor were enough to bring the drop pod to a halt.

Like an egg twirling slowly on its side, the Dreadclaw came to a slow halt. As it did, the surviving pictcasters told Occam all he needed to know about the havoc he had caused outside. As planned, the approach of the *Serpent's Egg* had gone unnoticed. The Dreadclaw's landing, conversely, was a bombastic announcement. The launch bay was littered with battered attack craft bearing the colours and markings of the Marines Mordant. The Adeptus Astartes themselves, however, were nowhere to be seen. Instead, the flight deck was decorated with the broken bodies of bonded servitors and Chapter serfs. Servo-automata and winged cherubim that had been working on the gunships as part of flight deck crew drifted over the lifeless bodies.

Occam could feel the detonations of upskittled munitions and shattered landers through the hull and flight deck below. Through the remaining casters he could see that fuel from impact-breached promethium barrels had caught light and was cloaking the disordered flight deck in a black haze. Klaxons were sounding, summoning serf sections from other parts of the battle-barge. While the smashed servitors remained on the deck, waiting for the assistance of compatriot constructs – as protocol dictated – Chapter bondsmen were already getting to their feet. Clutching shattered limbs and bleeding down their flak tabards and hooded tunics, the bondsmen were resilient. Occam knew them to be devoted servants of the Chapter cult and as such they would respond swiftly to the attack. He also knew each one to be an unsuccessful Space Marine aspirant. They were living embodiments of failure and untapped potential. The Alpha Legionnaires of the Redacted would be more than a match for them.

'Prepare to open hatch,' Occam said, prompting the machine-spirit of the Dreadclaw to release the pressure seals with a clunk. At the same time, the locks of the descent cradles cleared, allowing the Alpha Legionnaires caged within to extricate themselves with economy.

Lying on its side, the drop pod was not oriented for an effective dispersal. Climbing down through the cradles, the Redacted joined Occam as he knelt on the shattered instrumentation of the drop pod wall. The legionnaires dropped to one knee with their strike master. Each was a clandestine nightmare, garbed in renegade plate and clutching weaponry that was a heretical fusion of Imperial and xenos technologies.

The six renegades waited, clad in tarnished viridian. Their ghoulish forms were airbrushed in the neon-blue radiance of their plasma guns while adapted optics burned red in their serpentine helms. A cameleoline cloak was draped across one pauldron, while the other was emblazoned with the dread symbol of the three-headed hydra. The surface of the legionnaires' stylised armour was crafted to appear like scales, each plate sizzling with the static of an advanced optical field that shimmered across the cool ceramite.

'Ready hatch, aye,' Ephron Hasdrubal said, the Alpha Legion sergeant taking position at the egress. His helm was lost in the darkness of a cameleoline hood, with only his optics visible.

'Ready, aye,' Arkan Reznor and Carcinus Quoda confirmed, flanking the sergeant, the Alpha Legion warpsmith and sorcerer waiting for the order to disembark. While both were armed with their own equipment, the pair carried squad weaponry at their strike master's insistence. At a glance, at least, the Redacted were to be one: uniform in darkness, identical in purpose and indistinguishable in the sights of the enemy from one another.

'Aye,' Vilnius Malik said behind Occam, the young legionnaire clutching his combi-plasma gun in tight to his shoulder. The hulking Autolicon Phex knelt beside him but said nothing. Quetzel Carthach had cut Phex's tongue out and had done a lot worse to the legionnaire. Phex acknowledged his strike master with a tweak of his plasma cannon's coil regulator, causing the searing hum of the heavy weapon to die away briefly and then return to intensity.

'For the Emperor,' Occam the Untrue hissed, 'who knows not what is done in his name. Positions.'

The Redacted gathered about Autolicon Phex, who jangled with grenades and spare hydrogen canisters. Occam nodded. Sergeant Hasdrubal popped the manual release on the hatch. Like a fanged mouth, sections of the hatch began to retract, revealing the launch bay beyond. The tactical displays of Occam's helm zeroed in immediately on moving targets outside the drop pod. With each glowing blink of the lenses, augur-overlays cycled briefly through different spectra – infrared filtering, ultraviolet resonance, motion sensors.

'The welcoming party,' Arkan Reznor said, selecting three small servo-automata that sat like grenades on his belt. Their serpentine skulls were gilded, while their repulsor housing was a small clinkered shell. Like a child winding up a clockwork toy, the warpsmith activated his retinue of drones designated Beta, Zeta and Theta. Hanging in the air on powerful repulsors, the servo-automata allowed a small nest of mechatendrils to uncoil and writhe with serpentine motion.

While broken-backed servitors, auxilia and bondsmen littered the launch bay, deck serfs in Chapter colours ran forward from the section blast door, thumbing bolt shells into assault shotguns. Intent on repelling the boarders, the serfs converged upon the *Serpent's Egg* and hammered the Dreadclaw's hull and opening hatch with pump-action blasts.

'Introduce us,' Occam commanded as the hatch clunked open and a bolt-round shot by his helm. With a hiss of sub-molecular conversion, Autolicon Phex unleashed a raging blast of plasma out of the Dreadclaw. Almost as broad as the hatch opening, the furious orb shot out across the flight deck like a blue sun, leaving behind a glowing trail of hydrogen. The impact was devastating. The globe of plasma would not be stopped, blazing through throngs of Chapter serfs and wiping them from existence. The robes of those nearby caught fire at the intense heat of the blast's passing and became thrashing blue infernos.

'Away,' Reznor said, allowing his servo-automata to swoop out of the hatch.

'Centrobaric formation,' Occam ordered. 'Establish position and draw them in.'

'Aye,' the Redacted returned, lowering their helms and jumping through the hatch. Dropping down to the flight deck with a flourish of their cloaks, the renegades immediately set to work driving back the closing ranks of Chapter serfs. Rapid, staccato blasts sent small orbs of plasma far across the deck with unerring accuracy. Burning straight through bondsmen in their flak and fabric, the raging balls put attackers down on the deck, turning them briefly into mounds of thrashing agony. This didn't last long.

Arkan Reznor had long had a weakness for the heretical genius of xenos technologies. Such passion was evident in the Redacted's plate and weaponry. With the core warband only numbering six legionnaires, the squad favoured hard-hitting plasma guns over the ubiquitous bolter – associated with so many of their dark brotherhood. Occam also had the warpsmith adapt the weaponry for more effective operational use. Fusing forgeworld fare pillaged from the armouries of the defeated Nova Legion, with the martial technologies of xenos breeds carving out empires on the Eastern Fringe, Reznor had managed to solve the plasma gun's propensity to overheat and increased both the weapon's range and fuel economy.

'Brother Malik,' Occam said, allowing bolts to detonate against the retracted landing claws he was using for cover. He smirked to himself behind the fanged faceplate of his serpent helm. 'Bring the night.'

The joke was specially meant for Vilnius Malik, who was not an Alpha Legionnaire by genic heritage. A restless renegade, gifted beyond his years with boltgun and blade, Malik had been a willing recruit for Night Lords operating out of the storm of the Emperor's Wrath. Gene-sired and trained in the arts of terror, Malik lived to win but had a healthy distrust of corruption. Abandoning his Night Lords brothers as they increasingly became things of twisted logic and flesh, Malik wandered the core sectors.

Lending his talents to warbands of renegade Space

Marines, like the infamous Hounds of Horus and the Slaughtersworn, he inevitably survived them all. Occam the Untrue had encountered the promising killer when the Redacted worked in a joint action with the Shadow Pact against the Vindicators at Karpathia Corona. Surviving them also, Malik accepted Occam's offer to join the Redacted and take his place amongst lost brothers searching for similar purpose.

As Sergeant Hasdrubal ran through a hail of bolts spat from assault shotguns, he gave the young legionnaire furious cover fire from his plasma gun. Vilnius Malik, who carried the scoped length of a long-shot plasma gun, took a knee and shrugged his cloak off his shoulder.

'Power distribution nexus,' Occam heard Arkan Reznor tell the former Night Lord. 'Far bay wall. It distributes power to non-essential systems in the section. Look for the heat signature.'

Malik didn't even flinch. The warpsmith knew more about the capital ship's systems than the Marines Mordant Techmarines tending to them. Lining up the advanced optics of his helm with the scope, Malik sent a succession of plasma blasts up through the middle of a charging crowd of Chapter serfs. The crackling orbs blazed into the piece of nondescript equipment that Reznor had indicated, cutting between the bondsmen with incredible accuracy and timing. The distribution nexus flashed and sparked as it overloaded. Without local power, the huge blast door separating the launch bay prow section and the thorax gun decks crashed to the floor. The bulkhead came down with a boom, cutting off the thousands of servitor gun crew and deck serfs stampeding down the length of the cannon battery sections to reinforce their cult brothers in the launch bay.

The powerful lamps lining the ceiling of the bay flickered and then died, plunging the colossal chamber into a hazy murk of smoke and starlight. Promethium fires burned in the bay and the beams of boarding craft cut through the obscurity. Occam the Untrue felt both the impact of landing gears on the flight deck and the hammering footfalls of loyal serfs charging through the darkness. The blasts of the Redacted's plasma guns lit up the bay around the Dreadclaw in ghoulish blue. The glowing orbs revealed the faces of bondsmen, fiercely loyal to their cult masters in the Marines Mordant and intent on repelling boarders.

'Save your fuel,' Occam ordered across the squad vox. 'Dissemble.'

The deck became drowned in darkness. Onwards the serfs came, their charge slowing to a twirl of confusion as they blinked at the blackness, searching for renegade Space Marines who had been there moments before.

Like the members of his warband, Occam had become one with the darkness. About him he could hear the whine of his suit, dropping to low power – all non-critical systems shutting down in readiness for snap-rebooting. His optics had blinked to blackness, while his cloak had helped to break up the outline of his armour. The scales of the heretically enhanced plate had changed colour. Like a chameleonic lizard, the suit replaced the dishonoured colours of the Alpha Legion and flushed to the dirty darkness of its surroundings. Occam enjoyed the confusion of his enemies. He was close enough to slice their throats but they could not see him.

In the murk, an Alpha Legionnaire suddenly appeared amongst the small army of Chapter serfs. Shotguns were pumped and bolts unleashed as the serfs spun around and fired at the phantasm. The hololithic representation crackled and warped as a hail of bolts passed through it. In the darkness, Occam heard the screams of serfs blown apart by bolts in the crossfire. As the ghostly legionnaire faded, the representation being projected by Beta – the servo-automata hovering above the battle – another appeared on the far flank. Fewer serfs fell for Zeta's deception and even fewer for Theta's. Adapted bolts still shot wildly through the darkness, however, with one almost blasting the fanged servo-automata to raining shrapnel.

The distraction had served its purpose. Boarding craft that had put down on the deck some distance away kicked on their floodlights and emergency landing lamps. In the smoky light, the Alpha Legionnaires of the Redacted were transformed into silhouettes. They were not the only ones. Hordes of death cultists were among them, sprinting deftly from the ramps of lighters and assault boats. In their masks and clutching wicked blades and needle pistols, the Seventh Sons joined the fray. Like a river coursing about a set of boulders, the death cultists ran around their armoured masters and threw themselves at the deck serfs of the *Assiduous*.

'Onwards,' Occam announced across the vox, his modified suit systems rapidly firing back up to full functionality. The black shapes of the warband walked through the carnage. Shotguns barked bolts into the charge, while Seventh Sons cut through the loyal serfs with envenomed blades and flash-blasts from their needle pistols. Aiming for exposed flesh and faces, they ducked and weaved through the havoc. The Alpha Legion acolytes left serfs crashing to the deck and doubling up behind them, clutching wounds and writhing in the agony of fast-acting venom.

'Strike master,' Ephron Hasdrubal said as they left the vicious boarding action. The sergeant was drawing attention to the blast door closing off the launch bay from the cavernous gun decks. The sheer weight of numbers behind the section bulkhead – deck serfs, servitor cannon crew and hereditary auxiliaries – was lifting the door clear of the floor to flood the darkness with light and repelling forces.

'Autolicon,' Occam called across the vox-channel. 'Melta bombs.'

Holding the weight of his plasma cannon in one hand, the legionnaire snatched the chunky grenades from his belt and threw them forward through the darkness to Occam, Hasdrubal and Malik. Catching the melta bombs, the renegades twisted their plunger handles back and forth before skimming the grenades across the flight deck towards the oncoming rush.

For a moment, the darkness evaporated and a series of thunderous flashes dominated the bay. The grenades detonated with a sub-atomic whoosh. The flight deck beneath the charging serfs glowed red and then molten white. Unfortunates caught in the thermal blast turned to billowing clouds of fine ash. Others running across the melting deck sank into liquid metal, screaming their lives away before the bubbling flight deck popped like a growing blister and liquid metal gushed down onto the deck below. Bondsmen running near the crater put up their hands to shield themselves from the heat but their flesh caught fire and they turned into thrashing mounds on the floor, smouldering in the reasserting darkness.

Still, hordes of deck serfs and servitors ran on, spilling from the gun-deck blast door with a ferocious desire to see the interlopers banished. Like white blood cells attacking the source of an infection, the bondsmen came at the Alpha Legionnaires. Any ordinary Imperial wretch might have thought twice about such a foolhardy action. To specimens of miserable humanity, Space Marines – even those that had turned from the Emperor's light and embraced other paths – were veritable demigods to be feared. The Chapter serfs were fanatics of their own following – a cult honouring the Marines Mordant, devoted to both serving and protecting the interests of their Adeptus Astartes masters. The Alpha Legion were an enemy to be repelled, and if possible destroyed. Loyal serfs thought nothing of throwing themselves at such a fearful foe. They would die for their masters – and did so.

'They're insistent, aren't they?' Sergeant Hasdrubal said.

'Close quarters, brothers,' Occam said. 'Be the mistake that our enemies have made.'

With the exception of Autolicon Phex, who lit up the benighted launch bay with blazing orbs that cut through the ranks of serfs, the Redacted slapped their plasma guns onto the backs of their mag-lock belts. With a fluid motion they snatched up hand-to-hand combat power weapons that hummed to energy-sheathed lethality. With pumped bolt-rounds crashing through the air and the horde of bondsmen hitting the squad like a force of nature, the Alpha Legion held their ground. They advanced through the furious sea of bodies, even. Blasts from Phex's plasma cannon cleared a path through the attackers, while Occam's legionnaires stepped, twisted and cut their way through the loyal serfs.

Protecting each other from levelled shotgun barrels, combat blades carried by the serfs and chainswords hastily grabbed to repel the Alpha Legion boarders, the Redacted worked in slick balance – like the cogs of some ancient clockwork artefact. Hasdrubal and Vilnius Malik took the lead, the former Night Lord going to savage work with a pair of lethal power blades.

While he slashed and stabbed, the sergeant produced his own weapon artefact. It was a wicked, xenos blade – more torturer's device than weapon – recovered from an alien battlefield in the Garon Nebula upon which Hasdrubal had left many dead. The weapon's many blades sprung, flipped and clacked into place like the butterfly knife or switchblade of a hive ganger. Seizing serfs by their flanks and burying the multi-blade dagger into their bellies, Hasdrubal lifted them off the ground with the force of his stabbing motion. Serfs shrieked horribly as blades embedded with neural wires, energy sheaths and twisting chainblades visited unbearable agony upon each victim before Hasdrubal pressed the mercy switch on the handle that delivered oblivion.

Holding the flanks of the Redacted's close combat formation were the warpsmith Reznor and Carcinus Quoda – former Librarian and squad sorcerer. With precision movements, Reznor wielded a pair of short-haft Omnissian power axes. The crackling cog blades sheared off limbs and crashed down through the barrels of combat shotguns. Occasionally, the warpsmith's mechatendrils would slither out and strike, grabbing serfs and tearing them towards him before whipping back between pack and plate. As Reznor wheeled about, his cloak following him around, he threw the axes the short distance into the chests of charging serfs before turning, ripping them out and burying them in another oncoming unfortunate.

Quoda, meanwhile, flushed the azure crystal that formed the many-faceted head of his force sceptre with otherworldly power summoned from the empyrean. With each psychically enhanced blow, Quoda took off heads in a crystal-splattered haze of gore and broke attacking serfs, putting their shattered bodies down on the deck with warp-fuelled savagery.

While his legionnaires cut, bludgeoned and blasted a way through the ever-growing horde, Occam the Untrue unleashed his own nightmare. Snatching a hand-held power scourge from his belt, the strike master thumbed the weapon to life. He wheeled the scourge about his head before lashing out at attacking bondsmen, allowing the multi-tailed whip of joined blades to crackle and writhe. With a sizzle and a flash, the razored tails of the weapon slashed through Occam's victims. Combat shotguns were cut into sparking pieces. Heads and limbs were sheared from torsos. Shutting off the power at the handle, the strike master bullwhipped the tails of the scourge away, catching serfs in a bladed nest of agony. He brought the weapon back to life and turned his opponents into thrashing puppets of crackling torment. Expertly uncoiling the scourge with a rippling flourish, the strike master allowed his smouldering victims to fall dead to the ground.

Occam sensed more bodies about him. The cultist hordes had caught up to their masters and were meeting the army of serfs flooding in from the gun decks head on.

'Time,' Occam ordered, taking note of his helm's chronometer. 'Leave these unworthy wretches to the Seventh Sons.'

Accelerating into a powered run, the legionnaires brutally barged serfs aside before slipping down onto their cloaks and the polished flight deck. Sliding across the floor, one by one, the warband disappeared into the darkness of craters left behind by the melta bombs.

Exchanging weaponry mid-drop, the Redacted landed with a power-armoured thunk on the maintenance deck below. The blue glow of their plasma guns lit up the pipe-lined passageway. It bore the filth of age. The *Assiduous* was an ancient relic of a vessel. The walls were stained and the piping was encrusted with exotic corrosions. Beneath the grille panelling running the busy length of the maintenance corridor, Occam heard the trickle of liquid detritus. Oils and blessed unguents. Coolant and chemical spillage. The blood of Marines Mordant defenders and the ichor of enemy organisms intent on invasion. Across the centuries, filth had trickled down through the battle-barge, drawn on by the insistence of artificial gravity to pool in the bowels of the vessel and run along the sub-chambers and corridors running the length of the keel.

On the floor were several serfs who had fallen into the pit following the explosion. Bones protruded from knees where the ugly fall had broken their legs. Gritting their teeth, they still tried to get to their feet. Their continued efforts both impressed and annoyed the strike master.

'Malik,' Occam said. 'Take care of that.'

Holding his long-shot plasma gun under the breach with one gauntlet, Malik drew a scoped bolt pistol with an extended barrel from his holster and aimed it down at the bondsmen. Thudding silenced Stalker shells into the shaven heads of the serfs, Malik put an end to their agony.

'As I said, this will work for us,' Arkan Reznor said. He took several steps up the passage, the blue haze of his plasma gun revealing a mono-task servitor. The drone was all pallid flesh and augmentation. It used a long-handled scraper to shear encrusted alien parasites from the curved walls and piping that were quietly breeding in the foul darkness of the ship's bowels. 'These maintenance passageways intersect and run the length of the barge. We can avoid the gun decks and make it to within twelve decks of the command deck.'

Occam the Untrue nodded, walking up towards the miserable servitor. At an instruction from Reznor, his tongue clicking and rasping something approaching binary at his servo-automata, Beta, Zeta and Theta advanced up the passage on their repulsors. Their augurs hummed to a rhythmic scan while they activated socket lamps that lit the way ahead.

'It is imperative that we take the bridge,' Occam said, 'or Lord Carthach's efforts will be all for naught. He might take the fortress-monastery but this vessel – battle damaged and operating with a skeleton crew – could still level Salina City and the Bas-Silica with one salvo from its bombardment cannon.'

'Why not take out the cannon instead?' Malik asked. 'The dorsal section is closer.'

'Because that would be too easy,' Ephron Hasdrubal answered, his tone sharpened with the hint of a remonstration.

'The sergeant is, as ever, correct,' Occam said. 'We are the Emperor's test. Let our efforts purge the Imperium of the weak, leaving His dominion stronger than we found it.'

'As you wish, strike master,' Malik replied.

'If there is an actual Adeptus Astartes presence on this vessel,' Occam said, 'and Codex Astartes protocol suggests that there should be – then it will be found on the command deck. No member of the Marines Mordant is to be allowed to live. Quetzel Carthach demands it, and he is the Angelbane – a living end to the successor sons of Guilliman. If the Emperor wills it, then it will be so. Dissemble.'

Once more, the Redacted's adapted plate answered. A flush of colour rippled through the ceramite scales. The darkness that the Alpha Legion had previously been was now bleached to Ultramarine blue and silver, with one pauldron and half-suit devoted to each colour: the honoured Chapter colours of the Marines Mordant. Occam pulled his cloak around to hide the legionary markings on his pauldron.

'Quoda,' Occam said. 'The details.'

The squad sorcerer banged the base of his force sceptre against the floor. The azure crystal that made up the head of the weapon rang with mind-aching intensity, the serpentine psi-convector running through it amplified by Quoda's telepathic powers. The former Librarian stared into the crystal, his faceplate reproduced in the crystal's many facets. While cloaks and chameleonic plate could hide the Alpha Legion's identity and give the impression that the renegades of the Redacted belonged to a different Chapter or warband, the devilry was in the detail. Carcinus Quoda used his powers to ensure that those encountering the Redacted saw what they expected to see. Details and expectations drawn from their own minds and therefore beyond reasonable suspicion: appropriate weaponry, insignia and honours, the acid-splash scars from the *Assiduous'* battle with the tyranids.

Occam the Untrue stood before the servitor, which had stopped scraping the encrusted walls of the passage. The drone stared up at him, its blank face and oil-black eyes fixed upon the strike master's plate. Occam waited as what was left of its brain and its simple cogitator processed what it was seeing. Gently, the servitor's head bowed, as protocol dictated – as it might before one of its Marines Mordant masters.

'Let's go,' the strike master said.

γ

TURNING TAIL

Captain Sol Ventor moved between runebanks and attendant deck serfs on the bridge, his scar-cracked features furrowed. He looked across the command deck of the venerable battle-barge *Assiduous*. It was awash with activity.

A small army of robed bondsmen was breaking protocol and calling out from their stations, while serf armsmen stood either side of the bridge elevator doors with their combat shotguns. Console-interfaced servitors blurted in binary while Master Zamander and Techmarine Arkadii collated the datastreams. Brother Arkadii had responsibility for the *Assiduous*, while Zamander was the Chapter's Master of the Forge and had taken personal responsibility for overseeing the honoured battle-barge's punishing schedule of repairs. Zamander was followed around by a small huddle of lexomat servitor units, bringing the computational power of their cogitators to the data flooding into bridge runebanks.

Shipmaster Darrius had reported to the bridge and stood

by his command throne, his hood down and shaven head glistening with reflected red lighting. Captain Ventor had just sounded a Vermillion Alert. The shipmaster's aged features were contorted with incredulity as deck serf after deck serf brought him data-slates of unfolding information. Earpsichor, the battle-barge's astropath, hovered nearby.

All about them, Ventor's honour guard stood to attention in their blue and silver artificer armour and ornate helms. Their Marines Mordant plate was decorated with honours and loincloths of leather and chain. One even held a company banner, replete with new recognitions of the Chapter's encounter with Hive Fleet Leviathan. Each silent veteran held his primed boltgun aimed at the deck, ready to defend the Space Marine master. As captain of the Marines Mordant Fourth Company and master of the Chapter fleet, Ventor warranted such an escort.

The leader of the honour guard was Brother Orthrius – a taciturn warrior and company champion of the Fourth. He stood by his captain with arms folded above a pair of short power swords that criss-crossed at the hilt.

'What in Guilliman's name is going on?' Ventor demanded, running his ceramite fingers through his Vitrean-white hair before reaching for the pulpit rail with his left gauntlet. The captain had no right arm. He had lost it to a tyranid monster that had stormed the corridors of the *Assiduous* during the horrific boarding action that had sent the battle-barge back to Vitrea Mundi for repairs. Ventor had been so busy with his reports to Chapter Master Pallidax and his responsibilities as master of the fleet that there had simply been no time for the surgery to fit a bionic replacement. 'Prow section – status?'

'The boarding action is yet to be put down,' Orthrius admitted, 'but the numbers look small.'

'Pirates?' Ventor asked. 'The Tyrant's reavers?'

'I've never known the Red Corsairs to take such wild risks. Lufgt Huron knows better. He hits with force. Who ever heard of a battle-barge being stormed thus?'

'The *Assiduous* is not herself,' Ventor admitted, 'and we are fielding a skeleton crew. Tell me this is nothing.'

'It is,' Orthrius said, 'and it will be over soon. Sooner if you let me go down there.'

'No,' the captain said. Orthrius gave an imperceptible shake of his champion's helm before continuing his assessment.

'The fighting is restricted to the launch bay. The gun decks remain secure. I have reinforced the section with armsmen and crews from the batteries.'

'How by Holy Terra did they get past our augur fields?' Ventor demanded. The master was given to cursing and taking, among other things, the Emperor's name in vain.

'That I do not know,' Orthrius grizzled, pointing between runebanks and over the shoulders of bridge bondsmen. 'It's isolated and contained.'

'No, it's not,' the battle-scarred Ventor said, surveying data-slates brought to him. He called across the command deck: 'Report.'

'Vitrean Planetary Defence Auxilia report the mass movement of people on the streets of Salina City, my lord,' a deck serf told him, standing up at his station and lowering his head.

'Orbitals?'

'Captures and augur scans show a huge cloud of gas or vapour rising from the Great Soda Lakes,' another robed officer told him. 'The population are fleeing the city and arriving at the gates of the Bas-Silica for shelter.'

'How can this be?' Ventor demanded. 'How can we be only learning this now?'

'I fear, up until now, communications from the surface have been blocked or disrupted,' the deck serf offered.

'An attack has been unfolding below us...' Ventor said grimly.

'And we didn't even know it,' Orthrius said.

Ventor turned to a serf at a master vox station: 'Well, we know it now. Get me the Chapter Master – get him now.'

The serf struggled to raise the Bas-Silica, citing a continued disturbance at the source. In the significant amount of time it took him to establish a static-shot channel between the *Assiduous* and the fortress-monastery, more bad news had reached the bridge. The astropath Earpsichor and Shipmaster Darrius had confirmed that all other Marines Mordant vessels, system stations and star forts had failed to meet long-range vox and astropathic communication protocols. Outer system defence platforms, patrolling rapid-strike vessels, sub-sector frigates and remaining Marines Mordant-manned star forts, watching over the outskirt regions of the Maelstrom, had all gone silent.

'Captain,' an officer bondsman piped up, 'orbital captures show evidence of explosions and fire fights conducted within the city and the fortress-monastery itself.'

'Vox station!' Ventor roared at the attending serf. Techmarine Arkadii, however, had been working at the runebank for some time.

'Channels are being jammed from the surface,' he told the captain. 'I have penetrated the interference and isolated limited vox and hololithics. Chapter Master Pallidax for you.'

'Chapter Master?' Ventor called as nerve-shredding static boomed across the command deck. A hololithic representation of Tarro Pallidax warped and sizzled in and out of focus before the captain. Pallidax stood before a throne of clouded quartz in a blue and silver suit of Tactical Dreadnought armour – a relic from the Chapter's inception. Serfs and Marines Mordant battle-brothers kept moving into hololithic representation, bringing their Chapter Master new intelligence.

Pallidax cut a grim figure. His white hair was cropped short and missing about the long-healed crater in his skull where the Overfiend of Octarius had buried a hammer. Where his eye was missing also, the cold blue of a bionic twinkled lazily. A long time had passed since his crusading days against encroaching ork empires. The Chapter Master's face bore the deep lines of responsibility and more recent tragedies.

Pallidax had lost two companies of honoured warriors on what had already been a penance crusade through the Tempest Hippocrene. Another had been decimated defending recruitment worlds from the predatory expansions of another greenskin Overfiend.

Star forts stationed on the borders of the Maelstrom and fleet patrols had been mercilessly hit by pirates, renegades and Red Corsairs operating out of the warp storm, as the Tyrant of Badab turned his attentions rimward. As the Marines Mordant lost company after company, requests for assistance from brother successors had gone unheeded. The Nova Legion, Vindicators and Crimson Consuls were all sons of Guilliman who shared some of the responsibility for guarding the rimward frontiers of the Maelstrom – as the doomed Maelstrom Wardens had done with the coreward sectors before the Badab War. The Nova Legion didn't reply at all. The Vindicators were found to be in the throes of their own calamity. In answer to a surprise astropathic distress signal from the Crimson Consuls, Pallidax sent a demi-company and some of his finest remaining captains to help them fight off the Alpha Legion at Carcharias. They never returned.

All the while, the Marines Mordant had lost two further companies on the Kontradorn Drift from fighting a splinter fleet of Hive Fleet Leviathan – a gruelling engagement that had nearly cost the Chapter their only remaining battle-barge, the venerable *Assiduous*.

'Bas-Silica, this is *Assiduous*, please respond,' Ventor called.

At first there were no words: only static. Pallidax's mouth went to work on reports and orders that the command deck could not hear, before his battle-weary features formed a furious scowl in recognition of the communication difficulties. When sound did cut through the static it revealed to Sol Ventor gunfire and the thunder of nearby explosions.

'Captain,' Brother Orthrius said, moving between the glow of runebanks. Techmarine Arkadii's efforts were paying off. 'We're getting reports of armoured renegades on the planet surface. Traitor Guard and terror attacks throughout Salina City. The cloud rising from the soda lakes is probably an engineered chemical reaction. It is drifting through the city. Sources on the ground are claiming thousands dead.'

Ventor and his champion locked grim gazes.

'Continue,' the captain said.

'People are fleeing the city,' Orthrius said. 'The Chapter Master opened the Bas-Silica's gates to admit them...'

'Which is what the renegades were waiting for,' Sol Ventor said.

'Yes, master.'

'The attackers are within the perimeter defences?'

'And are laying siege to what is left of the veteran First Company,' Orthrius told him. 'Eyewitness accounts tell of a myriad of xenos mercenaries supporting the assault. Our brothers are struggling to both mount a defence against such different enemies and defend the refugees from the city.'

'And who is responsible for this?' the captain demanded. 'Or do these craven renegades hide their markings as they do their intentions? The Tyrant's Corsairs? Lord Bythoss and his Apocalypse Watch? Word Bearers out of Ghalmek?'

'*For once, they do not hide their markings,*' Chapter Master Pallidax said, his words and hololithic representations crackling to clarity. '*It is the Alpha Legion.*' Boltfire and detonations continued to carry across the transmission. The name of the dread Legion echoed nastily about the command deck. For a moment, the transmission was lost.

'Chapter Master?'

'*Captain, can you hear me?*'

'Yes, Chapter Master,' Ventor said. 'We're receiving you.'

'*Good,*' Pallidax said, '*because I want no confusion about my next order. The enemy are in. Alien mercenaries. Renegade Guardsmen. Warp-tainted altereds. Traitors clad in bilious blue and green. The scum of the galaxy, all under the foetid banner of the hydra. The Alpha Legion have us. They are led by the one they call the Angelbane. The self-same monster no doubt*

45

responsible for the silence of our brother successors. He talks to us now, through our own fortress vox casters. He offers us a living hell – a place in his ranks, in exchange for our surrender. The game is over and the sons of Guilliman are played out. There is one piece on the board he has missed, however. A sacrifice waiting to be made. You know of what I speak.'

'Chapter Master,' Ventor said, his voice cracked with fury and pain. 'The *Assiduous* has been–'

'*The* Assiduous, *aye,'* Pallidax said, not seeming to hear the captain. *'What we have taken for misfortune and tragedy has a name. The Angelbane. This fiend and his Alpha Legion filth cannot be allowed to escape the Bas-Silica. You know what I am asking you to do, old friend?'*

'I do,' Ventor answered gravely.

'This is the last you shall hear from Pallidax of Vitrea Mundi,' the Chapter Master said. *'The final lament of the Marines Mordant. Let our name echo through the ages as warriors of the Emperor's Space Marines, terrible and true. Loyal sons of Guilliman and avengers of our brothers' blood. Let our dirge be the thunder of the Assiduous' bombardment cannon and our tomb these hallowed halls. I am giving the order to lower the Bas-Silica's void shields… now. Captain, do your duty.'*

With that, the hololithic representation warped and died. A terrible silence descended upon the command deck. One by one, Chapter serfs, crew and Marines Mordant looked to their captain.

'My lord,' Brother Orthrius said. 'We cannot do this.'

'And yet we must,' Ventor said, his face a pale blank.

'What? Become the final weapon wielded by the Alpha Legion against our brothers?'

'We have no choice,' the captain told him, his voice low and heavy with responsibility.

'We can choose not to fire upon our own brothers,' Orthrius called, his desperation echoing about the cavernous bridge.

'You heard your Chapter Master,' Ventor said. 'We were fighting side by side against the enemies of the Imperium before you were even born. Tarro Pallidax is not given to hyperbole. When he announces that this is the end of his Chapter, he damn well means it. I have an order from my Chapter Master – as protocol dictates, I intend to follow it.'

Ventor looked around the command deck. At the ornate helms of his honour guard hanging in shame. At Brother Arkadii and Master Zamander's sombre acceptance. At serfs staring in disbelief at the horror unfolding on their consoles. At Earpsichor and the shipmaster waiting grimly by.

'Orthrius,' the captain said finally. 'If we do not do this, this Angelbane – once he has taken the fortress-monastery – will turn its defence lasers upon the *Assiduous*. You know in her present condition she cannot withstand such an attack. Call it the dying wish of an honoured Chapter Master or self-preservation, this must be done. Status?'

'The fortress-monastery's void shields are collapsing,' Master Zamander confirmed from a runebank.

'Then please be so good as to inform the section ordinators and dorsal gun crews of our target and intention,' the captain told Zamander. 'I want magma-bomb warheads primed and the bombardment cannon trained upon the fortress-monastery. Full spread, if you please. No consideration is to be given to Chapter forces at the impact site or collateral citizenry in the adjacent city. Make sure they understand. Repeat the order twice. I want the target and the enemy within completely obliterated.'

'As you command,' Master Zamander said, turning back towards the runebank.

It all happened so fast that Sol Ventor, already numb at the news from Vitrea Mundi, couldn't make himself act. The command deck, the runebank unit and Master Zamander suddenly disappeared. The polished metal floor glowed red and then white, bubbling about the Techmarine's boots as he backed away. The console station melted before him and a screaming Zamander – already aflame and sinking as if into a mire of molten metal – dropped down through the deck. The runebank and melting floor followed him, leaving behind a dark crater that revealed the deck below.

Ventor felt the whoosh of heat on his face as another sub-atomic detonation turned the deck nearby into a fiery pit. He felt Brother Orthrius push him back before the champion ran forward to help members of the honour guard. Marines Mordant were aflame and roasting within their plate. The company's standard turned to ash, while its bearer fell down through the white-hot inferno with two of his veteran brothers. Orthrius managed to pull the final surviving member of the honour guard out of the superheated blast.

The Alpha Legion were not just on the planet surface. They were not contained, as Orthrius had suggested, in the launch bay. They were here – intent on taking the battle-barge's command deck. Sol Ventor shook the stunned realisation from his addled mind and found his way to action.

'Suppression fire!' he roared across the bridge at the surviving Marines Mordant. With a wave of his gauntlet he directed deck serfs from their runebanks and consoles.

'We are under attack. Follow your protocols. Lock down the bridge.'

As the remaining member of the honour guard blasted his boltgun back into the darkness of the pit, Techmarine Arkadii did likewise with his pistol into the crater that had swallowed the Master of the Forge. Bridge serfs, up from their stations, snatched laspistols from their robed belts and joined them. Orthrius tore his power blades from their scabbards and brought them to sizzling life, assuming position in front of his captain. Shrugging back his silvered cloak, Ventor went to draw his own bolt pistol but found it to be missing.

Turning furiously, he found Shipmaster Darrius standing behind him. The senior serf held the weight of the ornate weapon in both hands, leaning into the pistol. As the master's scarred face creased with imperious incredulity, the bolt pistol fired. Brother Orthrius was thrown forward by the force of the bolt round's impact, his helm blown open at the back. Brains and skull blasted forth through his ornate faceplate, while the champion's short power blades clattered to the deck.

The shipmaster thrust the bolt pistol at Ventor, forcing the Marines Mordant captain back. Behind Darrius, he could see the dead bodies of the serf elevator sentries and the astropath Earpsichor, their slit throats leaking lifeblood all over the deck. Ventor tensed in his plate, the hydraulics and servos straining. With a single power-armoured strike he could break the serf shipmaster's spine. Darrius stared at the master of the fleet with dark eyes, holding the bolt pistol on Ventor's furious figure.

'I believe you're fast, captain,' Darrius told him, 'with your genetically enhanced reflexes, your training and plate. But do you really think you're faster than a bolt round?'

Snarling, Ventor turned to the Marines Mordant and serfs firing down into the holes in the command deck. As bolt weapons ran dry, the Space Marines held up their gauntlets, indicating that the light show the deck serfs were visiting upon the darkness below should also come to an end. After several seconds, a grenade vaulted up out of the darkness. Spinning in the air, the melta bomb reached up into the bridge.

'Fire in the–' Arkadii managed before the melta bomb detonated. As it did, another grenade was tossed up out of the second hole. Exploding at shoulder height, each grenade blossomed into a blinding, sub-atomic blast that could be felt by Ventor on the other side of the bridge. The captain watched with horror as the melta bomb blasts wiped the deck serfs and the last of his Space Marines from existence. Bridge bondsmen disappeared in a stream of ash and screams, while the Marines Mordant became ghastly sculptures of melted plate and scorched flesh. As the intense flare of the detonation faded, the two Space Marines managed a few more seconds of dreadful, twisted life before dying.

'Darrius,' a stunned Sol Ventor said. He had used his gauntlet to shelter his face from the heat. He now raised it above his head.

From the deck below, the captain could hear equipment being moved. Without moving the barrel of the bolt pistol, the shipmaster gestured towards the smouldering openings melted into the floor. Looking down, Ventor saw the impossible. Marines Mordant Space Marines in faded blue and silver, stepping up mounds of piled equipment to climb through the holes in the deck: three proceeding from each. Ventor knew the Space Marines. He recognised their markings and even the scars on their plate, caused by acid-splashes, fangs and claws. These were Marines Mordant that he had fought beside against the chittering hordes of the alien tyranid.

'Brothers, no,' the captain said, his voice brittle. He looked between Darrius and the arriving Space Marines. 'What have you done? Do you know what you have done? You have sided with traitors and in doing so have become one of them. You have sold out your primarch to the highest bidder and betrayed your blood. Think, brothers, of what you do. Think on what you would say to your Emperor, if you were before him now – your souls as easy for him to read as an open tome.'

The lead Space Marine cleared the seals of his helm and took it off as his compatriots closed in the plasma guns trained on the captain.

'Dissemble,' the leader ordered.

As he approached Sol Ventor, his plate began to blot and darken. Like a death world reptile changing colour, his power armour lost its silver and blue patterning, its scars and markings. Revealing the scaled ceramite and besmirched viridian beneath, the sizzling transformation made the captain's eyes blink and his mind ache. For a moment, the patrician features marking a successor son of Guilliman and white hair of a Vitrean were visible. With the fading ache came a revelation. These were not the Marines Mordant he had fought with. He had only imagined them as so. They were warriors of the Alpha Legion.

The face beneath the helm belonged to no brother of Sol Ventor. His skin had a copper hue, while hologrammatic tattoos of serpents danced with angle and movement above the interloper's ears and around the back of his bald head. Unsmiling but satisfied, the leader had eyes that burned both with intelligence and a piercing darkness, making his gaze hard to hold. Despite this, Ventor's own eyes picked out in the stranger's appearance the subtle signs of surgery and face-transplantation.

'I do think of what I might say to the Emperor,' the Alpha Legion commander told Ventor. 'In fact, I speak to Him every day. I hope that my hearts and soul are as easy to read as yours, captain. For I tell Him that, unlike the Marines Mordant, I fight for Him still.'

With the slickness of a striking snake, the Alpha Legion commander drew his scoped bolt pistol and aimed its elongated barrel at the captain's chest. There was not the crash Sol Ventor expected. Bolt rounds thudded through his breastplate with an almost silky hiss. He felt them, hot and terrible, tearing through his chest. His multi-lung and hearts. Staggering back, the Marines Mordant captain fell. Agony lanced through his chest. He coughed up blood, thick and warm. He heard his ruined hearts beat no more. Staring up, he could see the Alpha Legion commander standing over him. There was no malice in those eyes, only understanding and cold necessitude.

Sol Ventor felt the darkness closing in. It was a darkness that he knew would claim not only him but his genic brothers also – for the Marines Mordant had fought their last battle and they had lost.

δ

THE VIPER'S NEST

'Mina,' Occam the Untrue said to the operative. 'The doors.'

The Assassin, still disguised as the ageing shipmaster, stepped over the body of the dead Marines Mordant captain. As she moved across the bridge she hooked the toe of a boot beneath an abandoned combat shotgun on the deck. She scooped up the weapon and stepped through the smouldering bodies of serfs. Working the pump action, she took her place by the elevator doors.

Occam's legionnaires didn't need instructions. The difficult section of the operation was over. Now they slickly fell to completing the mission. As Beta, Zeta and Theta rose from the holes in the floor to attend on their master, Reznor got to work on an auxiliary console. He double-checked that no order had been sent to the dorsal gun decks to fire the barge's bombardment cannon and began re-establishing orbital vox communications. While Malik and Autolicon Phex aimed their plasma weaponry down into the pits, ensuring the bridge could not be retaken the way the Redacted had entered, Sergeant Hasdrubal opened a vox-channel with the High Serpent to update him on their situation.

'Well?' Occam asked.

'I have ordered the Seventh Sons to disengage and retreat back to the boarding craft,' Hasdrubal told him.

Occam nodded. The death cultists had only ever been a distraction. He had never intended them to blood-and-guts their way through even the skeleton crew of an Adeptus Astartes battle-barge.

'Send my regards to the High Serpent,' Occam said. 'Tell him that his flotilla is cleared to withdraw. He is to leave the *Serpent's Egg* and one lighter for our convenience.'

'What of the bonded crew?' the sergeant asked.

'Where are they?'

'Large numbers are concentrated on the gun decks, drawn there from the rest of the ship by orders to repel boarders.'

Occam the Untrue nodded to Hasdrubal and himself.

'Jam vox communications between sections,' Occam ordered. 'Then seal the batteries off from the launch bay and the rest of the battle-barge. I want you to open the airlocks on the thorax gun decks and drop the battery integrity fields. Let the crew feel the embrace of the void.'

'Aye,' Hasdrubal said. It was a cold order to carry out but Occam and his sergeant both knew that the Marines Mordant would have done the same to the attacking Alpha Legion in a heartbeat.

'Anything from Lord Carthach?' Occam asked.

'Nothing on the Bas-Silica open channels,' Arkan Reznor confirmed. With his mechadendrites extended and moving across the shattered runebanks, he was already reinstating operations to several of the least damaged consoles.

'Perhaps they are having trouble taking the Librarius or the last of the First Company veterans.'

'Unlikely,' Occam said, checking his chronometer. The Angelbane's merciless actions usually ran like clockwork. Such synchronicity was the reason it had been so important that the Redacted take the command deck of the *Assiduous* when they did. If Carthach had experienced problems with the Marines Mordant psykers or if Chapter Master Pallidax had managed to hold off the Alpha Legion's overwhelming attack, then Occam would have expected word from the Angelbane.

'Perhaps the Angelbane has succumbed,' Carcinus Quoda said, looking out through the great lancet screens of the bridge. Occam joined the sorcerer there.

'We should be so lucky,' he said to the psyker. 'Do you know something that I don't?'

'The sheer tonnage of what I know that you do not could stop a formation of Land Raiders in their tracks.'

'Fair,' Occam admitted to the sorcerer. 'Now answer my damn question.'

'No,' Quoda said. 'For now, the Angelbane lives.'

'Encoded channel,' Occam ordered, turning to Arkan Reznor. 'Inform Lord Carthach that we have completed our mission. The *Assiduous* resides under the control of the Alpha Legion. Ground forces are shielded from attack. We await his orders.'

Occam shrugged his pauldrons. It was a redundant communication. Carthach must already have known that the Redacted's operation had been successful. The battle-barge's bombardment cannon hadn't fired. Still, the strike master expected the report might garner a response from madmen and deviants amongst the Alpha Legion ranks – Quetzel Carthach included – distracted by the opportunity to terrorise and torture the last remaining members of a decimated Chapter.

The sons of Guilliman had a talent for attracting the Angelbane's attention.

Occam looked to Autolicon Phex, who was aiming his plasma cannon down into the depths of the pit melted into the deck. Phex had been a member of the Nova Legion – brother successors to the Crimson Consuls, Vindicators and Marines Mordant. A newly promoted Scout, he had possessed a talent for destruction and had assumed a position in one of the Chapter's many Devastator squads. After Lord Carthach's Sons of the Hydra had ended the Nova Legion at Scintil-Novax, Phex had been discovered in one of the Reclusiam penitoria-cells, where he had been punished for transgressions in his operational interpretation of the Codex Astartes.

Initially slated for exile and to carry out a death oath by the Chapter's Master of Sanctity, he instead became the last surviving battle-brother of the Nova Legion and a plaything for Quetzel Carthach's amusement. Experiencing misery, persecution and torment at the hands of the Angelbane, including having his tongue cut off, Phex was perversely given to Occam to replace a legionnaire that the Redacted had lost during the hard battle to take the fortress-monastery on Scintil-Novax.

As part of an insult Occam felt he had to endure, Carthach claimed that he would not tolerate a son of Guilliman in his own ranks. Since the Redacted were already made up of what he termed second-rate renegade pretenders – rather than truefoil Alpha Legionnaires like Carthach himself – it was decided that Occam was to carry the burden.

As the artificial atmosphere was vented through the gun decks, taking thousands of serf crew members with it, Occam paced the command deck, waiting for Carthach's response. The Angelbane was not wrong. The Redacted were made up of renegades who had joined the ranks of the Alpha Legion rather than those who bore the genic heritage of the Last Primarch. What they lacked in blood, they shared in the perversity of the Legion's operational aspirations and myriad dark objectives.

Occam wouldn't have it any other way. While the Redacted fought with the zeal of converts – attempting to honour and harness some of the professional potency of the Legion's past – Carthach's Sons of the Hydra were, by and large, legionary butchers. Pirates. Madmen. Warp-tainted altereds. Quetzel Carthach was indeed the Master of Harrows. By joining disparate Alpha Legion warbands under his banner and throwing them into coordinated actions, he had succeeded in wiping out the successor sons of Guilliman on the rimward borders of the Maelstrom, and earned the title Angelbane.

While the Angelbane was the puppet of his pathological hatred, Occam was driven by a harsh and uncompromising love of his Emperor. The priests of the Ecclesiarchy might have thought themselves austere and the agents of the Inquisition unflinching in their prosecution of His will, but none had the adamantium faith required to embrace the traitor and carry out the Emperor's work from within the enemy lines. To be the true check and balance. To fan the flames of heresy and temper the resolve of a brittle empire.

Such pursuits brought Occam into company with renegades like Quetzel Carthach. Carthach was both madman and genius. He was too dangerous for his bitter cause to be either ignored or fully embraced. Like many in the fragmented Legion, Carthach had long lost his way. An ancient lie twisted to the harshest of truths, the arch-lord had reputedly been present upon cursed Eskrador, the day the twin primarch fell. While Occam doubted this was true, Carthach lived for the suffering of Guilliman's sons and devoted his considerable talents to their extermination, Chapter by successor Chapter.

The Angelbane favoured the old ways, reproducing in his own rancid fashion a ghostly shadow of the Alpha Legion's infamous Harrowings. The culmination of many months of planning and preparation, Carthach and his gathered Alpha Legion warbands launched mass lightning attacks of synchronised force and unstoppable variety. Planetary assaults were complemented by piratical deceptions. Cultist mobs rose up amongst the populations of loyal Imperial worlds, while Assassins stalked planetary leaders. Psycho-indoctrination and orbital bombardments spelled doom in their different ways, while xenos mercenaries and daemonic allies were unleashed upon the Emperor's servants. While the Tyrant of Badab had announced his hatred of the Imperium through a bombastic war that had dominated the coreward sectors, the Angelbane had been quietly snuffing out Adeptus Astartes home worlds on the other side of the warp storm.

In doing so, Quetzel Carthach satisfied his cruel obsession and the Sons of the Hydra contributed to the Legion's murky objective of further destabilising a tottering Imperium. The insurrectionists, monsters and piratical marauders placing themselves under the Master of Harrows' command meanwhile prospered, pilfering victim Chapters of their finest plate, much-needed Adeptus

Astartes weaponry and fleet assets. Occam knew not how many of the Ultramarines' successors Quetzel Carthach had truly ended. The demise of the Crimson Consuls on Carcharias had been a crude kind of merciless artistry and the Redacted had taken part in the harrowing actions that had destroyed both the Vindicators and the Nova Legion.

Still, Occam did not rate the Chaos lord. While he was a ruthless figurehead, driven by an ancient legionary hatred, Carthach's strategies and those he committed the Redacted to were not half as accomplished as the Angelbane liked to think. Occam knew he could do better for his Emperor and that one day he might.

'What do orbital captures show?' Occam called across the command deck, as he paced between lancet screens. He was getting impatient. Arkan Reznor obliged his strike master. Superimposed on the arched bridge ports, Occam could see the dirty, white surface of Vitrea Mundi rotating slowly and silently. He could see that the vapour cloud that had risen from the soda lakes was now all but obscuring Salina City. It threatened to swallow the structure of the Bas-Silica fortress-monastery next.

'And augurs?' Occam asked.

'Fires from terror attacks and detonations across the city and within the fortress-monastery's perimeter walls,' Reznor said, studying his runescreen.

'Time?'

'Nothing new.'

'Small arms fire? Troop movements?'

'Difficult to tell through the vapour cloud,' the warp-smith said, adjusting magnifications and filters. 'Beyond smoke trails and fires from recent detonations, the Bas-Silica looks quiet and still.'

'What in the warp is going on down there?' Occam said, almost to himself. 'What can you tell me?'

Arkan Reznor shrugged his plate.

'I can tell you that most of the fortress-monastery's void shields are back to full intensity,' Reznor said, 'and that I'm getting heat signatures from the defence laser auto-motives and battery silos.'

'What?'

'Perhaps the Marines Mordant still hold the towers,' Quoda hypothesised, looking out through the lancet screens.

'Or the Angelbane ordered the surface-to-orbitals warmed up as a defensive measure,' Sergeant Hasdrubal pitched in.

Occam looked at them and then back at the screens.

'Defence against what?' he said. 'We're the only ones up here.'

Something wasn't right. Occam might not have been a genic member of the Alpha Legion, but his instincts were still warning him there was something off. Lack of com-munications. Absent activity. Timing issues...

The Angelbane's plan had been proceeding right on time. Three days before – standing on the benighted strategium deck of Carthach's ancient flagship, the *Omega-Echidnax* – the Sons of the Hydra, Legion operatives, cultist leaders and the arch-lord's xenos advisors had gathered to make final preparations for the attack on Vitrea Mundi.

It had been agreed that Carthach would lead the assault on the fortress-monastery personally, at the head of the Alpha Legion Terminators and the monstrous xenos mer-cenary hordes that usually accompanied his actions. The Master of Harrows favoured a variety of alien breeds for maximum strategic flexibility: Tarellian dog-soldiers, Morralian Deathsworn, Galg freedom fighters, Fra'al marauders, serpent warriors of the sslyth and eldar out-casts. Such xenos would ordinarily be an unwieldy rabble. They were united in one thing, however: their seething hatred of humanity.

Accompanying Carthach by arrangement in his assault upon the Bas-Silica and the veteran companies of Marines Mordant that held the fortress was Vhospis Voyteq and his warband 'the Kyndred'. Alpha Legionnaires grotesquely warped by the environs of the Maelstrom, Voyteq and his tainted warriors provided the Sons of the Hydra with the shock troops required for the inevitable hand-to-hand car-nage to be undertaken in the fortress-monastery courtyards.

It was the responsibility of another of Carthach's cap-tains, Sisyphon Vail, to dump chemicals in the soda lake upon whose shores Salina City rested. The poisonous cloud that Occam had seen rising up through the city and the coordinated actions conducted by both Vail's war-band 'the Honourless' and their Traitor Guard terror cells had worked perfectly – driving the city population towards the fortress-monastery. The moment that the Marines Mordant had opened the mighty gates of the Bas-Silica had been the signal for Carthach and Vhospis Voyteq to attack. While Voyteq was a twisted thing, Sisyphon Vail a soulless creature and the Angelbane a madman, Occam couldn't help but admire the rank and file legionnaires of the Sons of the Hydra. In the quads and courtyards of the fortress-monastery, the fighting would have been bloody.

While most of the Alpha Legion warbands under Carthach's command had been given the dubious honour of facing what was left of the Marines Mordant with him down on the planet surface, warbands like The Chain Unbroken under Captain Naetrix Krayt and Occam's own Redacted had been assigned supporting roles off-world. Occam was now questioning the motivations behind that decision.

'Lord Occam,' Mina Perdita called from beyond the pulpit throne. She had her ear to the bridge elevator doors. Withdrawing to one side, she rested the combat shotgun against one shoulder, aiming the barrel at whoever might venture forth from the magnelevator car. Their plasma weaponry priming with a hum, the Alpha Legionnaires took cover and aimed at the elevator doors.

When the doors shuddered open, the Alpha Legionnaires could see that the sparking lamp in the car was out. The cycling filters of Occam's optics picked out a hunched, skeletally-thin figure in a hooded cloak, haunting the car interior. As the figure advanced from the elevator, his footsteps thudded metallically and with unexpected weight on the command deck.

The figure didn't get far. Ramming the muzzle of the combat shotgun into the side of his hooded head, Mina Perdita pinned the gaunt face of the new arrival to the side of the wall. As the figure scraped his downturned head upwards, Occam heard the squeal of metal upon metal. A single, large optic, unnatural in its intensity, burned green from the depths of the hood. With the twitch of a snarl, Occam recognised the interloper.

'You are not cleared to be here, abominable machine,' he said with annoyance. Mina Perdita and the legionnaires of the Redacted took note of the fact that Occam hadn't indicated they should lower their weapons. When the thing spoke it communicated in a stilted Gothic, as though it were always searching for the right words. Its alien voice sounded like arcing electricity.

'I neither give nor take orders, fleshling,' the xenos said.

'Not from you. Not from my own kind. My counsel is given freely. My reasons, my own.'

Carthach kept both the warped and the xenos within his close circle of advisors. One such alien wretch was Omizhar Vohk. The thing was a hunched nightmare of ancient xenos technology, its burnished silver frame draped in a ragged black cloak. A living artefact, Vohk's cyclopean optic burned its ghoulish green light into all upon whom he turned his gaze.

While repugnant to be around, his timely predictions had become valued by Quetzal Carthach. It was upon the ancient alien's insistence that Krayt and the pirate flotilla of The Chain Unbroken had been despatched to delay the arrival of the Angels Eradicant and the Astral Fists. Vohk predicted that contingents from both Chapters would respond to astropathic calls for assistance from Vitrea Mundi unless intercepted and drawn away.

The xenos advisor settled a metal claw on the barrel of Perdita's shotgun and pushed it slowly away, freeing his gaunt machine head.

'Malik,' Occam said. The xenos had an unsettling habit of appearing and disappearing as he pleased. He would skulk around corners and back into shadowy alcoves, vanishing like some kind of feudal world conjurer. No one among the Legion, including the warpsmith Reznor, understood the powerful technology that allowed such movement. Vohk had been reticent about discussing such secrets. He was much more interested in the Legion's own.

'In my sights,' the legionnaire said, the muzzle of his long-shot plasma gun following Vohk across the room.

'You are a violent Legion, amongst a violent race,' the xenos machine told them, stepping through bodies.

'Don't flatter us,' Occam said. He had little time for the advisor's games. 'What are you doing here?'

Omizhar Vohk stomped his hunchbacked way across the command deck. From behind, Occam could see that the metal vertebrae of his curved spine had punctured his ragged cloak and hood, creating sail-like spines.

'I bring word from the surface,' Vohk told him. 'From your arch-lord. Not mine. Yours.'

'Why hasn't Lord Carthach answered our communications?' Occam put to the metal nightmare. 'Has something gone wrong?'

'You might say that,' Vohk said cryptically.

'I did,' Occam replied. 'What do you say, xenos?'

Vohk peered out of the lancet screens and down at Vitrea Mundi with his green optic. He turned to face Occam with a flourish of his rags.

'The fortification of your genic enemies has been taken,' Vohk told him finally. 'The Angelbane is once again victorious.'

'That sounds like a good thing.'

Vohk nodded his narrow cranium, his features like a mirror-polished skull. Occam could see himself in the horrific visage.

'All who call the galaxy their home define themselves by what they are not,' Vohk said. He gestured at the strike master with a wicked claw. 'Human, alien. Those that fight for the Primordial Annihilator, those that do not. Victor, victim. Binary oppositions. Choices, if you will.'

'The Alpha Legion prides itself on resisting such narrow interpretations,' Occam hissed. 'For us, there is always another way.'

'That remains to be seen, fleshling,' Omizhar Vohk said.

'Let us see what you do with this choice. You are monitoring the fortification below, no?'

Occam looked to Arkan Reznor, who looked back at his rune screen. Like everyone else on the command deck, he had been distracted by the alien's arrival. Occam heard the warpsmith curse under his breath.

'The defence lasers have powered up,' Reznor confirmed, 'and the emplacement is reorientating.'

'Talk,' Occam said to Vohk.

'You need not me to tell you what you already suspect to be true,' Vohk said. 'What you have always suspected to be true.'

'The Bas-Silica is going to fire upon the *Assiduous*?' Occam asked, but the question came out more like a statement.

'Almost certainly.'

The Alpha Legionnaires unconsciously took several steps towards the xenos advisor, while Mina Perdita slipped into the elevator car, her finger hovering over the button.

'At Carthach's order?'

'Of course.'

'Why?'

'What reason does he need?' Vohk put to the strike master. 'The Angelbane's gift has been in bringing the lesser-race scum of the galaxy together, so that he might drown the sons of the Eastern Primarch in your myriad talents and motivations. He is, however, a being driven by hate. The Primordial Annihilator has long had its hooks in him – drawing him on. And he hates you, Occam – 'the Untrue'. He hates you, what you fight for and those who choose for their own reasons to fight with you.'

Vohk gestured at the legionnaires of the Redacted.

'Why?' Ephron Hasdrubal demanded, closing in with his bolt pistol clutched in his gauntlet.

'Because we are different,' Quoda the sorcerer said, 'and we define ourselves by what we are not.'

'The Alpha Legion has made an art out of pretending to be something they are not,' Vohk told them, 'but you aren't pretending. Your primarch isn't your own. Your blood betrays you. The least treasonous thing about you all is the paint on your plate. At least that can claim to belong to the Legion. Your arch-lord employs renegade Space Marines, but you are the only ones in his ranks to desecrate the colours of his Legion by wearing them.'

'The defence laser array?' Occam put to Reznor, turning away from the alien advisor.

'Still reorientating,' the warpsmith said, 'but approaching our target trajectory.'

'Void shields?' Occam asked.

'Cannot be activated in void-dock,' Reznor told him. 'The scaffold-platforia. The repairs.'

'Like the universe, fleshling,' Vohk said, 'you are running out of time.'

'Quoda, tell me you can read this abominate thing,' Occam said, turning his back on the alien.

'He cannot,' Vohk assured the strike master, tapping his silver skull with one claw. 'His warp-born powers have no dominion here.'

'Everything you have said, Carthach knows,' Occam said. 'None of us originally belonged to the Legion. Malik was one of the Night Haunter's attack dogs and my sergeant a hunted member of the Fallen. Quoda there is an excommunicate member of the Relictors and my warpsmith was run out of the Mentors Chapter by the Inquisition for unsanctioned technological experimentation. Carthach himself recommended Phex for service in my ranks and he *is* a successor son of Guilliman.'

'Because he hates you,' Omizhar Vohk told him. 'He hates your blood and he hates the hearts that pump it, for he knows that in their own ways and for their own reasons, such hearts still beat *for the Emperor*. Even the attack dog, who cares little for whom he fights.'

'Again,' Occam said, with no little frustration, 'Lord Carthach knows this. The Sons of the Hydra all strike in their different ways. It has been the hallmark of the Angelbane's success – to this very day. Xenos-lovers. Altereds. Seditionist cells. Pirates. And yes – even loyalists. We all have our uses.'

'It seems that you have outlived your usefulness, fleshling.'

'Go back to Lord Carthach,' Occam told Vohk, towering over the hunched machine in his plate. 'Tell him that we have accomplished our objective in good faith and in his name. That as true Sons of the Hydra, we await his further orders.'

'Listen to yourself, renegade,' Vohk said. '*Good faith. True sons.*'

'Tell him!'

'I cannot.'

'Why not?'

'Because it was I that advised him to fire upon you.'

Stunned silence settled upon the command deck.

'I indulged a little in the untruths that your Legion revels in,' Vohk said. 'I told him, now with the successor sons of Guilliman defeated, that you intended to usurp his command. I told him of your little secret concerning your shape-changing Assassin there. That you intended to set her upon him again – to finally finish what she started. I find that lies are best hidden amongst truths, no?'

Sergeant Hasdrubal brought up his bolt pistol and levelled it at Omizhar Vohk's silvery temple.

'We should end this xenos abomination and leave,' the sergeant said.

Occam stared at the ancient. Vohk stared back with the green intensity of his cyclopean optic.

'It's too late for that,' Occam said. 'This alien thing has kept us talking and seen to that. Right?'

'They almost have us,' the warpsmith confirmed.

'You said most of the fortress void shields are back up and operational,' Occam checked, not taking his eyes off Omizhar Vohk. 'Which ones aren't?'

'The ones through which the defence lasers would have to fire in order to strike this vessel,' Reznor told his strike master.

'It is time to find another way. It is time to make a choice, Occam the Untrue,' Vohk said. 'Have you outlived your usefulness or has Lord Carthach?'

'Usefulness to who?' Occam demanded.

'To me, fleshling,' the ancient said. 'To the gods and emperors of this galaxy. To the species who might prosper here and to your Legion, who ten thousand years ago made the most difficult of choices. Can you make the same, I wonder?'

'Sir?' Sergeant Hasdrubal said.

'My lord?' Arkan Reznor asked.

Occam looked around the command deck. From Mina Perdita's false face to the serpentine helms of the Redacted and on to the leering skull-face of the mechanical monster before him.

'Is the bombardment cannon's target trajectory still set?' Occam asked finally.

'On the fortress-monastery, yes,' Reznor said. 'With the dorsal section gun crews still standing by. We can exploit the void shield opening if–'

'Have them execute their captain's final order,' Occam said, cutting the warpsmith off.

In the silence that followed, the Redacted heard the bombardment cannon fire and felt the buck of the linear accelerator through the deck. The Alpha Legionnaires moved towards the lancet screens and waited for the inevitable. Either the magma bomb warhead would hit the fortress-monastery first or the Bas-Silica's defence lasers would blaze the defenceless battle-barge out of the heavens. As an apocalyptic glow rose up from the planet surface, Occam felt his plate sag slightly. Whether this was relief or the weight of responsibility for the atrocity he had just committed, he could not tell. Regardless of the hundreds of thousands of Imperial citizens that had just been vaporised, the bombardment cannon had buried hundreds of Alpha Legion Space Marines and their cult followers beneath them. For a moment the spectacle held the legionnaire's gaze.

'Sir,' Ephron Hasdrubal said. Occam turned.

Omizhar Vohk was gone.

Behind his faceplate, Occam snarled. Had Carthach intended on celebrating his victory by finally purging the Redacted? Or had the alien ancient simply convinced the Angelbane of imminent betrayal, as he had done with Occam?

The strike master felt the optics of his legionnaires on him. An explanation was required. A direction, at least – even if Occam didn't know what that direction was.

'Whichever way you look at this,' he told the Redacted, 'we have done the Emperor's work here today.' The Alpha Legionnaires nodded their helms slowly in sombre agreement.

'Your orders, strike master?' Reznor asked.

'It will not be long before the Astral Fists and the Angels Eradicant break system,' Occam told them. 'Krayt and his pirates will not be able to delay them for long. We are not going to be here when they arrive. Quoda, accompany the sergeant. I want the armoury checked on our way off this hulk for anything useful to replenish our own – specialist ammunition and equipment, rare grenades and artificer weaponry. Check with Reznor regarding our needs. Reznor, I want you to re-establish atmospherics and pressure on the thorax gun decks. Then have the sub-light engine columns engaged. Push this beast into a fast-deteriorating orbit. Phex, go with Perdita and prep the drop pod and lighter. Malik, with me. We'll all meet back at the *Serpent's Egg* and abandon the ship.'

As members of the Redacted took to the elevator car and dropped down through the holes in the command deck, Occam took one last look through the lancet screens at the glowing crater that had been the Bas-Silica. Vilnius Malik joined him.

'Looks like we're on our own,' Occam said.

'It won't prey on my conscience,' the former Night Lord answered.

'Mine neither,' Occam assured him. 'For I can't afford to have one.'

PART II

GHOST LEGION

ε

SNAKE EYES

The Assassin assumed the identity of another. It was her way. It hurt just to be herself and such inner torment drove her to seek solace in the shapes of other people. Everyone. Anyone but herself.

Mina was a mistress of shadow and suggestion. Aboard the *Iota-Æternus* she did not bother with polymorphine. Every agonising transformation under the powerful drug's influence cost her. The temple, however, had equipped her with many skills. Silence. Stealth. Agility. Even when she could be seen, she made herself unremarkable. Unobtrusive and part of the pattern.

Even without wasting the chameleon-like properties of the drug, her arts of deception were considerable. She was a keen observer of human behaviour. She also had an exquisite control over both body and voice – the kind of skills that an actress or performer could only dream of wielding. She moved like a phantom in flesh, stealing props and clothing to aid her presentation as she went.

She was presently a robed young man. Lithe. Muscled like a killer but with the glinting eyes of a hooded, religious deviant. One of the Seventh Sons trusted by the super-human sorcerer Carcinus Quoda to work at his beck and call in the librarium. The Assassin used serpent and death cult tattoos on her skin, as well as penal colony identica codes from Korsino 421, where the Seventh Sons had been radicalised and recruited.

She crossed the small command deck of the *Iota-Æternus* with her gorgon mask hanging from the belt of her robes. The Alpha Legion vessel was a refitted Q-ship – a sprint freighter outfitted with hidden heavy weaponry. Typically, such Q-ships would be mixed into freighter convoys to act as a deterrent and surprise defence against pirates. The Redacted had found the *Iota-Æternus* – with its cargo holds outfitted with concealed batteries and extra decks for housing their cult armies – perfect for their needs. The Q-ship made for a versatile base of mobile operations for Occam the Untrue and his Alpha Legionnaires.

Perdita passed between the cultist-manned runebanks of the cramped bridge, her robed shape cutting a silhou-ette into command deck lancet screens. Upon the orders of Lord Occam, on the return of the *Serpent's Egg* and cult boarding craft to the Q-ship, the *Iota-Æternus* had taken position in the nearby Kraal Nebula. The Alpha Legion vessel was holding hidden station in the nebula, monitor-ing the Vitrea Mundi system in the aftermath of the attack.

The Assassin passed beneath the gaze of Torghai Naga-Khan, shipmaster and captain of the *Iota-Æternus*. A Chogorisian, Naga-Khan was a verbose character full of charm and intellect.

In the interests of extra security and perverse indulgence,

Perdita made it her business to move unrecognised amongst the ship's cultist crew and trusted operatives like Freydor Blatch and Captain Naga-Khan. The Assassin even occasionally chanced her hand with their enigmatic overlords, the renegade demigods of the Alpha Legion, especially if she sensed there was something particularly significant and unshared transpiring among them.

Perdita knew, for example, that Naga-Khan had been first officer on an Imperial Navy frigate during the Damocles Crusade. There to check the aggressive expansion of eastern xenos empires, Naga-Khan was unfortunate enough to get caught up in a mutiny against a tyrannical, spire-born captain. Taking control of the vessel and knowing that a court martial and a commissar's noose awaited him back with the Imperial fleet, Naga-Khan gave himself and his frigate up to their enemies, the alien t'au. Finding employment with the xenos collectivists, Naga-Khan became a Gue'vesa privateer, using his inside knowledge to prey on military convoys supplying Imperial forces in the Damocles Gulf. Ever the free spirit, the successful privateer began selling his talents to the highest bidder, finding himself finally in the employ of Occam the Untrue.

Climbing the starboard pulpit staircase, Perdita moved past Naga-Khan. The shipmaster was drinking some kind of Chogorisian horse-swill from a wineskin, droplets of which dribbled down the luxurious black length of his moustache, beard and hair. Naga-Khan drank almost constantly, feeding the shipmaster's ego and pushing him and his vessel on to ever more audacious feats.

Behind the shipmaster's throne, Perdita entered the librarium, which occupied the rear section of the command deck. As Perdita shuffled past printed vellum and ducked beneath jawless servo-skulls spewing it out from their quill-mounted mandibles, she moved through other trusted members of the Seventh Sons. The Assassin knew that loyalist Space Marine Chapters manned their libraria with powerful psykers responsible for interstellar communications and warrior-clerics who maintained the Chapter's repositories of wisdom and history. Such Space Marines kept reports, researched treatises and maintained the memoirs of the Chapter's greatest martial minds.

Alpha Legionnaires like the Redacted had precious little need for such repositories. Instead, the sorcerer Carcinus Quoda ran his intelligence-gathering operation out of the librarium command centre. Perdita moved through the hololithic displays and runebanks, which were covered in vellum scrolls and data-slates. Under Quoda's authority, calculus logi, lexomats and linguitor units went to work on data gathered by cultists, operatives, code-scrubbers and the sorcerer's small astropathic choir-coven. Seemingly drawn to the other warp-sensitive mutants on board, Ghesh – the ship's Navigator – also frequented the librarium.

Like all witchbreeds, Carcinus Quoda was odd. Reserved and cautious, he was like a blind man feeling his way through the galaxy's secrets – sifting for anything of use to the Redacted. Perdita watched the twitchy sorcerer move about the intelligence centre, his towering figure dressed in ship's robes. While displaying no obvious corruptions, despite his sorcerous dabblings in the warp, Quoda had a weakness for artefacts – both alien and those tainted by Chaos – that might help the Redacted serve the Emperor. His Chapter had been excommunicated for such heresy. Perdita knew that he kept dangerous relics in a secure vault, adjoining his private suite of cells, but had never managed to gain admittance. She monitored the sorcerer out of the corner of her eye as he riffled through scrolls, consulted attendant cultists and communed with his astropathic choir.

'Anything from the *Omega-Echidnax*?' a Seventh Son asked her. The deep lines of his face and the glint of bridge lamps off the short silver bristles of his close-cropped head betrayed the cultist's age. A former prisoner, just like the rest of the Seventh Sons, his abilities had been put to work in the librarium rather than as part of death cultist boarding actions. Perdita looked down at the vellum scraps she was absently flicking through. She handed him a piece that detailed a lack of vox-contact and returns from the Angelbane's flagship. As they had concluded for other vessels belonging to the Sons of the Hydra, Quoda's logi and intelligence analysts had determined that in all probability their crews – thinking all had been lost on the surface of Vitrea Mundi – had fled the system.

'What about other vessels in the region?' the silver-haired cultist asked, squinting at the report Perdita had handed him. She passed him a data-slate this time, identifying vox-intercepts from an Astral Fists strike cruiser that had just broken system. The Astral Fists' communications would go unheeded. There was a glowing crater where the Bas-Silica and Salina City used to be. The aged Seventh Son shuffled off to show the reports to his master, Carcinus Quoda. Quietly, the Assassin left the bridge and librarium.

It was easier indulging in the art of being others. She had done so many terrible things during her time in the Officio temples. She had murdered men and women, the

young and the old. She had been the personified end
to defenceless aliens and humans tainted beyond use to
themselves. In training she had even killed sister Assassins:
girls with whom she had lived and trained. Perdita sometimes thought that she might be hiding from the terrible
things done to her, rather than those she had inflicted
upon others. Horrors experienced in infancy, before the
temple surgeons had experimented upon her flesh and
frame with muscle-rupturing chemicals, pop-up plates
of carapace and pneumatic bone extensions. Things she
could not remember or recall.

She was no longer some temple tool to be unleashed at
another's choosing. Conversely, she had no intention of
becoming like others she had seen – an acolyte of some
Ruinous Power promising gifts of change that she already
possessed. She was not interested in coin, opportunity or
protection – all of which she could procure for herself.
In breaking her, the Alpha Legion had given her purpose.
Occam the Untrue was her compass and his objectives
her true North.

In reality, the action above Vitrea Mundi had consti-
tuted a brutal coup rather than a purge. The Redacted,
among other Alpha Legion cells operating loosely under
the Angelbane's banner – like Naetrix Krayt's pirates –
were still technically Sons of the Hydra, only now with
the usurping Occam the Untrue as their de facto leader.

Perdita had no idea what Lord Occam's next move might
be. So far, it just seemed to involve hiding in the Kraal
Nebula. Perhaps he planned upon joining forces with
Krayt. Perhaps he would run down the *Omega-Echidnax*
and transfer his operations to the flagship. Perdita considered he might even follow through on the Angelbane's

operations in the Vitrea Mundi system and attack the arriving Astral Fists. Before deciding whether or not to stay with the Alpha Legion, the Assassin intended to find out – and she wouldn't simply wait for a fork-tongued announcement from the ship's demigod overlords.

Moving through the Alpha Legion vessel, Perdita indulged another identity. Her next choice was one of the slight, bright-eyed girls she had seen on the dormitory decks.

While the renegades busied themselves with the lofty prosecution of labyrinthine schemes, and operatives were either recruited or imprisoned on board for the utilisation of their talents, the Seventh Sons ran a small, self-sufficient colony on the converted decks of the freighter. They were not cult slaves to be organised into meatshield formations or regiments being transported aboard Navy carriers to their deaths. The *Iota-Æternus* was their home and the Alpha Legion overlords walked among them like household gods. On Korsino 421 the prisoners were too deadly and unified by the death cult faith to be segregated. The penal colonies were close-knit criminal communities, where order was maintained not by walls and wardens but by cult structures established by the High Serpent and his Alpha Legion sponsors.

Moving from the trudging step of a librarium attendant to the light tread of a colony courtesan, she adjusted her hair and cult robes in a savage design to frame her harsh but attractive features. She showed off other tattoos. By the time she turned into one of the colony's open deck thoroughfares, containing serpent shrines, fighting pits and communal galleys, her disguise was complete.

Brushing shoulders with other brothers and sisters of

the Seventh Sons, Perdita could smell spicy food being prepared and felt the spray of blood from death cultists competing for sport in shallow fighting pits crafted from cargo crates. She passed individual cells where cultists were indulging in sense-heightening narcotics, being tattooed and ritually scarred. She stepped over poisonous serpents that slithered across the deck. Collected from myriad worlds, their venom was used in temple ceremonies. Many had escaped their containment to infest the ship.

Moving down through the decks, she looked in on the High Serpent's personal quarters. It was here that she had sometimes found Freydor Blatch drinking with the shipmaster or playing regicide with Ghesh the Navigator. She found him this time discussing cult business with his seven disciples. Among the most deadly of the death cultists and influential among the former prison population, the disciples were the High Serpent's eyes, ears and mouthpiece among the cultist colony. Unlike Perdita herself, the Seventh Sons cared little for the events above Vitrea Mundi and possible repercussions to come. They would follow their Alpha Legion masters – to whom they owed everything – into the raging eye of a warpstorm. They were content to do as they were asked.

The Assassin moved lightly through the chamber. It was more lavishly decorated than the rather sparse environs of the rest of the colony. She took up a carafe of wine and refilled the chalices of the disciples and the High Serpent himself. Blatch was in mid-diatribe and was more than distracted. While Perdita trailed her fingertips suggestively along one girl's shoulders and the back of the High Serpent's fat neck, Blatch barely noticed her. Confident that the Seventh Sons were discussing little of note, the Assassin pushed on.

She retained the disguise of the cultist girl as she came across Ephron Hasdrubal. The Alpha Legion sergeant was where he could usually be found when not attending upon Lord Occam or off-ship on a mission: the practice cages. While many renegade Space Marines allowed corruption to take root in their genetically engineered flesh or their prowess to wither through the ages, the demigods of the Redacted maintained at least some rituals of their previous lives.

As she tended briefly to the injuries of battered and broken Seventh Sons in the antechamber, Perdita watched Sergeant Hasdrubal go toe to toe with ten death cultists within the practice cages. Peering surreptitiously through the bars, she saw the bare-chested sergeant – his ship's robes like skirts about his waist – dance through his opponents with the grace of a demigod.

Improvising and moving from technique to exotic combat technique, Hasdrubal wielded his torturer's multi-blade like a practice-cage gladius. The vicious death cultists – all chosen for their own differing techniques and physical talents – swung, sliced and stabbed at the legionnaire with venom-slick blades of their own. Time and again, Perdita saw the sergeant dodge razored edges of smouldering lethality, his pale skin untouched.

While the death cultists were fast and deadly enough to cut a buzzing fly in two, the Alpha Legion sergeant's superhuman reflexes made them appear like they were swinging through syrup. Turning the multi-blade in his hand, Hasdrubal batted aside his attackers' lunges. Blades edged with neural mesh turned cultist weapons into contact-instruments of shrieking torture. Chain-blades pranged envenomed swords from grips while energy-sheathed power blades sheared cultist weapons in two.

With the face of a hunted man – a man with no intention of ever being taken by his loyalist Dark Angels brothers – Ephron Hasdrubal snatched up disarmed cultists and threw them down onto the deck. Others he backhanded across the practice cage with the contempt of a demigod, while the last got the legionnaire's heel jackhammered straight into the abdomen, breaking the Seventh Son.

The sergeant stood there, barely breaking a sweat and fine-tuning his torturer's blade. All about him, cultists groaned and crawled over the deck in a daze.

'Again,' the sergeant ordered, prompting replacement cultists to enter the practice cage. Perdita ran in with several others. She had no intention of going blade to blade with the demigod, although she did suspect that with her temple training she might fare better than the penal colony killers being dragged out of the cage. Instead, she took the broken cultist under the arm with another Seventh Son, and helped the unfortunate away.

The ship infirmary was mercifully not far away. Unfortunately, it was small and already overrun with injured cultists from the boarding action on the battle-barge. Seventh Sons, bandaged and recuperating, swung from hammocks that had been set up on pipes lining the corridors outside the infirmary.

The Assassin handed the broken death cultist off to a medicae-servitor. Under the watchful gaze of two Seventh Sons minders, hostage medical staff tended to the injured.

While the cultists were willing servants of the Alpha Legion and operatives like Perdita engaged in service to the renegades, the talents of some were less than voluntary. The Redacted didn't boast an Alpha Legion Apothecary and so penal colony medics, nurses and servitors were taken hostage by the liberated Seventh Sons and put to work in the ship infirmary. Moved between the medical facilities and the brig, the medical staff and chirurgeons were treated well in exchange for use of their life-saving talents when the circumstances required it. Perdita suspected that the colony medics were simply waiting for the day an Imperial cruiser might capture the *Iota-Æternus* and finally free the hostages. What made the medical staff even more pliable and cooperative, however, was the insistence by their Seventh Sons patients that even should that come to pass, they would only see the inside of another cell – this time in some backwater Inquisition stronghold.

Not far from the practice cages, Perdita could hear the shooting range. The single thunderclaps of a boltgun echoed up the passageways, prompting the Assassin to change her disguise once more. Selecting the appearance of the broken cultist she had just delivered to the infirmary, she brought up her hood. Utilising props and abandoned clothing from the crowded infirmary, she changed her gait and the confidence with which she carried herself. She passed through the range to find the renegade known as Vilnius Malik there. Like his Alpha Legion brothers he was dressed in ship's robes and aiming a Stalker-pattern boltgun down the length of the shooting gallery.

Cultist wranglers had manhandled several mutants into the plasma-blasted range. Such creatures, never in short supply on the fringe worlds of the Maelstrom, were no good to themselves or anyone else. As they ran awkwardly between bolt-blasted cargo crates, Malik – his eye to the Stalker's scope – picked them off. Blowing the heads off the mutants might have seemed a mercy but for the delight clear on the legionnaire's face. As Seventh Sons cultists wrestled another grotesque mutant from storage incarceration, Perdita gave them room. Picking up a pair of ammunition crates, she moved on.

The Assassin found the Redacted's warpsmith hard at work in his workshops, overseeing the workmanship of a small army of interfaced technical servitors. His mechadendrites snaked about him, making small recalibrations and adjustments before whipping back into his plate. Not unlike the sorcerer Quoda, Perdita always found Arkan Reznor hard at study and work. Torghai Naga-Khan might have been shipmaster of the *Iota-Æternus* but the vessel really belonged to the arch-experimenter Reznor. His servitors and upgraded servo-automata maintained the converted freighter, while the Q-ship's concealed weapon and sprint engine columns both benefitted from customisation with alien technologies.

Unlike Quoda, who always maintained a haunted, detached air, Reznor was happy to share enthusiasm for his work and technical passions. His invaluable contribution to the Redacted had undoubtedly enhanced the small warband's effectivity and allowed them to achieve much more than their numbers might suggest.

As Perdita entered the workshop, she found herself barred by the appearance of the warpsmith's personal servo-automata – Beta, Zeta and Theta. Using their underbelly nest of serpentine mechatendrils, they took the ammunition crates from her and hovered before the Assassin, prompting her to leave the workshop.

Finding herself in the aft-section of the ship, Perdita pulled her hood up over her head and walked down a dark corridor from which adjoined the private cells of the Alpha Legion overlords. Outside the chambers belonging to Autolicon Phex, the Assassin's excellent hearing picked up a sound. She slowed, taking a furtive look up and down the passage before listening closer at the metal of the door.

Within, Perdita could hear muffled whimpers, harsh whispers and the sound of banging, like a head against a wall. Phex had been the latest addition to the Redacted. The Assassin knew of Phex's treatment at the hands of the Angelbane and the arch-lord's insistence that he join Occam the Untrue. As she listened to the demigod's suffering, Perdita considered how each member of the Redacted was a madman in his own way and that the addition of another would make little difference.

At the rear of the ship, situated between the customised engine columns of the *Iota-Æternus*, were the private chambers of Lord Occam. Of the Untrue, the Assassin knew almost nothing. He was unusual, even for a member of the Alpha Legion. Perdita knew precious little of the Imperium of ten thousand years ago but understood that like the rest of the Emperor's Space Marines, the Alpha Legion had once been loyal. Like the Imperium itself, the Legion had been shattered by the events of the galactic civil war and even more by a short eternity of stagnant disintegration.

Perdita understood from working amongst the renegades that the once proud Alpha Legion – worthy, proficient and loyal – now shared the same fate as other fallen Legions. The Legion was a nest of knotted serpents, an entity as one but with every fanged head pulling in a different direction. Cells operating on their own. Alpha Legion warbands, forming brief collectives under charismatic arch-lords like Quetzel Carthach. The rare sub-sector wide Harrowing – crude cataclysms coordinated under the cover of Black Crusades.

As Perdita entered Occam's vaulted chambers she heard her master within.

'Priest,' the strike master said, his words like a warning, 'there is nothing to fear here. Pray, enter.'

The Assassin listened to the lie. She knew that as well as the medics, Occam had taken a priest. Confessor Kressnik had been sent to the penal colony to use his skills in oratory to draw the prison population from their serpent worship and back to the Emperor's light in readiness for regimental processing – the Seventh Sons were to become part of a cannon-fodder penal legion.

Occam had taken an interest in the priest, routinely having him brought to his chambers. What the strike master didn't know was that Kressnik had hanged himself in his cell within hours of being taken prisoner and that Perdita had been impersonating the priest and keeping the legionnaire's counsel ever since.

Perdita let her cultist robes slip off to reveal the ragged remains of the priest's filthy white cassock. She pulled up the priest's voxhailer half-mask to cover the bottom part of her face and produced his limp mitre from a pocket. Arranging her hair beneath the mitre, she took a moment to assume the priest's limp and moved on inside.

Inside the chamber was dark, which worked well for the Assassin. A stained-glass window in the rear of the chamber threatened to bathe its gloom in a multitude of colours whenever the Q-ship's sub-light engines fired. Perdita entered a room within a room. Incongrously, a tiny chapel lay within.

She knew the history of the shrine from Occam. When reports had reached the strike master that Word Bearers ships out of Ghalmek had hit the shrine world of Canticula, he had ordered the *Iota-Æternus* diverted there. All the Alpha Legion had found was smouldering ruins and suffering.

The precious artefact denoting Canticula as a shrine world was the tiny, unassuming Chapel of the Immaculate Ascension. The chapel had been built upon the supposed site of the Emperor's landing there, early in his crusade to spread humanity's dominion throughout the stars. It even incorporated a partial impression of the Emperor's armoured boot, left behind by his visit and preserved by natural processes.

The Assassin didn't know whether the artefact was fake – as many claiming such heritage were – but the little, backwater world had become a destination for pilgrims who wanted to walk in their God-Emperor's footsteps. Claiming that where the Master of Mankind had been the dark forces of the galaxy could not follow, Canticula – and the Chapel of the Immaculate Ascension in particular – had become a magnet not only for exorcists and daemonhunters but also those believing themselves tainted or even possessed. On the flags about the altar and on the sides of the holy object itself, Perdita had noted the faded markings of ancient hexagrammic wards, purity seals, chiselled extracts from the Lectitio Divinitatus and sigils of banishment. She suspected that many pilgrims arrived at the chapel with shackled loved ones who were merely suffering from mental afflictions or delusions brought on by toxic hive world environments. In reality, the Assassin knew little about such arcane rituals and protections and for all she really knew, a thousand polluting entities might have been banished upon the altar.

The Word Bearers had certainly believed in the shrine world's significance and had decimated its small cities from orbit. Arriving on Canticula, Occam the Untrue discovered the ruined chapel to be partially intact and the altar untouched by the destruction that had rained down from the heavens. Using lighters and the Seventh Sons as labour, the strike master had what was left of the chapel transported up to the *Iota-Æternus* and rebuilt in his chambers.

As Perdita walked through the derelict chapel and approached the altar she could see the partial impression of the boot print inset in the surface. It looked like nothing to her, but for billions across the Imperium – including Lord Occam – it was a visual reminder of the Emperor's enduring presence in the galaxy. It represented the difficult path walked by the Master of Mankind and the truest of his subjects. The symbol of a destination as yet unreached.

Perdita looked up. Through the doorless archway of the shattered chapel she saw Occam the Untrue sitting in the chamber's command throne like a troubled king. Crafted of jet, in the slithering semblance of a many-headed hydra, the throne glistened in the gloom. Dismissing a servo-skull and the Seventh Sons assigned to his personal needs like assembling his plate and preparing weaponry, Occam got up from the throne. His ship's robes trailed along the polished floor as he approached the chapel. Even without his armour, his footsteps sent quakes through the deck that Perdita felt through the cold soles of her bare feet.

Marching in through the archway, the demigod knelt before the altar and made the sign of the aquila across his chest. Even now, the Assassin considered, it was such a strange thing to see a renegade Space Marine do.

'Confessor,' Occam said, his words bouncing unnaturally through the shattered architecture of the rebuilt chapel. 'Hear me.'

With a theatrical look of dread crossing her false features, Perdita assumed the role of the priest once more. She readied her voice and became the priest in manner and syllable.

'If I must.'

'Gracious, as always,' Occam said.

'For all the grace allowed a prisoner,' Perdita replied.

When the strike master didn't reply immediately she thought she might have pushed the confessor's disdain too far. Confessor Kressnik was a man of the God-Emperor, kept incarcerated aboard an Alpha Legion vessel for its captain's amusement. Perdita had decided that the priest would be proud but still fearful – as indeed she was in the presence of Occam the Untrue. 'Whatever good grace I am allowed, is yours.'

'You are wise beyond your years, confessor,' Occam said.

'Speak unto me,' Perdita said, 'as you might before your God-Emperor.'

'And he will listen?'

'He listens as a father to His children.'

'His wayward children,' Occam said.

'The unfavoured are not forgotten,' Perdita told him, trying her best to emulate the priest and a hundred others she had known with their dry sermonising. 'Unburden your hearts, Space Marine.'

Perdita watched as Lord Occam flicked his gaze up at her briefly. It felt like the sights of a sniper's rifle aimed at her head.

'I have served the Master of Mankind,' Occam said, 'in a life long forgotten and I serve him still.'

'Yet you keep company with deviants and heretics,' Perdita interjected.

'They are weapons to be wielded,' the strike master said, 'and a weapon is nothing in itself. A razored blade. An undetonated charge. A shell, silent and unrealised within its magazine. A weapon needs a hand to direct its destruction. To decide who will live and who will die by its agency.'

'And you are that hand?'

'No,' Occam the Untrue told her. 'The Emperor is – for I am a weapon also and he had directed me towards his enemies.'

'The heretics you fight beside...'

'If that is what the Master of Mankind wills, then yes,' Occam said, his words growing keener and sharper with every utterance.

This is what Mina Perdita had learned about the strike master from such conversations. He wanted to be questioned; he wanted to be challenged. He was unsure of which direction to take. Occam the Untrue was no less lost than the madmen and corrupted souls under whose banners he had fought. In a galaxy of confusion, uncertainty and lies, Perdita decided, even a member of the Alpha Legion was allowed doubt. Standing before him in the semblance of a priest, she was a living embodiment of such a principle.

'The Imperium in its present state is not the dominion the Emperor intended,' Occam said, his voice laced with accusation. 'It forever totters on the precipice of destruction, is infested with alien empires and riddled with the taint of corruption.'

'Do you not share in some of that responsibility, renegade?' Perdita put to him.

'I do not,' Occam said. 'The lords of the Holy Ordos, the Ecclesiarchy and the battle-brothers of the Adeptus Astartes do. Through their every feeble action, they sustain the ailing beast that is the Imperium. I want to put it out of its misery. I want to purge the rot and the stagnation. I want what the Master of Mankind wants – the empire we were promised.'

'How can you know the mind of the God-Emperor?' Perdita pressed. She backed from the altar as Occam suddenly got to his feet. The Assassin cursed herself. Instead of venting his imperious fury, the strike master narrowed his eyes at her in thought and recognition. Perdita's heart thudded in her chest. She had responded to the legionnaire's sudden movement with the reflexes of an Assassin, not an elderly priest.

'The blood that runs through these veins,' Occam told her, his voice low, 'belongs to my genic father and my father's father. I am engineered of the Emperor's flesh. What are you, priest, but the detritus of humanity washed up on the shores of some cardinal world, bloated with its own self-importance? You stand in those rags and in the ruins of churches and think that qualifies you to speak on His behalf? You are but charlatans puppeting the cadaverous remains of a tyrant you barely understand. His tyrannical spirit burns on in brothers brave enough to prosecute the cold complexities of his will.'

'And you are one of those brothers?'

'I am,' Occam seethed across the altar. 'He will deliver the promised empire – a dominion humanity can be proud to call its own – but for such an Imperium to exist, both the tainted meat of the body Imperial and the useless fat must be cut away. The weak and faithful of the galaxy are just as much an impediment to such an outcome as the powerful and traitorous.'

'And that is what you intend to do?' Perdita asked the Alpha Legion strike master. 'Wield that knife and cut away the tainted and feeble?'

'In the Emperor's name, yes,' Occam told her.

'Even without the aid of your legionary allies?'

Occam gave Perdita snake eyes. His lip curled into a slow snarl.

'A small blade can do a lot of damage,' Occam said, 'if you know where to strike. Any Assassin would be able to tell you that.'

When the strike master sprang, Mina Perdita was expecting it. It didn't help her. Neither did her Assassin's reflexes or temple training. She was slower than she might have been. Unsure of when to break character. Waiting until Occam confirmed his suspicions with violent conviction. His arm shot out and grabbed her by the scruff of her robes, his fist like a vice of bone and muscle.

Occam the Untrue lifted her off her feet and slammed her down on the surface of the altar with merciless force. Holding her with one hand, he pushed the other into her robes. Perdita kicked, hit and thrashed in the Space Marine's grip, attempting a series of locks, holds and defensive manoeuvres, as dictated by her training. Each had its own lethal follow-up, but fight though the Assassin might, she couldn't get any to stick on the demigod.

Running his hand through the robes, Occam found the blade Perdita had secreted there – a weapon she had surreptitiously picked up from the practice cages. As Occam pulled it from the rags and held the venom-slick blade above her, Perdita fell still in his grasp.

'Is this for me, Assassin?' he put to her. He gestured to his own features. 'You think I don't know a false face when I see it? Have you come to finish what you started? The Angelbane is dead. Are you here ensuring that I don't take up his mantle?'

'No,' Perdita insisted, 'a thousand times, no. I don't expect you to believe me, my lord, but it remains the truth.'

Occam peered into her eyes before his face creased with anger and frustration. He slammed her against the surface of the altar before lifting her off and pitching her across the chapel chamber. Usually a creature of precision and grace, Perdita tried to regain her balance but by the time she got her feet to the floor, her face was flying into the stone wall.

Getting up, she felt the warmth of blood down the side of her face. It was seeping from a gash on her head. She turned and put her back against the wall. As she did she heard the clang of metal against the flags of the floor. Lord Occam had tossed the envenomed blade down at her feet.

'You're right,' the strike master said. 'I don't believe you. Take your weapon and do what you came here to do. You have been a good servant to the Legion. I'll kill you quickly. I owe you that much.'

Perdita kicked the blade away, sending it skidding noisily across the flags and out of the chapel archway.

'I swear,' Perdita said, 'by the Emperor, on some serpent shrine or to the Dark Gods – I am not here to harm you. I am Perdita. Your agent. Your operative. Your blade to strip the carcass Imperium of the feeble and the damned.'

'Then what are you doing here, Assassin,' Occam put to her, 'in the private chambers of a renegade who needs little reason to end you? Consider your answer carefully. It may well be your last.'

Mina Perdita licked her lips.

'I thought myself accomplished,' she said, 'when I first infiltrated the Sons of the Hydra. I have learned a lot from you and your Legion. Like all in the Alpha Legion, I wanted to know. I wanted to understand and I'll admit – to use such knowledge to my advantage. A great deal changed above Vitrea Mundi. So much depends upon what you decide. I'm not ashamed to admit that I would like to know what happens next. That is why I tried to deceive you. One way or another, I assure you that it won't happen again. I just wanted to know the mind of the man who holds my fate in his hands.'

The Alpha Legion strike master stared at the Assassin, the snarl contorting his face fading.

'When I am ready to share my mind with you,' Occam the Untrue said, 'with the Seventh Sons or my legionary brothers, you will know about it. Now get out of my sight and frequent these chambers no more.'

ζ

SNAKE OIL

'Is there a problem?' a metallic voice proceeded from the darkness.

As Mina Perdita left his chambers, Occam looked down at the partial imprint of the Emperor's boot set in the surface of the altar. Following in the Master of Mankind's footsteps was proving difficult indeed.

The sons of Guilliman. Renegade madmen. The corrupted. Devout servants of the Emperor. All were out for Occam's blood. Now his own operatives seemed to be stalking him and xenos abominations were trying to get him killed.

'As she said,' Occam answered, 'the Alpha Legion teaches its operatives to be curious and to take the initiative.'

The hunched figure of Omizhar Vohk ventured forth from the shadows of the chapel. He gave Occam the sickening green glare of his single optic.

'You are fortunate, fleshling, that she didn't take the initiative earlier with that blade,' the xenos advisor said.

'You overestimate her as you underestimate me, monster,' Occam told him, leaving the chapel and crossing the chamber. 'You have your predictions. The Legion has its games, its tricks and deceptions. She did well to get as close as she did, all things considered. The Legion can use such skill and audacity.'

The xenos creature hung back and dug at the crumbling stone of the chapel with its metal claws.

'It is interesting,' Vohk said, 'the fleshling preoccupation with stone. Everywhere you go you feel the need to erect your false temples and tiny tombs. Perhaps we are not so different, you and I. The worlds of my people are similarly dominated by such buildings – albeit on a much grander scale. Perhaps one day, I shall get the opportunity to show you such wonders.'

'Perhaps one day, abomination, you'll get to the point.'

As Occam turned and sat back in his throne, the legionnaire heard the metallic thunk of the alien's footsteps following him across the deck.

'I understand, fleshling,' Vohk said. 'In a life as short as yours, I appreciate that you have little patience for such delays. I apologise. You see, all I have is time. Time and what it tells me.'

'It's the only reason you are alive to haunt the corridors of my ship,' Occam told the alien. 'You like tombs? If you pull something like that again, you are assured to see the inside of one.'

'I saved your life,' the alien taunted.

'That is yet to be seen,' Occam told him. 'Now, as you were saying, monster.'

'Ah, yes. Before we were rudely interrupted,' Vohk said, standing beside the throne like a dutiful advisor. 'I served as advisor to Quetzel Carthach – such colourful names you have.'

'Before you had me drop a magma bomb warhead on him,' Occam interjected, 'the necessity of which you will also explain to me.'

'Where I come from, fleshling,' Vohk said, 'I am called many things.'

'I don't doubt it.'

'Astraturge,' Vohk continued. 'Stellasayer. Chronomancer. I read the stars and harness their gravitational governance of the past, present and future. Lord Carthach benefitted from my talents in exterminating the sons of the warlord you call Guilliman – in that, the objectives of the Angelbane and my master overlapped.'

'Your master?'

'We all have masters, fleshling, do we not?'

'I don't.'

'You do,' Vohk assured Occam, 'you just don't know it yet. I foresaw for the Angelbane – further madness, obsession and the persecution of brother Space Marines.'

'So you thought you would help such insanity along,' Occam said with a baleful gaze.

'Indeed, fleshling,' Vohk told him, unfazed. 'At my instigation, you became the focus of such obsession and the beneficiary of its tragic outcome. For now it is the objectives of the Redacted and my master that overlap.'

'Until you advise someone to drop a magma bomb on me,' the strike master said.

'I will not be lectured on the rare necessitude of duplicity by a member of your Legion,' Omizhar Vohk told him evenly. 'We are both creatures of opportunity, are we not – and make opportunities where they fail to materialise?'

'Fair enough, abomination,' Occam said. 'But tell me this – what are your master's objectives? Because we no longer have the manpower to challenge Adeptus Astartes Chapters – no matter how depleted their ranks might be. You saw to that.'

'My master wants something.'

'What is this thing?'

'A piece of alien technology, more ancient than your entire species,' Omizhar Vohk said.

'Most of the best technology is,' Occam the Untrue agreed. 'Is this artefact dangerous?'

'Very.'

'And he needs this piece of technology locating?'

'We know where it can be found,' the alien advisor assured him.

'Then why don't you go fetch it for him, lapdog?' Occam asked. 'You seem pretty adept at ghosting your way into places into which you have not been invited. My ship and chambers, for example.'

'The artefact is located in a place where such techno-sorcery is compromised. A fleshling is required for this task. He wants the Alpha Legion to retrieve it for him.'

'Only the Legion?'

'He trusts few others with such an important undertaking.'

'Why not send Carthach?' Occam put to him.

'The Angelbane's approach would have been... unproductive,' Vohk told him. 'This undertaking requires a light touch and the sensibilities of a thief, not a butcher.'

'I am no thief, xenos.'

'I beg to differ,' Vohk said. 'Everything about you is stolen, from your ship and plate to your face and your purpose.'

Occam grunted.

'Is your master too polite to go and recover this piece of technology himself? Why does he need the Redacted?' the strike master asked.

'The Lord Dominatus issues orders and the Alpha Legion follow them,' Omizhar Vohk told him.

'What did you just say?' Occam said, rising out of his throne.

'I see that I have your attention,' the abomination observed.

'The Lord Dominatus?'

'My master,' Vohk said, 'and yours.'

'You work for a member of the Legion?' Occam asked, turning his head to one side to peer into the dark hood of the alien machine.

'Quetzel Carthach is not the only arch-lord of the Alpha Legion to gather your dark brotherhood under his banner,' Vohk said. 'As emissary of the Lord Dominatus, I engaged the Angelbane and the Sons of the Hydra – as I have many Alpha Legion cells, warbands and lone legionnaires. Since you belonged to the Sons of the Hydra also, it could be argued that you are already engaged in my master's service.'

'The destruction of Adeptus Astartes Chapters,' Occam said, 'the retrieval of artefacts, the gathering of legionnaires – what does this Lord Dominatus want?'

'A great many things,' Vohk said, 'one of which is for you to be a Legion again. A single, unified fighting force, rather than a scattered network of terror groups, all waging your own wars for your own reasons. The Lord Dominatus believes that the Legion can once again be more than the sum of its parts – that it can once again play its part in the destiny of the galaxy.'

'Who is he?' Occam demanded.

'His identity is not mine to divulge,' the xenos advisor said. 'What I can tell you, Occam the Untrue, is that you and he are the same.'

'What does that mean?'

'It means, that you are both believers,' Vohk said. 'That despite a civil war that tore your empire asunder and ten thousand years of taint and degradation, you both wear the colours of the Legion and beneath them both still harbour loyalty to the corpse Emperor.'

Occam turned away. His mind was a whirl. He absently shook his head.

'How is this possible?'

'Should you pass my master's test,' Vohk said, 'then perhaps you could ask him face to face.'

'Test?' Occam said. 'The artefact?'

'It belongs to the Lord Dominatus,' the alien said, 'and he wants it back. He offers the Redacted the honour of returning it to him.'

Occam's eyes burned with questions. His hearts beat with the excitement of possibility. The opportunity to be truly part of the Legion rather than some crude harrowing or attempt at former glories sounded interesting enough. To serve with an arch-lord that shared Occam's objectives, however, was an opportunity not to be passed up.

The strike master felt the ghostly echo of caution flutter through his chest. He rubbed at his chin with his fingers and thumb before turning back to the alien advisor.

'Why should I trust you?'

'Lord Carthach trusted me,' Vohk told him.

'And look where that got him,' Occam said. 'One of the

greatest renegade warlords of the Eastern empire, undone by a single lie, uttered from the mouth of a faithless xenos.'

'The Lord Dominatus trusts me,' Omizhar Vohk said.

'Why does he trust you?'

'You might not know this, fleshling,' the alien said, 'but the Alpha Legion has a long tradition of working with xenos interests for common aims. I'm not talking about mercenaries, alien cultists and indentured wretches. I'm talking about long-term strategic cooperation between xenos collectives and the leaders of your Legion.'

'Leaders?' Occam said. 'You mean the primarch?'

'I mean the primarchs...'

While keeping his eyes on Vohk's optic, Occam began to stalk around the machine. Before joining the secretive ranks of the Alpha Legion, Occam had spent years in the Reclusiam, librarium and forbidden archives studying their victories, their methods and history. As an outsider to the brotherhood – a non-genic legionnaire – he prided himself on understanding more about the Legion than most. Amongst warped warlords, lost to the Chaos gods and maniacs devoted to the anarchic destruction of the Imperium, Occam was a veritable expert on legionary culture and past glories.

The strike master was shocked by the depth of the alien's knowledge of the Legion's most intimate secrets. During Occam's researches he had pored through contradictory accounts of split loyalties within the Alpha Legion, dating back to the great betrayals of the Horus Heresy and even possibly further. There were ghosts of rumours concerning Alpha Legion involvement with clandestine alien groups who shared their objectives.

The fact that convinced Occam the concept of collaborating with Vohk and his master was truly worth entertaining was the revelation of the twin primarchs. Two primarchs: one soul in two bodies – neither of whom had been seen in millennia. Sightings of the pair, like regular reports of their deaths, had largely been regarded as legend. It had been variously reported that Alpharius, the figurehead father of the Legion, had lost his life at the hands of both Rogal Dorn and Roboute Guilliman of the Ultramarines – both of which, if either, could not be truth. Quetzel Carthach, like many legionary lords, claimed to have been there the day the primarch fell but such incidents had little, if any, basis in fact. Similarly, in a propaganda war perpetuated by Imperial authorities, the entire Alpha Legion – primarch and all – had been erroneously declared destroyed at least three times by the High Lords of Terra.

'Abomination,' Occam said slowly. 'Tell me, is the Lord Dominatus–'

'Fleshling,' Omizhar Vohk said. 'You are a member of the Legion. You know better than to ask questions, the answers to which I cannot give. Pass the test. Bring the Lord Dominatus what he desires and I'm sure that he will provide the answer to all of your questions.'

'He had better,' Occam said.

'Then we have an accord?' the alien advisor said. 'A legionary compact.'

'With the Lord Dominatus,' Occam said. 'Not with you, faithless xenos.'

'Agreed.'

'Now tell me,' Occam said. 'What is this artefact and where can we find it?'

'I will not embarrass us both by trying to describe it to you,' Omizhar Vohk said.

'It must have a basic function.'

'In terms you might understand,' Vohk said, 'it is a containment field generator.'

'Does this thing have a name?'

'The Tesseraqt.'

'And where can I find this ancient piece of xenos technology?' Occam the Untrue asked.

'That's simple,' Omizhar Vohk said. 'The Tesseraqt currently resides on the daemon world of Ghalmek... in the Maelstrom.'

η

ONCE BITTEN

The Crozier Worlds. Lord Occam stood on the bridge of the *Iota-Æternus*, staring out into the void. Having left the cloaked confines of the Kraal Nebula and the devastation of Vitrea Mundi long behind, the strike master had Naga-Khan make for a cradle of star systems linked by a web of busy trade routes and pilgrim trains.

The Chogorisian shipmaster had cautionary words for Occam, reminding him that the region housed the capital world of the sub-sector, was densely populated and served as operational hub for the Adeptus Ministorum in the area.

Occam appreciated that from the shipmaster's point of view, having been a mutineer, privateer and pirate, it was a foolish destination. With the worlds of the important Badab system and coreward sectors still ablaze from the Tyrant's rebellion and Quetzel Carthach snuffing out home worlds belonging to the successor sons along the rimward border of the Maelstrom, the presence of the Adeptus Astartes was severely depleted in the galactic region. Added to that was the massive reassignment of regimental forces and sector fleet assets of the Imperial Navy in recent months. Such forces had joined the Astral Fists, the Angels Eradicant and the Black Templars as part of a battlegroup initially to combat the aggressive expansion of the Overfiend of Octarius. The crusade force had then been diverted to halt the progress of splinter fleets peeling off from Hive Fleet Leviathan and rising up through the galactic plane.

As Naga-Khan had insisted to the strike master, this meant there were huge swathes of Imperial space in the rimward sectors going largely undefended. Frigates now patrolled where Imperial Navy battleships kept the peace. Following the exodus of regiments in the area like the Pharaghast Hive Rifles, the Valhallans and Darsine Patricians, regional security was largely in the hands of penal legions and the relatively inexperienced and poorly equipped local militia. Even the forge strongholds of the Adeptus Mechanicus, like Brontal-Maxima, Tanthrax and the Arx worlds – highly fortified in themselves but with no remit for sub-sector defence – had lost their Titan Legions to combat the tyranids.

When Naga-Khan had told Occam that there had never been a better time to be a pirate or renegade warlord in the area, the strike master had agreed. Alpha Legion, like the Sons of the Hydra, had not been the only ones to pounce on the opportunity. Huron Blackheart's Red Corsairs were running riot across the region. The mutant hordes of the Ménage were striking out from Chimerica on the fringes of the Maelstrom. The activity of eldar raiders in the region had intensified while daemon ships of the Word Bearers visited the dark righteousness of orbital judgement on the faithful of the Imperium.

It perplexed the shipmaster, therefore, that Lord Occam had him navigating the crowded systems of the Crozier Worlds. Several times the Q-ship had almost run afoul of cardinal world monitors and Adeptus Ministorum system ships. When challenged over the cardinal world of St Clements, Naga-Khan had transmitted that the armed freighter was transporting pilgrims to Inviolata-Proctor.

This explanation, and the sub-light blizzard of other pilgrim ships moving between worlds and systems of the Crozier Cradle, had meant the *Iota-Æternus* had been sent on its way, only to almost collide with a sleek unregistered corvette that the shipmaster suspected belonged to the Holy Ordos. It too seemed intent on reaching its destination and went swiftly on its way.

This was one of the many reasons that Occam employed the privateer as his shipmaster. Naga-Khan was calm in a spot. In all the time the Redacted had employed his services, the ship had never been boarded once. It had come close the time a heavy cruiser of the Imperial Navy and its accompanying pirate-hunter squadron of frigates mistook the *Iota-Æternus* for a corsair. The pirate ship had been terrorising merchant shipping between the nebulous Pillars of Heaven. As a case of mistaken identity, Occam could hardly lay that at the shipmaster's door. As ever, Naga-Khan had kept his cool and navigated his vessel through the trouble.

If the Q-ship was ever boarded and searched, Occam was confident that the legionnaires of the Redacted could evade detection and capture. Operatives could assume roles in the deception. Identica, paperwork and logs were maintained to keep up the illusion that the *Iota-Æternus* was one of a billion unremarkable transports plying their trade about the Imperium. The Seventh Sons might even be able to pass for pilgrims. The Q-ship's hidden weaponry, however, and its enginarium – customised using xenos technology – were another matter entirely.

'Anything?' Lord Occam asked.

Naga-Khan moved along the runebanks, checking in with cultists and servitors.

'No vox-chatter,' the shipmaster said, 'no augur returns. Looks good.'

'Quoda?'

The sorcerer came forth from his small choir of astropaths.

'No long-range communications,' he confirmed, 'as far as we can detect.'

'Give me a pict-angle on the planet,' Occam ordered.

Within moments, several of the lancet screens sizzled to an exterior pict-feed. Before the gathered operatives, cultists and legionnaires of the Redacted on the bridge was a heavily forested world, the continents of which were choked with the variegated foliage of colossal trees. Beyond, the crew could see the sunburst smirch of the distant Maelstrom.

'My lord?' an uncertain Ephron Hasdrubal asked.

'You are looking at the fruits of your labours, sergeant,' Occam told him. 'Intelligence gathered by Blatch and Perdita on Saint Clements, from the penitents they brought you and your *interrogation* of them, has led us here.'

'And here is?'

'Sub-sector Trinitus – spinward crook of the Crozier Cradle,' Naga-Khan interjected.

'Specifically the forest world of Nemesis Spectra,' Occam

told him. 'Mostly Titanwood barrens and shallow seas – all but uninhabited, bar a few isolated abhuman populations.'

'So what are we doing here?' the sergeant asked.

'Give me a close-up on quadrant forty-four east, one hundred and twelve north,' Occam said. As the pict-image began to formulate, he added, 'Centre and pull back.'

As the bridge was flushed with the seasonal greens, browns and blues of a close-up on the canopy expanse, a colossal tract of deforestation and damage was revealed. Black streaks of hazy devastation. Clustered patterns of craters across leagues of primordial woodland, focused around a huge hole in both the forest vastness and the crust of the planet surface.

'Opinions?' Lord Occam asked.

'If I didn't know any better,' Hasdrubal said, 'I'd say that was the work of the Legiones Astartes.'

'From the collateral damage,' Arkan Reznor said, the warpseer giving his professional assessment, 'the pattern and spatial distribution, I'd say we were looking at an orbital strike from a capital ship. A grand cruiser – perhaps even a battleship. The bombardment was very targeted. Insistent, also. The primary crater must be deep, the result of consecutive strikes.'

'We've seen this before,' said Sergeant Hasdrubal. 'On the Canticula shrine world.'

'Word Bearers?' said Carcinus Quoda.

'They have been getting increasingly adventurous,' Lord Occam said. 'Sending out demi-Chapters, warbands and planet-smashing battleships from their daemon forge.'

'Surely we are not desperate enough to pick at the leftovers of such daemon-worshippers and fanatics,' Hasdrubal said.

'Fanatics have their uses,' Lord Occam said, 'as our Legion well knows. This strike, as well as those on Canticula and the archive worlds of the Zosima Crucizoid is the work of the *Dissolutio Perpetua*, a daemon ship out of the Ghalmek forge world. Big. Ancient. Afflicted. She's been sighted smashing a path through the Crozier Worlds. As confirmed by Perdita's investigations and your own interrogations, sergeant – her tour of destruction took her here, where she dumped her ordnance upon Bastion-Conundra.'

'Which is?' Sergeant Hasdrubal probed.

'We have been searching for Conundra on and off for years,' the sorcerer Quoda said. 'A secret Inquisitorial fortress-repository, containing countless banned artefacts of xenos and cursed origin.'

'And the Word Bearers beat us to it,' Lord Occam said, 'which doesn't reflect well on the Legion.'

'The artefact we're looking for,' Hasdrubal said, pointing to the lancet screen, 'was down there?'

'Yes.'

'So we're too late.'

'You can tell,' Arkan Reznor indicated, 'the ordo's real high-security installations from just their barracks and processing facilities. Many are underground and even then, the first twenty levels or so are a fortified front. I'd say that the orbital bombardment probably took care of them, opening the way for a Word Bearers raid on the maximum security repository below.'

'Perdita,' Occam indicated. The Assassin retained her own appearance, which pleased the strike master after the conflict in his quarters. Her head was clean-shaven and serpentine tattoos slithered down the side of her face. The

Alpha Legion operative was leaning against the hololithic projection plate and now got to her feet.

'The High Serpent and I infiltrated the chambers of the chartered captains on Saint Clements,' she told the gathering. 'The merchant fleets operating in the area largely have responsibility for running the pilgrim trains or transporting victuals between the agri worlds of Provenda Arcturo and the Crozier Worlds. Some are retained for the personal use of the cardinals astra and dioceses. We gathered intelligence from a number of shipmasters and fleet operators who claimed that their vessels had been urgently reassigned by their sponsors and sent into restricted space in Sub-Sector Trinitus. Some of the loose-lipped captains revealed that their services have been commandeered by the lord of the Holy Ordos for the transportation of high-security cargoes off Nemesis Spectra.'

'Where did they transport such cargoes to?' Quoda put to her.

'That's the question,' Occam told him, pointing at the sorcerer.

'The consignments received Inquisitorial escorts and the flotillas were shadowed by reserve Navy cruisers brought in from the sector base at Strontia Primis,' Perdita said. 'They delivered their cargo to a small, uninhabited world two systems away.'

'Tell me you have the location,' Quoda said.

'The agri world freighters were forced to offload their cargoes at the edge of the system,' the Assassin told him.

'Which probably saved their lives,' Sergeant Hasdrubal interjected. 'If they had borne witness to the destination, the Inquisition would likely have had them executed. The local lord of the ordo must have an agreement with the cardinals.'

'One curious captain told me he saw vessels of Martian registration leaving the system,' Perdita said, 'from its outer region.'

'Mechanicus arkfreighters,' Reznor said, 'probably transporting heavy mining equipment for the excavation of a temporary installation.'

'Warpsmith?' Lord Occam said, as Reznor moved across to a navigations runebank.

'The outer regions boast three worlds,' he told Occam. 'Two gas giants and a rocky dwarf planet recognised by the Adeptus Ministorum as a minor shrine world.'

'It won't be there,' the strike master said. 'The Inquisition won't want the attention. Do the gas giants have moons?'

'Only one large enough to sustain atmospherics and workable gravity for a temporary installation,' Reznor said, scanning through the data flashing up from the runescreen. 'Fifty-Four-Thermia. Uninhabited.'

'So this xenos artefact,' Sergeant Hasdrubal said, 'this Tesseraqt, has been transported there?'

'No,' Occam said. The answer drew furrowed brows from the gathered legionnaires. 'The Tesseraqt is gone. Intelligence I have from another source confirms that it was amongst the artefacts the Word Bearers pillaged from the repository on Nemesis Spectra during their raid.'

'So why aren't we running down the *Dissolutio Perpetua*?' Arkan Reznor asked.

'Because the daemon ship,' the sorcerer Quoda said, beginning to understand, 'its mission complete, has returned to Ghalmek with its prize.'

'Then the artefact is lost,' the sergeant said.

'Perhaps not,' Lord Occam told him.

'You want to make a suicidal run into riftspace,' Hasdrubal

said, 'and raid a daemon world crawling with Word Bearers and entities for an artefact we know next to nothing about?'

'No, brother,' Occam assured his sergeant. 'I do not. Your assessment of the dangers and the likelihood of mission success is an accurate one.'

'Then what are we doing here, my lord?'

'Perdita?' Occam prompted.

'The merchant captains confirmed that along with the freight transported offworld from Nemesis Spectra, one shipment contained prisoners,' the Assassin said.

'The installation on Nemesis Spectra was a repository,' Arkan Reznor added.

'Yes,' Occam said. 'It was not outfitted for prisoners. The Word Bearers' raid might have been successful but as the freight shipments prove, they were unsuccessful in taking the installation. It seems that some of their number were taken by Inquisitorial forces and abandoned by the *Dissolutio Perpetua*. Those prisoners have been moved to this new facility on Fifty-Four-Thermia with the transported artefacts. The ordo lords are on the back foot. They are unprepared, as their temporary installation is, for a second attack. We shall capitalise on their weakness and free these Word Bearers prisoners. They shall be the key to unlocking the secrets of Ghalmek, as the Tesseraqt will be the key to finding the Lord Dominatus – an Alpha Legionnaire with whom the Redacted's destiny is intertwined.'

Occam looked around the bridge. Operatives like Naga-Khan and the High Serpent knew better than to offer any challenge to their Alpha Legion overlord. Malik and Phex, for their own different reasons, seemed uninterested in the mission's details. Both were more at home in the execution of such details. Quoda and the warpsmith knew the extreme dangers inherent in what their strike master was proposing but Occam knew that both desired entry to the Inquisitorial repository, with its treasure trove of heretical technologies and damned artefacts. Only Ephron Hasdrubal seemed to hold any doubts but as sergeant of the Redacted and second to Occam's command, he did not advertise them beyond the most necessary of questions.

'As you wish, my lord,' the sergeant said.

'Now tell them the bad news,' the strike master said to Mina Perdita.

'Several freighters were already carrying assignments when they arrived at Nemesis Spectra, which were taken on with the cargo and prisoners.'

'What were they carrying?' Hasdrubal asked.

'A detachment of Battle Sisters from the Citadel-Preceptory on San Sacrista.'

The sergeant grunted. 'Then I hope they are ready to die for what they believe in.'

'Shipmaster,' Lord Occam commanded, 'make way. I want a sub-light speed approach to the system with concealed weaponry primed.'

'Will you be requiring the Seventh Sons, my lord?' Freydor Blatch asked. Occam looked to Arkan Reznor.

'It's too cold on the surface,' the warpsmith told him.

'Assist the shipmaster,' Occam ordered. 'I suspect that it is too soon to expect augur stations and monitoring platforms. Perdita's contacts reported two battle-scarred Inquisitorial corvettes assisting in freighter escort duty. They must have survived their encounter with the *Dissolutio Perpetua*, with one or perhaps both holding some kind of clandestine station in the system. The *Iota-Æternus* will be ready for such resistance and if required the Seventh

Sons will assist in manning the gun decks and repelling boarders. Perdita, you too. The Redacted will handle this mission – alone.'

θ

COLD BLOODED

It was dark. Occam's optics cycled through different visual spectra. As they did so the strike master was treated to a vision of 54-Thermia's frozen desolation. The Inquisitorial base was located on the night side of the planet but the darkness was intensified further by the black ice and snow that covered the planetoid's surface.

Occam trudged through the lightless oblivion, his plate working hard to fight off the sub-zero bitterness. Primordial winds howled across the icy plateaux and through the valleys of stunted black mountains that rose up about the Redacted. With their camo-cloaks and the scales of their armoured suits matching the darkness, the Alpha Legionnaires made their slow progress through the black snow, the storm and the desolation.

Progress had been equally cautious into the system. Naga-Khan had brought the *Iota-Æternus* up through the shadow space created by the dark side of the system's colossal gas giants. He had expertly picked the Q-ship's path through systems of rings, debris fields and moonlets, all the while using the freighter's enhanced long-range augurs to feel out vessels in the crowded region before such craft detected them. Occam had been impressed with both the shipmaster and Arkan Reznor's xenos modifications, as the augurs picked out the ghostly presence of an Inquisitorial corvette boasting its own advanced technologies in the form of scanner-resistant hull plating. Essentially cloaked, the ordo corvette was stationed within the colossal crater of a shattered moon. Hiding within the impact site of a collision that had long ago destroyed the moonlet, the ship seemed to wait like some predatory fish on a reef.

Avoiding the Inquisitorial vessel, the Q-ship similarly concealed itself among the smashed bodies of the debris field. Masked by regular meteorite activity in the region, shallow descents and impacts on the ice world, the *Serpent's Egg* fell towards the surface of 54-Thermia. Exiting the Dreadclaw some distance from the unmaskable heat signatures of the Inquisition repository, the Alpha Legionnaires made their approach on foot.

Vilnius Malik and the warpmaster Reznor were out in front. Malik was utilising his excellent night vision to follow frozen tracks he routinely uncovered beneath a layer of fresh snow. The compacted tracks crunched beneath his armoured footfalls, while Reznor scanned for devices that might give the presence of the renegades away.

'I have nothing,' he reported back to Occam over the encoded suit vox-channel. 'No augurs, motion detectors or trip beams. No evidence of minefields either.'

'Perhaps it's too soon,' Occam voxed back. 'Perhaps the installation is more temporary than even we suspect, with

resources going to another permanent facility being prepared elsewhere. Either way, this is good for us.'

'They're relying on patrols,' Malik added, kicking at the
frozen tracks beneath the soft blackness being deposited
by the blizzard. 'Vehicles pass through here regularly on
their way back to base.'

'How long?'

'By the depth of the imprint,' Malik said, 'every three
or so hours.'

'Vehicles?'

'Something modelled on a Rhino chassis,' the former
Night Lord told him.

The legionnaires of the Redacted all turned their helms
as they heard something through the noise of the storm.
The haunting shriek had a mournful quality, as though
something large and not too distant was suffering out in
the storm with the renegades.

'Should we get off this trail?' Sergeant Hasdrubal asked,
trudging up behind. Tearing his gaze from the direction
of the sound he looked back along the path of the frozen tracks.

'No,' Occam said, thoughtfully. He reached out towards
Autolicon Phex, who knew the gesture well. Unclipping
a melta bomb from his belt, Phex handed the grenade to
the strike master. 'We should definitely stick to the trail.'

Sister Superior Invioletta rode out the rolling motion of
the *Pyra-Sanctora*. The Immolator was a relic-vehicle of the
Order of the August Vigil. A tracked transport, sections of
its thick plating were carved into bas-relief and shallow
representations of the Emperor's great deeds. Its dozer
blade cleared black snow from its path, while banners of

the Orders Pronatus trailed behind it in the blizzard gale. As the Immolator's engine plant growled, pushing the transport on through the frozen landscape, fire drizzled from the burnished barrels of its turret-mounted heavy flamers.

'I have a faint return, Sister Superior,' Sister Eupheme said, her breath misting on the gelid air of the compartment. She sat in the driver's nest of gears and flickering runescreens. Invioletta leant in, her brutally shaved scalp brushing up against the driver's own. Their bone-white plate lightly clattered. In the dull reflection of the scratched screen, Invioletta saw the glint of the staples across her missing right eye. She took in the ghostly augur reading. Squinting into the storm with her single eye, the Sister Superior peered through the slit of the viewport.

'Probably some creature indigenous to this ice ball,' the Battle Sister said. 'Ursula.'

Sister Ursula came forward from the rear of the compartment, leaving three other armoured Sisters. The Sisters Dominion cradled unprimed flamers in their white gauntlets. Sliding her helmet down over her shaved skull, Ursula popped the top hatch and admitted the howling storm.

'Full stop!' Invioletta called out as a hulking shape, darker than the surrounding oblivion, filled the viewport. Sister Eupheme hauled at the Immolator's gears, back-thrashing the tracks. Invioletta saw that the Sister was struggling and felt the transport drift on the ice. Ursula was almost thrown forward by the force but managed to hold on to the open hatch and driver's cradle.

'Target,' Invioletta called out, pulling on her own white helm. She slapped her gauntlet against the Immolator's side door and threw it open, allowing the other three

Sisters Dominion to exit the vehicle. The compartment was filled with the hiss and welcome warmth of flamer primers, to be almost immediately lost in the roar of the icy storm.

The Sister Superior followed them, resting her gauntlet on the Inferno pistol sitting in her fur-lined belt holster. Outside, her armoured boots squelched through slush. Looking up she saw the shape of a large xenos creature, one of 54-Thermia's wasteland predators. Larger than the Immolator, the small mountain of shaggy, barbed fur stood its ground, all yellowing claws and icicle-lined tusks. The Inquisition forces on the ice world had encountered several such creatures, one having found its way into the carved caverns of the ordo installation seeking shelter. Squaring up to a Sentinel powerlifter, which had been moving crates of classified cargo, the beast had killed the walker's crew.

After it had been put down by Invioletta's squad of Sister Dominions, Palatine Sophirica and the lord inquisitor's high explicator – Inigo Valdex – ordered all such monstrosities destroyed if found within the base perimeter.

'Purge,' the Sister Superior commanded. The wasteland gloom was suddenly lit up by two fat streams of sputtering promethium. Alight and guttering against the force of the surrounding storm, the streams coated the shaggy monster with sticky fuel and writhing flame. Spreading out about the alien predator, the Sisters of the August Vigil unleashed their flamers and hit the beast in the flanks with their own swirling streams of fiery death.

'Cease,' Invioletta called across her suit vox, 'and save your holy fuel. The beast burns. Let the Emperor's light take it.'

The Battle Sisters stood there for the time it took the inferno to destroy the monster. Strangely, the creature did not shriek and wail like its waste-wandering kindred. Instead, it seemed content to sit there and burn until the storm doused its black, smouldering bones.

Taking a long look around her, Invioletta stared into the depths of the blizzard. The cold was creeping in through her plate and chilling her bones. Finally satisfied, the Sister Superior directed her Dominions back into the *Pyra-Sanctora*. As Sister Ursula climbed down and locked off the top hatch, Invioletta laid a gauntlet on Eupheme's pauldron and directed the driver on. Sister Eupheme gunned the Immolator's engine. As before, the transport seemed to struggle.

'What is it?' Invioletta demanded.

'I don't know,' Sister Eupheme told her. 'Perhaps we are throwing a track. Hang on, that's got it.'

The *Pyra-Sanctora* lurched forward, its tracks biting back into the frozen ground. The vehicle's dozer blade struck the scorched bones of the alien cadaver blocking the Immolator's way, smashing the pyre to one side.

'That's it,' Eupheme confirmed. Invioletta threw a few switches on the ceiling panel above the driver and patched in to the installation's encoded vox-channel.

'*Pyra-Sanctora* to Nemesis base, respond,' the Sister Superior said, the signal crackling and warping with the surrounding storm. '*Pyra-Sanctora* checking in. Nemesis base, respond.'

'Pyra-Sanctora, *this is Nemesis*,' a sizzling voice returned finally. '*You missed your transmission window. Protocols have been initiated.*'

Invioletta's lip curled behind her faceplate. It was Sister Superior Assumpta. Sister Assumpta handled liaison between the Adepta Sororitas and Inquisition forces at the repository installation. While all Sisters considered themselves daughters of the Emperor and equal in His esteem, there were still tensions. Assumpta was a Sister-Chamberlain who belonged to the Order of the Veiled Mantle – one of the Orders Famulous. The Sisters of the Veiled Mantle had a special care for the Holy Ordos, Inquisitorial installations and the ordo lords who presided over them. Fielding for them diplomats and advisors, the Sisters Famulous were a point of contact between the clandestine agents of the Inquisition, the Sisterhood and other commandeered forces of the Imperium. As a Battle Sister, Invioletta – like Palatine Sophirica – did not enjoy taking orders from non-militants such as Sister Assumpta and the lord inquisitor's aide, High Explicator Valdex – especially on matters of security.

'Stand down protocols,' Invioletta said. 'Our patrol was delayed by an encounter with an indigenous lifeform. The threat has been purged and the base perimeter secured.'

'Sister Superior,' Assumpta said across the warping channel, 'please ensure that all reports are delivered in pre-assigned transmission windows. High Explicator Valdex will expect an audience upon your return. Nemesis out.'

Invioletta grunted, flicked the vox-switch and sat back down in the compartment. Eupheme turned to say something but Invioletta shook her head gently in response.

It took another thirty minutes to reach the installation. Beyond the twinkling blue of arc lights in the storm, there was little to identify the site as a base at all. As the Immolator crunched through the old, frozen tracks of hundreds of previous patrols, the great rime-coated blast doors of the entrance began to rumble aside. Built into a hollow in a low, fat mountain and carved into the depths of the ice below, Nemesis base was all but hidden. As the transport churned its way through accumulating snow and into the cavern within, another Immolator left the base to go out on patrol. Flashing lamps at each other, the tracked transports passed, the blast doors closing between them, shutting out the storm. Compared to the black wastes beyond, the hangar within was a hive of activity.

When the lord inquisitor had requested reinforcements from Cardinal Trazier, following the renegade attack on the ordo's secret base on Nemesis Spectra, Invioletta and her palatine had been sent with one hundred Sisters Dominion to secure the temporary facility. As Sisters of the August Vigil, their duties included security of shrine worlds and some of the Ecclesiarchy's most prized artefacts. On 54-Thermia, however, they were tasked with securing a frozen repository, freshly cut into the ice by Adeptus Mechanicus work crews, and ensuring the safe transport and instalment of heretical artefacts. Recovered by inquisitors and operatives of the Ordo Hereticus, these cursed items – many corrupted by Chaos and infused with xenos power – had to be kept safe from heretics and renegades who might use their potential against the Imperium. At least until the repository fortress on Lodovica IV had been refitted for the ordo's permanent use.

As well as the heretical artefacts and technologies, Invioletta and her Sisters had responsibility for the security of several prisoners who had been captured in the attack on Nemesis Spectra. These were renegades that Lord Inquisitor Van Leeuwen had wanted to interview himself, rather than turn over to another inquisitor or facility. He had instructed the Adeptus Mechanicus work crews to carve out oubliettes in the frozen bowels of Nemesis base for the express purpose of interrogating the renegades, to discover who it was who had attacked the Ordo Hereticus on Nemesis Spectra and why.

As Eupheme brought the *Pyra-Sanctora* in to a maintenance station next to several other armoured transports, Invioletta could see Battle Sisters and Inquisitorial staff going about their business through the viewport.

The cavern walls were ice and rock, while the centre of the large chamber was dominated by thousands of crates stacked in small mounds, with snow-lined walkways left in between. Generators struggled in the extreme cold and the ceiling lamps above the stacks filled the chamber with a flickering gloom. Sisters of the August Vigil in white plate patrolled the chamber in pairs, holding their primed flamers at the ready, while a small army of bonded servants, Mechanicus magi, priests and servitors moved through the massive collection. The crates came in various shapes and sizes, some no larger than a jewellery box while others were bigger than the *Pyra-Sanctora*. Each contained some damned artefact or piece of alien technology confiscated by the Ordo Hereticus from the many thousands of renegades and heretics they had persecuted in the sector. The crates were stamped with hexagrammic runes and hummed with small stasis field generators operating within.

Ordo notaries were shadowed by servo-skulls, all working for High Explicator Valdex and the lord inquisitor. They catalogued the crates before having heavy servitors and sentinel power lifters move the containers to freight elevators that took the cargo down to frozen repositories far below the planet surface.

As a Sister Dominion pulled aside the door for Invio-letta, the Sister Superior stepped outside. Taking off her helmet, she took in the scene. It was still face-scaldingly cold in the cavern and her breath frosted on the air. She could hear the cacophony of hard work echo about the chamber. Sentinel walkers trudging by. Immolators idling. Bonded servants calling out to each other, their quills scratching on vellum and beeping off data-slates. Servo-skulls hovering overhead. Inquisitors with special interests could be heard shouting at their own notaries and servitors who stood silently by.

'Have that track checked with the enginseers,' Invioletta called back through the door at Eupheme, then to Sister Ursula, 'and refuel the turret tanks.'

'As you wish,' the Sisters replied.

'The same with your weapons,' Invioletta said, turning to the Sisters Dominion who had exited the vehicle after her. 'Then evening prayers, vespers and take your supper. Weapons check and meet back here for midnight patrol. Understood?'

'Yes, Sister Superior,' the squad answered.

'Where will you be?' Eupheme asked.

'Where else?' Invioletta said. 'Making my report to the high explicator.'

I

A BREED APART

The Redacted moved through the entrance chamber like ghosts.

Their movements were slow but certain, their muffled servos and hydraulics carrying them through the crate stacks almost like dancers. With their plasma weaponry deactivated and concealed within their camo-cloaks, each Alpha Legionnaire clutched a silenced bolt pistol in his gauntlet. Every decision was considered. Each movement was undertaken with caution. They could not afford to be seen, and as such the warband moved as one. Their optics flashed everywhere, ensuring that their armoured forms did not enter the overlapping lines of sight of either the Battle Sisters sentries or the army of Inquisitorial repository staff.

Entry to the installation had been difficult and no member of the squad wanted to be responsible for the Redacted being detected. Having hunted down and killed a xenos creature of the wastes, Occam had had his renegades drag the body across the ice and position it on the well-worn tracks of the base patrol. Setting off a melta bomb in the centre of the frozen tracks, before the hulking corpse, the legionnaires of the Redacted waded into the resulting crater of slush and allowed it to rapidly refreeze about them.

When the next patrolling Battle Sisters transport stopped to dispatch what they took to be a threat blocking their path, Occam and his legionnaires had reached up from the freezing ice and tethered themselves to the underside of the vehicle. Allowing themselves to be dragged through the ice and snow, the Redacted had entered the Inquisitorial installation unnoticed. Unhooking themselves from the belly of the tracked transport while servitors attended to refuelling, the legionnaires escaped into the maze of crates and cargo dominating the centre of the cavern. One by one, avoiding the dull senses of the servitors and the pairs of Battle Sisters patrolling the periphery of the cavern, the renegades melted into the stacks.

Inside the cavern, the legionnaires had detected no augur fields, trip beams or pict-streamers. With the base still in a state of unpacking and organisation, there had clearly been no time for such security measures. Occam led the way through the narrow gaps between the mounds, using stasis crates to hide his presence. His renegades followed, their armoured steps light and auto-senses helping them to pick their way through the cavern unseen. Hissing warnings across their suit channel and pointing out threats to one another, the legionnaires negotiated the labyrinthine stacks with stealth and superhuman patience.

'Retreat and watch those corners,' the strike master instructed under his breath.

Moving back between two large humming containers

to avoid a data-slate-consulting notary and his hydrauli-
cally clawed servitors, the legionnaires had to pass across
an arterial route through the collection. Ensuring that no
Battle Sisters sentries were about to cross the route on
their patrol and glance down through the cargo stacks,
the Redacted moved into a small cul-de-sac and knelt
down in the snow.

'Reznor,' Occam uttered as a pair of servo-skulls glided
overhead, scanning crate identica with their optics and
recording notations with mandible-quills on draped vellum unspooling where their lower jaws had previously
been. The warpsmith unhooked Beta, Zeta and Theta from
his belt and activated the servo-automata. Moving with
the same serpentine stealth as the warband and allowing
a nest of mechatendrils to slither down out of their own
skulls, the drones went hunting. Stalking the Inquisitorial
servo-skulls through the crates like octopoid predators,
Reznor's servo-automata seized the drones one by one.
Within seconds the servo-skulls had been taken apart and
destroyed.

As the squad waited for bonded servants and consulting
priests and Mechanicus magi to move on, the legionnaires
produced their hand-to-hand combat weaponry.

'Dissemble,' the strike master hissed, provoking in the
Redacted a chameleon-like change. As legionary colours,
scales and cloaks turned dark crimson like the spreading
gore of fresh wounds, the renegades assumed the surface
appearance of Word Bearers Chaos Space Marines. Occam
nodded his approval as the transformation completed. If
the Redacted were to be captured by Inquisitorial forces,
then Occam wanted them to be identified as Word Bearers.
As far as the Imperial authorities were to be concerned,

the Alpha Legion never set foot on 54-Thermia. Occam pointed with a single digit of his gauntlet: 'Go.'

The movement of the Redacted through the stacks and across the cavern was a thing of lethal beauty, all but unseen and unknown. Where cornered by converging Inquisitorial staff, the Alpha Legionnaires were forced to improvise with savage decisiveness.

While Quoda and the warpsmith prised open stasis crates, taking an interest in the heretical contents, Malik and Sergeant Hasdrubal went to work with their powered blades. Grabbing bonded servants, notaries and priests with speed and power-armoured force they dragged their stunned bodies behind crates and slipped the soft crackle of their assassin's weaponry through the flesh of their victims' throats. Silent. Quick. Economical. Within moments, the corpses had been hastily buried in the ice and snow of the cavern floor and covered with crates or dumped in the stasis containers themselves.

Where small groups had to be dispatched quickly, the legionnaires brought up their bolt pistols and punched silent Stalker rounds through the centre of chests or clean took off heads. During one desperate entanglement, near the cavern edge, Occam garrotted a young inquisitor with the crackling tendril blades of his power scourge. He held the agent of the Holy Ordos in a vice-like power-armoured hold, the scourge cutting slowly through the gristle, tendon and bone of his neck. All while the inquisitor's acolytes and autosavants were put down with silent bolt blasts and the throat-stabbing thrust of blades.

Putting their pauldrons against a large crate, the legionnaires heaved. They obscured the entrance to a freight elevator – one of several set in the ice wall of the cavern – and moved the stasis container across the snow. Watching for patrolling pairs of Battle Sisters, the Redacted made their move. Autolicon Phex slipped across to the elevator car. With Phex kneeling down under the weight of his heavy plasma gun, hydrogen flasks and grenades, the legionnaires – one by one – ran across and received a boost from the renegade. Launched up at a rough hatch in the sizeable elevator car, the legionnaires climbed up onto the roof before pulling Phex up with them.

In the silence and gloom of the ice-carved elevator shaft, the Redacted paused. Positioning themselves behind the car's bulky cable assembly, they waited in silence, kneeling on the roof of the elevator like statues. The car didn't boast anything as sophisticated as mag-locks in the ice shaft: its controls simply operated a heavy-duty winch system situated above the renegades. It was noisy but reliable and carried the car up and down the shaft, between the cavern-repository and various sub-levels that had been carved into depths of the ice. As they moved, Sergeant Hasdrubal listened at the elevator hatch and Reznor's servo-automata hovered on their repulsors, scanning the different levels with their enhanced augurs. They fed their data back to the warpsmith, who in turn relayed it to Occam when the elevator car was on an empty return.

'Feedbacks confirm that the upper levels are dominated by heavy machinery,' Reznor confirmed, 'which makes sense. Installation would have been easier and it could have been put in place earlier while the lower levels were still being excavated.'

'Generatorum?' the strike master asked.

'Yes, as well as some kind of operations complex,' the warpsmith suggested.

'Below that I suspect are the quarters and garrison levels for the Sisters,' Reznor said. 'Fewer returns there. Little activity.'

'And beneath those?'

'Repository levels, utilising the greatest concentration of security features,' Reznor said. 'Blast doors, hexagrammics, basic augur sweeps, sentry stations and patrols – at least as far as these readings suggest. No promises.'

'We have no interest in those,' Occam said, 'now we know that the Word Bearers have the prize they came for.'

'The warpsmith and I disagree,' the sorcerer Quoda reminded his strike master, but in the planning stages of the venture Occam had overruled the pair's request to investigate the secured treasures of the Inquisitorial repository.

'Anything below those?' Occam pressed the warpsmith.

'At the very bottom, a smaller complex,' Reznor told him.

'Except no stasis containers have been transported down there in the whole time we've been monitoring,' the sergeant said, lifting his helm up from the hatch. 'Only personnel.'

'Best guess?' Occam put to him.

'Mostly priests, I'd say,' Hasdrubal informed him, 'senior acolytes and Sisters – along with inquisitors. Agents have made regular trips down there.'

'Prisoners?' Occam asked.

'I'd say so,' the sergeant said.

'It's settled then,' Occam decided. 'Sergeant, take Quoda and the warpsmith. I want you to infiltrate the upper level and make your way to the generatorum. Use whatever strategies necessary to disguise your presence.'

'Even Quoda?' the sergeant asked. 'Won't use of his abilities set off some kind of alarm?'

Occam nodded. As well as training, stealth, silent slaughter and the chameleonic properties of their plate and cloaks, the strike master was sending them with their only psyker. People saw what they expected to see and Quoda's powers might just be enough to make even devout Sisters and staunch inquisitors blind to the renegades' presence.

'Augurs are most likely concentrated in the repository levels to monitor the corruption of the cargo,' Reznor reassured them. 'Little use for them in the operations section or generatorum.'

'Once in the generatorum,' Occam continued, 'I want the warpsmith to engineer a controlled overload. Nothing explosive. As far as the installation is concerned, we're looking at a reactor malfunction. They will send their enginseers.'

'But they won't reach the reactors,' Sergeant Hasdrubal said. 'We'll see to that.'

'You want a meltdown?' Reznor clarified.

'Of the surrounding ice,' Occam said. 'Warm meltwater should melt further channels on the upper level and drain down the open elevator shafts.'

'That follows,' the warpsmith said, 'but once it begins there will be no stopping it.'

'I'm counting on it,' Occam told him. 'The dungeon level will become flooded...'

'...forcing the security forces down there to evacuate the prisoners,' Hasdrubal added with approval.

'Malik, Phex and I will ride down to the dungeon level,' the strike master said, 'and will take possession of the transported prisoners in the car. All rendezvous in the cavern-repository for a tactical withdrawal. Installation to *Serpent's Egg*. The Dreadclaw back to the *Iota-Æternus*. Understood?'

The legionnaires nodded silently.

As the car shuddered up towards the cavern-repository to collect another consignment of cargo, the Alpha Legionnaires got ready. Positioning themselves either side of the doorway opening onto the operations level, Hasdrubal leant his helmet to one side and risked a brief glance. With the broad corridor of ice empty, the sergeant led Arkan Reznor and the sorcerer Quoda off the roof of the moving car and down the freezing passage towards the distant boom of the generatorum. Beta, Zeta and Theta drifted close by after them.

Occam, Malik and Phex remained hidden on the car roof as it went down the shaft. They held position as the car came to a stop and unloaded a consignment of crates on a repository level. From there it carried agents of the ordo, notaries and Battle Sisters down into the depths. The strike master couldn't hear any klaxons or the hammer of boots into the elevator car that would signify security forces had been scrambled to the operations level.

It soon became apparent that the sergeant had succeeded in his mission, as meltwater began to seep, trickle, and then gush down the wall from the operations level opening. Warm water began stripping away the ice wall of the shaft and filling it with steam. Listening through the hatch, they heard the Battle Sisters vox the base enginseers with instructions to inspect the environmental controls and the generatorum. Occam knew, of course, what they would find was a quietly overloading reactor that despite their best efforts would continue to heat the ice about it.

'Not long now,' the strike master told Malik and Phex. 'Prime your weapons.'

Holstering his pistol and blades, the former Night Lord brought his adapted plasma gun to life. With some calibration, Malik brought the sound of the weapon's deep hum down and concealed the blue glow of the barrel with a sliding shutter. As Occam followed suit, Autolicon Phex did the same with his heavy plasma gun.

As a waterfall of black meltwater gushed down the shaft wall, the strike master brought his helm optics down to a crack he had set up between the hatch and car roof. Observing in silence and angling his view, Occam took in the occupants of the car.

He immediately saw the white plate of Battle Sisters. Promethium sloshed about in the canisters of the flamers they were carrying. Two were bereft of helmets and shaved. One had an eye that had been stapled shut while the second, some kind of officer in an ermine cloak, had black symbols of reverence and devotion burned into her teeth. She was speaking into a vox headset.

'Double the perimeter guard,' the officer said with a snarl. 'I want reports from all patrols out on the ice and security logs for the repository levels triple-checked.'

'It could be just a malfunction,' her compatriot with the stapled eye said. 'The cold – nothing much seems to work on this ice ball.'

'Such naivety is not your reputation, Sister Superior,' the officer spat, holding the receiver of her vox headset. 'You know as well as I, there is no such thing as *just* a malfunction, but I expect that is what the ordo's forces on Nemesis Spectra thought before the apocalypse rained down on them from orbit. The renegade and heretic are not to be underestimated.'

'Never, palatine,' the Sister Superior answered.

Occam saw that the pair carried chains of barbed silver and manacle restraints – the kind that might be used in transferring dangerous prisoners.

When the elevator arrived at the bottom of the shaft, Occam felt a shudder and resistance. The meltwater that had collected in the dungeon level of the complex slowed the elevator down before gushing in from the connecting passageway and flooding the car up to the Battle Sisters' thighs. Holding their flamers and hissing primers above the water, the Sisters cursed and waded into the darkened depths of the frozen dungeon.

After they left, Occam could hear voices and shouting from the oubliettes. Here, the Inquisition had secured their prisoners: dangerous heretics, nullified witchbreeds, altereds and Traitor Space Marines. The strike master hooked his ceramite fingertips under the hatch and quietly opened it. Motioning for Phex, Occam directed the legionnaire to position himself above the hatch with the barrel of his heavy plasma gun pointing down. The strike master and Malik positioned themselves either side of him, criss-crossing their aim down into the car.

'Move, you heretical scum,' Occam heard the palatine say as the Battle Sisters splashed their way back through the rising waters.

Through the open hatch, Occam saw that the Battle Sisters had their flamers slung and were holding a lone prisoner in chains between them. Occam could tell from his size that he was an Adeptus Astartes legionary. A pale and battered specimen of genetic engineering, whose armourless body was splattered with blood and filth.

With his bloodied wrists manacled behind him and his

ankles chained loosely together, the hulking prisoner had a brace around his bulging neck and a caged bridle about his head. He was struggling to walk and his hands rattled in their chains like his head in its cage. Patches of skin across the prisoner's body were black with the withering effects of frostbite. It became clear to Occam that the ordo torturers had made effective use of their frozen surroundings. As the prisoner was moved into the centre of the car, Occam could see that his face was in a terrible state.

Chains radiating out from links on the neck brace were held by the Battle Sisters, keeping the prisoner in place between their number. While the Sister Superior held an Inferno pistol pointed up at the back of the huge prisoner's caged head, the palatine held the wicked curvature of a chainblade against his muscular side. She tapped the teeth of the weapon against his chest.

'One move,' she snarled at the prisoner, staring into his skull-cage. 'You so much as blink at me the wrong way, traitor...'

Angling his view through the hatch, Occam looked down upon the prisoner. He could see that he was a Word Bearer. Though carrying himself like a whipped dog, the proud defiance of his Legion could still be seen in the glint of his bloodshot eyes and the set of his jaw. His flesh was like an unholy text. Those patches that were not frostbitten and black were a contested space of words and symbols tattooed into the skin. Faded beneath were sigils and incantations that Occam recognised as ruinous markers and honoraria. These covered his whole body, while over the top – in bloody ink much fresher than the heretical flesh-scripture – were hexagrammmic symbols and writing in High Gothic.

With the prisoner secure, an inquisitor entered the elevator car. His ordo robes and the small mountain of exotic furs cascading down from his armoured shoulders made wading through the meltwater difficult. A bionic claw tapped nervously against the grip of a holstered bolt pistol, while the other clutched his helm. He treated the occupants of the elevator car to his skull-face. The beneficiary of many rejuvenat treatments and surgeries, the inquisitor's face was mottled, threadbare skin stretched across the sharp bones. It was almost transparent in places. His eyes were orbs misty with age, behind which bionic optics had been implanted, making his pupils and the surrounding transparency of his skull glow red. He also no longer had his own teeth, instead baring implanted fangs of sanctified silver. Somehow the agent of the Holy Ordos managed to make a seemingly permanent scowl with the tight skin of his face – a mask of prejudice and hatred.

'Lord inquisitor,' the palatine asked, 'what about the others?'

'One did not survive the exorcism,' the inquisitor said, 'the other, the interrogations that followed. I will not allow this wretched specimen the mercy of drowning. Get him up to one of the repository levels, somewhere this flood cannot reach him. I want him secured in one of the empty reliquaries. Then, lady-palatine, I shall expect a full report regarding what on Holy Terra is going on.'

'Yes, my lord,' the palatine replied, throwing the crank that activated the elevator.

Once again, Occam felt the winch struggle. It wasn't just carrying the passengers, it was trying to lift half a car full of meltwater. The elevator shuddered back up the ice shaft, water draining from the car as it moved. Occam knew they couldn't wait much longer. With every passing moment the chance of the Redacted being discovered on top of the elevator car or in the generatorum increased. Between floors, the occupants of the car were stranded and beyond the help of Battle Sisters sentries in both the dungeon and on the repository levels above.

'Now,' Occam ordered.

The Battle Sisters heard the sub-atomic whoosh of Phex's heavy plasma gun and looked up. There was nothing they could do to stop the cataclysmic blast of blue fury that raged down through the car. Phex pumped orb after blistering orb down through the hatch, blasting screaming Sisters down through scorched holes in the car floor. Occam and Malik joined the mayhem, sending streams of furious plasma balls down into the car that burned straight through plate and flesh. About the prisoner, Sisters of Battle died – the victims of the Alpha Legion's expert aim and unrelenting destruction.

In the moments that followed, everything was havoc. Battle Sisters disappeared in blinding eruptions of plasma while others clutched holes burned clean through their chests and abdomens before crashing down onto their knees and toppling over. The unsteady prisoner was dragged down with them and both the palatine and Sister Superior had to rescue themselves from falling through wide holes melted through the car floor.

'Word Bearers!' the palatine roared, her lips contorted about the ugly exclamation. As she pointed her chainblade up at the hatch, the occupants of the car returned fire. The Sister Superior's Inferno pistol melted blast holes up through the roof of the car, while the lord inquisitor's bolt pistol – fast out of its holster in his bionic claw – punched bolts wildly up at the Redacted. As a column of fire from a Battle Sister's flamer raged through the hatch, the legionnaires were knocked back. Malik stumbled and Phex's camo-cloak caught light. When the flames evaporated, Occam could see that the lord inquisitor was standing over his prisoner.

'You return, enemy of the Emperor,' the inquisitor called up through the hatch, his bolt pistol wavering before the Word Bearer's head. 'Surrender, or I shall deny you your prize.'

Occam knew he had to act. He could gun the inquisitor down from the elevator car roof, but now he had stated his intention, Occam could never hit the Sister Superior and palatine before they ended the prisoner.

Thudding across the roof with powered steps, the strike master jumped and dropped down through the hatch. Appearing from the gloom of the ice shaft, Occam landed on the inquisitor. Using the weight of his plate and the force of the drop, the strike master smashed the inquisitor's frame, bionic workings and ornate suit into the floor. Aiming his plasma gun down at the metal claw clutching the bolt pistol, which Occam now had pinned, he blasted both weapon and appendage to steaming oblivion.

Besides the palatine and her Sister Superior, only one Battle Sister had survived the plasma onslaught. In her scorched white plate she turned on Occam, aiming the nozzle of her flamer at him.

'So, you're going to burn us all, Sister?' Occam taunted.

'Do it!' the palatine commanded, as the Sister hesitated. Her commander had no such qualms about sacrificing everyone in the elevator car to destroy the Word Bearers.

'Malik,' the strike commander called. A second later, the

Battle Sister's head was gone – blazed from her shoulders in a flash of plasma. As her body dropped, Occam could see the former Night Lord through the hatch, kneeling on the car roof, peering down his weapon.

Barging the corpse of their falling Sister aside, the palatine and Sister Superior threw themselves at Occam.

'Die, heretic!' the palatine bawled, as the strike master brought his plasma gun up. Sparks flew as she batted the barrel of the weapon aside. Carried off by the thrashing teeth, the plasma gun was torn from Occam's grip and flew at the elevator wall. As the blade slashed back, he felt its barbs bite into the surface of his plate.

Turning with the motion, Occam snatched his power scourge from his belt and thumbed it to crackling agitation. Whipping the tendril blades around, the strike master struck the curved chainblade. Sparking pieces of the weapon hit the opposite wall. As the Sister Superior shot a superheated blast of energy at the strike master from her Inferno pistol, he snatched the palatine up by her breastplate and used the Battle Sister as a shield. Occam watched the expression on the palatine's face change as the melta blast cooked its way through her.

Throwing her corpse to one side, he passed the scourge between his gauntlets, bringing the snaking tendrils up and over his head. Ripping them down through the Sister Superior, he paused as he completed the manoeuvre. The scourge had cut the one-eyed Sister into pieces. Clean cuts through plate and bone meant that the Sister Superior swiftly became a mound of toppling flesh.

Occam allowed himself a moment as the carnage settled. Coiling up his power scourge and recovering his battered plasma gun, the strike master picked his way through the bodies. Drawing his bolt pistol, he thudded Stalker rounds into any body still quivering. As he did so, Occam saw that he was being watched by the Word Bearer.

'We have come for you, brother,' Occam told him.

'You really haven't,' the Word Bearer told him, rasping through the ruin of his face.

Occam looked down at his plate and cloak. Perhaps it was his accent. Perhaps it was the meaningless sigils that were part of his disguise or the surface patches of scaled plate that had been torn up by the chainblade and were betraying the true colours of his Legion. Occam turned the bolt pistol on the Word Bearer.

'What do you care?' the strike master said. 'You're getting rescued.'

Scooping up the prisoner's chains he threw them up to Phex and Malik, who unceremoniously hauled the Word Bearer up through the hatch. Holstering the pistol, Occam leapt up for the hatch and Malik's offered gauntlet, the legionnaire helping to pull his strike master up onto the roof.

'Sergeant,' Occam said, changing his suit's vox-channel. 'The prisoner is in our possession. Status report?'

At that moment the ice shaft began to echo with the bleat of a distant alarm. When Hasdrubal finally returned the communication, his voice was all but drowned out by gunfire.

'We've run into a few problems, strike master…'

κ

SLITHER

By the time the elevator car reached the operations level, all hell had broken loose. Klaxons carried through the thin air. The corridor floor was a rapids of fast-moving meltwater and fallen armoured bodies. Notaries and bonded servants splashed this way and that across junctions, while Battle Sisters in white plate created gauntlets and bottlenecks, filling the corridor with gouts of fiery brilliance from their flamers.

From around the corner, Occam saw Beta, Zeta and Theta appear. Blazing towards the elevator on their repulsors, they were clearly trying to escape gunfire. Zeta was aflame. Then came the sergeant and Quoda. While the sorcerer held his plasma gun in one hand, he supported Hasdrubal in the other, guiding him around the corner and pushing him on towards the rising elevator car. As the sergeant got closer it became clear that the faceplate of his helm had been smashed. His optics were cracked and his grille an ugly mess. The helm was sparking, as though it had been hit by a glancing bolt round or swipe of a chainblade. From the way Quoda was guiding him, the sergeant had clearly been blinded.

As the two made their desperate way up the corridor, they were followed by streams of flame licking their backs and bolt blasts sending up fountains in the meltwater deluge. Occam and Malik returned fire, sending a storm of plasma blasts back up the corridor that skimmed the wall. These and furious balls of energy unleashed by Autolicon Phex's heavy weapon drove the Battle Sisters back behind the cover of corners.

Several were suddenly blasted off their feet and into the junction, falling faceplate first into the shallow waters. As orbs of plasma blazed in the backs of the fallen Sisters, Arkan Reznor appeared behind them. He was holding his own plasma gun in one gauntlet and Ephron Hasdrubal's in the other. Pumping plasma blasts back the way he had come, he turned and ran with powered steps towards the elevator. The corridor behind him became an inferno of flame as the Battle Sisters chasing him down closed with their quarry. Meltwater rained from the ceiling and streamed down the walls. For a moment, the warpsmith was lost in a haze of black steam until suddenly he appeared. Sliding through the meltwater torrent, Reznor was down on his side – the ice and water carrying the weight of his suit along until finally he entered the elevator car and hit the back wall with the soles of his armoured boots.

Quoda hit the crank, sending the car back up towards the entrance chamber.

'Grenades and spare canisters,' the strike master ordered, prompting Phex to start pulling melta bombs and plasma gun hydrogen flasks from his belt and hand them to Malik and Occam.

The strike master nodded and the three of them began priming melta bombs and hurling them up at the fast-approaching doorway to the cavern. They followed these with the hydrogen canisters.

'Down,' Occam ordered, lowering his head and prompting the legionnaires to drop through the ruined hatch and into the car with the others. As he dropped down himself, the detonations began. The walls of the shaft shook and fractured, while the freight car trembled, swinging on its cable and banging against the ice.

The legionnaires of the Redacted knelt down on the floor of the car with Reznor and the Word Bearer. Knowing what was coming, Reznor tried to shield the prisoner the best he could. Explosions and an intense wave of heat passed over the top of the car, followed by the flame of the exploding hydrogen canisters. The legionnaires felt the heat wash across their heads and their backs.

As the explosions died away, the warpsmith lifted his head to check the Word Bearer.

'Are you hurt, brother?' Reznor asked.

'He knows,' Occam informed the warpsmith across the vox, prompting Reznor to abandon the charade, pull his bolt pistol from his holster and put the muzzle under the Word Bearer's chin.

'I've got the prisoner,' Occam said, scooping up his chains and standing up. 'Quoda?'

The sorcerer looked down at the wretched Word Bearer and reached into the foetid recesses of the traitor's mind.

'Hatred,' the sorcerer told Occam, reading the prisoner's

muddled thoughts. 'Confusion. Pain – a lot of pain, both physical and spiritual.'

'Not surprising,' Reznor said, using the bolt pistol under the Word Bearer's chin to get him up off the ground.

'Well, that will be nothing compared to what we'll do to him if he interferes with our objectives,' Hasdrubal said, his gauntlet on the hilt of his multi-blade dagger.

'I don't think he's in much of a condition to do that,' the sorcerer Quoda said as the car shuddered up the shaft towards the open doorway.

'Sergeant?' Occam asked. 'What about you?'

'Can't see anything,' Hasdrubal admitted.

'Don't worry,' the strike master told him. 'You're not missing much. Reznor, have your automata guide the sergeant. Phex, blast us a path. Malik, point. Warpsmith, you have the rear. Be ready for anything. Don't stop until we've cleared the facility.'

As the car rocked by the melted doorway, Phex blasted away with his heavy plasma gun, lighting up the steam-shrouded stacks of the cavern.

'Go!' Occam commanded, sending his legionnaires out into the decimation. The Redacted slipped and slid down into the craters left behind by the melta bomb detonations. The hydrogen canisters had caused further destruction by knocking down stacks and setting fire to stasis-containers. As their shapes were detected in the black mist, the Battle Sisters holding the cavern opened fire.

Bolt blasts and fire streams erupted from all directions as Sisters fired upon the renegades from strategic hold points and as they exited elevator freight cars further around the cavern wall.

Taking cover in the craters and stepping through the flame-swathed and half-melted bodies of bonded servants and notaries, Malik led the way. He took the Redacted from cover to cover. Melted depressions. Half-demolished stacks. Large containers. While Malik dropped advancing Sisters with his expert aim and rocketing orbs of plasma, Phex moved up behind, blasted stacks apart to reveal Sisters in white, waiting in ambush.

Dragging the stumbling Word Bearer along on a short chain, Occam pulled the prisoner down close to the ground to avoid ricocheting bolt rounds and streams of blessed flame. Pumping balls of plasma between Malik and Phex, the strike master blasted fallen Sisters getting to their feet back into the floor of ice.

As Malik led them swiftly on, pushing through the havoc and confusion of the cavern-repository, Occam could hear the screams of dying Inquisitorial staff above the klaxons. He could also make out the rabid calls of their ordo masters, intent on destroying the Word Bearers who they believed had mounted an assault on their temporary base of operations and were attempting to free their prisoner.

Out of the bank of black steam, Occam saw a white shape accompanied by the sound of thrashing metal teeth. Swinging a chainsword above her head, a Battle Sister charged towards him. Occam hauled the Word Bearer around and went to point his plasma gun, but Carcinus Quoda got there first. Swinging his force sceptre, he smacked the thrashing chainblade aside before sweeping the heavy, glowing crystal back. Charged with psychic power, the weapon smashed the broken Battle Sister off her feet and back through the mist.

Another came at the strike master and his prisoner from

the other side, running around a large stack of crates. Some kind of officer, she carried a short power blade that hummed its vicious intent. Pulling the Word Bearer back around the other side, Occam blasted the oncoming Sister. As plasma balls blazed into her breastplate, she was knocked back and her lifeless armoured corpse came to a skidding, steaming halt before the strike master.

Looking behind, Occam saw that the scorched shape of Theta hovered before Hasdrubal, leading the way, while Beta and Zeta – their mechatendrils wrapped under his arms – guided the Alpha Legion sergeant through the wreckage, bodies and gunfire. Bringing up the rear was Arkan Reznor. He carried one plasma gun slung over his shoulder and held another empty weapon in his hand. Drawing his bolt pistol, he sent silenced Stalker rounds back at pursuing Battle Sisters. Pointing the weapon down at collapsed stacks of containment crates, the warpsmith shot at their stasis-field generators. Ruptured crates spilled their heretical contents, forcing Battle Sisters to retreat from the corruptive influence of such dangerous artefacts. Where unstable stasis fields crackled, merged and spread across the carnage, Battle Sisters were caught. Frozen in the struggling stasis fields, Reznor sent bolts their way. Frozen also, the rounds hovered before the Sisters, ready to end their lives as the fields collapsed.

Ducking beneath columns of flame, the Alpha Legionnaires changed their hydrogen canisters and pushed on through the havoc. Putting Sisters down with close-range energy blasts and stabbing slashes of his power dagger, Malik led them towards the cavern blast doors. As Phex blazed the pair of Sisters guarding the exit back into the scorched metal of the giant door, Occam knelt down.

'Reznor,' the strike master called, drawing the warpsmith up from behind. 'Bypass the controls.'

As the warpsmith went to work on the blast door, the Alpha Legionnaires laid down a merciless hail of plasma, forcing the Battle Sisters back behind tracked transports undergoing maintenance.

'Now, Reznor,' Occam called to the struggling warpsmith, as bolt rounds sparked spectacularly off the blast door.

'It's encoded,' Reznor called.

'*Now*, warpsmith,' Occam roared, pulling the Word Bearer behind him and emptying his plasma gun at the Battle Sisters.

'Got it,' Reznor said finally as the blast doors began rumbling aside.

'Go!' Occam called, pushing his prisoner out into the freezing storm. As one by one the legionnaires struck out across the ice, they became aware of lamps bleeding through the storm.

'Vehicle,' Malik called, prompting Phex to throw him a melta bomb. Priming the grenade, Occam slid it across the ice and under the oncoming armoured transport. With a flash, the front of the vehicle was turned to dribbling slag. As screaming Sisters opened the side door and fell out of the vehicle, the legionnaires trudged past without mercy and became one with the black storm.

'Where is it?'

'Port-side aft,' Arkan Reznor reported from one of the Dreadclaw's runescreens. 'Coming up fast.'

The image displaying an exterior pict-feed showed the receding dark ball of 54-Thermia and the advancing shape of a sleek, Inquisitorial corvette. It had taken several hours of evasive manoeuvres and doubling back through the storm to avoid the tracked transports of the Battle Sisters hunting them through the deep freeze. When they had finally reached the *Serpent's Egg* and achieved lift-off, they found that the Ordo Hereticus corvette they had observed earlier had been brought out of hiding to mount an orbital patrol. The Dreadclaw benefitted from a head start but couldn't hope to outrun the corvette.

While the rest of the Redacted were locked in their cradles alongside the chained Word Bearer, Occam drifted about the interior compartment in the zero-gravity.

'Where is the *Iota-Æternus?*' Quoda asked.

'On station, where she was instructed to await out return,' the blind Hasdrubal said, sure that Naga-Khan would follow his orders.

'Warpsmith?' the strike master said.

'Torpedo away,' Reznor called out.

'On target?'

'On target,' Reznor confirmed.

'Evasive?'

'Not a chance,' the warpsmith said.

Occam waited precious seconds. With each passing moment the corvette's righteous torpedo was streaking towards the Dreadclaw.

'Escape isn't enough,' Occam decided, announcing his intention to the compartment. 'We're going to have to turn this around on our pursuers. Warpsmith, what do we have that can take down a torpedo?'

'Nothing offensive has range,' Reznor answered.

'What about non-offensive?' Occam asked. 'Can it be neutralised?'

'Perhaps...' the warpsmith said, unlocking himself from

his cradle and swimming through the zero-gravity to the compartment floor.

'Talk to me,' Occam called.

'Electromagnetic pulse,' Reznor said, snatching the cog blade of his Omnissian power axe and tearing up the flooring and silver insulation. 'I'm going to rig the piezoelectric crystals in the engine and pod systems for overload.'

'And this electromagnetic pulse can nullify the torpedo's own systems?' Occam said.

'In theory.'

'Our plate?'

'Will recover,' Reznor said. 'The machine-spirits will activate auxiliary systems.'

'What about the Dreadclaw?' the sorcerer Quoda said. 'Like the torpedo, we'll lose control also.'

'One crisis at a time,' Sergeant Hasdrubal warned.

'*Iota-Æternus*,' the strike master called across the vox-channel, 'encoding.'

'Iota-Æternus, *receiving*,' Naga-Khan responded.

'Shipmaster, listen carefully – we are shortly going to lose vox-communications and power,' Occam said.

'*Receiving, Lord Occam*,' the shipmaster said.

'We are being pursued,' the strike master said. 'I want you to plot an intercept course and prime your weaponry. We'll lead them straight to you.'

'*On our way*,' Naga-Khan told him across the channel.

Looking down, Occam saw that the warpsmith was hard at work, tearing out cabling and making his heretical modifications.

'Quoda,' the strike master said. 'We are going to lose life support. Get the insulation and wrap up our prisoner.'

'And you thought it was cold down on the planet,' the

blind Hasdrubal said to the Word Bearer, leaning across from his cradle.

'How close?' Reznor called up from the mess of floating cables.

Occam pulled himself through the weightlessness of the Dreadclaw compartment, down to Reznor's runescreens.

'Close,' the strike master warned, watching the torpedo streak through the void towards them.

'I'm going to need a countdown,' the warpsmith said, tearing out more cabling and holding two sparking interfacia in his gauntlets. 'I need to set off the pulse about one to two hundred metres out.'

'That is going to be close,' Quoda said.

'Ready?' Occam asked. The warpsmith didn't look it.

'Standing by.'

'Three...' the strike master called, not taking his optics off the exterior pict-feed. 'Two... one. *Now*.'

When Reznor struck the interfacia, the cables sparked spectacularly. As the flash filled the compartment, the flooring about the warpsmith exploded as though the Dreadclaw's cells had overloaded. Reznor was blasted back and hit the wall, letting out a roar of pain. Everything happened so fast that it was difficult for Occam to follow. Runebanks set in the Dreadclaw's wall sections sparked furiously. Screens blazed white and then shattered. A sequence of smaller ruptures made their way through the engine compartment before one final overload killed the light of every lamp and system in the drop pod.

Occam's auto-senses briefly cut off and his optics blinked to blackness. The strike master felt the struggle in the darkness about him – his plate's belligerent machine-spirit fighting for its continued existence. With a flicker, the optics returned, followed by auto-senses, hydraulics and servo-automotives.

Almost immediately Occam felt the impact of the torpedo. Instead of detonating in a brief, oxygen-fuelled explosion, both torpedo and Dreadclaw simply collided. The electromagnetic pulse had burned out the torpedo's priming mechanisms and instead turned the weapon into the equivalent of a giant, bullet-shaped slug.

The high-speed impact smashed into the drop pod's armour plating with a thunderous clang that could be felt through wall, cradle and plate. Occam bounced off the wall and was thrown through the weightlessness of the compartment. He could feel the Dreadclaw tumbling off course through the void. As he steadied himself, he could see that the sickening motion was being made worse by a hull breach in a crumpled wall about the site of the impact. The *Serpent's Egg* was bleeding atmosphere into the void, propelling the Dreadclaw on in its dizzying tumble. He felt the pull of the expulsion and considered attempting to block the breach. The strike master decided against it. Nothing would stop them losing atmosphere now: air, warmth and pressure.

The strike master looked about the darkened compartment, his suit lamps cutting through the gloom. He saw Reznor's unconscious body floating in his plate and being drawn to the narrow hull breach. Smoke drizzled from one blackened gauntlet where the torrent of power from the Dreadclaw's battery cells had flowed back through the warpsmith. Beta, Zeta and Theta had fared little better, the servo-automata clanking about the compartment in zero-gravity – their workings burned out by the electromagnetic pulse.

About him, Occam heard the pumps and life support die away. The rumble of the Dreadclaw's thrusters could no longer be felt through the drop pod's superstructure. *The Serpent's Egg* was now nothing more than a coffin tumbling through space.

All the legionnaires could do was wait. Occam pulled himself around the compartment, checking on the unconscious Reznor and putting him back in his cradle. He checked on Ephron Hasdrubal also. The sergeant assured him that beyond getting sparks directly into his eyes when his helm was hit, the cracked optics and faceplate itself showed no sign of a breach. This was the same with Reznor's blackened gauntlet.

The Word Bearer was not so fortunate. Without his plate, the Traitor was exposed to the fierce hostility of the void. A drop in pressure. A lack of oxygen. Murderous cold. Checking the prisoner, who already looked like he had been beaten and tortured into a private hell, Occam saw that his genetically engineered body was already responding to its glands and implants. The Word Bearer was entering a state of suspended animation, preserving his vital functions, while his skin had started to bleed a parchment-like second surface – a thin organic veil of scabby threads that Occam knew would form into a cocoon-like covering, protecting the prisoner from the ravages of the environment.

The Redacted bided their time. Without ports in the armoured Dreadclaw and with the exterior pict-feeds dead, the renegades knew nothing of what was happening in the void outside. Occam even tried to peer through the cracked breach in the compartment wall but could see nothing. The *Serpent's Egg* could be at the epicentre of a desperate space battle between the *Iota-Æternus* and the

Inquisitorial corvette – and probably was – but locked inside the drop pod, the legionnaires knew nothing.

From time to time the strike master's plate registered ghostly readings suggestive of activity outside – energy feedback from what could have been an exchange of laser beams and cannon fire. He felt the slightest inertial nudge of the Dreadclaw adjusting trajectory, probably caused by the drop path crossing the path of an engine trail or sub-light turn where the two vessels outside were desperately trying to position themselves for a devastating broadside.

Naga-Khan had been a privateer for the alien races of the Eastern Fringe and had engaged Imperial vessels in piratical actions many times before. More recently, the strike master had been on the bridge while the shipmaster had sprung such ambushes. Naga-Khan favoured drawing his victims in, presenting the *Iota-Æternus* as a harmless freighter broadcasting false identica on all channels. As inquisitive vessels approached, he would present the unarmed Q-ship's flank. Without weaponry, such a manoeuvre failed to register as a threat. That was until the shipmaster ordered compartment doors rolled aside on the vessel's port and starboard sides, revealing to an attacker hidden cannon batteries instead of freight holds. Firing as each cannon bared, the *Iota-Æternus* overloaded the enemy's forward void shields and blasted powerful energy beams down through the length of the target vessel, Naga-Khan ultimately crippling his foe.

Occam had seen the captain expertly spring the same successful ambush a hundred times. He could think of no reason why such a scenario wasn't playing out at that moment. The shipmaster had the element of surprise, as well as xenos-modified weaponry and sub-light engines. The strike master bet, however, that Naga-Khan had never faced the captain of an Inquisitorial corvette before. Such ships benefitted from some of the best technology the Imperium had to offer.

The Redacted's long wait finally came to an end with the subtle reintroduction of gravity. As Occam's boots drifted back down and the drop pod thunked to the floor of a hangar flight deck, the strike master considered to whom the deck belonged.

'Pattern Asteron,' Occam ordered. Quoda and Malik joined their strike master about the compartment walls, their glowing plasma guns pointed at the hatch. Hasdrubal, Reznor and the Word Bearer were still locked in their cages but the sergeant had his multi-blade dagger out. Autolicon Phex had taken position behind the cradles, his heavy plasma gun pointing between the legionnaires and down the length of the drop pod.

As a plasma torch went to work on the exit hatch of the *Serpent's Egg*, filling the inner compartment with sparks, Occam and his legionnaires hugged their weapons against their pauldrons. There was no time for grenades, or to allow such weapons to be thrown into the Dreadclaw from outside. As soon as an enemy presence was confirmed, the Redacted would need to turn the hatch into a monstrous mouth vomiting forth a storm of murderous plasma.

'Stand by,' Occam said as the plasma torch finished its work. 'Remember – do not be taken alive. That's an order.'

Occam saw the legionnaires nod their agreement. They only had to look at the Word Bearer to see what a vengeful Inquisition had in store for them.

As the hatch fell away and thunked to the deck, smoke obscured the opening. Occam's cycling optics revealed figures beyond. One came forward through the obscurity.

'The shipmaster's compliments,' a voice carried into the compartment. It belonged to Mina Perdita. As the smoke cleared, the Redacted could see the Assassin, the High Serpent and members of the Seventh Sons on the hangar deck beyond – the deck belonging to the *Iota-Æternus*. 'He is glad to report that he has crippled the enemy vessel, my lord – with superficial damage to our own.'

'Very good,' Occam told the Assassin, allowing the barrel of the plasma gun to drift down. The legionnaires in the compartment did likewise. 'My compliments in return.'

'Your orders, my lord?'

'My orders,' Occam told her, 'are to get us out of here – best possible speed.'

PART III

UNITY AND LIES

λ

TURNING THE SCALES

The Cathedra Crosium was definitely impressive.

Even a man like Archimedis Van Leeuwen – no stranger to the segmentum's wonders – found himself staring.

Towering high above the low-gravity world of Incandesica, the cathedra's crown of steeples and chapel towers reached for the heavens. Incandesica was situated at the heart of the Crozier Worlds and was the hub of Adeptus Ministorum affairs in the sector. The mighty Cathedra Crosium sat at the heart of Incandesica's high-rise continental expanse of City-Sanctus. One fat hive, expanding for thousands of kilometres and dominated by dormitory spires, temple complexes and the magnificence of gothic shrines, the City-Sanctus was swarming with priests and pilgrims.

Doubling as a palace of planetary governance, the great state rooms of the cathedra were vaulted chambers of ornate stonework – ancient and beautiful. Colonnades of statues ran up the centre, depicting cardinals and other high ecclesiarchs heralding from the sector, and saints that had inspired the faithful of the Crozier Worlds.

The colonnade came to an end at the centre of the cavernous chamber. Situated there was the pulpit throne of the cardinal incumbent, framed by a colossal tapestry bearing a fanciful depiction of the God-Emperor carrying the globe of Incandesica on his armoured shoulder. Above the throne, the cathedra's highest steeple remained open like a crown of its own, revealing the starlit firmament and the passing of the cardinal world's devotional moons.

Even at a brisk pace, it took half an hour to make one's way through the palace's many massive ante-chambers, ambulatories and transepts. Fraters, pilgrims and confessors stopped in their tracks to allow the party to pass, while boltgun-wielding Battle Sisters, in full ceremonial palace plate, gave the visitors the narrowing of their eyes.

Leading the way in his robes and furs was the Lord Inquisitor Van Leeuwen, a member of the Holy Ordos. The sigil of the Ordo Hereticus emblazoned on the breast of his ancient powered plate told all that even in a place of important men, he was a man of singular importance. The inquisitor carried his ornate helm at his side and tapped an empty belt holster with a bionic claw – the bolt pistol that usually resided there had been left with the dean of the palace gate as a sign of respect.

Several Sister-Vestals gasped as they saw his gruesome face up close. The mottled transparency of his face and the skin stretched across his skull were evidence of several rejuvenat treatments too many. The silver fangs that replaced his teeth and the red pin-point optics burning through his misted eyes and glowing through his wasted flesh added to the inquisitor's grotesque appearance.

He was not alone. The flagstones shook beneath his own step as an honour guard of recruited penitents flanked him. The last surviving members of the Nova Legion, the five Angels of Death had painted over their legionary colours with the black of mourning and pledged their superhuman talents to Van Leeuwen and his hunt for their sworn foes. Like the inquisitor, they too had left their weaponry with the dean.

Attending upon Van Leeuwen in the form of diplomatic aides were a native son and daughter of the Crozier Worlds. Sister Superior Sabine of the Order of the August Vigil had been part of the secondment sent from Incandesica with two hundred of her devout kind to support the inquisitor in his work on the Cradle's edge. Confessor Karolco, meanwhile, had worked for Van Leeuwen as an exorcist, extracting the secrets of possessed heretics.

As the inquisitor and his entourage arrived before the pulpit throne, it began to turn on its mighty dais. Van Leeuwen noted the presence of Battle Sisters up in the raised stone galleries, pointing scoped and targeter-mounted Stalker-pattern boltguns through embrasures and down at the new arrivals. The inquisitor felt the scopes of the weapons follow him and the dot of targeters pass across his ornate plate. It seemed to Van Leeuwen that bringing weapons into the cathedra only breached Adeptus Ministorum diktats when they were carried by visitors.

Choirs of voxhailer-mouthed servitors flanked the throne chamber, filling its vastness with hymnals and cogitator-fed recitations from the Lectitio Divinitatus.

In the throne was the husk of a man, twice even Van Leeuwen's age. Buried in an ornamental cassock and towering mitre, the cardinal astra's skeletal hand looked as if it were fossilised to the ceremonial crozier he held upright. The inquisitor suspected that the wizened cardinal rarely left his throne, if the nest of medical tubes, pumps and monitors was anything to go by. As the dais turned, the cluster of clergy and attendants gathered about the cardinal came around with it. While Sisters Hospitaller attended upon the cardinal's person, a Sister Famulous stood before a runescreen-mounted lectern. A crusader in ancient plate stomped forward, his steps heavy on the dais. As he rested the tip of his notched ceremonial power sword against the stone the sound reverberated around the chamber. With him stood a Battle Sister, some kind of canoness, the inquisitor suspected. Her head was brutally shaved like Sister Sabine's. Van Leeuwen watched her flick untrusting eyes from his entourage up to the Sisters behind the embrasures. An extravagant cloak covered her ornate plate and the canoness held a sceptre in her gauntlets. Although the sceptre was ceremonial, it looked as if the Battle Sister were ready to brain anyone getting too close to the ecclesiarch.

'Lord Inquisitor Archimedis Van Leeuwen, of the Ordo Hereticus,' the Sister Famulous announced from her lectern, before presenting her master: 'Cardinal Astra, Planetary Governor and Sector Arch-Ecclesiarch – Josephat Hieronemo Trazier the Third. State your business and go in peace, Lord Van Leeuwen.'

'My business,' the inquisitor announced, his voice echoing eerily about the vaulted throne chamber, 'concerns not just the cardinal astra but also his people. He is shepherd to billions across the Crozier Worlds, guiding them in body and soul towards the God-Emperor's benevolent light. He must know that packs of rabid dogs are tearing their way through his flock.'

'It is my understanding...' a gaunt priest said, stepping forward.

'The honourable Arch-Deacon Faizel Scamander,' the Sister Famulous announced, 'Protector of the Creed.'

'...that the people look to the Emperor's servants to protect them from such savagery and the Holy Ordos to root out the cause of such disease.'

Van Leeuwen stepped forward also. He heard the creak of plate up in the elevated galleries.

'Don't lecture me, sir, on my duty,' the inquisitor said, 'and I shall not lecture you in return about your own responsibilities.'

'Have we not already fulfilled our responsibilities to the Inquisition?' the canoness said.

'Canoness Preceptor Mauratania Kendriss...'

'The cardinal astra,' Kendriss continued in her heavy accent, 'in his eternal wisdom, sent you two hundred of my Sister Dominions, to aid the Ordo Hereticus in its good works. I see that you have brought one of my Sisters before me.'

'What more could you want from us?' a portly priest with a ragged, silver tonsure and beard called out with more incredulity than, by the fearful expression that crossed his face, he originally intended.

'Vandrach Guzzman – Pontifex Urba of the City-Sanctus...'

'Everything you have,' Inquisitor Van Leeuwen seethed back through his silver fangs, 'if I so choose and the Master of Mankind demands.'

A moment of uncomfortable silence descended upon the chamber.

'We did not mean to give offence, inquisitor lord,' the cardinal astra rasped between breaths on a rebreather.

'And you, your holiness, did not give any,' Van Leeuwen said. 'For my hasty words in this divine place, I apologise also.'

'The physical and spiritual safety of the God-Emperor's people has, is and always shall be of paramount importance to His most trusted servants,' Cardinal Trazier said with effort. 'Men like you, lord inquisitor, and men like me.'

'I am very pleased to hear you say that, cardinal,' Van Leeuwen said. 'To address the canoness preceptor's question, her Sisters do excellent work guarding artefacts of ruin and dangerous xenos technologies – keeping them safe from heretics, damned sorcerers and those corrupted by the warp. But I come to you not to talk of a defence against the darkness, for it lays siege to the Imperium on all fronts. No, I wish to talk to you – a stalwart subject of the God-Emperor – about taking the fight to our enemies and carrying His light and destruction into such darkness.'

'You talk of the Tyrant's turning,' the cardinal astra said, his voice a crackling whisper, 'and the tragedies of Sector Badab.'

'Tragedies indeed,' the inquisitor said, 'but fortunately they are the concern of the Emperor's loyal Space Marines and others within the Holy Ordos.'

'Speak on.'

'The Tyrant might have fled for the environs of the unholy Maelstrom,' Van Leeuwen said, 'but I speak of other… traitors who have long made their home there. A dark brotherhood that strikes from the darkness and whose atrocities demand action from men such as you and I.'

'Bearers of the Word, your excellency,' Confessor Karolco

called up to the cardinal. 'Perverters of the creed, spreaders of heresy and butchers of the faithful.'

'These good brothers of the Adeptus Astartes are all that are left of their honoured Chapter,' Van Leeuwen said, presenting the Space Marines of the Nova Legion, 'now pledged with me to finding the dread renegades responsible for such slaughter. And they are not the only ones. My researches have revealed three other Chapters – three other lights extinguished by the darkness.'

'And these Bearers of the Word,' Cardinal Trazier said, 'though I hate to even speak their name, are the ones responsible.'

'Yes, mighty ecclesiarch,' Confessor Karolco said, 'and much more besides. I have personally aided the inquisitor in his interrogations and exorcisms of such warp-spawned deviants. They are a threat to everything the Imperium stands for.'

'The confessor does not exaggerate,' Van Leeuwen said.

'I know of the historical treachery the Word Bearers committed,' the cardinal astra said, 'and the present threat they pose with their otherworldly pacts, their heretical poison and apocalyptic arts.'

'Then you know that they routinely send out ships from the Maelstrom to rain destruction upon the God-Emperor-fearing planets of the Crozier Worlds and that they must be stopped.'

'But lord inquisitor,' Arch-Deacon Scamander piped up, 'surely Adeptus Astartes warriors like the ones present before us are best equipped to fight such an evil, as they did during the dark days of the Heresy.'

'The God-Emperor helps those who help themselves,' Van Leeuwen told the gathering of ecclesiarchs. 'I have sent word to the warmasters of the Astra Militarum, the High Admirals of the Imperial Navy, the Martian priesthood and Adeptus Astartes Chapters across the region. The story is the same. Cardinal, it is the story of all times. Threats from within and without. Too many, with too few forces to combat them. The expansion of barbarian empires, xenos invasions, piratical opportunism and the ever-present dangers spewed forth by the unholy Maelstrom.'

'Indeed,' the venerable Trazier said.

'The faithful of the Imperium must play their part, too,' the inquisitor said. 'It is not enough to wait for wildfires to appear across the storm-bordering sectors. The inferno must be doused at the source. This is why I have been touring the Crozier Worlds, speaking to the ruling ecclesiarchs of cardinal, shrine and cemetery worlds asking them to raise frater militias and pilgrim armies.'

'In the name of what, lord inquisitor?' the cardinal astra asked.

'A White Crusade, your eminence,' Van Leeuwen told him. 'Billions of the fighting faithful, from High Temperance, St Sorcha, Fleur-de-Phasmi, Ignatius Crozier and many worlds besides. All travelling with fiery preachers along pilgrim trails as we speak, to rendezvous at Suspiria Proctor.

'From there, they shall launch a crusade into the Maelstrom and take the fight to the Word Bearers, their abominate sponsors and their cultist hordes on their own soil. They shall be the hammer that shatters the dark faith of the traitors and puts an end, once and for all, to their ancient threat.

'I am close to discovering the location of the dread planet from which the Word Bearers launch their raids.

Even then, the frater faithful and preachers of the Crozier Worlds will not embark. For a White Crusade needs a figurehead. A name, beyond the God-Emperor's, to give good men spiritual strength in the face of darkness. *Your* name, Cardinal Trazier. Only when your priests and the fighting fraters of Incandesica join us at Suspiria Proctor and your blessing is given, shall the White Crusade be undertaken and the deviant Word Bearers of the Maelstrom be destroyed.'

'I have never heard such insanity,' Arch-Deacon Scamander said.

'Madness,' Pontifex Guzzman agreed.

'You invite the slaughter of billions,' the canoness preceptor hissed.

'As we invite the same,' Cardinal Trazier said, 'if we stand by, cower inside our chapels, our churches and do nothing. As the good inquisitor says, we must lead by example. So, Lord of the Holy Ordos. You may go to Suspiria Proctor. Await the frater faithful I will send. Then tell all that Josephat Hieronemo Trazier the Third gives his blessing to this White Crusade – an undertaking that receives the God-Emperor's benediction also.'

'As benevolent as you are wise, cardinal astra,' Van Leeuwen told Trazier. 'Your reputation is well deserved. And now, I take my leave. May the God-Emperor go with you, mighty ecclesiarch.'

'And with you, my son,' Cardinal Trazier told him.

As the inquisitor and the Adeptus Astartes mounted the ramp to an orbital lander bereft of identica and markings, the craft's thrusters engaged and started lifting it off the cathedra landing pads. Leaving behind the Battle

Sisters sentries and dusty priests of the palace, the lander spiralled up above the bell towers and spires, punching a hole through Incandesica's spectacular layers of cloud before striking out for the darkness of the void.

'Dissemble.'

Occam the Untrue turned around in the carrier compartment. While the exterior of the stolen lander was plain, the interior was plush. The scales of his plate, like those of the other members of the Redacted, changed back to their legionary colours from the penitent black of long dead Space Marines of the Nova Legion and Inquisitor Van Leeuwen's ancient suit. Freydor Blatch threw off the heavy robes of the exorcist, while Mina Perdita simply took off her Battle Sisters helm. The Alpha Legion and their operatives felt the change as the sorcerer Quoda abandoned his efforts and the aura of telepathic manipulation that surrounded the renegades and played upon the prejudices, imaginations and expectations of those observing them, collapsed. The Redacted were the Inquisitorial entourage no more.

Sergeant Hasdrubal took off his refurbished helm, revealing fresh scarring across his face, an eye that had been surgically saved and a bright green bionic optic that replaced the one that could not. He hadn't been the only one to benefit from an upgrade. In the time the Redacted had been touring the planets of the Crozier Worlds, garnering support for a supposed White Crusade, the warpsmith had replaced the right hand and gauntlet he had lost in the *Serpent's Egg* with the bionics of an impressively dextrous appendage.

'Right,' the strike master said to the Alpha Legion renegades. 'We have assembled the pieces – now it is time to play the game.'

μ

SECOND SKIN

Lord Occam's chambers were filled with the sound of hushed whispers and the beating of dark hearts. While the strike commander sat in his throne, decked in plate, figures moved in and out of the reconstructed Chapel of the Immaculate Ascension. His armour had assumed legionary colours, while his helm sat on the arm of the throne. Ghosting about the dark recesses of the chamber were Vilnius Malik and Sergeant Hasdrubal. The legionnaires wore helms with full plate. While Malik cradled his long-shot plasma gun like some kind of sentinel, the sergeant stood at ease, his gauntlet resting on the pommel of his sheathed, multi-blade knife.

Within the chapel, chirurgeons and medicae servitors were hard at work at the stone altar, which had been covered with transparent plastek sheeting. While medical-tooled servitors cut away at the subject lying there, the chirurgeons consulted, pointing as their drones went to work with las-scalpels and monomolecular chainblades.

Occam knew one of the bearded chirurgeons to be Mina Perdita, the Assassin offering further security in the chamber. Since she knew more about taking life than saving it, the strike master assumed that she was the quiet figure in surgical robes lurking near the rear of the gathering.

The form on the altar was large. Like a mummified corpse recovered from a burial site, the figure was sheathed in a cocoon. In places the material was thin, like scabby parchment stretched across the musculature of the figure within; in others it was thick and horny, forming nubs, whorls and patterns of daemonic suggestion. Cutting away the second skin under the instruction of the chirurgeons, who stood some way distant, the medicae-servitors moved about the evil thing undaunted.

Gossamer wires ran from sensors on the husk to mobile runebanks that monitored the subject's vital signs and filled the chapel with the sound of heartbeats. As sprays were issued and injections given through the shell of the cocoon, the servitors cut away more of the material from the subject's face. The soft thunder of beating hearts accelerated and the runebanks spewed forth data, which the chirurgeons consulted with interest.

Now that the Word Bearer's face was revealed, Occam could see that despite the infernal suggestion of his cocoon, the traitor Space Marine was not an altered underneath. He was as disgusting as he had been when Occam had found him – the Word Bearer's black, frostbitten face a mess. He was not, however, warped by daemonic presence. The Ordo Hereticus exorcists had long driven any monstrous entity from the Word Bearer's body and soul. The strike master was not inclined to be complacent. Quoda had insisted that the chapel's hallowed influence would go some way to subdue the damned flesh of the Word Bearer. Perdita was nearby, ready to slit throats and stab hearts. Vilnius Malik and the sergeant had orders to put the Word Bearer down brutally if he showed signs of daemonic intrusion, while Autolicon Phex waited on the door to the strike master's chamber, his heavy weaponry ready to be called upon.

As the Word Bearer's hand came up suddenly, the chirurgeons and even their servitors jumped back. The cocoon cracked and tore at the movement, allowing the Traitor Space Marine to grab the wired sensors from his chest and kill the sound of hearts rapidly beating. Sitting up on the altar, the Word Bearer sloughed the encrusted sheath off like a second skin. Occam found himself up out of his throne. Malik and the sergeant closed in, while the chirurgeon the strike master suspected was Perdita pushed his way through his startled colleagues.

The Word Bearer glowered about the interior of the chapel, the whites of his eyes writhing in the black ruin of his face. He was clearly not comfortable, his frost-withered lips retracting about his teeth. He stared down at his naked body and grabbed at his chest, as though missing the damnation of his plate. Occam narrowed his eyes, watching the Word Bearer. It seemed something more to the strike master. As though the Traitor Space Marine was missing more than just his armour.

Finally, the Word Bearer looked around, prompting the medicae staff to back away even further. Then his gaze settled on Occam, flanked by Malik and the sergeant. While the muzzle of Malik's glowing plasma gun was aimed at the Word Bearer, Hasdrubal merely stared back at the prisoner, his gauntlet grasped about the hilt of his multi-blade.

The Word Bearer grunted his derision.

'Serpents…'

'Serpents that saved your life,' Malik said dangerously, staring down the length of his aimed weapon. 'And don't forget that.'

'Where are we?' the Word Bearer demanded with the imperiousness of a zealot.

Occam and the sergeant frowned. The phrasing of the question sounded odd.

'You are…' Occam said, 'aboard my vessel – as a guest. My legionnaire here speaks true. You were a prisoner of the Holy Ordos.'

'And now we are *guests*,' the Word Bearer said, 'of the Alpha Legion.'

'Honoured… guests,' Occam told him, picking up on the Word Bearer's strange way of referring to himself. He turned to the gathering. 'Robes and water – for our honoured guests.'

Servitors brought robes for the Word Bearer, a carafe of water and a chalice. The Traitor Space Marine looked suspiciously between the offerings and the strike master. This time it was Hasdrubal's turn to grunt his derision.

'If we had wanted it, you would be dead already,' Occam told the Word Bearer. 'We might be serpents, brother, but you need fear no poison from us.'

The Word Bearer ignored the offered chalice and took the carafe, downing the contents. Gesturing for another, he drank deep: his time as an Inquisitorial prisoner combined with time spent cocooned against the elements, or lack thereof, had visited upon the Traitor Space Marine a mighty thirst. Then came the robes, and his toes reached tentatively for the deck. He looked down at the altar and around at the crumbling architecture of the Chapel of the Immaculate Ascension. His eyes fixed upon the hexagrammic wards adorning the flags, the purity seals carved into the stone of the altar, holy scripture and sigils of protection and banishment.

'An attempt at humour?' the damned Space Marine said.

'No,' Lord Occam said. 'It is meant for the solace of the faithful – not the amusement of heretics. That seemed to be lost on you when your vessel brought its apocalyptic thunder to the Canticula shrine world.'

'It seems you missed one,' Hasdrubal said, gesturing to the ruins of the chapel.

'Now, let's begin,' Occam said, moving towards the Word Bearer. 'How about your name and rank?'

'You think us afraid to reveal such details,' the Word Bearer said. 'You think us some terrified soldier, obeying orders and saying nothing to withstand interrogation? I'll tell you freely, as I told the Emperor's pigs, the names of those that cost them their lives.'

'Pray do,' Occam said.

'I am Goura Shengk,' the Word Bearer told him, 'Dark Apostle of the Barbed Oath and spiritual leader of the Varga Rax, those warp-tempered of flesh.'

'And…' Occam said, sensing more.

'Morphidax the Primordial.'

'If I may make an observation,' Sergeant Hasdrubal said, 'you speak with a pride and defiance ill-befitting your present circumstances.'

'And you speak like a legionnaire of little understanding,' Goura Shengk said. 'A warrior with experience cleaving flesh asunder but with little comprehension of the darkness operating within.'

'Enough,' Occam commanded. 'Lord apostle – Primordial One – the truth of the matter is that we find you far from home, at the mercy of your Imperial enemies and abandoned by those you would call brother.'

'Truth?' Goura Shengk said. 'What would the Alpha Legion know of truth?'

'More than you would think,' Sergeant Hasdrubal warned the Word Bearer.

'Your brotherhood abandoned you,' Occam accused. 'The traitors under your command.'

'Again,' Goura Shengk said, 'you think you can manipulate us with details half understood. Those brothers obeyed our orders. They have a thousand decrees, precepts and commandments to follow from a thousand dark tomes – and they followed them to the letter. There is no wedge to be forced between the Bearers of the Word. The duty was carried out. Our sacrifice ensured success.'

'But they left you,' Occam pressed.

'Failure is not tolerated in the ranks of the Dark Brotherhood and the Daemon Council is not forgiving.'

'You have a new brotherhood now,' the sergeant said. 'A new duty – to us, your saviours.'

'Think not to threaten us,' Goura Shengk told Hasdrubal. 'We share this delicate vessel, this miserable flesh – warping it for our own amusement and purpose. You really think we care what you do to it with your paltry blades? You put too much faith in your skill and a razor's edge.'

'You can never put too much faith in that,' Hasdrubal told him.

'But you don't share that vessel, lord apostle,' Occam said, confronting the Word Bearer with the reality of his predicament. 'Your flesh is home but to one presence. The

Inquisition exorcists saw to that. Your daemon – the entity you live to appease – is gone. Banished to the beyond. You are alone, Goura Shengk – but it need not be so.'

The Dark Apostle seemed to consider Occam's words.

'We will not join you,' Goura Shengk said, 'and your band of faithless traitors.'

'We are far from faithless, lord apostle,' the strike master said. 'Besides – I am not recruiting.'

'We set you at liberty, you thankless wretch,' Hasdrubal reminded the Word Bearer.

'This does not look like freedom,' Shengk said.

'And it isn't,' Occam assured him. 'Your flesh is your prison. I offer you something else. A way back – to your brothers, to your home, to your daemon.'

'To punishment for our failures.'

'Better than a bolt round to the skull,' the sergeant assured him. 'Which is what you would be facing among our number.'

'And why would the Alpha Legion wish such kindnesses upon a brother of the Word?' Goura Shengk asked.

'We share common goals,' Occam the Untrue told him.

'You speak of an alliance.'

'I speak of an exchange,' the strike master said. 'We shall take you back to your daemon world, lord apostle, to rejoin your Legion, your brothers and your darkness. To face your punishment and beg for forgiveness.'

'Take us to Ghalmek?' Goura Shengk said. 'The Daemonforge? The Shrine of Iron? You could never reach such an unholy place. The Maelstrom would chew your vessel up and spit you out.'

'That is why we need your guidance,' Occam told him.

'What do you want with the daemon world?'

'Truth?' the strike master asked.

'We're not sure you can manage it,' the Word Bearer told him.

'The artefact your traitors stole from Nemesis Spectra,' Lord Occam said.

'What do you want with the Slaughterlord?'

'The Slaughterlord?'

'The daemon Kar'Nash'gahar,' the Dark Apostle said, 'Lord of Glorious Slaughter and Slayer of Worlds. The infernal volumes of the *Daedronicron Malefest* foretold of his coming. That those who freed him from imprisonment could count on his thunder in the trials to come.'

'And you seek to engage this daemon's thunder?' Occam asked.

'You don't?'

'We care nothing for your dusty tomes and their prophecies,' the strike master promised. 'The Alpha Legion deal in the here and the now. We seek the ancient technology that holds your rancid daemon – and that is all. Keep your monstrous entity and the doom he brings but give us the technology, in exchange for your life.'

'We do not believe you,' Goura Shengk said. 'Besides, the Grand Apostle, the Daemon Council and the Brotherhood of the Dark Word will never barter for such a prize. Its dread promise will only just have reached Unholy Ghalmek. Why should they give it up?'

'I can be persuasive.'

'You will be dead,' Goura Shengk said. 'The Grand Apostle will have you stellafied – your hands and feet nailed to the half-points of a Chaos Star – while you slowly roast in the light of Ghalmek's blood-red sun.'

'Leave the Grand Apostle to me,' Occam assured him.

'Then I shall kill you myself,' the Word Bearer promised. 'We are not like you, faithless legionnaire. Our word means something – in this existence and the one beyond. We will not betray our brotherhood or give up our prize. Our names shall be carved into the mighty Animus, atop the Malevolent Mount, crafted from the black stone of a thousand temples fallen.'

'No,' Occam told him. 'It will be forgotten. Your prize will be delivered to the Shrine of Iron by another. It will be his name that will adorn this monstrous monument you speak of. Who knows, Goura Shengk – perhaps your successor will be rewarded with a daemon of his own. Perhaps an eternity is too long for your own daemon to wait and he will favour another with his presence.'

'You are wrong,' Goura Shengk said. 'I might have failed but my First Acolyte and captains, in turn, failed me. They return to punishment – as is decreed.'

'Aye, they return – as decreed,' Occam said. 'As you must, Goura Shengk.'

'I will not be goaded, serpent,' the lord apostle said.

'Then be persuaded,' Occam the Untrue urged. 'Be bribed and bought with a future that awaits you. Whatever appeases your dark soul. We want not your daemon prize, Word Bearer – only the artefact prison that holds him. If you would die rather than deal for yourself, then bargain for the benefit of your brothers.'

'What can you possibly offer the Daemon Council?'

'The only currency your dread council deals in,' Occam said: 'souls. We might be small in number but our reach is far. For weeks now we have been touring the Crozier Worlds – a region that knows the wrath of the Word Bearers well.'

'You know it does,' Goura Shengk said.

'Disguised as the very Inquisition authorities your daemon ship hit on Nemesis Spectra and who, in turn, enjoyed your company on Fifty-Four-Thermia, we have been taking meetings with the ruling ecclesiarchs there.'

'And why would you do that?'

'Recruitment, lord apostle,' Occam the Untrue told him. 'The Word Bearers of Ghalmek and the apocalyptic attacks of their ungodly daemon ships are to be tolerated no longer. There is to be a White Crusade – a holy war the likes of which you have never seen, to be waged against your dark brotherhood. It will find your daemon world and destroy you there.'

'Snake…' Goura Shengk spat. 'You applaud your own efforts and place too much faith in the Corpse-Emperor's weakling priests. Such human frailty is nothing compared to the daemon legions that fight for the Dark Brotherhood.'

'Perhaps,' the strike master said, 'but entertain this thought, for a moment. Such a force exists and is amassing in an undisclosed location in the Crozier Worlds as we speak. I have sent my Low Servant and his cultists to meet each pilgrim transport as it arrives from different parts of the Crozier Worlds and begin the process of infiltration. Naturally, my operatives intend to recruit the most promising of the frater militia for the Alpha Legion's ranks. The rest, lord apostle, can be yours. A devout army of the faithful, corrupted to the will of your Daemon Council before frater ships ever set sail for the Maelstrom. A billion souls, delivered straight to the Shrine of Iron. Enough even to satisfy the wrath of your Daemon Council.

'Think on it, Word Bearer. But don't take too long. I did

not break you out of that ice hole for nothing – but if it is nothing that you offer me then I'll be damned before I let you see your daemon or your daemon world again.'

Occam nodded, bringing Vilnius Malik forward. The plasma gun hummed to priming as the legionnaire aimed it at Goura Shengk. It bathed Word Bearer and legionnaire both in its blue brilliance.

'Damnation or oblivion,' Occam said. 'You choose. But choose now.'

After a proud delay that made Sergeant Hasdrubal smirk, the Dark Apostle answered.

'I cannot in dark conscience,' Goura Shengk said, 'deal doubly with the Daemon Council. I have taken oaths before the Ruinous Powers. My hearts are enslaved to their dread will. It is not in my power to betray them or their interests in the name of saving my miserable life.'

Occam heard Malik's plate creak as the legionnaire leaned in with his plasma gun.

'However,' the Dark Apostle said. 'There will be ceremony and ritual to observe upon our arrival at Ghalmek. This distraction might offer a resourceful individual time to lift an ancient artefact from our catacomb-archives unnoticed, if he were pointed in the right direction.'

Lord Occam placed his gauntlet on the barrel of Malik's plasma gun and lowered it slowly towards the floor.

'Good enough.'

PART IV

THE THIN VEIL

v

SEA SERPENTS

Occam paced the tiny command deck of the *Iota-Æternus*.

The strike master could feel it on the bridge, in the hangars and along the freighter's winding passageways. There was a tension – not just in the faces and voices of the Seventh Sons but also in the vessel superstructure. While the High Serpent's cultists were nervous about entering riftspace, the Q-ship itself was making its displeasure known. Occam's superhuman hearing picked up the high-pitched ring of unnatural vibrations through metal struts, girders and decking. Like a tuning fork, the *Iota-Æternus* was singing, and the tune wasn't pleasant.

The Q-ship had held her immaterial course for days, ploughing on through the storm-wracked ether and the warped reality beyond. While Arkan Reznor had made many upgrades and customisations to the vessel, incorporating xenos technologies into the sub-light drives and weapons systems, the warp engines and Geller field generator were thoroughly Imperial. Reliably old, the field generator and warp drive had never failed Naga-Khan and the Alpha Legion. Reznor and the shipmaster's own enginseer both considered them dependable. The warp engines and integrated field generator had never been under so much stress before, however.

Striking out from the Crozier Worlds, the *Iota-Æternus* made for the aberrance of the Maelstrom. At Goura Shengk's instruction, the Q-ship entered the raging storm at the Sinistral Gate. This was an area of calm favoured by pirates and renegades striking out from the Maelstrom. Shengk insisted that his personal daemon ship, the *Dissolutio Perpetua*, used the Sinistral Gate for slipping out of the warp storm and running down on the Crozier Worlds and the fabricator moons of the Koronado Cradle.

From there Quoda's choir of astropaths begged permission to retire to their quarters, insisting they were suffering mind-splitting headaches and the fact that the sorcerer couldn't rely on their abilities in the storm. Quoda and Navigator Ghesh, meanwhile, took on a haunted look as the freighter traversed the vicious tempest. It didn't need a psyker to feel the rancid effect of the Maelstrom on the vessel. A wave of lingering nausea swept through the cultist crew, like an extreme form of motion sickness, and even Occam felt something horrible in the pit of his stomachs.

Skimming through the tumultuous mayhem of the Maelstrom, the freighter made short warp jumps interspaced with storm-running cruises at sub-light speed. Naga-Khan and Ghesh wouldn't risk engaging the warp-drive for too long within the storm for fear of plunging into its monstrous heart. Naga-Khan warned the strike master that they could end up getting hopelessly lost, emerge on the other side of the galaxy, become trapped in some kind of temporal distortion or be torn apart upon emerging into a region of the Maelstrom where reality was storm-shredded – fused with the strange weather of the immaterium.

The Geller field was operating constantly, with Arkan Reznor stationed in the enginarium to deal immediately with any problems – such problems having the potential to present the defenceless vessel to the innumerable immaterial entities and predatory daemons like bloody bait to a swarm of sharks. Every time the warp-drive disengaged and the sub-light engines found purchase in the strange and varied realities the *Iota-Æternus* found itself in, the Geller field generator struggled, causing the field to momentarily flutter. In those heart-stopping seconds, the cultist crew and members of the Redacted would stop what they were doing and look around warily at the brief dimming of the deck lights.

For Ghesh the Navigator skimming through the storm in this way was like flashing a lamp on occasionally in the darkness and describing to their Word Bearers guest what he saw. Naga-Khan would then course correct based upon the Dark Apostle's recognition of the different streams, eddies and tempest phenomena he expected to encounter.

Unlike Occam's legionnaires, operatives and cultist crew, Goura Shengk seemed perfectly at ease. Looking like a small mountain wrapped in robes, the Dark Apostle stared out through the lancet screens into the havoc beyond, his eyes and teeth white in his blackened face. While the Word Bearer had consented to assist the strike master in his proud and limited way, Occam still had Vilnius Malik ghost him, watching over the former prisoner from a distance, his long-shot plasma gun at the ready. As an extra precaution, Autolicon Phex stood guard by the elevator door with his heavy plasma gun. Ephron Hasdrubal was present also, never far away from the Dark Apostle, even though Occam hadn't issued the sergeant with such a duty.

For the most part, Occam stood to one side. He was in command but the responsibility of getting the *Iota-Æternus* through the dangers of the Maelstrom largely belonged to the shipmaster, Navigator Ghesh, the warpsmith and Goura Shengk. While Reznor kept in contact from the enginarium and Naga-Khan oversaw matters on the tense bridge, the Dark Apostle interpreted the monstrous phenomena outside the ship. Goura Shengk had names for features described by the ashen-faced Ghesh, both occurring in the warp and the confused realities of the storm traversed by the Q-ship – the Ghostmare, the Storm of Maws, the Vassago Stream, Perdition's Gate, the Phorneus Rapidity…

Beyond the Maelstrom and the storm's nightmarish environs, Occam could see the spectral impression of predatory warp entities and monstrous daemons in the sizzling Geller field. They were a constant presence, testing the integrity of the field and pressing their mind-scalding forms up against the bubble of reality that enveloped the *Iota-Æternus*.

'Identify,' Occam ordered. His eyes fixed upon a horrific cyclone churning up the immateriality about it. Like Jupiter's great red spot it was a blood-red storm raging within the havoc of other tempests, warpstreams and currents. A crimson haze spewed continuously from its abominate mouth, casting everything around it in obscurity. As it washed up against the lancet screens, the strike master

SONS OF THE HYDRA

saw that the haze was made up of tiny globules of rich, red liquid that looked very much like blood.

'The Mawtex,' Goura Shengk said. Even the Word Bearer looked concerned at the appearance. 'A storm within the storm that appears and disappears at whim.'

'Ghesh?' Occam said.

'It's deep,' the Navigator said, entranced. 'Bottomless. Its currents are strong but the structure volatile.'

'Even we don't risk our vessels in the Mawtex,' the Word Bearer said. 'There are pirates and renegades who do, however, using it to traverse the Maelstrom.'

'Your orders?' Naga-Khan said. Occam looked to Goura Shengk.

'There are safer routes,' the Dark Apostle said.

The strike master grunted at his use of the word *safer*.

'Skirt it.'

As the Q-ship pushed on through the haze, the vessel became submerged in a backwash of cloudy blood, the twisted wreckage of storm-smashed vessels thunked against the hull.

'I can't see anything,' Naga-Khan complained, moving between cultist-manned runebanks. 'Augurs.'

'Not functional,' one of the Seventh Sons reported.

Occam stared into the red mist. Within the Maelstrom the scanners returned warped readings, phantasmic traces and evidence of the impossible. Here they didn't even return that.

'It's the Mawtex,' the Dark Apostle said. 'Your instrumentation's readings are being drowned out.'

'By what?' the strike master asked.

'Open a short-wave vox-channel,' Goura Shengk said.

'What channel?' the shipmaster asked.

'Any channel,' the Word Bearer said.

As Naga-Khan put the channel on loudhailers, the command deck was filled with an unearthly roar. The crew's faces creased in a nerve-shredded wince. A Seventh Son screamed out while several others vomited onto the deck. To Occam it was an annoyance but a loud and insistent one. He didn't know whether or not it was some colossal daemon entity of the unnatural flux of the storm that created the sound but he knew that he didn't want to listen to any more of its furious madness.

'Enough,' he commanded, prompting a deck officer to kill the loudhailer. He looked from the red lancet screens to Sergeant Hasdrubal and the shipmaster. 'Blind and deaf. We're not even able to feel our way through this muck. Status?'

'We're running with shields raised,' Naga-Khan told him, trying to assure the strike master that precautions had been taken, 'and batteries primed.'

Occam wasn't convinced. This was the Maelstrom: anything could happen.

'All stop,' he commanded.

'All stop,' the shipmaster repeated to the command deck crew.

'Roll aside the compartment doors,' the strike master said, 'and present cannons.'

'Sir,' Naga-Khan protested, 'aren't we giving away–'

'Do it,' Occam said.

Without question, the shipmaster carried out the order. As the Q-ship slowed, the cloud of red globules settled about the lancet screens. A metallic boom reverberated down the length of the armed freighter as plating rolled aside to reveal the hidden batteries in the converted cargo sections.

'Cycle pict-streams,' Naga-Khan ordered. Occam nodded his agreement. As the lancet screens crackled from forward to aft, port to starboard views, the same red obscurity fogged up every angle.

Occam came forward, peering through the red murk. As the views cycled, the strike master looked for something but found nothing. Occam turned around to find Goura Shengk doing the same. Meanwhile, the command deck crew waited patiently.

'Sir?' Sergeant Hasdrubal said.

'It appears I have made an error,' Occam said finally.

'It doesn't happen often, my lord,' Naga-Khan said.

'Shipmaster,' Occam said, 'stand down the batteries and prepare to make way...'

Occam's voice trailed off as the port-side pict-feed revealed a disturbance in the bloody globules and then the ghostly silhouette of a vessel. The strike master could make out the reinforced prow of a Chaos raider. The ship was dirty red and black, bearing colossal sigils splattered unceremoniously across its armour plating. The vessel had clearly seen recent action, its hull pock-marked with blast craters and the ragged damage of cannon fire.

'Enemy vessel,' Naga-Khan called out, 'approaching port-side aft at ramming speed.'

'As you were,' Occam said.

'Port-side batteries, fire as you bear,' Naga-Khan commanded, stabbing at the buttons on a runebank and opening a channel with the gun decks.

Occam watched as cannon beams lit up the red obscurity of the blood haze. The encounter was too close to rely upon void shielding, and thick streams of energy tore into the attacking vessel's prow at almost point-blank range. With a flash, they punched through the reinforced armour plating and blazed along the length of the raider.

'Stand by for impact!' the shipmaster announced.

Occam grabbed for the pulpit with a gauntlet and engaged the magnetic soles on his armoured boots. The Q-ship had ripped through the Chaos raider, turning its decks into a blizzard of light and destruction before blasting the vessel's engineering section out through its aft.

The raider attempted a last moment evasive manoeuvre, only to smash into the side of the *Iota-Æternus*. As the cultist deck crew were knocked from their feet and cradles, Occam kept his balance, his boots locked to the deck.

Within moments, the fat muzzle of Malik's plasma gun was pressed between Goura Shengk's shoulder blades. Sergeant Hasdrubal's multi-blade was clear of its sheath and against the Word Bearer's throat.

'Leading us into an ambush, brother?' Hasdrubal put to the Dark Apostle.

'They're not Word Bearers,' Goura Shengk said.

'Cycle pict-streams,' the strike master ordered.

As the lancet screens left the scene of destruction and crackled to starboard, the bridge was greeted with evidence of another attack. The reinforced prow of another raider, its hull smeared red and black and covered with spidery sigils and blasphemous decoration. There was no time for a response from the batteries. The Chaos raider slammed into the starboard flank of the *Iota-Æternus*.

Runebanks sparked. The lancet screens crackled. Deck lamps flickered. Occam looked back at the feed. The raider had hit them amidships, ramming into their side. Bulldozing the armed freighter with inertial certainty through the blood cloud, the Chaos raider ploughed on at maximum sub-light speed.

'Is the hull breached?' Occam called through the emergency lighting and klaxons. Righting himself, Naga-Khan repeated the question through the vox-system to engineering.

'Not according to any of my feeds down here,' Arkan Reznor called back. 'Integrity and environmentals are maintained.'

'Thank the God-Emperor,' the shipmaster said.

'We have damage to the starboard batteries, however,' Reznor informed the strike commander.

'Power?' Naga-Khan said, eager to fire upon the ramming vessel.

'I would not advise priming weaponry on such decks,' Reznor said. 'With damaged weaponry, we are more likely to visit further damage on ourselves.'

'Geller field?' Occam called.

'Holding.'

'They are pushing us into the Mawtex,' the strike master observed. 'Engines?'

'Won't be enough,' Naga-Khan told him honestly.

Occam understood. The Mawtex was huge. Even with forward movement, the ramming vessel would still drive them into the gaping maw of the blood storm.

Occam moved towards the elevator doors. 'Sergeant, Malik, with me. Phex, take care of our guest. Shipmaster, ready the *Iota-Æternus* to repel boarders.'

While Reznor made his damage report and Naga-Khan sent word across all sections for the Seventh Sons to repair to the gun decks ready to resist a boarding action, Autolicon Phex grabbed Shengk's shoulder from behind with a gauntlet. Supporting his heavy plasma gun with the other, he aimed it at the Word Bearer's back.

Snatching melta bombs from the legionnaire's belt, Occam marched towards the elevator doors, flanked by Malik and his sergeant.

'What's the plan?' the sorcerer Quoda called out from strategium.

'We are going to introduce ourselves to the enemy captain,' the strike master told him.

Occam's boots hammered along the passageway. Followed by Sergeant Hasdrubal and Malik, he made his way to the freighter's thorax section. A sea of Seventh Sons parted for them as they ran to their stations, bathed in emergency light. While Malik already had his plasma gun, two cultists waited by the thorax section bulkhead with the sergeant and strike master's weapons. With their shaved, tattooed heads down and plasma guns offered, the Seventh Sons stood to one side, allowing the legionnaires to snatch the weapons out of their hands as they ran by.

'Thorax airlock,' Occam called across his suit's vox-channel, 'starboard-central.'

'Standing by,' Carcinus Quoda returned from where he was stationed on the command deck.

As Occam and his legionnaires reached the airlock, they threw themselves through several antechambers, a receiving chamber and an open bulkhead. Inside the lock, Hasdrubal went to work securing the pressure bulkhead and sealing the compartment from the rest of the ship. The last thing the *Iota-Æternus* needed in the middle of an attack was an accidental depressurisation.

'Ready,' Occam put to Malik and his sergeant. The pair hugged their weapons in close and fell in behind their strike commander. Occam positioned himself in front of the airlock door. 'Purge.'

As Quoda popped the lock from the bridge, the air explosively evacuated the chamber, blasting the three members of the Alpha Legion out into the dreadspace of the Maelstrom. Everything became a kaleidoscopic nightmare as Occam and his renegades tumbled through the haze of blood globules and afflicted void. As they shot across the distance between the two vessels, Occam could see the damage that the ramming action had done to the *Iota-Æternus'* starboard flank and weaponry. Through the bloody murk, the strike master saw the blaze of the attacking vessel's sub-light engines. With its armoured prow still resting against the smashed section of hull, the raider intended on driving the armed freighter into the Mawtex.

For a moment, everything became immaterial fury, spectral claw and maw. Leaving the Geller field surrounding the *Iota-Æternus* and entering the pocket of rancid reality protecting the Chaos raider, for a second Occam and his Alpha Legion renegades were at the physical and spiritual mercy of daemons. Horrific denizens of the warp storm swarmed about them, drawn like moths to the flame of the legionnaires' mortal existence. Occam's auto-senses registered their alarm as beasts of the beyond moved in with talons, tentacles and daggered jaws. His hearts thundered in his chest. A moment later it was over, as they entered the aegis of the other ship.

The legionnaires tumbled along the length of the Chaos raider, over baroque mouth-muzzled turrets and monstrous chains that criss-crossed the ruinous obscenities plastered across the red and black hull. Hurtling towards the tower and command decks situated towards the aft of the vessel, Occam reached out for augur arrays, ether vanes and trailing chains that enveloped the ship. Smashing through arrays and snapping vanes with his tumbling velocity, the strike master reached out and locked the hydraulics of his suit's powered arm. With his gauntlet grasping the links, Occam allowed his grip to run for a while – slowing him down, before locking onto the chain and allowing the bundled servos and hydraulics of his plate to soak up the recoil.

Drifting with the force of the raider's acceleration, the strike master proceeded to haul himself arm over arm up the length of chain. As he reached the hull of the Chaos ship, he found that Malik had locked onto the same length of chain, while Sergeant Hasdrubal had managed to anchor himself to a smashed augur array. Mag-locking the soles of their boots to the hull, the Alpha Legionnaires made their way towards the cathedralesque lancet ports of the raider's bridge. Like the rest of the vessel, the command deck had received a mauling. Battle damage had left the section a mess of twisted scrap and ugly repairs. Ports nearest the damage were scorched black, with colossal cracks running through the armourplas.

Remaining concealed, Occam peered inside. The bridge beyond was cramped, like that of the *Iota-Æternus, and b*athed in emergency lighting. Servitors and pirate crew had been brutally interfaced with their station cradles and runebanks. Cabling and spiked chains draped from the ceiling and ran across the deck. Groups of piratical raiders were gathered about the bridge like the members of a hive gang staking out their territory, sitting on railings and leaning against burned-out runebanks. Their flesh was a battleground of warp-ravaged affliction and ritual scarification, the symbols of Dark Gods cut into their mangled features.

Occam cast his cycling optics across the command deck. While the interfaced deck crew suffered in silence, the Maelstrom pirates were roaring their insanity and jubilation at having rammed the *Iota-Æternus*. Then he saw it. The pirates were not alone. They were not even in command. Occam made out the nightmare shapes of power-armoured figures. Hunched in the filthy crimson of their plate, their suits were decorated with hanging hooks, chains and mail skirts. Goura Shengk was right. These were not Bearers of the Word. Scored brutally into their ceramite, the renegades wore the sigil of the Tyrant of Badab. These pirates haunted the immaterial havoc of the Maelstrom, preying on the vessels lost within and raiding Imperial shipping in the sub-sectors surrounding the warp storm. Occam could see that the ramshackle bridge still bore signs of battle damage, possibly from engagements of secession as the Tyrant led them from the light of the Emperor's benevolence into the darkness of self-serving heresy.

'Red Corsairs, out of Hell's Iris,' Occam told his legionnaires across the suit vox. Magnetically anchored to the hull with every step, the strike master presented himself – walking out before the great lancet windows. He was joined by Vilnius Malik and Sergeant Hasdrubal, their plasma guns primed and aimed at the ports. 'They have embraced heresy – let them feel the embrace of the storm that follows.'

Within, the vessel's captain stood up from his pulpit throne as he saw the impossible. Alpha Legion Space Marines, standing on the exterior hull, pointing their weapons at the armourplas of the bridge viewports. The Red Corsairs captain was draped in threadbare furs and had a patch riveted across one of his helm optics. On a brazen chain attached to the deck the captain restrained a grotesque hound of red scale, daemon fang and claw. With its spiked hackles up and leathery frill sprung, the monster snarled at the intruders it saw through the towering lancet ports.

Pulling on the trigger, Occam pumped a blast of plasma at the armourplas. The sphere of raging hydrogen sailed through the void and struck the damaged port with a flash. A molten blaze spread out from the site of impact and seared through the spidery cracks in the plas. Beyond, the strike master could see the confusion and horror of the bridge. Pirates scrambled instinctively back from the lancet ports while the Red Corsairs moved aggressively forward with their boltguns. As the plasma broke through, burning a hole through the thick plas, the bridge of the raider evacuated. Air rushed from the hole and a storm of suction passed through the command deck, knocking pirates off their feet. Clawing for anything, they were torn from handholds and dragged across the chamber. Smashing through the railings and runebanks, broken bodies flew at the breached lancet screen.

As Malik and Sergeant Hasdrubal opened up similar holes in other command deck windows, a hail of bodies was sucked towards them with the evacuating atmosphere. When the force of the bodies hit the breach, the lancet windows shattered. Anything not secured was shot out into the void, past Occam and his two legionnaires. Data-slates. Servo-skulls. Servitors torn from their interface cradles. Pirates. Even Red Corsairs who had failed to anchor themselves in time.

The stream of souls shot away from the Chaos raider, passing out of the sheath of reality protecting the vessel, and the Tyrant's chosen became a feast for thousands of swarming warp entities.

With the lancet ports gone, Occam joined his legionnaires in shooting blazing balls of plasma into the bridge. Smacking such blasts into runebanks and bridge architecture, the Alpha Legion advanced. While several Red Corsairs had managed to anchor themselves, they had been caught off guard. The appearance of the Alpha Legion, the evacuation of the chamber, and the zero-gravity environment they suddenly found themselves in, made demands on the pirates that Occam was only too willing to exploit.

With the howling storm of atmospheric evacuation gone, the strike master clumped his mag-locked way in through the shattered lancet port and across the command deck. Using runebanks as cover, the Redacted advanced, feverishly blazing away with their plasma guns at anything that moved.

Everything seemed to move in silence and slow motion. Wild boltfire rocketed across the bridge at the legionnaires. The strike master took brief cover, avoiding the worst of the gunfire, with several bolts taking apart a runebank and another glancing off his pauldron. Zeroing in on the positions of remaining Red Corsairs, Occam burned a hole straight through a renegade struggling in the absence of gravity. Hasdrubal turned a runebank into a molten mess of dribbling metal with repeated blasts of his plasma gun, forcing a Red Corsair out of hiding. Malik was ready with his own long-shot weapon, putting a sizzling globe of sub-atomic hydrogen straight into the side of the Red Corsair's helmet.

With the armoured bodies of dead renegades floating away, the Alpha Legion pushed on across the command deck. Holding onto the wall and launching out from behind a runebank, a chain-draped Red Corsair swung out with the thrashing barbs of a curved sword. Malik was forced to turn it aside with a side-smash of his plasma gun. As the weapon was torn from his grip and spun at the wall, Malik savagely tore his bolt pistol from its holster. The Red Corsair kicked away from the wall and came at him. They grabbed each other's armoured wrists in their gauntlets, and Malik and the pirate held the pistol and chainsword at arm's length, tumbling through the zero-gravity of the chamber.

Occam and his sergeant stomped on towards the throne, where they discovered a Red Corsairs captain taking cover. As the throne soaked up the sizzling blasts of plasma, the pirate captain pulled a massive chainaxe from where it was sheathed across his back. Swinging down in slow motion, the Corsairs captain smashed the chain with which his daemon hound was restrained.

The monstrous hound bounded off the floor and into the zero-gravity of the bridge, moving with infernal speed and grace. Landing and launching itself from the pulpit rail, the daemon beast bounced off the chamber ceiling and straight down at Ephron Hasdrubal.

As the sergeant wrestled the abomination, Occam finished the throne with the last of the hydrogen in his flask, turning it into slag. The Red Corsair burst through the remains of the throne, covered in strands of melted metal, and swung the gigantic chainaxe furiously. With a floating savagery, the Tyrant's champion tore the weapon's thrashing head through runebanks and railings, forcing

Occam back. The strike master didn't have time for such an engagement. Letting the Red Corsairs captain pull himself across the architecture of the bridge, demolishing runebanks and columns with swipes of his axe, Occam pushed away, floating out of the weapon's barbed reach.

Abandoning his plasma gun, Occam lurched back. He kicked the shaft of the chainaxe to one side and spun around, his armoured elbow smashing into the Red Corsair's helm. As the seals popped, Occam brought up his fist with powered force to blow the helmet clean from the captain's head.

As the red helmet flew upwards and struck the ceiling, Occam was treated to the horror of the Red Corsair's ravaged features. A pallid, warp-smeared skull-mask of ritual scars and tumours, the captain's face leered at him through the frozen nothingness of the void. His misting breath was stolen from between his needle teeth and black lips. One eye was missing, a stapled mess, while the other bulged and was iced over. Rather than stop the blind pirate in his tracks, it turned him into a frenzied machine – swinging his axe about like a thing possessed.

Looking back down the length of the command deck, Occam saw the lamps above the bridge elevator change. Klaxons erupted across the rest of the ship, and he imagined that reinforcements were making their way up to aid their masters. He put another console between him and the furious renegade, buying a few precious seconds. Pulling himself up by floating chains and cables drifting from the ceiling, Occam moved out of the wild path of the axe. The strike master allowed the Red Corsair to bury the monstrous weapon in the mangled runebank, grabbed for a bridge column and swung himself around.

As the elevator doors opened, a small horde of warp-scarred pirates were ripped from the car with the evacuating atmosphere. Their flailing bodies shot across the command deck.

The Red Corsair struggled to free his axe. Occam landed a kick on the captain's breastplate and sent his enemy tumbling. The pirate captain smashed into the stream of evacuating bodies. Occam watched the Red Corsair go, carried out into the waiting void.

Sergeant Hasdrubal, meanwhile, was cloaked in a mist of rancid ichor. Holding the daemon hound as it clawed at his plate and snap its monstrous jaws shut around his helm, the sergeant stabbed his multi-blade repeatedly into the creature's belly, using every torturous application of the weapon as he thudded it into the struggling beast. Finally, he tossed the twitching body of the hound after its master.

'Fire in the hole,' Vilnius Malik called out across the vox-channel as the legionnaire rested the soles of his boots on his opponent's chest and kicked away. Disengaging and flipping backwards out of the arc of the curved chainblade, Malik left the Red Corsair with a melta bomb locked to his plate. In a moment of panic, the renegade reached down and tried to tear the explosive off. Detonating in an optics-searing flash, the Red Corsair disappeared – vaporised from reality. In the zero-gravity, the blast reached across the bridge. Heat washed over Hasdrubal, clearing the cloud of daemon blood from about the sergeant.

Bringing himself back down to the deck and mag-locking his soles to the metal, Malik recovered his weapon and joined the sergeant by the main bank of consoles.

'Reznor?' Occam asked across the vox.

'*Standing by,*' the warpsmith reported.

As Reznor spoke to Malik and Sergeant Hasdrubal through the rudimentary controls on various runebanks, Occam issued his orders.

'Kill the engines,' he said as he recovered his own plasma gun. He stared out of the blasted lancet screens. The *Iota-Æternus* was still there, its starboard battery smashed, with the reinforced prow of the Red Corsair raider bulldozing it on through the red globular mist: on towards the Mawtex.

As the Q-ship began to drift away from the ramming prow and disappear through the haze, Occam realised that Hasdrubal had managed to cut power to the raider's sub-light engines.

'Malik,' Occam called. 'Scuttle the vessel. Purge locks on all levels and drop the hangar integrity fields. Empty this crate into the Maelstrom.'

'Affirmative,' the former Night Lord said with relish, before using his runebank to execute the order. Occam could only imagine the horror taking place down through the decks of the pirate raider. Mortal crew members would be dragged across chambers and along corridors, their bodies broken against the twisted, unfeeling architecture of the Chaos vessel before being blasted out of section air-locks by the streaming hundred. Occam nodded to himself. The daemon entities haunting the Mawtex would feed well on such a bounty.

'*Iota-Æternus,* respond,' Occam said across the vox.

'*Here, strike master,*' Carcinus Quoda returned, the sorcerer's voice crackling with the growing distance.

'Status?'

'*The shipmaster confirms that we have steering way,*' Quoda said. '*Reznor is preparing a damage report for your return.*'

'Our guest?' the strike master asked.

'*Is still our guest,*' the sorcerer said.

'Very good,' Occam said, satisfied. 'Send a lighter. We're coming back.'

ξ

THE SHREWDNESS OF SERPENTS

The ship felt different.

It was as apparent to Mina Perdita as it was to all on board the *Iota-Æternus*. The Seventh Sons were like the crew of any vessel entering the immaterium. Superstitious sayings were uttered, rituals were observed for good fortune. Thanks would be given as the vessel broke the warp at the end of its journey, however long or short it might have been. Entering the Maelstrom was something else, though.

Even in the service of their Alpha Legion overlords, the Maelstrom had been a phenomenon to be skirted and avoided. Its radiance was always there, dominating the void.

Lord Occam had committed the *Iota-Æternus* and its crew to plunging into the depths of the deadly storm with only a traitorous Word Bearer as their guide. Sayings and rituals were not enough to comfort the cultist crew this time.

Passing through the living quarters Perdita could see that the Seventh Sons were suffering. They were as stalwart as ever in the prosecution of their duties and murderously loyal to Lord Occam, but days riding the perverse currents of the storm had left many cultists ashen-faced and the corridors were tinged with the sharp tang of vomit. Even the charlatan Freydor Blatch found it hard to keep up appearances, the High Serpent having lost his appetite for private revelry. He still took a bottle of amasec to his chambers at the end of the watch, however, claiming that the potent liquor served to calm his stomach.

As for Perdita, she grumbled and vomited with the rest of them but mainly to keep up appearances. Every time she endured the effect of polymorphine burning through her veins she had to suffer the bending of bones, the stretching of skin and the rupture of flesh. The first few times she had attempted such transformations at the temple she had emptied her stomach onto the polished stone floor. Now, it took a little more than the sickening roll of the ship in a perpetual storm to unsettle her.

Ordinarily the death cultists of the Seventh Sons were unshakeable. Their faith was sustained, like Perdita's own, by the expectation that they were always mere moments from the end, expecting death to come for them in the form of a bolt or blade. The Maelstrom represented something else, however. The entities howling through the storm, dragging their claws along the hull or whispering seductive horrors to the cultists through their dreams did not promise anything. Their gift was a thousand wishes granted and the eternity of torment that came with them. The cultists were ever fearful that the Geller field might collapse and their flesh would be torn to ribbons by the daemon monstrosities rampaging through the ship. Their ultimate terror, however, was that they might answer the call of such entities and surrender their souls. Such were the fears of mortals in the crushing depths of warp-churning oblivion.

Perdita was dressed like a female menial, a member of the Seventh Sons the High Serpent had assigned to attend upon their Alpha Legion overlords. Carrying clean cloths and a metal bowl of water, she approached the demi-god known as Autolicon Phex. The legionnaire stood as still as a statue outside a door in the corridor. Dressed in full plate and carrying a monstrous heavy weapon, he was guarding the cell housing the Word Bearers prisoner. Lord Occam had commanded that the renegade not be referred to as such. As a *guest* on board the *Iota-Æternus*, however, the Word Bearer still warranted a legionnaire keeping watch on his quarters, Vilnius Malik on constant stand-by and, of course, Perdita herself. As a menial, the Assassin tended upon the Dark Apostle, ready to take the necessary measures to end the Word Bearer should his intentions turn hostile.

'You again,' Goura Shengk said as she entered. Acting as a menial might, Perdita bowed her head before the hulking traitor. Getting up from one knee in his deck robe, the Dark Apostle brought back his hood to reveal the black mess of his face. The Assassin said nothing. What could a menial possibly have to say to such a being?

As she placed her bowl and cloths down on a stone pedestal, she noticed that the Word Bearer was still staring at her and that he was bleeding. There were speckles of red on his sharp teeth and a wound, seemingly self-inflicted, on his hand.

'You don't speak much, do you, serpent girl?' Goura

Shengk said. He followed the question with a mocking hiss, like that of a snake. Perdita ignored him and tore a strip off one of the clean cloths. Moving in on the towering Dark Apostle, she began to bandage his wound and tie the dressing off in the palm of his hand.

The Word Bearers were fanatical warriors, keepers of the dread word and each an acolyte to the ruinous gods. Dark Apostles were unholy warlords at the head of such monstrous hosts – their minds were archives of forbidden knowledge while the flesh of many was thrice-damned by the presence of daemons feeding from their dark souls.

Perdita had every reason to fear Goura Shengk but she did not. It was hard to fear a foe whose death you had practised a million different times in a million different ways.

'You are more than you seem, I suspect,' the Word Bearer said, flexing his bandaged hand. 'Like all who serve your master's Legion. You needn't worry. We have given our word – and nothing is more important to a son of Lorgar. The strength of our word survives the ages, given as it is to deities and dark princes. You can expect no trouble from us, girl.'

Perdita's eyes flashed down at the cell floor. Blood had not merely dripped there. The Word Bearer had used it to make glistening signs and symbols about his kneeling form.

'Nothing to worry about, I assure you,' Goura Shengk said, stepping out of his circle of blood. 'Just servants of Chaos, honouring their gods. Your master has his chapel. We have the Shrine of Iron and the darkness of the warp all around us.'

The Assassin sensed the Dark Apostle's arm reach around

her and felt his huge hand on her shoulder. She tensed, as she might anyway. She could not give herself away by reaching for a weapon or assuming a combat stance. At the temple she had been trained to exploit the weaknesses of even those opponents seemingly without them – opponents like Space Marines. Motioning her around, Goura Shengk pointed out several key symbols on the floor. They were hard for Perdita to look at, filling her head with an existential dread.

'The Dark Pantheon,' the Word Bearer said. 'Gods that are ever before us and behind us. Within and without. Men like your master are fools to fight without their blessing. Other renegades are fools still for choosing one dread deity to the insult of all others. Bearers of the Word worship all dark forces in all their wondrous manifestations. The Shrine of Iron was built to honour such patrons.'

'My lord,' Perdita protested, keeping her voice weak and pleading. She tried to push against his hand but the traitor's grip held her firm.

'Do not turn your back on the Ruinous Powers, girl,' Goura Shengk warned. 'Look and you will truly see. Open your heart to their darkness and you will be rewarded – for only gods have the power to grant your heart's desire.'

'You are hurting me,' Perdita said, fighting the Dark Apostle as a menial might, reaching behind and scrabbling at his girder-thick arm. At the same time she slipped a stiletto dagger free from where it was concealed in the sleeves of her robe. She held the narrow, envenomed blade within her other sleeve, ready to strike.

'There,' the Word Bearer pointed, moving his finger around the circle: 'The Changer... the Great Lord of Decay... the Prince of Excess... the Blood God... All are there to serve your desires and in turn be served by them.'

Perdita blinked. The final damned sigil drawn in the Dark Apostle's blood began to boil on the floor as she stared at it, and she was finding it hard to drag her gaze away. Her grip tightened about the stiletto blade. She thought of all the places she could plunge it. Into the Dark Apostle's eye. His temple. One of his hearts. Through the flesh of his throat.

'Yes,' the Word Bearer said. 'The Blood God. He calls to you, sister.'

Perdita heard a hum in her ears to match the veil forming before her eyes. Somewhere in the back of her mind she knew she was losing control and hated herself for it. The spitting sigil seemed to respond as much to that as her desire to end the Word Bearer.

'Yes...' Goura Shengk said, before he was interrupted. The dread seduction of the moment broken, Perdita felt someone else standing over her. Autolicon Phex was there, holding the humming barrel of his heavy plasma gun above her head, the muzzle against the side of the Dark Apostle's head.

Blinking the confusion from her eyes, Perdita tore her gaze from the sigils on the floor and whipped the envenomed blade up to rest under the Word Bearer's chin. She felt an unconscious snarl slip from the mask of her features.

'Ah, a successor son of Guilliman,' Shengk said, his voice dripping with derision. 'Here to avenge your kindred, brother?'

The Word Bearer backed from both the legionnaire's barrel and Perdita's blade. The Assassin heard the sound of armoured footfalls in the corridor. With Phex away from his post, Vilnius Malik had moved in. He paused next to Phex.

'The strike master's orders,' the former Night Lord said. 'This filth is wanted on the bridge.'

At the mention of Lord Occam, Perdita got a full hold of her emotions. The burning rage guiding her blade evaporated. She served her master with her deadly talents and not herself. She hadn't killed for herself in years.

The legionnaire's indication that Occam was on the command deck surprised her. The bridge had belonged to Sergeant Hasdrubal for the past day, with Lord Occam having taken to his quarters. The Assassin suspected that he was praying to the God-Emperor for spiritual guidance in this dark place.

Perdita, who made it her business on the ship to know most things, had heard his last request was of the High Serpent. Blatch subsequently sent for twenty of the best needlers and artists from amongst the Seventh Sons, with inks and their crude equipment. This was another way Perdita knew the strike master to spend his time – adorning his flesh with the symbols and markings of his chosen Legion. It appeared to help him think. In that way he was little different to Goura Shengk with the patterns on his floor.

The Dark Apostle smiled at Perdita.

'Summoned to the bridge – that can only mean one thing,' he told her. 'We have arrived.'

Occam gripped the pulpit railing of the bridge. The *Iota-Æternus* was holding station in between a roaring warpstream of immaterial energy and the choppy radiance of an unnatural star. The system's afflicted sun flickered between blazing white light and a darkness, like a malfunctioning strobe, momentarily lighting up the Q-ship and the surrounding system before plunging it back into gloom. With each pulse of unnatural radiation the warped star made the *Iota-Æternus* roll.

'This is it?' Occam asked.

Ghesh, the ship's Navigator, came forth and confirmed the location with a bow of his mutant head.

The strike master stared out across the void. This was where the Word Bearer's directions had taken them. While hundreds of moons rode out the rough immaterial weather of the region, each appearing as though dread runes and continental sigils had been carved across their rocky surfaces, Occam could see no planet orbiting the system's strange sun.

In a glittering miasma orbiting the star, however, the strike master could see a nebulous cloud of crystals hanging in the void. Occam hadn't noticed it at first. Naga-Khan's bridge crew had fared no better, returns from long-range augurs – already struggling in the storm – being bounced straight back off the reflective surface of the crystal cloud. Like a billion shattered mirrors, the crystal shards reflected the colour and bizarre features of the Maelstrom around it.

'Yes,' Goura Shengk said, as he was escorted onto the command deck by Malik and Phex. Occam turned to see that Perdita was with them, in her disguise as a cultist menial. 'In answer to your question, that is unholy Ghalmek, daemonforge and Shrine of Iron. We just don't like to advertise it.'

'Our augurs show nothing,' Occam said.

'And they won't,' Shengk said.

'I expected more in the way of defences,' Sergeant Hasdrubal said, although it wasn't clear if he was talking to Occam, the Dark Apostle or both.

'Ghalmek is well fortified,' Shengk said, 'as it needs to be, situated here in the Maelstrom – to defend itself against mutant migrations, daemonic incursions and pirates. Again, we tend not to advertise it. If a host breaches the crystal cloud, it will soon discover its mistake. Even given such precautions, thousands have tried across the ages and thousands have failed, for mighty Ghalmek still stands. This is why, legionnaire, if you hadn't bartered, your White Crusade would have been for naught.'

'Unbeknownst to the frater legions,' Occam assured the Dark Apostle, 'the Alpha Legion fights on their side – and the Alpha Legion always finds a way.'

'How do you know we haven't already?' Ephron Hasdrubal said over Shengk's shoulder, taking a little of the pride from the Word Bearer's ruined features.

'What of your own arrays, augurs and monitoring stations?' Occam asked, noting that he hadn't seen any orbiting platforia either.

Goura Shengk stepped forward and pointed through the lancet ports at a nearby moon.

'Look.'

As Occam peered up at the cursed moon he saw a colossal daemon eye open on its surface. Massive and bloodshot, the infernal creature sat like a tick buried in the rock of the moon's rune-carved surface. As the strike master stared about at the other moons, he saw more predatory eyes open to watch the progress of the *Iota-Æternus*. The daemonic gaze made Occam feel uncomfortable.

'Shipmaster,' Occam said, 'prime the batteries.'

'We shouldn't do that,' Goura Shengk said. 'If you come to Ghalmek in peace, then act like it.'

Occam looked from Hasdrubal to Naga-Khan.

'Prime the batteries,' the strike master insisted, 'but do not run out.'

'Proceed towards the northern pole,' the Dark Apostle said. 'We shall need to present ourselves. There are rituals to observe. You had better let me do the talking.'

'That's why we brought you,' Occam said, nodding to his sergeant. Hasdrubal moved up behind the Word Bearer and rested the tips of his multi-blade against his side. 'But if what proceeds from your mouth displeases me, you shall come to know suffering like no other. We shall find another way in and you can bleed your last on my deck, a short distance from the unholy soil of your daemon home world. We can all win here or you can lose. Am I understood, Word Bearer?'

'Crystal clear,' the Dark Apostle said with a black smirk.

As the *Iota-Æternus* moved on through the system, more daemon moons opened their eyes, watching the Alpha Legion vessel proceed through the flickering light of the sun. The command deck was silent and tense. Heading for the top of the cloud, as instructed, the *Iota-Æternus* found itself reflected in the shattered, silvery crystal. The shards seemed to have an unnatural sentience of their own, parting like a swarm to admit the ship's prow and dimensions. Within the cloud, Occam saw that some of the smashed pieces were tiny slivers while others were chunks of crystal almost as large as the *Iota-Æternus* itself.

Daemon faces glowered from within the crystal, staring through the silvery surface like ghostly nightmares, looking hungrily at the Q-ship passing through the cloud and the souls within.

As the crystals parted, Occam could make out structures

beyond. A wall of burnished metal and rows of guns came into view.

'All stop,' Occam called, while Hasdrubal allowed his torturer's blade to dimple Goura Shengk's robes.

The Q-ship came to a halt above the daemon world of Ghalmek. In front of the Alpha Legion vessel lay a monstrous Word Bearers battleship. Warp-encrusted. Battle-scarred. Ancient. Occam suspected that its pattern dated back to the dark days of the Heresy, perhaps even earlier. Its hull was covered in unholy scripture while parts of its metal architecture, including its colossal rows of antique cannons, were afflicted and warped with daemonic possession.

Occam stepped forward. He could feel the fear on the bridge. It would take nothing for the battleship to turn the *Iota-Æternus* into a flaming wreck or a vaporised cloud of nothingness. He looked about through the lancet screens and down at the daemon world.

The flickering light of the damned star felt its way through the crystal cloud, bathing the daemon world in intermittent gloom and complete darkness. The surrounding shards created a shattered sky. A billion daemon entities looked down from their crystal prisons, feasting upon the deviance and devotion of Ghalmek's citizenry.

The Shrine of Iron was a relatively small planet, but appeared larger due to the ancient cage of void docks, planetary scaffolding and monstrous platforia that surrounded it. Rusting in their age, some of the structures had been painted a dirty crimson while others bore dark symbols of summoning. The shrine fleet sat at anchorage about the planet, docked with the surrounding structure like magnificent, unhallowed cathedrals in the void.

Occam could see Word Bearers battleships, grand cruisers and grotesque daemon ships, docked alongside bloated carriers that were spiked like sea urchins and used for transporting pilgrim labour. He could see a blizzard of lost and captured Imperial shipping amongst the larger vessels, repurposed for the traitors' own profane use. Dark Mechanicum factory ships and ark tenders were also in sight, moving between new ships under construction, indulging in daemonic rituals and making blasphemous adaptations.

The planet's surface reached up to meet the orbital scaffolding. The daemon world was buried in thousands of years of architectural accretion. It was like a single, fat hive that covered the entire surface of the small planet. Nests of spires housing pilgrims, workers and deviant constructs reached up from the architectural malaise. Infernal forgeworks and manufactoria blazed across the surface. Rising above the smog of damnation and industry were continental cathedra – entire regions busy with the towers, spires and steeples of unholy temples, all built to honour the Chaos Pantheon.

The four dread Powers were very much in evidence on Ghalmek. Forges raged to create weapons of war for the Word Bearers and their pilgrim armies of the afflicted. At the tolling of stratospheric bell towers, rivers of cultists seeped downhill like diseased effluence from vaulted churches. Twisted temples grew out of cathedral structures like mutations, while within unholy Bearers of the Word indulged their daemon overlords with veneration and worship.

Occam looked back at the fanged mouths of battleship cannon aimed at the *Iota-Æternus*.

'Open channel,' the strike master commanded. He gave Goura Shengk the hardness of his eyes. 'Time to talk to your brothers.'

The Dark Apostle bowed his head and approached a runebank. Adjusting the channel, he spoke across it in a strange language. His words were ancient, uttered in an accent of flint and sparks.

As different voices filled the bridge from the voxhailers, there was an exchange. Although Occam didn't understand the language he could tell by the intonation that the voices were surprised and cautious. After completing the exchange, Shengk was handed over to another. Backing from the runebank and Hasdrubal's blade, the Dark Apostle bowed his head once more to Occam.

'Renegade vessel,' the voice said. It sounded like iron scraping through crackling embers. 'My name is Sor Tandrach, First Acolyte to Malthusa Vho'tek – the Lord High Apostle and Herald Orbital. The *Lex Diabolitora*, the battleship under whose guns you find yourself, as well as the void infernal and daemon skies of Ghalmek, are his. The punishment for your trespass is a death to flesh and the imprisonment of your eternal soul. However, Apostle Shengk informs me that your miserable band of renegades have been of some service to him and ensured his return to face trial on mighty Ghalmek. For that, you will receive passage to the surface and an audience alongside Goura Shengk to plead for your existence with his unholiness, the Grand Apostle and Abyssal Prince of All-Ghalmek.'

'I applaud your mercy and wisdom,' the strike master said, looking at his sergeant. Hasdrubal nodded.

'The one known as Occam,' First Acolyte Tandrach continued, 'and only he, shall accompany Apostle Shengk to the surface. Your vessel shall dock in the adjacent bay. Any attempt to deviate off course and the *Lex Diabolitora* will open fire. Run out your weaponry and the *Lex Diabolitora* will open fire. Attempt to leave this place unsanctioned and the *Lex Diabolitora* will open fire.'

'I think we understand,' Occam replied. 'Extend my appreciation to the Grand Apostle. I look forward to an audience with his unholiness.'

0

FORKED TONGUES

Occam took the controls of the stolen lighter himself. It was a battered agri world craft, formerly used for transporting grain between surface silos and freighters in orbit. He had asked Arkan Reznor on the flight deck for something disposable but reliable. The warpsmith had asked Occam if he could accompany the strike master and share the risk of the daemon world. It was regrettable he could not, since Reznor would have been much more comfortable behind the controls of the lighter. The strike master usually had one of the Seventh Sons perform such a duty, as there were a number of talented pilots among their number. By comparison, Occam's skills were rough. He could get the craft from orbit and put it down fairly harshly on a landing pad. It was everything in between that was the problem.

As the lighter spiralled down through the thin atmosphere, a billion daemon entities looking down on its progress from the shattered sky above, Occam guided the craft towards a colossal polar structure. While the *Iota-Æternus* was docked above, amongst half-constructed daemon ships and under the guns of the *Lex Diabolit-ora*, Goura Shengk directed the strike master towards the Cathedra Nox – an architectural nightmare spanning a small continent. The structure was part cathedral, part fortress. Amongst its skyscraping bell towers, spires and warp-encrusted steeples Occam could also see courtyards and surface-to-orbit laser silos. Sacrificial plazas, warped statues and domed libraria were decorated with heavy weapons emplacements. Magnificent stained-glass windows depicting Dark Gods sat in thick walls.

Guiding the lighter down through swarms of spiked transports carrying cultists to dark prayer and mutant labour to their shift in the manufactoria districts, Occam avoided the scaffolding of new daemon-honouring shrines built amongst the horror of older devotional structures. He weaved around high-tension cables stretched between pocket hives and chains supporting Titan God Machines under construction. He dropped down through heavy metal smog banks that were settled above manufactoria complexes and the slum habs that fed them with cultist workers.

Goura Shengk pointed out a landing pad atop a cathedral tower, the crenellations of which were lined with curved metal spikes like fangs. The pad itself was a pentangle lined with ruinous sigils and huge electro-candles. Ragged cultists rushed up from a stone stairwell. They were followed by a squad of hulking, spiked shapes in dirty red plate. Their welcoming party, the strike master assumed.

Occam opened an encrypted vox-channel: 'Coming in to land.'

'*Standing by*,' Sergeant Hasdrubal returned from the bridge of the *Iota-Æternus*.

Drifting over the landing pad, Occam allowed the descent to overshoot slightly, scattering the cultists and putting the Word Bearers escort on edge, as he wanted them. Putting the lighter down heavily, off the pentangle's centre, Occam shut down the craft's engines and life support.

'Shall we?' the Dark Apostle said. Occam said nothing, but led the way through the cargo compartment, hitting the stud for the ramp. Taking his helm off, he mag-locked it to the rear of his belt. As they descended the pair of them found the squad of Word Bearers had fanned out about the craft. They were all armed with boltguns of ancient design. Occam could see that their armour was fused to their warped bodies, gaps in the cracked plate revealing daemon brawn and glowing runes. Among their number was a helmetless acolyte who sported a daemonic half-face, one side belonging to a bald, bronze-skinned Word Bearer and the other an infernal monster of sharpened teeth, warp-glazed eye and single horn. The half-mouth of the daemon seemed perpetually curled in grinning self-satisfaction while the other was downturned and unsmiling.

'You are Goura Shengk,' the being rasped, 'late apostle of the Barbed Oath, Honoured of the Varga Rax, Captain of the *Dissolutio Perpetua*. Warp-tempered of flesh and host to Morphidax the Primordial.'

'We are still all those things,' Shengk told the acolyte. 'And you are…'

'Zothrac of the Graven Gate,' the monster told Shengk. 'Acolyte to Drach'Var Tal, first of his name, First Apostle of the Daemon Council and right hand to the Abyssal Prince of All-Ghalmek.'

While Occam let the formalities wash over him, it became clear that Shengk and the daemon Word Bearer heralded from different companies or Chapters. There was clearly no brotherly love lost between them.

'Search them,' Zothrac said.

Two Word Bearers came forth to check Occam and the Dark Apostle for weaponry. While Shengk still wore his deck robes, Occam wore his legionary plate. He had forgone all weaponry, however. Knowing that he would be searched, Occam had decided not to risk the offence a bolt pistol or secreted close-combat weapon might offer.

Within the ancient plate and helm of the Word Bearer searching him, Occam could hear the ugly breathing of another daemon monstrosity. Like Goura Shengk, it seemed the Word Bearers of Ghalmek favoured their daemon allies with flesh. Their own. They shared their ageing, superhuman frames with beings of the warp, so that such allies might travel with them beyond the safety of the storm.

It did not surprise Occam to be searched, but he was surprised with the equally distrustful treatment of one of their own. As a Dark Apostle, Occam suspected that Goura Shengk outranked every Word Bearer on the landing pad and yet they treated him with the same caution as a member of the Alpha Legion. The Word Bearer searching Occam went so far as to lean in and smell the strike master. Through the helmet's grille Occam heard a bestial snuffling. Moving across to Goura Shengk, the Chaos Space Marine did the same.

Occam stood there in the sights of the daemon Space Marines as the acolyte and the searchers conversed in a guttural, infernal tongue.

'You have been purified, brother,' the acolyte said to Shengk, the disgust clear on both sides of his flesh. 'Your flesh is without blessing and your soul unfavoured. You are untempered and like this one, you carry the stench of weakness.'

Shengk gave the acolyte a flash of his perfect teeth from behind black, ravaged lips.

'The Abyssal Prince awaits us,' Shengk told him. 'It would be unwise to keep our lord waiting.'

'Indeed,' the half-faced acolyte said. 'I thought the same thing when you failed to return with the *Dissolutio Perpetua*. You have kept your prince waiting. He is… displeased. I suspect bringing this fork-tongued serpent before him will do little to improve his disposition. The pair of you will not be alone. I have sent for your host captain and honoured First Acolyte – now Dark Apostle of the Barbed Oath in your place. A reward for fulfilling the prophecies of the *Daedronicron Malefest* and returning Kar'Nash'gahar – Lord of Glorious Slaughter and Slayer of Worlds – to the Shrine of Iron. I am glad to be the one to reunite you.'

'Does this thing ever break for breath?' Occam asked. 'Or is that his talent on the battlefield – talking his enemies to death?'

The acolyte snarled his daemonic displeasure, prompting Word Bearers to lean in with the muzzles of their boltguns.

'Zothrac is a brother of the Graven Gate,' Goura Shengk said, 'and as such hasn't seen a battlefield for a long time. He hides with his fiends among library stacks and black altars. He is a dark and true servant of Ghalmek, pledging to never leave his daemon world – and certainly not the safety of the storm. He likes the Graven Gate firmly closed, with his host firmly on this side of it.'

'You will die for that, untempered thing,' Zothrac spat.

'Aye, we will,' Goura Shengk said, 'but not by your unworthy hand. Now, be a good herald and walk us to our end.'

Out on the landing pad, the strike master noticed that it was raining. Slivers of silvery crystal drizzled from the sky and pitter-pattered against his plate. Occam and the Dark Apostle were escorted down the stairwell and into the main body of the Cathedra Nox. It was a haunted place, filled with gloom and foreboding. Every anteroom and vaulted chamber venerated daemon princes and Dark Gods: colossal statues of honoured entities loomed over them, while sigils of summoning were carved into stone floors stained red with sacrificial blood and black with the infernal fires of manifestation. The stone of the structure was cracking and ancient, held together by warp encrustation and darkness. Occam passed through vast halls constructed from mortar and skulls. He walked through the living light of ghostly entities cast in the colours of stained-glass windows. He heard the screams of the sacrificed as they were burned on great pyres of black bones beneath towering chimneys.

All the while, choirs of lesser daemons filled the chambers with madness, alongside the mournful tolling of cursed bells in the belfries. Cultists in black robes went about their business, chanting, summoning and reading from forbidden tomes. Black priests plotted in benighted crypts. They conducted dark rituals on warped altars. Some fell into mumbling insensibility, standing in their own mess and proceeding to rot in their pulpits. The bloodthirsty whispering of daemons prompted others to make sacrifice of friend and foe with kris blades buried in backs.

Dark cardinals in different transept temples, twisted beyond recognition, gave sermons before colossal barbed stars, in honour of the Dark Gods of Chaos. They favoured ghoulish priests with their wisdom, who in turn would spread the dread word to their damned flocks in the hive chapels and church manufactoria.

In the gloom of the cathedra corners, behind blood-drenched tapestries and in the catacombs below Occam's feet, the strike master felt daemons stalking his path. Fiends and horrors hungered for him, while the vast building itself seemed alive with infernal sentience. Eyes opened in lecterns. Fanged archways drooled their expectation. The red and black stone of walls creaked and seemed to lean and listen for the strike master's coming.

While daemons went about their dark business, favouring the shadows, barbican-archways were guarded by cultist soldiers. Some were dressed in blood-stained ceremonial robes. They leaned against serrated halberds, their clawed hands resting on the holsters of baroque autopistols. Those guarding the pulpits and cardinals were caged in clattering plate that sizzled with smouldering runes. They knelt before daemon-possessed great swords and axes used in ritual sacrifice.

The strike master observed with a tactician's eye the deployment of Word Bearers throughout the structure. Some were warped monstrosities and willing vessels for daemonic entities like Goura Shengk and his Varga Rax. It seemed to be a dark blessing reserved for officers, warlords and favoured units. Most of the Word Bearers on Ghalmek appeared relatively unchanged, their rune-encrusted plate merely smoking with the malevolence of the unholy place and their own black hearts.

As Occam and Goura Shengk were marched up polished obsidian steps and into the cathedra-palace, the strike master was exposed to deviancies of all kinds, committed with solemn reverence in the private chambers of the Grand Apostle. Word Bearers stood guard on vast landings, lit by windows bearing the most blasphemous of stained-glass depictions and twisted daemonic statues of living iron. The Word Bearers sentries were clad in barbed Terminator armour, carrying boltgun-mounted chain-glaives. Their helms were horned and warped about the bestial features of the Word Bearers within.

At the top of the stairs, the strike master and Goura Shengk were walked into a domed throne room with black walls and without windows. An infernal glow was created by runes and damned scripture that burned in the walls. In this gloom, Occam could make out an audience of warped clerics, Dark Mechanicum priests, robed daemon heralds and high-ranking Word Bearers. Dark Apostles, dressed in the dread glory of ornate plate, bore symbols of different unholy Chapters. Heavily armed host captains stood in attendance, while possessed acolytes bled the warp into the chamber from their glowing eyes and mouths.

A pair of misshapen Terminators shuffled their spiked forms and crossed the barbed blades of their glaives before Occam and Goura Shengk. Spindly cardinals sprang forth to offer dark blessings and baptise the new arrivals with daemon ichor flicked from their long fingers. Occam looked down at the filth as it sizzled on his plate. Unholy prayers were offered and chalices brought forth by daemon wretches.

'Drink of spiritual pollution,' a horror-faced cardinal

encouraged, 'so that you might be unpurified in the presence of the Abyssal Prince.'

Shengk took the chalice and drank deep the black blood that bubbled within. Taking the jewelled cup tentatively, Occam put it to his lips. His superhuman physiology had been engineered to subsist on virtually anything. The contents of the cup not only raged a physical revulsion down through his body, but they seemed to sear his very soul. Spitting the contents out and dropping the chalice, Occam could hear the infernal mirth of the throne room.

Apostles and armoured acolytes, their features horribly warped by daemon sponsorship, laughed through sharp teeth before standing to one side. A throne of barbed bone and iron was revealed, in which sat a monstrous daemon prince. What little remained of his legionary plate was rune-scored, encrusted and embedded in armoured red flesh. It was all daemon brawn and grotesque sinew. The hulking creature wore a crown of twisted horns and breathed intermittent gouts of fiery steam from a helm grille that still remained part of the daemon prince's elongated snout.

Zothrac made formal introductions, as he had done on the landing pad. These were translated into a dark daemon tongue by a herald at a twisted lectern, which multi-tasked with its many limbs. As it made its announcements, the creature dipped a quill into the darkness of its single eye and scribbled unfolding events down in a living tome. Occam waited under the burning gaze of the daemon prince as two other Word Bearers were admitted to the chamber. The plate of one had the markings of a host captain, while the second, trailing a cloak of stitched skin and holding a spiked staff of office, carried himself with the confidence of a senior officer. They carried their helmets at their side and Occam saw their ugly faces change as they beheld Goura Shengk. Shengk, for his part, gave them the hostility of his frost-ravaged features. His gaze lingered particularly on the barbed ball that formed the head of the ceremonial crozius his opposite carried.

'Apostle,' the host captain said, taking a knee. 'By the tri-fold blessings of the Dark Gods, you are alive.'

'I am,' Goura Shengk said. Occam watched the second Word Bearer. He seemed less pleased to take a knee but finally did so.

'Apostle,' he said. 'You must know that everything was done to secure your freedom.'

'Everything *was*,' Occam interjected, 'and your master's freedom was secured.'

The Word Bearers seemed to ignore the strike master, while the daemon prince looked on with displeasure.

'The mission was a success?' Shengk asked coldly as they got back to their feet.

'The prophecies of the *Daedronicron Malefest* have been realised,' the Word Bearer told him, 'and at long last the Slaughterlord returned to Ghalmek.'

'Where is Kar'Nash'gahar?' Shengk asked. 'If I might be so bold.'

'He has been taken to the catachives,' the Word Bearer told him, 'beneath the cathedra, so that the prince's diabolists and warpsmiths might investigate the xenos technology that is his prison and prepare the rituals for his coming.'

As they talked, Occam noticed Zothrac move through the audience and speak quietly to a number of fell daemons and Word Bearers who bore the same Graven Gate markings as the acolyte. His helm boasted an extravagant plume and the dun glory of his red plate was inlaid with rune-inscribed bone. He too carried a crozius. The weapon boasted a huge head created from the impossibility of interlocking geometric frames, which formed a Chaos star. Its thick iron haft was so heavy that it took all four of the Word Bearer's four arms to wield it.

'Enough of this,' the senior officer rumbled.

'Silence,' Zothrac commanded. 'Drach'Var Tal, First Apostle of All-Ghalmek speaks.'

'Success,' the daemon First Apostle said, 'failure. You are not fit to judge such things. Only the Abyssal Prince can do that. For my part, the brothers of the Barbed Oath have not kept their word – to each other or to the Daemon Council. Goura Shengk, you promised our master Kar'Nash'gahar, the Slayer of Worlds. Instead, you return with slithering vermin of the void. Renegades of half heart, who favour not the Dark Gods with a Legion's loyalty.'

Goura Shengk lowered his head.

'As for your host captain and the First Acolyte – now Dark Apostle of the Barbed Oath in your miserable stead,' Drach'Var Tal said, 'he indeed succeeded in carrying back your prize and claiming your rewards. He did not return with his master, however. To leave a corpse behind is one thing. To leave man and daemon to the mercy of our sworn enemies is something else entirely. What faith can the Daemon Council have that their own members might be served similarly?'

Once more the Word Bearers were on their knees.

'My lords...' the host captain pleaded.

'I appeal to your infernal wisdom, my Abyssal Prince,' the newly promoted Dark Apostle said, 'and the mercy of the Dark Gods.'

'The Dark Gods know nothing of mercy!' the daemon prince roared, coming up off his throne and spuming flame.

As the Word Bearers got up and stumbled back, a barbed Terminator stomped forth and rammed the screaming chainblade of his glaive through the Dark Apostle's body. He trembled on the thrashing blade while daemons vaulted from the audience, pouncing on the host captain and tearing him to pieces.

Occam stood rigid, ready to react should a blade rage at him or an infernal claw reach out for his shoulder. Goura Shengk, meanwhile, kept his head down – accepting his fate and the Daemon Council's judgement.

As the host captain was torn to pieces, the Word Bearers Terminator heaved the Dark Apostle away from himself, simultaneously firing his boltgun at his victim, blasting his body against the wall.

Occam took a step back. He didn't want the hulking palace guards behind him, but if the daemon prince's court of abominations began leaping at him he wanted to be able to put Goura Shengk between him and any danger.

As the Word Bearers trembled their last on the stone floor, the Abyssal Prince settled back in his throne. Terminators pointed the lengths of their glaives over his shoulders, aiming their boltguns at Occam and Shengk.

'What to do...' the daemon prince said, his words burning on their air, '...with you?'

The creatures of his infernal court chattered in their dark tongue, contributing their own opinions.

'Skin the serpent,' Drach'Var Tal said, 'and take his ship.'

'Surely the Dark Apostle must be punished for his failures,' Zothrac said to his master.

'Agreed,' Drach'Var Tal said, turning to the Abyssal Prince. 'Goura Shengk must be made an example of. We cannot have Bearers of the Word returning to Ghalmek empty-handed.'

'What say you of this, apostle?' the daemon prince asked.

'He contests your judgement, dark lord,' Occam said.

'What makes this scaled vermin think he can speak in my presence?' the Abyssal Prince said, venting flame through his flesh-embedded grille.

A Terminator stepped forth to smash Occam in the midriff with the haft of his glaive, but the strike master kicked it away. Spinning around behind the armoured hulk, Occam used him for cover.

'He has not returned empty-handed,' Occam insisted. 'He offers you one billion innocent souls as recompense for his failure and intelligence of an attack averted on the unholy soil of this very daemonworld.'

The Terminator turned, his chainblade shrieking as it wheeled overhead. At the legionnaire's revelation, the Abyssal Prince's claw came up. The chain-glaives at his shoulder rose and the roaring blade gunned by the Terminator looming over Occam chugged and died.

'Does the serpent speak true?' First Apostle Drach'Var Tal asked.

'A White Crusade gathers beyond the storm,' Goura Shengk said finally. A hiss of infernal hostility passed through the gathering. 'The Corpse-Emperor's priests intend to avenge the pious worlds they have lost at our hand. This lord legionnaire has infiltrated their number.'

'My warband is small,' Occam admitted to the daemon prince and his council, 'and my resources limited. Although it might be heresy for a son of Alpharius to admit it, my capabilities do not match my ambitions. The frater armies of the Crozier Worlds can be delayed and with sufficient manpower, corrupted. Why waste blighted souls in a fight with the Emperor's hordes, when you can have them join you above Ghalmek? You can watch the failure of the cardinal warlords from your very throne. The Alpha Legion would, of course, expect to choose the most gifted for our own cultist ranks.'

'You are in a position to demand nothing,' Zothrac said. The acolyte and the First Apostle looked to the Abyssal Prince with the rest of the Daemon Council. Occam, too, watched the prince. The monstrous thing had once been a Word Bearer and tactical intelligence still glinted in its horrid, narrowing eyes.

'We have a pair of prophets before us,' the daemon prince said, 'telling us of doom to come and how victory might be snatched from the snaggle-toothed jaws of defeat. Well, prophets must be tested, trust earned and worth measured. We must know the untruth of their flesh and the strength of their spirit. Let them be tested on the star, out on the Constellation Fields. Let them feel the light of our benighted sun and the gaze of the primordials.'

'What of the serpent's ship?' Zothrac asked. 'It sits under the High Apostle's guns.'

Drach'Var Tal looked between his prince and his acolyte.

'Let them be tested also,' Drach'Var Tal said. He nodded at the hulking sentries.

As Occam and Goura Shengk exchanged unreadable glances, Word Bearers Terminators grabbed them from behind, the chainblades of their glaives resting on their shoulders. Dragged around and out of the presence of the

Abyssal Prince, the pair were marched out of the throne room and down the obsidian steps.

Under Occam's breath, he said: 'Did you get that?'

The encrypted vox-channel he had opened with the Redacted as he came in to land had been kept open, allowing Occam's legionnaires to eavesdrop on the judgement of the Daemon Council.

'*We'll be ready,*' Hasdrubal promised the strike master.

'*Let me follow you,*' Vilnius Malik said, his vox signal much stronger than the sergeant's struggling from orbit.

'No,' Occam hissed. 'Proceed with the plan. Do your duty. Allow me to do mine. Occam out.'

π

SHEDDING SKIN

Up on the command deck, Mina Perdita stood with the lord sergeant and the sorcerer Carcinus Quoda. With the shipmaster, they all watched as daemon constructs and diabolists in ritual environment suits gathered along the girders, transepts and platforia of the orbital docks. The *Iota-Æternus* had taken its place there under the guns of the monstrous battleship and among the half-constructed daemon ships of the Word Bearers fleet.

The Redacted watched as runes glowed to life along the length of the partitioning structures, while deviant constructs and diabolists encircled the Q-ship and began conducting dark rituals. Holding plasma torches, daemon constructs drifted across to the *Iota-Æternus* and burned sigils into the painted hull.

'What are they doing?' Naga-Khan asked, fearful for his ship. Sergeant Hasdrubal looked to the sorcerer for guidance.

'What they are doing to the metal and machine-spirits

of these other unfortunate vessels,' Quoda said. 'The Word Bearers are preparing *Iota-Æternus*. Polluting it. Making it a host for daemons.'

'We cannot just stand here while they force this vessel to be possessed by some monstrous entity,' Perdita said.

'Agreed,' the shipmaster said.

'Let me put on a suit and clear them from the hull,' the Assassin suggested.

Hasdrubal watched the cybernetic creatures scuttle across the hull and burn into it their dark runes of daemonic summoning.

'We cannot risk provoking the Word Bearers,' the sergeant said. 'Not while Lord Occam is on the surface and the prize is still in the enemy's hands.'

'Also not while we sit under that battleship's guns,' the sorcerer Quoda said.

As klaxons erupted across the bridge, Naga-Khan rushed back to his cultist-manned runebanks.

'What is it?' Hasdrubal demanded. 'What have they done?'

'The Geller field is collapsing,' the shipmaster called, his alarm obvious. Perdita watched as he moved from bank to bank giving orders. He moved to an engineering runebank and tore the cultist manning it aside. Frantically pushing up on a thick-set handle that appeared locked in a downward orientation, Naga-Khan attempted to reinstate the field from the bridge. Through gritted teeth he called: 'Can't raise the field from here.'

The sergeant turned to Quoda.

'What can we expect?' Hasdrubal said. As he did, channels opened and voxhailers shrieked with the sound of warp entities infecting the ship's communication systems with their madness.

'Expect anything,' the sorcerer said. 'The daemon enti-ties of this benighted place will make the *Iota-Æternus* their own.'

'Sound the alarm,' Hasdrubal told Naga-Khan. 'I want all operatives and Seventh Sons armed and on high alert.'

'Affirmative.'

'Can we get word to the warpsmith?' the sergeant asked.

'The ship's vox system is overrun,' the shipmaster said, moving from runebank to runebank.

Hasdrubal turned to Perdita. 'Get down to the enginar-ium,' he ordered. 'Appraise the warpsmith of the situation. Tell him we need the Geller field back online or we're going to lose the ship.'

Taking a last look at the diabolists and daemon con-structs conducting their rituals about the *Iota-Æternus*, Perdita turned and bolted across the bridge. The ship was in uproar. Alarms had alerted the cultist crew to the emergency. As she bolted down passageways and across chambers, the Assassin took advantage of her petite form and quick step. Darting left and right through throngs of heavy-set cultists and hurdling equipment, she moved through them with slick ease. Loading needle pistols with their deadliest toxins and drawing blades from enven-omed belt sheaths, the Seventh Sons prepared themselves for what they could only expect to be a boarding action. Perdita pounded down the corridors of the Q-ship and began to realise how mistaken they were.

The *Iota-Æternus* felt as if it were in pain. The voxhail-ers howled insanity while deck lamps flickered. Bulkheads opened and closed. Electrics sparked. The excruciating sound of metal warping rang through the superstructure. The vessel was hurting. Changing.

As the Assassin moved through the havoc the calls of death cultists echoing down the corridors turned to screams. Cultists fired their needle pistols into the sentience of walls and floors and slashed at grasping tendrils of cable. Everything creaked horribly as the metal of chamber walls and floors warped and became ribbed like the interior of an animal. Corridors spasmed and quaked. Cabling that ran across mesh floors began to sliver.

Perdita accelerated, leaping over lines and cables that reached out for her. She rolled under closing bulkheads that were sprouting huge daemon fangs and cleared ladderwells that closed on climbing cultists, shearing them in two. Seventh Sons reached out for her in panic and terror as cells swallowed them whole. The metal of the walls stretched about the claws and horned faces of daemon creatures materialising within the body of the ship.

The Assassin rolled across the trembling deck. As she did, a cultist sank down into the metal as though it were quicksand, dragged down by daemon claws slurping up out of the floor. Completing the roll, Perdita snatched up the needle pistol and blade left behind by the sinking Seventh Son.

By the time the Assassin reached the enginarium section, the entire ship seemed possessed by rampant daemonic entities infecting its spirit and violently warping its architecture. When she arrived at the section doors she found that a huge smouldering hole had been blasted through them. Within she could see Autolicon Phex with his heavy plasma gun blazing globes of sub-atomic energy into any part of the walls and floor that moved.

'It's Perdita!' she called before hooking her fingers about the blasted doors and pulling them open. As she did, odious tendrils reached out for her from the opening.

Entwining themselves about her limbs, the tentacles of the monstrous door aimed to hold her in their web. Flashing left and right with her recovered blade, the Assassin slashed at the appendages. Pieces dropped and writhed on the floor, and snaking stumps splattered Perdita with ichor as she tore herself free.

'What are you doing here?' Arkan Reznor demanded, the warpsmith moving between colossal pieces of equipment. He alternated between working feverishly with his tools and burying his Omnissian axes in the flesh-metal of machinery gaining daemonic sentience.

'The lord sergeant sent me,' Perdita said, ducking beneath Beta, Zeta and Theta, who drifted about the engineering chamber attempting to aid their master in his futile repairs and recalibrations.

Reznor gave her an imperious glare – the indication that he had little use for an Assassin in the enginarium.

'The vox system is down,' she said.

'I know that,' the warpsmith told her, indicating with the blade of an axe. The section voxhailers were screaming and chanting their insanity all around. Reznor retreated from an infernal maw that had opened in the pipe-lined section of wall he was working on. Swinging one of his crackling axes around, he buried it in the monstrous face forming in the piece of machinery. 'Phex!'

As Reznor indicated the ceiling over the legionnaire, Phex looked up to see another daemon orifice opening above him. Chitinous claws and feelers reached down for the renegade but Phex aimed his heavy plasma skyward and pumped several blinding orbs into the manifestation. Swallowing the raging blasts, the daemon shrieked before drenching Phex in a shower of steaming blood.

'The Word Bearers are conducting some kind of ritual about the ship,' Perdita told him, moving through servitors and deck seers that had been assisting the warpsmith. 'The Lord Sergeant and the shipmaster say they need the Geller field back online.'

'What do you think we have been trying to do?' Reznor called, turning to chop a horrific talon from an appendage reaching out for him. The deck beneath the boots of several servitors appeared to spoil and soften. The servitors sank in the liquid metal while inhuman eyes opened in the walls, entrancing enginseers and drawing them towards the morphing horror of the possessed machinery. As deck cabling writhed to serpentine life and coiled about Perdita's slender leg, the Assassin stabbed her blade into the rancid tentacle, pinning it to the floor. Infernal runes spread across the surfaces of the engineering chamber like a rash, while a howling mouth opened in the wall beside Perdita. It blazed like a furnace and threatened to vomit forth sickly flame. Pointing her needle pistol into the maw, she emptied the weapon into the soft flesh-metal of the mouth, causing it to shrivel and close.

Leaping over bubbling sinkholes in the deck, the Assassin took position between Phex with his raging heavy plasma gun and the warpsmith.

A tentacle-like appendage, thick and covered in barbed suckers, erupted from the wall nearby, forcing Reznor to duck and Perdita to lean out of its rancid path. Phex was not so fortunate. The grotesque, muscular limb slithered about the legionnaire's armoured form and lifted him from the deck. The tentacle smashed Phex brutally back and forth against the walls and up and down between the ceiling and deck. With his plate rent and crumpled, the legionnaire dropped his heavy weapon, allowing its cable to become entwined with the tentacle. Perdita watched in horror as the daemon appendage broke Phex against the compartment wall.

'Grab it!' the warpsmith roared, reaching out for the tentacle with his gauntlet. It was the absolute last thing that Perdita wanted to do. Burying her cultist blade into the unnatural flesh of the manifesting entity, she used it to try to anchor the appendage. It bucked and writhed like a great serpent. Reznor seized its length with one gauntlet before going to work with a power axe. The weapon bit through the daemonic brawn of the thing, spilling ichor on the deck. With the appendage finally cut in half, both Reznor and the Assassin stumbled back. One half retracted horribly into the pulsating wall while the half around the groaning Phex writhed on the deck.

'There,' Arkan Reznor said, pointing down the section with his axe. Perdita followed the line of the weapon to see a huge piece of arcane machinery at the far end of the engineering compartment. Crackling, fat power cables ran from the system and surrounding auxiliaries. The pipes reaching up out of the piece of machinery like an organ glowed hot with overloading power. The arcane system itself, meanwhile, was trembling and transforming before their eyes. Shaking with rage and affliction, it seemed to be fighting itself and everything else, emitting roars of agony and frustration from fang-filled maws opening in its grotesque flesh-metal body of the thing.

'What is it?' Perdita called back.

'That,' Arkan Reznor said, 'is the Geller field generator.'

The Assassin shook her head.

'We have to abandon ship,' she said.

'And go where?' Reznor replied. 'Trust in the strike master – he will fix this.'

'Lord warpsmith,' Perdita said, looking back at the pulsating horror of the Geller field generator, 'I'm not so sure that this *can* be fixed.'

ρ

SERPENTS BENEATH

Vilnius Malik crunched across the Constellation Fields. As a Night Lord he had been one with the shadows, bringing terror to masses. As a member of the Alpha Legion he had honed his death-dealing skills further, managing to hide in the light of day and bring doom to his enemies. Moving across the surface of the daemon world, even he felt exposed.

The skyline was a stabbing silhouette of spires, steeples and architectural magnificence: colossal cathedra and temple accretia dedicated to the Dark Gods of Chaos. In the distance, hellish forges and manufactoria glowed with the fell light of industry. Magna-machinery rumbled with daemon possession, while assembly lines manned by legions of warped servitors and cultist workers spewed forth entity-infested machines of war. Malik had even seen half-constructed God-Machines. The dread Titans – part daemon monster, part abominate machine – festered in their scaffolding, swarming with diabolists performing dark consecrations.

Caustic ash drifted on the foul breeze downwind from the industrial centres. Malik had dissembled his sophisticated plate, the ceramite scales bleeding into the soot-stained red of Ghalmekian Word Bearers. He had travelled down with the lighter piloted by the strike master. Holding on to the exterior hull and protected from the worst excesses of the descent by Lord Occam's angling of the craft, Malik had arrived on the daemon world without the knowledge of Goura Shengk or his Word Bearers brethren on the surface.

Leaving the craft and landing pad, Malik had committed to a second dangerous descent, climbing down the tumbledown architecture of the dark cathedra tower in full plate. Hiding from Word Bearers sentries, warped priests and the daemon fiends that stalked the colossal building, Malik made it to the surface – if such a thing existed. Beyond the manufactoria and daemon forges, the cathedra and temple districts appeared to be vast edifices of infernal worship built on top of the ruin and rubble of former structures.

Walking along a glowing channel of molten iron, Malik's confident strides took him up through groups of ragged pilgrims, their warped flesh further afflicted with studs, spikes and tattooed runes that smouldered. Moving aside for their Word Bearers overlord, the cultists allowed Malik to pass unchallenged. The channel and the beaten ash track that ran alongside seemed to be a bifurcating thoroughfare taking cultists, sacrificial victims and dark cardinals in wretched finery between the mighty transepts and private chapels of the Cathedra Nox. Even servo-skulls, built into the flesh-stripped horror of horned daemon heads, travelled noisily back and forth along the track.

Fortunately, there were precious few Word Bearers out on the thoroughfare. The ruling traitors of Ghalmek largely restricted themselves to the unholiest of structures, leaving the unremitting industry and dark worship of the daemon world to the cultists and constructs.

About the track, Malik could see the Constellation Fields. Eight-point stars of Ruinous significance turned like spiked, iron wheels on spindle-axles buried in the blood and ash. Spread-eagled and lashed to the slowly turning frames were figures. It was difficult for Malik to tell who they were. Some appeared to be priests and others mutant-cultists. A number even appeared to be decked in twisted plate while many were disfigured by daemonic possession – horns, monstrous claws, warped forms.

At a junction in both track and magma channel, Malik was forced to cross a crumbling stone bridge. Pushing his way through a gathered throng of chanting cultists, the legionnaire saw diabolist-priests with glowing green censers move about several new additions to the Constellation Fields. While most of the figures on the Chaos stars and the squealing wheels themselves were caked in caustic ash like statues, the pair of new additions were merely dusted grey. They had been presented before the thousands of daemon entities staring down from the shattered sky.

Malik paused as the throng parted, their diabolical chanting filling the air. On the first wheel he saw a face he recognised – or rather the absence of one. Lashed to the revolving star, with his head leant back, was the Dark Apostle, Goura Shengk. The ruin of his face had assumed the hellish nobility of a daemon entity. The Dark Apostle's head now boasted a magnificent set of iron horns growing out of his skull and his muscular body was enhanced further by daemon bulk. His flesh was a nest of iron barbs – like the horns, growing out from what Malik suspected was a daemon-warped skeleton of iron. The Dark Apostle's face was a mask of indescribable ecstasy and torment. His daemon was once more one with his flesh, Malik realised.

The legionnaire could guess who the second figure was. Clad in ash-smeared plate, Lord Occam turned slowly on the star beneath the gaze of dread daemon entities. Ragged cultists chanted. Diabolists went about their rituals. As the strike master's head lolled around on the creaking wheel, Malik's body tensed within his armour. Malik had listened to his commander's fate over the open vox-channel. He had his orders but Lord Occam was before him now. A prisoner, whose flesh was being offered – like Goura Shengk's – for daemonic possession.

Malik looked around. His cloak – disguised as stapled daemonhide – covered his weaponry. He felt for his long-shot plasma gun, his boltgun, grenades and power blade. He was surrounded by cultists and censer-swinging priests, but they were nothing to a renegade Space Marine. Within moments, the crowd would be a mound of broken bodies. The legionnaire hesitated. Looking through the forest of Chaos stars staked out across the Constellation Fields, Malik could see all manner of daemons – like watchdogs – stalking through contested souls and warping flesh. Grotesque servo-skulls hovered overhead, their pict-feeds no doubt feeding back to the Word Bearers who had ordered such punishments. Beyond them, in the shattered sky above, daemon monstrosities could be seen. Eyes, inhuman in their vigilance and full of predatory intent, were everywhere. They looked down on the Shrine of Iron, ever watchful.

The strike master's head came back around again. Malik was relieved to see that as yet, Occam had not suffered spiritual invasion and a damning of the flesh. The ash about his eyes and head was dark with moisture. Malik could only imagine the physical exertion of the wheel, the spiritual resistance required by the strike master and the torment suffered on the star, as daemons tried to claim their offered victim. Tears and dirty beads of sweat rolled across Lord Occam's shaved head to drop to the daemon world earth.

As the strike master's head lolled back and upside down, Malik saw his eyelids open. At first, the legionnaire thought his master was dead – or worse, that his body had become home to some parasitic daemon entity. Malik didn't find lifeless eyes or the black doll's eyes of a possessed warrior; he saw glistening eyes still full of fight and determination. As the wheel turned, Lord Occam shook his head slightly – imperceptible to the diabolists offering his Alpha Legion flesh as a vessel to daemons hungry for the taste of mortality. Malik saw it, and nodded his helm slowly in return. Drawing his cloak about the bulk of his plate, the legionnaire pressed on as a drizzle of crystal slivers began to fall from the sky.

Following directions that Goura Shengk had shared with the strike master on board the *Iota-Æternus*, Malik made his way through the Constellation Fields, through the ruins of the long-collapsed Church of the Righteous Darkness and broke into the catacomb-archives beneath the Cathedra Nox.

In his disguise, hunched beneath his daemonhide cloak,

Malik explored the labyrinthine nightmare of the Word Bearers' secret repositories. The passageways twisted and turned. Some sections had collapsed under the weight of the fallen structures above and the mighty cathedral on top.

The legionnaire moved down through the infernal tombs and catacombs. Thousands of Word Bearers had been interred there. Warped bones and horned skulls sat in coffins of blasted plate. High-ranking cultists and benighted priests made offerings in sacrificial chambers. The final screams of victims slaughtered on obsidian altars and the laughter of appeased entities rang through the depths.

Malik passed diabolists dragging feral daemonhosts in silver chains. Cultist archivists busied themselves recovering dread texts for their Word Bearers masters and cataloguing dark artefacts. Daemon creatures stalked through the labyrinth on their own foetid business, the unholy glow of their eyes visible in the distant darkness. As a Word Bearers acolyte appeared out of the same impenetrable gloom, marching in the other direction to Malik, the legionnaire kept his head down. Speaking in a strange tongue that the Alpha Legion renegade didn't understand, the acolyte came to a creaking stop in the faded infernal glory of his ornate plate.

Looking about for skulking daemons and tome-laden archivists, Malik stepped into a catacomb alcove and directed the acolyte to follow with his gauntlet. Even in his daemon world dialect, the legionnaire could tell that the Word Bearer was upset. Stepping after him with rasping remonstrations spilling from his helm grille, the Word Bearer closed with him.

Spinning around, Malik grabbed the traitor about his armoured throat and pushed him back against the crumbling stone of the alcove wall. Pulling his power dagger out from beneath the folds of his cloak, Malik brought the weapon up with force and precision, hammering it into the Word Bearer's chest. He held him there for a moment like an assassin, intending his foe to die quietly in the corner. As the Word Bearer heaved back with the strength of an altered, Malik began to realise that he had underestimated his enemy. Forcing the Alpha Legionnaire against the opposite wall of the alcove, their armoured boots scuffling in the dust of the catacombs, the acolyte plunged his gauntlet down into his holster to produce an ancient bolt pistol.

Slashing the power blade down like a machete, Malik hacked the pistol and gauntlet off at the wrist. With the weapon on the floor, the legionnaire batted the Word Bearer back. Slamming him into the wall once more, he held him there and stabbed the traitor again and again in the breastplate. With his corrupted hearts ruined and gore cascading down his plate, the acolyte slipped down the wall. Malik held him the precious seconds it took for his rasping breaths to come to a haggard stop. Heaving the armoured corpse into an empty catacomb, Malik kicked at the disintegrating wall to bury the puddle of tell-tale gore in rock dust and rubble, before swiftly moving on.

Crooked corridors led the legionnaire to vast libraries, where the stone shelves crumbled beneath the weight of damned tomes, grimoires and tracts written by corrupted cardinals, Dark Apostles and daemon princes.

As he descended down through the cursed earth of the daemon world, reality began to break down. Up became down, with dislodged stones falling towards the ceiling. Shadow turned to a blinding daemonic light. The twisting corridors became filled with a ghostly fire, through which Malik walked.

Goura Shengk's directions eventually led the legionnaire through sentient stone gates and a portcullis that rumbled at his approach. In the depths of the catacomb-archives, with the walls, floor and ceiling covered in the scribbled madness of incantations, Malik came to a network of half-collapsed caverns. The air was thick with ancient evil and the very stone of the crumbling structure felt infested with the presence of infernal entities. The floors of the archives were covered in Chaos stars, pentagrams and circles of glowing, unholy runes. They overlapped and intersected like a diagram. In each, Malik saw there were collections of mouldering artefacts. Ancient weaponry possessed by evil spirits. Blasphemous representations, draped with charms and religious icons venerating Dark Gods. Heretical technologies of human and xenos origin that crackled and interacted unnaturally. Cursed objects and containers leaking foul corruption into one another.

As Malik progressed through the caverns, objects moved of their own accord. Artefacts seemed to whisper their depravity to him. Chambers seemed to repeat themselves. Eventually the legionnaire came to a central hub – a cavern whose obsidian pillars held up the strata of crushed ruins and the weight of the Cathedra Nox. The darkness of the obsidian swirled with the strength of horrific entities.

The chamber was busy with cultists. Senior diabolists in robes of black and gold chanted unholy litanies about altars and Dark Mechanicum technologies. Daemon cyborgs in ragged robes, leaking the filth of corruption, worked on ruinous artefacts and entity-infused technologies. Hideous, horned monsters watched their progress while a pair of Dark Apostles in bleeding plate gave instructions in the same Ghalmekian tongue Malik had heard spoken by other Word Bearers.

This wasn't going to be easy, the legionnaire decided, moving back into the adjoining chamber. Looking about, Malik started pulling melta bombs from beneath his cloak. Priming their timers, the legionnaire crept carefully about the circles of damned artefacts and began setting them up on crumbling pillars and the rusted structural supports about the entrances.

Advancing into the central hub and around the choirs of cultists, Malik marked time by watching the daemon priests of the Dark Mechanicum work on one of their foul instruments. On an altar contained within a framework-globe of interlinked Chaos stars, Malik spotted the piece of ancient xenos technology that the strike master had described to him. It was small enough to be held in a gauntlet. A midnight black polyhedron in slick motion, with sections continually revolving, unlocking and interlocking to form new shapes. With moving edges outlined in an eye-stinging green radiance, the alien object hinted at a strange source of energy within.

This was the Tesseraqt – the object Omizhar Vohk had described to Lord Occam and Lord Occam to the legionnaire. Understanding it to be some kind of containment field generator, Malik tried to get a better look. Goura Shengk's Word Bearers had stolen the artefact from the Inquisition and returned it to the Shrine of Iron: now Dark Mechanicum priests, diabolists and daemon creatures had taken an interest in the dread item. Bombarding it with curse-fields, rancid augurs and ritual ceremony, the catacomb archivists were intent on finding a way into the piece of alien technology.

With his back to one of the obsidian columns, Malik attached a final melta bomb to the impossible structure. With all eyes on the Tesseraqt he then edged unnoticed towards a chamber exit not rigged to blow. As he did, one of the daemon monsters observing the delicate investigations of the priests momentarily sniffed the air – as though he could smell Malik's intentions or the stench of unwarped flesh.

The detonations in the first chamber went off, melta bombs vaporising the structural supports. The caverns shook. A thunder rolled through the catacombs, followed by a dust cloud that billowed through the hub. The air thick with the sound of pulverising rock and dust, Malik withdrew further and cycled his optics. Moving between spectra filters that showed the cultists, priests and daemonic entities, the legionnaire's augmented vision cut through the murk. He watched the gathering back away from the entrance to the collapsing chamber in shock. Even the robed daemons seemed skittish, the malevolence of their brute forms standing no more chance of survival if the Cathedra Nox came crashing down on them than the weakling cultists.

As the rumbling faded and the air thickened, the priests of the Dark Mechanicum began to take stock of the disaster. Malik heard the Dark Apostles on their vox-links, communicating with brothers on the daemonworld surface. While surprised by the event, none of the gathering panicked. The detonation had been lost in the unfolding thunder of the collapse, which Malik supposed was inevitable from time to time. Also, given the volatility of the possessed artefacts and xenos technologies stored in the catacomb-archives, explosive interaction was always a possibility. When the final melta bomb took out part of the obsidian pillar, however, caution prevailed. Cultists fled the chamber. The Word Bearers withdrew, their communications with the surface becoming ever more urgent. Daemonic creatures slunk back into the shadowy murk of other chambers while Dark Mechanicum priests hastily started to prepare the Tesseraqt for transportation.

Malik ventured forth. Having partially collapsed the adjoining chamber by design and leaving all other mighty pillars of the hub intact, the legionnaire was confident in his advance. Striding through escaping cultists, who simply took his armoured outline to be one of their Word Bearers overlords, he moved in on the priests. As their sickly optics blinked incomprehension, Malik put them down one by one. Thudding silenced Stalker rounds from his bolt pistol into the hooded, cranial cogitators of the Dark Mechanicum priests, the legionnaire scooped up the barbed globe of Chaos stars dropped by the senior construct. He smashed it into the ground and the iron cage fell apart. The forces suspending the Tesseraqt within were broken. Picking up the black cube, Malik saw that it continued to transform on the outstretched palm of his gauntlet.

As he stared at the alien object, the Alpha Legionnaire heard the infernal growl of daemons stalking him through the murk. They sniffed at his betrayal with flared nostril-slits and watched him with the burning of their eyes. He secured the Tesseraqt on his belt. Positioning his bolt pistol under one arm, he aimed the weapon through his cloak at their skulking approach. Malik could hear claws scraping on the archive floor and knew he was being rushed. The legionnaire blasted at the monsters, pumping bolt rounds that tore through the material of his cloak. Feeling one fell creature at his back, he spun around and dropped his pistol. He grabbed his plasma gun, turned and blazed a staccato of close-range orbs into the thing until, shrieking and thrashing, the daemon was blasted back.

Bounding over the bodies of its infernal kindred, a red-fleshed fiend barged the suffering creature aside and launched itself at Malik. Moments later, the legionnaire found himself crashing to the floor – the savage daemon tearing into him with snaggle-fanged jaws and claws.

With his plasma gun knocked aside, Malik grabbed the thing by the throat and tried to push it up and away from him. The beast was wild with infernal strength and fury, clawing and snapping at the legionnaire. Patting the rubble-strewn ground nearby with his other gauntlet, Malik found his way to his abandoned pistol. Snatching it up, he thrust the muzzle into the red flesh of the creature's side and thudded round after round into the daemon's unnatural flesh. Still, the monster came at him. As the pistol clunked empty, Malik allowed it to fall away. Slipping his power blade from its sheath on his belt, the legionnaire stabbed at the cratered ruin of the beast's midriff. With ichor streaming down his gauntlet, Malik thrust the weapon deep into the monster, ripping through its innards until finally its savagery subsided and it slouched still on top of him.

Heaving the daemon's corpse off his torn plate, Malik got back to his feet. Sheathing his blade and recovering his battered plasma gun, the legionnaire recovered both his pistol and the alien Tesseraqt. He aimed the glowing barrel of his weapon through the murk and dust. All about him, the structure creaked and cracked. The stone of columns and ancient walls was being slowly pulverised by the colossal weight of the Cathedra Nox. Confident that the Word Bearers had withdrawn to safety and that no more daemon entities stalked him through the obscurity, Malik left the chamber. His mission complete, the legionnaire scrabbled through the thick dust and rubble, making for the surface.

σ

POLITICAL ANIMAL

Occam became aware of deviant souls gathering out on the Constellation Fields. He had little idea how long he had been turning on the creaking iron wheel. With his armoured wrists and ankles lashed to the Chaos star, the strike master had been offered to the daemon swarm glinting in the shattered skies of Ghalmek. The malevolence of corrupt entities, reflected in the shards of crystallised warp smothering the planet, hungered for Occam's spirit. They fought for possession of the strike master's soul as his plate and the revolving star became encrusted with a mixture of ash drifting down from the manufacturing districts and a drizzle of silver slivers.

It hurt to open his eyes. The lids were heavy with a fatigue both physical and spiritual. Under a mask of settled ash, his face ached as the perpetual spiritual agony twisted his expression. About him, Occam saw that priests, warped pilgrims and robed daemons had gathered on the track running alongside to observe his torment. Diabolists chanted and droned, while armoured Word Bearers stood guard nearby.

As time passed the numbers and interest grew. Turning on another star next to him, Occam was aware of Goura Shengk. While the strike master fought off the soul-starved attentions of daemonic entities with every ounce of his being, the Word Bearer had freely offered himself to the corrupting darkness. He groaned continuously, his gasps and cries a haunting catalogue of unimaginable experiences, a simultaneous agony and relief that wracked the Word Bearer's body. Entities had fought over Shengk's soul like some kind of prize. Occam had listened as a conquering daemon wormed its way into the Word Bearer's being. Taking residence in his flesh and becoming possessed of Shengk's soul, the monstrous entity made the Word Bearer its home. Occam heard its voice mixed in with the Dark Apostle's own – its glee threading through his sufferings. The strike master listened to the horrible rupturing of flesh, the warping of bone and the growth of claw and horn. All the while, Goura Shengk became something else: a thing he had been before Occam had rescued him from the exorcists and interrogators of the Inquisition.

As for Occam himself, he had felt the tug of daemons tearing at his soul. His ears were full of infernal threats and promises, while a living nightmare of daemonic visions played before his eyes. He felt the predatory intentions of entities attempting to corrupt his soul and infest his flesh. All failed.

Occam's soul was strong. Fortified by his secret faith and with his soul still pledged to the God-Emperor, the Alpha Legion strike commander withstood the temptations of darkness and futures promised to him, and the monstrosity of daemons attempting to force their way into his being with spiritual savagery. Despite the torments of soul and flesh, Occam managed to resist them all. He had taken precautions.

Summoning the High Serpent and the best inkers among the Seventh Sons, Occam had lain naked across the altar within the Chapel of the Immaculate Ascension. With needles stabbing across the surface of his skin, Occam had ordered that the death cultists transcribe onto his flesh the ancient hexagrammic wards, purity seals, extracts from the *Lectitio Divinitatus* and sigils of banishment that decorated both the altar itself and the recovered flags surrounding the holy object. Like something unnatural in a sea of swarming behemoths, Occam was swallowed and spat out by creature after daemonic creature. His soul burned those entities attempting to smother it with their tentacled embrace, while his flesh was better protected from daemonic possession by the inked wards and sigils than by any plate or field.

Fighting to stay awake, Occam resisted the exhaustion of his continued efforts and kept opening his ash-encrusted eyelids. Every time he did, he saw that the gathering had grown about him. More cultists and dark pilgrims. Foul cardinals with the flocks, come to pray before the altar of afflicted forms.

Feeling hands and claws about his arms, the strike commander opened his eyes. The crowd was now punctuated with hulking figures in dull red plate. A number shared their genetically engineered forms with horrific entities. Monstrous daemonic brawn spilled from their armour. Amongst the reverential gathering of deviants and Word Bearers, Occam could see a party from the cathedra-palace. Members of the Abyssal Prince's court stood by, watching the strike master as he was taken down from the Chaos star. Daemon monstrosities waited in grand robes while overlords of the Word Bearers stood sentinel. Occam could see Zothrac of the Graven Gate and Drach'Var Tal, First Apostle of the Daemon Council. Neither looked pleased. On a huge iron palanquin, incorporating a barbed throne, sat the grotesque figure of the Abyssal Prince of All-Ghalmek. The palanquin was carried by hundreds of flagellant cultists and the weight of the monster above appeared considerable.

Cultists swarmed about Occam, flicking unholy oils at his ash-smeared plate and tracing dark symbols across its surface. Standing on the backs of two others, a cultist placed Occam's helmet on his head and locked the seals in place. As he did, Occam's head turned and he saw that Goura Shengk had similarly been taken down from his star. Cultists were gathered about the Dark Apostle, assembling a suit of spiked plate about his abominate form. Shengk looked different. Bigger. His body had been favoured with the warped blessings of Chaos. A daemonic entity had taken residence in his engineered form. The black ruin of his frostbitten face had changed. It was now an infernal nightmare of fang, nostril slits and straight horns vaulting forth from a malformed skull. A network of black scarring still afflicted the apostle's red cheeks and thin lips.

Zothrac of the Graven Gate stepped forth but Drach'Var Tal placed a clawed gauntlet on his pauldron and pushed forward instead. He looked up at the Abyssal Prince, who nodded his horned head.

'Goura Shengk,' First Apostle Drach'Var Tal announced, prompting the cultists about him to scatter. 'You have been offered to the beyond. You have been tested on the ruinous star, before a constellation of your daemon peers. Your failures have been forgiven and you are once more one with the darkness.'

Goura Shengk looked to Occam and gave him a fang-filled grin. In the swirling blackness of his eyes, the strike master saw the glinting presence of the daemon entity that now lived within the Dark Apostle.

'We are honoured to serve the dark powers,' Goura Shengk told the First Apostle and his Abyssal Prince, 'as both daemon and Bearer of the Word.'

'As we are honoured,' Drach'Var Tal said, 'to welcome Morphidax the Primordial back to the world of flesh and Goura Shengk to his rightful place at the Chapter head of the Barbed Oath.'

'This unnatural thing that you brought before us, however,' Zothrac said of Occam, 'has not been favoured by our daemon overlords. He has resisted their attentions. They are angered and insulted.'

'We are surprised that the serpent had such strength,' Goura Shengk told them.

'The Abyssal Prince has sanctioned your return,' Drach'Var Tal told Goura Shengk, 'as Dark Apostle of the Barbed Oath and to your daemon ship, the *Dissolutio Perpetua*. He wishes you to halt this White Crusade and to use your brothers of the Word, your cultists and daemons to spread our darkness through the ranks of the Corpse-Emperor's servants. Turn them against their priestly lords. Corrupt their purpose and lead them in pilgrimage into the storm and back to unholy Ghalmek. Will you do this?'

'I shall die trying, my Abyssal Prince,' Goura Shengk pledged.

'You had better,' Zothrac of the Graven Gate said, 'for if you fail us again, Goura Shengk, you shall be torn apart – body and soul – by the very daemon legions who fought for the right to infest your flesh. Even Morphidax will not be able to save you from them and the wrath of your brothers.'

'We understand,' Goura Shengk told them. 'What of the serpent?'

'Support for your reinstatement was not unanimous,' Drach'Var Tal said. 'Some among the daemon legions believe your hearts conflicted – that you do not have the strength to do what must be done.'

'The serpent will be offered to them in your stead,' Zothrac said. 'The spilling of his blood shall ritually anoint your new endeavour while the spiritual savagery of his end shall appease the wrath of our daemon over-lords. Already, his brother serpents fight body and soul above us as entities unleashed possess their pitiful vessel and metal turns on flesh.'

Occam stepped forward. As he did so, Word Bearers in Terminator plate stiffened and aimed their boltgun-mounted glaives at the Alpha Legion commander.

'You seem to have this all worked out, my lords,' Occam the Untrue said. 'But think on this before you sacrifice me and my men to your daemon lords and Dark Gods. Only I know where the White Crusade gathers. They wait to venture forth into the storm and hunt the sons of mighty Ghalmek down. Only I know where the combined frater forces of the Crozier Worlds are gathering and unless you know exactly where, you will not find the rendezvous in time to stop them. One word from me, utilising the same disguise as I used in gathering such a White Crusade, and they will wait – growing bored and impatient – fertile ground in which the Brothers of the Word can sow betrayal and spiritual dissent. You cannot convert an army already on the march to destroy you.'

The First Apostle and Zothrac of the Graven Gate stepped up onto the iron palanquin, making the trembling cultists carrying it wince. Approaching the throne, they conferred with the Abyssal Prince.

As they did so, Occam noticed that amongst the growing number of cultists gathering about the palanquin, another Word Bearer had arrived. The strike master recognised the markings on his plate straight away. It was Vilnius Malik. Surreptitiously, the legionnaire shrugged back his camo-cloak to reveal his plasma gun at the ready, should things not go according to the strike master's plan. As the gaze of their optics met, Occam saw Malik nod his helm slowly, indicating that his mission had been a success. He had the alien Tesseraqt in his possession.

'What are your demands, serpent?' Zothrac asked as he turned to face Occam with his master. 'Think before you speak. You are in no position to overplay your hand here.'

'Like the Dark Apostle,' Occam said, 'I only seek a way to serve – but with my flesh as my own and in my own way. Do not the dark and perverse Powers revel in such variety? Free my ship, my men and crew. I shall require them to meet your needs. Send us on our way. As he led me through the storm, like a guide, I shall lead Goura Shengk to the prize he has promised you. My pitiful vessel, as you call it, will be under the mighty guns of his daemon ship. I shall give the frater armies to Goura

Shengk and he to you. As recompense, the Alpha Legion asks to recruit only those most suited to the demands of service in our Legion – a small sacrifice. And, of course, we will all benefit from the havoc such a great gift shall bring the Corpse-Emperor's empire by your hand. My lords, this is an opportunity for all who fight under the banner of heretic.'

'Perhaps too good an opportunity,' Zothrac said before returning to confer with both the First Apostle and their Abyssal Prince. Finally the daemon bowed the extravagant horns on its head.

'Both the decision and associated burden is yours,' Drach'Var Tal said finally.

'Then we accept the burden,' Goura Shengk said, 'and shall take the serpent with us as we venture back beyond the storm. We will not allow him to fail us.'

'Good,' the Abyssal Prince said, flames roaring forth from his nostrils as he spoke. 'For further failure is your doom. Do not let the serpent slither away. The Word Bearers have forgiven you once but we shall not forget, Goura Shengk. Remember that.'

'Fear not, daemon masters,' Occam the Untrue told the Abyssal Prince and the gathering. 'You will get what is coming to you. The Alpha Legion will ensure it.'

PART V

HYDRA DOMINATUS

τ

TO CUT THE HEAD
FROM THE HYDRA

Suspiria Proctor was a cardinal world and sub-sector capital located on the edge of the Crozier Worlds. With only a few rocky shrine worlds and pilgrim waystations situated further stormwards, the planet was the closest of the Adeptus Ministorum's major fiefdoms. This had made the cardinal world a logical place for the frater forces of the Ecclesiarchy to gather before mounting their White Crusade.

Occam the Untrue walked the avenues and boulevards of the capital plate. Suspiria Proctor was a gas giant. Overhead, the sunburst smear of the Maelstrom dominated the sky, casting in silhouette a blizzard of pilgrim transports and Adeptus Ministorum carriers. They had arrived from all corners of the Crozier Worlds at Cardinal Trazier's request, each Ecclesiarchical planet sending a small army of frater militia to join the White Crusade.

The bilious blues and greens of the cardinal world's

upper atmosphere raged like a stormy ocean beneath the city. The capital plate was made up of an interconnected network of atmospheric platforia, each supporting a jagged stratoscape of spires, steeples and cathedral towers. Arched avenues ran between ornamental gardens and baroque architecture and over bridges connecting the network of plates. The air was full of the hiss of the storm below, the clouds of high-speed acidity roiling beneath like furious death.

'Inquisitor Van Leeuwen,' a cleric in trailing robes said as he met Occam on the avenue leading into the Cathedral-Primus. He was flanked by a ceremonial honour guard of armoured crusaders. 'My name is Deacon Borshach – I am aide-maximus to the lord cardinal and have been coordinating the arrival of frater forces above Suspiria Proctor. May I beg your indulgence – there are no weapons allowed in the cathedral. My men will hold onto them for you. This way please. My lord will see you now.'

Occam looked up at the sky swarming with crusader vessels. The *Iota-Æternus* and the *Dissolutio Perpetua* were not among them. The Alpha Legion armed freighter remained hidden in the system from the gathered armada and system monitors. It waited in the shadow of one of the gas giant's distant, pock-marked moons, close enough to reach the cardinal world by shuttle but not close enough to attract unnecessary attention from snooping system ships. The Word Bearers daemon ship did not benefit from the Q-ship's ability to disguise itself. It had been forced to wait on the edge of the system where its unholy presence could be hidden from the armada of Adeptus Ministorum vessels holding station above the gas giant.

Much closer, the *Iota-Æternus* had been sending forth an

assortment of lighters and hump shuttles carrying Frey-dor Blatch and the Seventh Sons to make contact with the Low Serpent and his cultist infiltrators. The Low Serpent had long been hidden amongst the frater billions, plant-ing the necessary seeds of doubt and recruiting operatives.

Occam and the Redacted had been upon one such lighter, their identities hidden by the psychic manipula-tions of Carcinus Quoda. Once again the sorcerer made the Emperor's devout servants think they were seeing Inquisitor Van Leeuwen and his Space Marine entou-rage, instead of a motley band of Alpha Legionnaires and heretic Bearers of the Word. While the warpsmith had remained behind on the *Iota-Æternus* to continue supervis-ing the warped vessel's repairs, Autolicon Phex was still in the infirmary recovering from his grievous wounds. Goura Shengk and a pair of possessed Word Bearers accompa-nied the Alpha Legion instead. They were hidden, like the Redacted, by Quoda's psychic talents and intent on every-thing proceeding smoothly so that the billion souls above Suspiria Proctor might one day fight for unholy Ghalmek.

Surrendering their substitute weaponry to the crusad-ers – loyalist boltguns that completed their disguise – the Redacted followed the deacon in through the grand entrance and across the vaulted chambers of the cathedral. When Occam saw that the episcopal throne was empty, he began to suspect something was amiss. The cathedral was vast but empty. The crusaders had dropped behind with the deacon and their weaponry.

Occam looked around at Quoda, who was concentrat-ing on manipulating surrounding minds and maintaining their illusion. While the strike master walked once again in the guise of Van Leeuwen, the renegades had taken on the appearance of loyalist Space Marines recruited to the inquisitor's cause. Sergeant Hasdrubal and Vilnius Malik flanked Occam and kept close watch about the chambers of the cathedral. Goura Shengk and his two daemon Space Marines were clearly suffering in the holy environs of the cathedral. Their bodies, twisted with infernal brawn and monstrous horns, sagged under the burden.

'Sergeant,' the strike master said.

'I don't like it,' Hasdrubal confessed. 'Enclosed. Too many entrances. Without our weapons. It's an ambush waiting to happen.'

'Malik?'

'Agreed,' the former Night Lord said. 'We should abort.'

'Bearers of the Word have come for the souls promised,' the Dark Apostle said. 'Do not lose your nerve now, serpent.'

'Something's not right here,' Occam said, the echo of his slowing steps carrying through the cavernous chambers. He stopped and turned but Goura Shengk grabbed his arm to stop him. Despite the draining effect of holy ground and the daemon Space Marine's suffering, the strike master could still feel his infernal strength.

'We go through with this,' the Dark Apostle said. 'We will not return to Ghalmek empty-handed again.'

Out of the corner of his optic, Occam saw a figure step out from behind the cardinal's throne. It was not the cardinal. Magnifying his gaze, the Alpha Legionnaire realised that he recognised the figure. He was staring at himself: Inquisitor Van Leeuwen – in the flesh and walking towards the new arrivals in his Ordo Hereticus plate. The inquisitor was escorted by two Celestian Sisters of the August Vigil.

'I think we may have overplayed our hand,' Occam said,

shrugging the Word Bearer off. He looked at his sergeant, who had spotted the inquisitor also.

Occam's gaze moved from the inquisitor to Goura Shengk but the strike master found it hard to believe that the Word Bearers would work with the Holy Ordos or vice versa. The Dark Apostle had too much to gain from Occam's plan. The strike master thought on the cultists under his control and even the renegade Space Marines that made up the Redacted. They were traitors all, to their own loyalist Chapters and had more than enough reason to suspect Occam himself – the strike master sharing with the Holy Ordos a devotion to the God-Emperor of Mankind.

No, Occam decided, but still such a double cross demonstrated the signature of the serpent. One way or another, the Alpha Legion were behind this. Perhaps Omizhar Vohk and the Lord Dominatus, impatient for their precious piece of alien technology.

As armoured shapes appeared at the archways and entrances, Occam began to comprehend the true depth of their doom. While Inquisitor Van Leeuwen and the Battle Sisters advanced, Space Marines in the magnificence of dark silver power armour marched forth from transept openings either side of the Redacted, levelling wrist-mounted storm bolters at the gathering. Their plate was decorated with the glory of etchings and purity seals. From the mighty archway entrance of the cathedral, Occam saw others approaching in formation: battle-brothers in immaculate Terminator plate, carrying halberds crackling with otherworldly power.

These were no ordinary battle-brothers of the Imperium. Their armour and weaponry gleamed with the honour of ages and they moved with a perfection of purpose. Occam could almost feel their dread confidence and power.

The strike master felt the quake of heavy footsteps through the cathedral flagstones as two towering walkers, boasting their own huge blades and heavy weaponry, stomped up behind the Terminators.

'Quoda?' Occam said.

'Grey Knights,' Carcinus Quoda told his strike master. 'Brothers of Titan, the righteous blood of the God-Emperor flowing through their veins.'

Occam suddenly felt the daemon claws of Goura Shengk about his armoured throat. The Dark Apostle had lurched for him.

'So you think to lead us back to the Inquisitorial dungeons,' Shengk roared, his voice assuming the dark reverberation of daemonic presence. 'And forfeit on the dread bargain you made with the Daemon Council.'

Sergeant Hasdrubal and Malik grabbed an arm each and desperately attempted to tear the Dark Apostle from their master. In turn, Shengk's Word Bearers escorts tried to do the same to the Alpha Legionnaires.

'I wish I had thought of that,' Occam managed, as the daemon Dark Apostle throttled him. 'It might have given us something to bargain with.'

The sound of clapping filled the cavernous chamber, the inquisitor's ceramite gauntlets clashing together in applause.

'There is no honour among traitors,' Van Leeuwen called, his voice bouncing about the cathedral. 'Here you fight, turning upon each other in the holy temple of the God-Emperor. Occam the Untrue, strike master of the foul Alpha Legion – from under which rock have you slithered? Goura Shengk, you should have remained in the storm, Word Bearer. You escaped my clutches once. It will not happen again.'

'They know our names,' Hasdrubal said.

'They probably know a lot more than that,' Occam said as Goura Shengk released him. He looked around at the closing Grey Knights. 'Which at least tells us something. They had help. Dissemble.'

There was no point in indulging the deception further. The Inquisition had them. The best Occam the Untrue could hope for was that the sight of renegades in Alpha Legion plate and the monstrous, daemon Space Marines of the Word Bearers might rattle the nerves of the Grey Knights. This was no hope at all, since the strike master knew better. The psyker sons of Titan were amongst the best battle-brothers the Imperium had to offer. Renegades and traitors were their quarry and in the Redacted they had such prey in their sights.

As Quoda's manipulations fell away, revealing the Redacted to all who had not already seen through his sorcery, Grey Knights Terminators spread out to circle them with the psychically attuned blades of their crackling halberds. Brothers in Aegis armour closed in, their optics lined up with their boltguns. Occam could see the glow of ammunition from the ejection ports of the various weapons – no doubt some kind of psychically enhanced bolts used by the Grey Knights to combat witchbreeds and daemons. Towering walkers piloted by Grey Knights pilots loomed overhead, aiming their appendage-mounted heavy weapons at the Redacted.

'So, serpent,' Goura Shengk said, his claw holding back one of his possessed Word Bearers who were roaring and

273

spitting at the Grey Knights. 'How are you going to slither your way out of this?'

'How indeed,' Occam said to himself grimly. Then, when the strike master could not conceive that the situation could get any worse, he heard a vox-channel crackle open in his helm. It was the *Iota-Æternus*.

'*Greetings, Occam,*' a voice said – a voice that made the strike master's hearts plunge within his chest. A voice he had not heard in some time and never thought to hear again. '*Have you missed me?*'

Impossibly, Quetzel Carthach – Angelbane, Master of Harrows and Arch-Lord of the Alpha Legion, was talking to him from beyond the grave. Worse, from the command deck of the *Iota-Æternus*.

Occam had buried Carthach on Vitrea Mundi, beneath the demolished ruins of a fortress-monastery and the hell-fire of a battle-barge bombardment cannon. How had he managed to survive?

Carthach didn't wait for the strike master to answer.

'*That was quite a surprise you had in store for me above the Adeptus Astartes home world,*' the Angelbane continued, his hate-strangled voice strained with pain. '*I didn't think you had it in you. I know better now. As you can see, brother, I have returned the favour. I leave you at the mercy of your enemies – as you left me at the mercy of mine.*'

v

POISONED HEARTS

It had all happened so fast, even for Mina Perdita. As an Assassin, she was used to situations unfolding quickly and the need for swift action. Her mind was a whirl of lethal immediacy, while her reflexes were honed to a razor's edge. She had lived among the dread Space Marines of the Adeptus Astartes long enough to know her limitations. They were genetically engineered to be superior. They were beyond human in body and mind. They were created to be stronger. Faster. To survive all that the galaxy could throw at them.

Perdita had, of course, killed members of the Adeptus Astartes. She had killed virtually every sentient thing that had lived and breathed within the borders of the Imperium. Her talents usually gave her the element of surprise. Poison-glazed blades. Weapons secreted in clothing. Death hiding in flesh. This time, however, it was the enemy that benefitted.

Perdita had been up on the bridge with Naga-Khan and

Ghesh, the Navigator. Together with the command deck cultists and the Sorcerer Quoda's astropaths, they had been monitoring the mission. There was a good deal to do. Lord Occam had led the Redacted down to Suspiria Proctor with Goura Shengk to meet the lord cardinal. Freydor Blatch had left with hundreds of Seventh Sons. They were ready to make contact with the Low Serpent and consolidate the infiltration of frater forces aboard the gathered armada of Ecclesiarchy transports. All the while, lighters arranged by the Low Serpent brought supplies back to the Q-ship.

With them they had brought uninvited guests. Space Marines of the Alpha Legion in shattered plate, led by the monstrous Quetzel Carthach. With their missing limbs supplanted with basic bionics and their horrific injuries patched up, the legionnaires – once exemplars of lethal grace and stealth – were in a sorry state. Their legionary colours were soot-smeared and crumpled, while cracked optics died before blinking back to searing life. Despite their terrible injuries, a handful of Alpha Legion survivors had stowed away on the visiting lighters and infiltrated the *Iota-Æternus*. Killing their way silently through the ship, they had burst forth onto the small bridge – their battered boltguns blasting apart Seventh Son sentries with the cool nerve and expert marksmanship for which the Legion was infamous.

With barrels of boltguns pointed at the command deck cultists and bridge crew, the Alpha Legionnaires ventured forth. Some were battered Space Marines while others were broken altereds in legionary plate. A limping Terminator with a replacement bionic leg moved aside to reveal his master. The Alpha Legion warlord's broken body had been pinned and braced within his shattered plate. One side of the Angelbane's skull seemed similarly reconstructed.

Perdita had been on board the Marines Mordant's battle-barge when it had opened fire upon Carthach's position down on Vitrea Mundi. The orbital strike had turned the fortress-monastery into a mountain of rubble and Alpha Legion bodies. Nothing could have crawled out of there alive – or so Perdita had thought. She, along with Occam the Untrue, had been wrong. They had under-estimated the Archlord of the Alpha Legion and now he stood on the command deck of the strike master's ship.

The Angelbane carried himself like an armoured puppet with cut strings. While half his face retained a trace of its genic nobility and one eye still gleamed with strate-gic brilliance, the other half was a mess of staples and stitching pins.

'Bring him forth,' the Angelbane hissed through his half-mouth.

Arkan Reznor stumbled forward and crashed to the deck on his armoured knees. His helmet was missing and his plate sparking and battered. Such damage had been sus-tained resisting Carthach's legionnaires, Perdita reasoned. His face was bloodied and bruised. When Autolicon Phex appeared behind him, the Assassin wasn't surprised. It made sense for Carthach to neutralise the remaining mem-bers of the Redacted on board the ship. What she did not expect was to see was Phex still carrying his heavy plasma gun and levelling its gaping muzzle at the warpsmith.

'You traitorous filth,' Reznor grizzled through broken teeth.

Phex could say nothing in return. Instead, he stepped

forth and smashed the warpsmith to the floor with the butt of his weapon.

'Good, brother,' Carthach said to Phex with strained appreciation. 'I couldn't have said it better myself. Now, who is the captain of this crate?'

When no one answered, Carthach used his remaining hand to draw a bolt pistol from a holster. He aimed the weapon across the bridge, fixing on one deck cultist after another before reaching Perdita. The Assassin froze. It was not the first time such a weapon had been pointed at her or even by a member of the Adeptus Astartes, but she thought it best to act like everyone else who fell under the Angelbane's sights.

'I am captain of this vessel,' Naga-Khan said, finally stepping forward. Carthach turned awkwardly and blasted the shipmaster back across a console.

'Not any more,' Carthach said, before issuing an order to one of his broken legionnaires. 'Round up the Navigator and astropaths. They will be needed.'

As the limping Terminator moved by, Perdita backed out of his path, using it as an excuse to put her back to the bridge runebanks and a line of consoles between her and the Angelbane. Her shoulder brushed up against the brawn of a death cultist nearby. His face was taut with expectation. The Seventh Sons were assassins all and Perdita could feel their desire to kill Carthach.

The Angelbane carried himself with obvious agony over to a cultist at a console and rested the muzzle of his pistol on the top of her shaven skull.

'Your strike master is off the ship on a mission,' the Angelbane said. 'We know this already. Open a vox-channel, please.'

SONS OF THE HYDRA

'Give them nothing,' Arkan Reznor spat, bringing himself back up off the deck.

'Phex!' Carthach ordered, as though issuing a command to a faithful hound. Perdita knew that the Angelbane had tortured Autolicon Phex horribly. She had heard his suffering through the door to his cell. While her strike master had used such treatment to secure Phex's seeming loyalty for the Redacted, Perdita could see now that the damage had run much deeper. Carthach had destroyed Phex's Chapter and had broken his victim both physically and psychologically. He had turned Phex into his personal plaything and still had the Space Marine under his control. Perdita came to the horrific realisation that Phex had been feeding his archlord information. Carthach had known of Occam the Untrue's plans and his intention to visit Suspiria Proctor.

Phex smashed Arkan Reznor back down to the deck. This time Perdita heard a crunch as the warpsmith's skull was fractured. As Carthach tapped the muzzle of his pistol on the deck cultist's head she opened the vox-channel with the Redacted down on the cardinal world.

'Greetings, Occam,' Carthach seethed across the channel. 'Have you missed me?'

Perdita watched the Angelbane uncomfortably pace the deck. His half-face was fixed in a mask of agony and vengeful glee.

'That was quite a surprise you had in store for me above the Adeptus Astartes home world,' the Angelbane said. 'I didn't think you had it in you. I know better now. As you can see, brother, I have returned the favour. I leave you at the mercy of your enemies – as you left me at the mercy of mine. The Inquisition has been informed of your many crimes – your devastation of Adeptus Astartes home worlds, your attack on their very own installations and the consort you keep with daemon-infested Bearers of the Word.'

'*Carthach,*' the voice of Lord Occam crackled back across the channel. '*Listen to me–*'

'No,' the Archlord of the Alpha Legion said. 'As we speak, your vessel resides under my control. Cultist contacts I have made among the frater armies are currently slaughtering your High Serpent and his infiltrators. Your warpsmith is coughing up pieces of that gifted brain of his on the deck. And you, brother Occam – you are facing eternity in the bowels of some God-Emperor forsaken, high-security Inquisitorial installation. There you will find others to listen to you. The Master of Mankind's stale agents have, as part of their torturous interrogations, an unending stream of questions for you, brother. You will not eat. You will not sleep. And you will not die. I have ensured it. Occam the Untrue will finally speak the truth. Perhaps we shall all learn something.'

'*Reznor?*' Lord Occam said.

'Here, strike master,' the warpsmith managed.

'*Phex?*'

'He's betrayed us to the enemy,' Reznor said.

'Enough of this,' Quetzel Carthach said, thunking across the deck and bringing up his bolt pistol. The vox went quiet for a moment as though Lord Occam was taking in the betrayal.

'*The shipmaster?*' Occam asked. '*Perdita?*'

'Perdita is here,' Arkan Reznor said, lifting his head. Blood from his scalp was raining down his face. 'The shipmaster is not.'

A single shot from the Angelbane's weapon blasted the warpsmith's head from his shoulders.

'*Reznor?*' Lord Occam called.

'Brother Reznor is dead, strike master,' Perdita said.

Carthach turned and unleashed another bolt from his battered pistol. It blew the cultist standing next to Perdita in half. While blending in with the other Seventh Sons on the deck, the Assassin had assumed a male voice.

'*Understood,*' the strike master said finally.

'Keep going,' Carthach dared Occam. 'I'll kill them all.'

'*I'm going to kill you, Carthach,*' Lord Occam snarled back across the crackling channel. The Assassin could hear other voices in the distance: imperious calls for the strike master and the Redacted to surrender.

'Not from where *you* are,' Carthach taunted.

'*Assassin,*' Lord Occam said. '*Can you complete your mission?*'

'I can't kill him,' Perdita said. Carthach killed another deck cultist, and another as the Assassin added: 'There are too many of them.'

With a haze of gore drifting across the bridge, Mina Perdita found herself standing alone.

Carthach's ravaged lips formed a half-snarl.

'Assassin, eh?' the Angelbane said, bringing up the smoking barrel of his pistol.

'*Then kill the ship,*' Lord Occam said gravely. '*My final order.*'

Perdita ran. Before her was the engineering runebank. She willed herself on, matching her Assassin's reflexes and morphing musculature to Quetzel Carthach's aim. One step. Two steps. Three. Skidding down behind a console she allowed the station to absorb the mauling boltfire.

She tried to clear her head. The Geller field could not be controlled directly from the bridge but the bank incorporated an override for emergencies. This qualified, the Assassin decided, as bolt rounds roared overhead and punched into the command deck about her.

With a snarl of determination screwing up her face, Perdita threw herself at the runebank. The seconds seemed to slow as she worked dials, hauled at the thick handles of levers and stabbed at studs with a finger. As bolt rounds crashed about her, the Assassin retracted behind a nearby console. The station was ripped apart in a shower of sparks. Perdita rolled across the punctured deck. Kneeling before the runebank she completed the complex sequence, tearing circuit boards out of their slots to slam them home in different ports.

With a clunk, a haptic interface opened in the runebank and Perdita plunged her fist desperately into the enclosure. Like an Iron Maiden for the hand, the biometric lock skewered her palm and the flesh of fingertips with needles. A shudder of pain and shock ran through the Assassin's body but she was beyond such sensations.

Perdita felt her body torn to one side like a rag doll as bolts from Carthach's pistol ripped through her body, turning the magnificence of the Assassin's surgical adaptations into butchered and blasted meat.

She hung there still, the interface emitting a dull ring as it completed its genetic sampling. Her head lolled back on her shoulder.

'Authorise and execute,' the Assassin hissed, the words escaping her trembling lips and reaching the runebank's vox horn. As her face relaxed, the muscles quivered. Somehow her face found its way back to the innocence of the girl who had originally been recruited by the Officio Assassinorum and had been sliced up on the Temple slab.

Mina Perdita smiled. She had shut down the Q-ship's Geller field, but in reaching the runebank, had ensured that the merciless accuracy of Quetzel Carthach's bolt round had disabled it. It could not be reinstated from the bridge and the Angelbane had no time to reach the Enginarium before the horrific consequences of her actions took effect.

As the Assassin's gore formed a fast growing pool on the deck below what remained of her blasted body, she felt a change in the ship. She had experienced this before. Above Ghalmek. She knew what dread she was looking for. The Word Bearers had possessed the *Iota-Æternus* and allowed the vessel to become host to daemon entities. Some of the superstructure and internal architecture still bore the evidence of the ship's traumas. Fang-lined doorways solidified in metal. The horror of twisted girders and passageways. The impression of claws and monstrous faces frozen in the hull. Ribbed chambers flesh-crafted to resemble the inside of some infernal beast. Daemons still haunted the dark corridors, while abominate entities waited in the shadows – ready for their chance to infest the ship once more with their madness and manifestation. Only the Geller field – running constantly to maintain a bubble of reality in and around the vessel – kept the daemonic possession at bay.

As Perdita felt the life drain from her a horrible new life took hold of the ship. A thousand daemonic heartbeats thundered through the superstructure, while foul ichor bled up through the decks. The vessel creaked and spasmed its torment as transformations ripped through its workings. Metal, darkness and flesh became one. Unreality swept like a plague through the *Iota-Æternus*. Entities, formerly denied, sank their claws into the ship and anchored their existence. The ship's entirety swarmed with the horrid impression of daemon creatures reaching out from the beyond. Pipes ruptured, filling chambers with steam, filth and the ghostly presence of monstrous beings. Runebanks trembled and sparked furiously before tendrils burst from screens and workings to seize the consoles from within.

Across the command deck, the Assassin heard the crash of boltguns. While deck cultists and astropaths were being eaten alive by daemonic maws opening in the deck and the souls squeezed out of them by barbed tentacles erupting from the walls and ceiling, Quetzel Carthach and his remaining Alpha Legion renegades were answering with firepower. Bolts tore through the infernal workings and metallic hide of the daemon ship. Carthach and his Sons of the Hydra put bolts between the many eyes of monstrosities manifesting upon the command deck. They cut through grotesque appendages reaching out for them and sated the appetites of rancid maws opening in the walls nearby.

Perdita listened to the Archlord of the Alpha Legion call out to the flesh-metal creatures emerging from the intensifying unreality of the ship. In the background his twisted brotherhood were dying. Legionnaires were being impaled on shafts of daemon tusk and horn growing up through the deck. Others were becoming one with the deck as they sank down through the liquefying horror of their surroundings. Retreating legionnaires were sheared in half by fanged bulkheads while Alpha Legion Terminators screamed as steaming ichor vomited at them from infernal orifices to melt thick plate and the flesh within.

Perdita heard Autolicon Phex grunt horribly as he was seized by the appendages of some abominate entity emerging from the wall of the ship nearby. Grabbed by muscular tentacles that snaked their way about plate and limb, Phex's convulsing fingers sent wild blasts of plasma across the command deck that burned into the daemon-hide branching through the metal walls. The heavy plasma gun crashed to the deck as his arms were prised apart by the unearthly strength of the daemonic appendages. A mangled scream erupted from his lips as the tentacles heaved at his arms, legs and head. The horrible sound was short-lived. Moments later, the traitor's armoured body was in six pieces, each being dragged covetously away.

As the boltfire died away, Quetzel Carthach's entreaties became louder and more desperate. There were no negotiations to be had or trickery that could be employed with such an enemy. The swarm of daemonic entities that the Assassin had unleashed in shutting down the Geller field were soul-famished and mindless in their savagery. The only interest they had in the Angelbane was to peel plate and flesh from his bones and feast upon his rancid spirit.

Carthach's words became a strangled roar as daemon teeth sprouted from the deck and ceiling about him. Lamps flashed and shattered, the corner of the command deck becoming a nexus of darkness – the depths of a monstrous throat. The Angelbane emptied the final fury of his bolt pistol into the oblivion before reaching to hold up the collapsing roof of the chamber. He hissed his hatred at the daemonic mouth closing about him, while the servos and hydraulics of his plate strained. One moment he was Quetzel Carthach – proud warlord, dark legend and Angelbane of the Alpha Legion – the next he was a shrieking mulch of plate and bloody flesh. Then, he was nothing at all.

Mina Perdita felt everything go dark. A nest of daemonic tendrils slithered from the sparking runebank and enveloped her ragged form with hooked barbs. She prepared herself for the horror to come. She had completed her Temple's mission. She had carried out her strike master's orders. She had brought an end to the galactic scourge that was Quetzel Carthach. It was now time to meet her own. As life left her, the Assassin felt the tendrils heave her blasted body into the daemon-haunted flesh-metal of the possessed ship. Now all Mina Perdita had to fear for was her immortal soul.

φ

SERPENTS CHANGE THEIR SKIN, NOT THEIR FANGS

Occam listened to the gunfire, death and horror.

As the screaming trailed off and the vox became a swarming plethora of daemonic voices, the strike master killed the channel. The *Iota-Æternus* and all on board – cultists, operatives, Space Marines – were lost.

Although it was difficult for the strike master to comprehend, he had even bigger problems to contend with. Quetzel Carthach might have finally met his end but he had left Occam at the mercy of his enemies. Those remaining of the Redacted and their Word Bearers allies were unarmed, within the sights and under the blades of the Grey Knights.

Occam looked up at a towering statue of the Master of Mankind, his mighty form standing astride the transept like a colossus and forming the arch under which the Redacted had just walked. His stone visage looked down on all in the cathedral with an imperious austerity – Alpha

Legionnaires, Word Bearers and Grey Knights in their magnificent plate and heavily armed walkers.

Regardless of his Chapter colours or the banners under which he fought, Occam had always been a committed servant of the God-Emperor. Such faith came easy within magnificent structures such as the Cathedral-Primus or encased within loyalist plate. It was something else entirely to be a loyalist in traitor's clothing: a renegade hated and hunted by all, whose heresy was a belief that the God-Emperor could be served from beyond such places. To fight deviants from among deviance. To battle evil shoulder to shoulder with the unholy.

Here Occam found himself once more. In consort with daemon Word Bearers while surrounded by those of the God-Emperor's blood: all under the fierce gaze of mankind's Master.

The strike master looked about him. The Grey Knights, their movements measured but fearless, were closing in. Their psychically charged blades crackled while the barrels of wrist-mounted storm bolters remained fixed upon the renegades.

'It seems you have us caught between an anvil and the Corpse-Emperor's mighty hammer of faith,' Goura Shengk snarled, 'and all the while your legionary brothers slither away like snakes.'

'Quetzel Carthach was no brother of mine,' Occam told him.

'Well, that's all well and good, strike commander,' the Dark Apostle said, 'but it seems your past failures with this Carthach have come to haunt us here in the present.'

'Haunt us is all he can do now,' Occam said, looking at Sergeant Hasdrubal, 'for now he is dead.'

'So I note,' Goura Shengk taunted bitterly. 'You are a twisted serpent, Occam the Untrue – proud and full of faith. We see, however, that you have finally made your pact with the darkness. That upon your order you unleashed the dread fury of the daemon storm.'

The Dark Apostle had listened to Occam's final order: the order that had damned his ship and brought forth daemonic vengeance upon Quetzel Carthach and his Sons of the Hydra.

'To utilise the power of the storm is not to become one with it,' Occam told the Dark Apostle.

'Orders?' Sergeant Hasdrubal asked. Unlike his master, he had no interest in a spiritual debate. Like Vilnius Malik, he could not stand by in the sights of the Grey Knights with no weapons of their own and no plan to prosecute.

'Pray tell us, serpent,' Goura Shengk hissed. 'What is your plan?'

'Quoda?' Occam asked, hoping to make use of his sorcerer's dread powers.

'The Grey Knights are psykers all, strike master,' Carcinus Quoda reminded him. 'Their combined powers have many times the potency of my own.'

With the Grey Knights like a closing trap of silver plate, intent upon taking both the Redacted and fell Word Bearers alive for Inquisitor Van Leeuwen, Occam's thoughts raced on.

Many times the potency…

'Strike master?' Vilnius Malik put to him.

Power of the storm…

'Occam?' Sergeant Hasdrubal said as the closing Grey Knights levelled their crackling halberds at the tight group of renegades, forcing them together.

Unleashed the dread fury...

Occam reached into an armoured pouch on his belt and retrieved an object heavy with its own alien darkness. The alien Tesseraqt Malik had retrieved from the bowels of the Ghalmek's polar cathedral. The black cube moved continually, sections opening and interlocking with one another in perpetual and fluid movement. The cracks in between the moving pieces glowed green with alien power. Occam knew it to be the generator of some exotic containment field – a piece of xenos technology that the Lord Dominatus desired for his own nefarious needs. Goura Shengk, however, had informed Occam that the Tesseraqt already contained a powerful entity in its alien field – a monstrous daemon that the diabolists and Dark Mechanicum priests of Unholy Ghalmek had made preparations to receive.

There would be no such ceremonies on Suspiria Proctor.

Occam jabbed his ceramite thumb into depressions on the six sides of the cube. As it transformed in his gauntlets, new surfaces presented new depressions which he pressed as fast as they appeared.

'Inquisitor,' a Grey Knights sergeant called as his brotherhood halted in a serrated circle about the renegades, the blades of halberds and barrels of storm bolters pointed inwards.

'Do your duty, sergeant,' Inquisitor Van Leeuwen said, his voice almost strangled with the satisfaction he felt at seeing the Alpha Legionnaires and Word Bearers captured. 'Secure the prisoners.'

'On your knees, foul servants of darkness,' a Grey Knights sergeant roared at the Redacted, his booming voice full of honour and hatred.

Malik was struggling. The former Night Lord did not like

being cornered and he would not be captured. He moved to rush forward at the line of crackling blades and gaping barrels but Hasdrubal stopped him, laying a gauntlet on the legionnaire's pauldron.

'Only at the strike master's word,' the sergeant growled.

'The word of a liar...' Goura Shengk said, his filthy daemon's claws growing longer and blood-red brawn flexing, '...a thief and a coward.'

As the Dark Apostle's daemon Space Marines also grew in ferocity and stature, spitting and hissing at the glittering cordon of Grey Knights, Occam continued to work the Tesseraqt. The black box transformed rapidly in his hands. The strike commander could hardly thumb the smooth depressions in the black, alien material quickly enough. Finally, something cleared. It wasn't a click or thunk like the opening of a lock. It was more like a change of pressure, but instead of being felt in ears and sinuses, the effect reverberated horribly through the mind. The Tesseraqt presented no more depressions to activate. Instead, the cube began to turn itself inside out and glow with a green darkness indicating that the containment field maintained by the ancient xenos technology was failing.

'I have two more words for you,' Occam the Untrue said, coming up behind one of the Dark Apostle's possessed sentinels. 'Get ready...'

Throwing the Tesseraqt between the Word Bearer's legs, Occam allowed the cube to skim across the marble of the cathedral floor.

'Grenade!' the silver-clad sergeant called out as the highly disciplined Grey Knights saw the object slide towards them and backed away. A Space Marine in grey plate opened fire with his storm bolter. Bolts rocketed across the transept, trailing ethereal power from the psyker's weapon.

Occam grabbed the warped pack of the Word Bearers sentinel and forced the creature forward. The daemon Space Marine roared its agony as the psychically charged bolts blasted into its cursed plate and infernal brawn. Holding the Word Bearer up like a shield, the strike master was pushed back by the Grey Knights' stuttering boltfire as it ripped into the thing.

A blinding green light filled the cathedral chamber. Even in the shadow of his Word Bearers shield, Occam's optics briefly blanked out as his auto-senses cycled through appropriate filters. For a moment the green light was everything. Muted thunder rolled through the transept, while unearthly energies crackled through the marble of the flagstones. Occam could hear shouting, more urgent than before. Calls tinged with a hint of superhuman panic.

The strike master was suddenly aware of the presence of something huge. Grey Knights were backing through the green brilliance, their gauntlets held up before the optics of their helms. The floor trembled. The walls shook. Dust cascaded down from the vaulted roof. As his plate registered a bank of heat – intense and unnatural – rolling out from the site of the opening Tesseraqt, Occam held up the daemonflesh of his Word Bearers meatshield. Furious, infernal flame reached for the cathedral roof. It writhed about the monstrous form of the daemonic creature that the strike master had unleashed.

'What have you done?' Goura Shengk shouted. He held up his claw before the wave of heat driving Inquisitor Van Leeuwen and his Grey Knights back. 'The Slaughterlord will destroy us all! He will not stop until the corpse of every soul on this doomed world lies at his feet.'

'Then I suggest we leave,' Occam the Untrue said, shoving the dying Word Bearer at the green tornado of fury and flame that was Kar'Nash'gahar, Lord of Glorious Slaughter and Slayer of Worlds.

As the alien containment field collapsed and the daemon monstrosity manifested fully, a tsunami of warped, crackling power crashed through the Space Marines in the cathedral, and Occam felt his power armour briefly die about him. Everything went black. All he was aware of was the muted roar of the daemon entity. Then he felt a distant thunder through the soles of his boots and the stone floor. The radiating energies of the monster's manifestation were overloading the power conduits, and not just in the cathedral; a chain reaction of explosions was spreading outwards into the machineries that powered the whole floating plate.

His optics crackled back to life after his suit had been momentarily immobilised by the shockwave of dark energy. Friend and foe alike had suffered the brief overload and one by one the Space Marines surrounding the greater daemon rediscovered mobility in their armoured suits, like statues coming to life.

The transept echoed with the gunfire of Grey Knights and the horrific bellowing of the greater daemon. A towering colossus of extravagant horn, claws and bulging muscle, its ugly face jangled with bronze rings through its snout, lips and ears. A pair of ragged wings unfolded like doom above the Space Marines below. The monster's features were uglier still for the insane rage it suffered upon being released from its prison and the spiritual torment of manifesting upon holy ground.

Psychically charged bolt-rounds ripped into the daemon's metal-threaded flesh from the line of Grey Knights. The beast roared, its anger shaking the cathedral's foundations as the mighty walkers unleashed their arm-mounted cannons at it. The thing attempted to shield itself using its wings but the fury of the heavy weaponry turned the leathery appendages into a mangled mess.

The colossal daemon doubled over and began to heave. A torrent of blood gushed from the monster's jaws and hit the cathedral floor. In amongst the deluge Occam could see something akin to the length of a huge, barbed tapeworm. Snatching up its grotesque length, the daemon twirled it about its huge form. Blood rained from the length of the thing and all too late, Occam realised that the monster was wielding some devastating weapon – a daemonic flail of black barbs and cruel hooks. Whipping out with the flail, the daemon turned an advancing line of Grey Knights into a scythed mess of mangled flesh and armour. Another great swirling slash of the daemonic weapon tore through the stone architecture of the cathedral and ripped apart the workings of one of the Grey Knights walkers.

'Sergeant,' the strike master called through the havoc, 'find us a way out of this.'

The cordon of Grey Knights closed about the Slaughterlord, the barb-like halberds of the silver-plated Terminators crackling as they advanced. Hasdrubal ran at the enemy; Malik and Quoda followed. A Grey Knights Terminator swung his force halberd around in a trailing arc of psychic might and the sergeant skidded to a stop across the marble flags before changing direction. Using the weight of his plate, Hasdrubal ran at the Terminator, slamming his pauldron into him. The Grey Knight was knocked back and as he was, Vilnius Malik did the same from the opposite direction.

As the Alpha Legionnaires grabbed an arm each, Carcinus Quoda slammed into the Terminator's chest. The Terminator brothers turned their own weapons to meet this new threat, and the sorcerer tore the force halberd out of the Grey Knight's clutches. With the weapon grasped in his gauntlets Quoda just managed to turn aside the smashing stroke of a Grey Knight before lopping the head off another weapon with a vicious back strike. Quoda dropped the halberd with a cry of pain as it burned his hands.

Running the stumbling Terminator back into the ranks of the Grey Knights, Malik and his sergeant let the Space Marine go. The other Grey Knights didn't see the danger until it was too late, concentrating all their fire upon the flame-swirling greater daemon instead. Crashing back messily through their ranks, the Terminator went down, taking several brothers down with him and opening a hole in the closing cordon.

'Dark Apostle!' Occam called, even as Goura Shengk's own warped sentinel tried to pull him away. The daemon Word Bearer ignored the strike master and shrugged his brother off. As a Grey Knight mounted a slow charge in his Terminator suit, his force halberd thrust forward like a skewering lance, the daemon Space Marine batted it aside with its huge, malformed claws. Defending his master, the creature leapt upon the Grey Knight and proceeded to savage him with horn and claw.

'Strike master!' Occam heard Ephron Hasdrubal call. The sergeant had his boot on a fallen Grey Knight's helm. Stamping down with a crack, the power armour seals gave and he broke the Space Marine's neck. With a grunt, the sergeant scooped up the cannon he was carrying.

Snatching a combat blade from the Grey Knight's belt sheath, he threw it to Malik. The former Night Lord immediately went to work savagely stabbing the downed Terminator in the neck, exploiting the seals between the warrior's helm and suit.

Quoda backed towards him, desperately smashing aside halberds swung with power and hatred by hulking Terminators. Every time the psychically charged blades clashed, they crackled with the Grey Knights' otherworldly energies.

Unleashing the fury of the cannon on the Terminators' armoured backs, Hasdrubal brought one silver-plated warrior down and distracted another long enough for the sorcerer to jab the Grey Knight in the throat with a crunch.

Occam started moving towards the opening his legionnaires had created. The Word Bearers sentinel protecting the Dark Apostle had become a skewered mess of daemon flesh and force halberds.

'Shengk,' Occam called. 'This is your last chance.'

The Dark Apostle had fallen to his knees before the immense destructive power of Kar'Nash'gahar. The greater daemon – furious, afflicted and aflame – was rampaging through the cathedral. Writhing in an inferno of green flame, the monstrous creature was infuriated by both its sacrosanct surroundings and the Grey Knights peppering its muscular form with storm bolter fire. As Terminators in grey plate closed on the abomination, corralling it with the presented blades of their halberds, the daemon stamped down on the annoyance. Splattering them into the cathedral floor with its hooves, the Lord of Glorious

Slaughter raged on, smashing one of the Grey Knights walkers into the wall with its horned shoulder.

Seeing the towering statue of the God-Emperor standing astride the chamber, the daemonic beast roared. As the horrific sound filled the chamber, Occam felt his soul shrivel. Kar'Nash'gahar tore the massive statue down with its flail and unrelenting fury. A small mountain of stone shattered across the remaining ranks of the Grey Knights. As the shadow of the falling statue buried Occam, the strike master made a decision. Instead of running for the withdrawing members of the Redacted, he made for Goura Shengk, who was stumbling towards the green brilliance of the Tesseraqt.

Occam felt the flags quake beneath his boots as the statue smashed to the ground. Stumbling and then skidding across the floor, the strike master found Goura Shengk on his knees before the daemon's glorious destruction. As they knelt there in the green light, bolts flying wildly and a cloud bank of dust enveloping them, Occam tried to tear the Word Bearer up onto his feet.

'We've got to go,' the strike master said. Occam cared little for the daemon filth but with the *Iota-Æternus* compromised, he needed the Dark Apostle and the *Dissolutio Perpetua* to escape the system.

'Go?' the daemon Space Marine seethed. 'Where would we go, serpent? Because of the sons of Alpharius, the souls we promised the Daemon Council are forfeit. Brothers of the Word will hunt us down. Because of your failures, strike master, there is nowhere to go.'

Occam looked up through the thinning haze of dust. He could hear screaming and the excruciating fracture of the cathedral cracking about them. The broken bodies of Grey Knights flew through the air. Through the murk and green light, Occam could see the greater daemon – a monstrous whirlwind of flesh and flame – break the back of a Grey Knights walker by stamping out with a cloven hoof. As bolt rounds ripped up through the abomination's back, the creature tore at statues and holy tapestries adorning the cathedral wall. Bombarding Grey Knights with rubble that surviving brothers used for cover, the daemon turned. Stormbolter fire ripped into the monster's metal-threaded hide. Roaring in pain and frustration, Kar'Nash'gahar threw itself at the Space Marines. The creature stamped Terminators into the cathedral floor and scooped up armoured victims in its great claws, crushing them with furious abandon.

It seemed suddenly to notice a figure taking cover behind the grand episcopal throne. Occam saw that it was Van Leeuwen, the inquisitor unloading his bolt pistol at the towering monstrosity. Obliterating the throne with a savage kick of its hoof, the Slayer of Worlds snatched Van Leeuwen in one great claw and brought the inquisitor up before its infernal ugliness. The inquisitor roared his hatred at the daemon beast before sending the last of his bolt-rounds into Kar'Nash'gahar's face, making the creature flinch. When the Slaughterlord roared back, the foul intensity of its breath melted the weapon in Van Leeuwen's gauntlet before turning the inquisitor himself into a withering husk. Tossing the body aside, the daemon once more raged into the gunfire of the remaining Grey Knights.

As the daemon stormed across the cathedral, Goura Shengk fell to his knees and held his arms outstretched.

'Mighty Kar'Nash'gahar…' the Dark Apostle called, supplicating himself before the greater daemon.

Occam shook his head. Unable to return to Unholy Ghalmek, Goura Shengk was looking for new daemon sponsors. Leaving the Word Bearer, the strike master ran into the blinding green light. He reached out and grabbed for the Tesseraqt. He felt the object moving. Reassembling. Once again, finding its form. As the Tesseraqt closed, the brilliant green light of the containment field disappeared and Occam found himself with the black cube once again in his hand.

As the light died, the Slaughterlord's gaze was drawn from its butchery of the Grey Knights. The monstrosity saw Occam with its prison in his hand. Its face contorted with hatred and fury as it associated the strike master with its incarceration.

Slipping the Tesseraqt into his belt pouch, Occam ran. Pounding his armoured footsteps across the cathedral, he risked a glance behind him as the greater daemon stomped forth in abyssal anger.

'Lord of Glorious Slaughter and Slayer of Worlds,' Goura Shengk called, 'we offer ourselves…'

A wrinkle of disgust passed across Occam's features at the Word Bearer's entreaty. The monstrosity stamped its hoof down on the Dark Apostle. The Word Bearer disappeared, replaced by a crater of shattered flagstones and fountaining gore.

The Master of Mankind's statue had fallen face first onto the ground and its colossal form lay in Occam's path. Skidding down onto his side, the strike master slid beneath the stern visage of the God-Emperor's face, mere moments before the Slaughterlord's hoof came crashing down to shatter the statue's back.

Occam ran past Grey Knights Terminators, whose optics

were fixed upon the Slaughterlord's spellbinding form. They held their halberds out to corral the monstrosity in a serrated gauntlet of psychically charged blades. Meanwhile, brothers in powered plate ripped into the greater daemon's foul brawn with the staccato blast of ethereal boltfire. These Grey Knights also seemed unconcerned at Occam's escape and the fleeing of the Redacted. Kar'Nash'gahar had their attention now and could not be allowed to leave this place to wreak havoc across the atmospheric plates of Suspiria Proctor.

Occam heard a gargling shriek across the vox-channel. A Grey Knights Terminator had managed to thrust the blade of his halberd into Malik's gut, bringing the former Night Lord down. The strike master could hear the suppressed gasp of shock followed by Malik coughing and spluttering blood up within his helm.

The Redacted were suddenly there at their brother's side. Occam ran at the Terminator, throwing the weight of his powered plate at the hulking Grey Knight's pauldron. Knocking him off balance and stumbling to one side, the strike master put the armoured warrior in Hasdrubal's sights, allowing the sergeant to finish their foe with a headshot from his boltgun.

A kneeling Malik roared as he pulled the skewering halberd blade from his side.

'Malik…' Occam said.

'I can make it,' the former Night Lord growled.

The strike master risked a glance behind him.

'Get him up,' Occam ordered. Between them, Hasdrubal and the sorcerer helped Malik to his feet.

'What's happening to the floor?' Hasdrubal said. Occam had detected it also. The gradient was changing. He could feel the ever increasing slant of the ground beneath his feet, had felt it since the storm of unnatural energy had been unleashed.

'I think the daemon's manifestation has knocked out the plate generatoria,' Occam told his sergeant. 'A chain reaction or system failure. The anti-gravity engines must be failing. This plate is falling out of the sky. We've got to get away.'

With an arm around each of them, Malik's armoured boots barely skimmed the floor. As the Alpha Legionnaires rushed him across the vaulted chambers, followed by their strike master, Kar'Nash'gahar smashed his way through the cathedral and the cordon of Grey Knights.

The greater daemon vented its monstrous fury upon the holiness of its surroundings, tearing architecture and the statues of saints down upon the battle-brothers in silver plate who sought to contain it. The cathedral drove the creature insane with the divinity of stone and sculpture. The Grey Knights demanded obliteration for the foolish assumption that they alone could contain the uncontainable. The Slaughterlord never took its fell gaze from the true object of its abyssal ire. The one who had unleashed the Slayer of Worlds once more upon the galaxy – a service that would not save him. The one who had kept the abomination prisoner in the xenos cube: Occam the Untrue.

'Do you have a plan?' Sergeant Hasdrubal called as they reached the cathedral gates.

'It barely qualifies,' Occam said, 'but yes – I have something.'

As Hasdrubal shouldered the towering doors open, creating the narrowest of gaps, the Redacted forced their way through. Occam followed, but outside the cathedral – gathered on the ceremonial entrance plaza – was a sea of cardinal world soldiers: planetary defence forces, storm troopers, crusaders and frater militia hordes, all dressed in devout black robes and armour. They surrounded the Cathedral-Primus, their weaponry aimed at the opening doors. At their head, in a Chimera mounting an armoured pulpit, was the lord cardinal's aide-maximus: Deacon Borshach. The Ecclesiarchical troops had all heard the thunderous horror coming from within the cathedral. They had felt the quake and crumble of foundations, and stained glass had rained down on them from the grandeur of shattered windows. Faced only with what was left of the Redacted, Borshach – like his cardinal world soldiers – seemed uncertain.

Occam was out of options. He pushed his legionnaires to one side. They had to clear the door. The action drew the fire of a militia trooper in black, his single stabbing beam going wide of the mark but enough to prompt a blinding cascade of others to sear across the plaza from the front lines of the cardinal's troops. Lasbeams cut across the path of the legionnaires, burning into the stone of the cathedral exterior. The strike master's armour registered a cluster of impacts. Some were glancing beams while others seared into the plate. He heard his sergeant call out as a beam struck him in the side of the neck.

In a monstrous boom of metal and stone, the cathedral doors exploded outwards. With a Titanic kick the greater daemon struck the doors with a hoof and sent one flying out across the plaza in a storm of masonry. Soldiers died in their hundreds as the colossal bronze door smeared their ranks into the plaza. Kar'Nash'gahar stood there, a nightmare made flesh, bellowing his bottomless rage at the Ecclesiarchical soldiers, the capital plate and the cardinal world at large. As the shock subsided and heart-thumping panic set in, the blinding hail of lasbeams left the Redacted and moved across to the greater daemon.

'Sergeant,' Occam said as the stone wall of the cathedral smoked about them.

'My lord?'

'Climb.'

'Climb?'

'For your lives,' Occam said as he backed from them.

'But my lord...'

'For the inquisitor's lighter,' the strike master said. 'The lord cardinal's barge. Some kind of craft up on the spire landing platforms. Anything that gets us away from that monstrosity. Now climb.'

As Quoda and the sergeant helped the wounded Malik up into the busy architecture of the cathedral wall, Occam followed.

Occam reached for ledges and hauled himself up through nests of stone gargoyles. Below on the plaza, the greater daemon was slashing at the ranks of cardinal world defenders with its flail, turning them into rivers of blood. The heaving, tilting plate made it impossible for the soldiers to retain formation. They flew up into the air and tracked vehicles left the ground. It was as though gravity was failing, when really the effect was being created by the freefall of the colossal plate. For Occam and the Redacted, at least, it sped up their climb and made surmounting the architecture of the cathedral exterior easier.

In the distance, the plate generatoria detonated. With the dropping capital plate now in the shadow of its higher neighbours, the rippling chain reaction of explosions lit up the dark undershell of the surrounding structures. The strike master could see that the main reactor had become a blinding flash of explosive mayhem. Silhouetted in the crackling destruction was the Slaughterlord Kar'Nash'gahar. It too had begun to climb up the walls of the cathedral. Its abyssal rage would not allow its gaoler to escape.

Occam pushed on. He could see Sergeant Hasdrubal and the sorcerer Quoda above, helping Malik up through the gargoyled architecture of the Cathedral-Primus and its main tower. Occam leapt for the ledges and sculptures. His engineered might and the servos of his armour carried him so far but the shuddering drop of the plate did the rest, carrying the strike master farther up the structure than he could have managed unaided. Latching onto crumbling stone sculptures and cloud-stained architecture he scrambled up the side of the cathedral: up, in pursuit of the Redacted; up, towards the cathedral tower tops that still descended parallel with the ragged edge of the city's surrounding plates.

Occam climbed for his life. A life that seemed worth so little in that moment. He had lost all. He had given up his ship to a daemonic entity. The Redacted were in tatters and the strike master's alliance with the Word Bearers of unholy Ghalmek replaced by a force of unnatural fury. Occam heard Kar'Nash'gahar's bellows of infernal anger and hatred rise above the screams of thousands. He felt the quake of the monstrous daemon as its bounding step took it up onto the cathedral side and its claws punched like grapnels into the thick stone of the ancient building. It flapped its ruined wings in frustration and bellowed its rage.

The strike master's climbing became increasingly wild. Hauling, scrabbling, he leaped from purchase to purchase. He quickly gained on Hasdrubal and Quoda, the pair negotiating the architecture with the broken Malik. They had made good time, however, having reached the tower's mighty steeple. Kar'Nash'gahar thundered up behind. It had almost reached him.

'Onwards!' Occam roared at his remaining legionnaires. Carcinus Quoda was heaving himself up a maintenance ladder that ran up the steeple's side, with Malik hanging off the back of his pack. Hasdrubal was holding back for his strike master but Occam called for the sergeant to keep going. Beyond the raging daemon that clawed and climbed, rumbling like a great furnace below him, Occam could hear fresh screams. These were not shrieks of horror at the sight of the daemon entity but calls of fear at the plate's sudden descent. Occam knew pain when he heard it. The lowest parts of the city plate were now sinking through the roiling clouds of acidic splendour that made up the planet's atmosphere. Lost in the colourful strata of death, the cardinal worlders of the capital plate were screaming and gargling as their flesh melted away and their lungs were turned to mush. Stone hissed as the acid did its worst and began eating through the foundations of the Cathedral-Primus itself.

'Go!' Occam called to his sergeant. He had drawn level with Hasdrubal. They could no longer see the sorcerer and Malik.

The Slaughterlord reached up for the renegade Space Marines, clawing away sections of stone. Uncoiling the great length of its flail from its spiked belt, the greater daemon slashed at the Alpha Legionnaires.

For horrible moments all Occam could hear was the shredding of stone and the thunder of rage as the flail tore through the architecture about them. Rock dust blanketed the scene of devastation until the winds whipped the cloud away. Through the destruction, he could see Hasdrubal hanging onto the shattered cathedral wall. They had reached the smashed edge of the spire landing platform some distance apart. Occam hauled himself up onto the platform.

'Sergeant,' Occam called. 'Hang on. That's an order!'

Hasdrubal hung on by his ceramite fingertips. He tried to haul himself up, the stone crumbling about him.

Suddenly Ephron Hasdrubal was gone. A mighty daemonic claw was in his place, digging deep into the stone. Encapsulated in the prison of hellish flesh, the crushed sergeant could do little and Occam could do little to save him. Another claw gripped onto the creaking edge of the platform and Kar'Nash'gahar heaved its daemon bulk up. The beast had leapt for its life and just managed to get a purchase on the edge of the platform. The strike master backed away as the abomination brought the horror of its horns and abyssal features up level with him. Its fangs were black with the fires of its ire. Its nostrils streamed burning steam with the exertion of its climb. The greater daemon's eyes burned bright for the years it had spent incarcerated in the alien Tesseraqt. Occam stared back. He was done running.

The strike master stamped down on the shattered stone of the platform. It did not take much. A single powered stomp sent cracks spreading through already loosened stone. A moment later, the daemon was gone.

Peering down past the broken stone edge, Occam watched

the silhouette of the daemon thrash away from the plate. Tumbling down, with sections of broken stone and the broken sergeant, Kar'Nash'gahar fell down through the atmospheric maelstrom, flapping the useless expanse of its shredded wings. The daemon raged and bellowed. The capital plate with all its population was vanishing into the bottomless storm of acidic hell. Occam watched as his loyal sergeant and the monstrous greater daemon followed it, until the raging storm had claimed them both.

Getting up and stumbling away from the smashed edge of the platform, Occam heard the roar of engines. An Inquisitorial lighter drifted in close. He could see Quoda in the cockpit. The craft drifted around, its ramp lowered. The strike master leaped up onto the ramp just as the upper reaches of the cathedral fell away. Occam gazed down for a few more moments as the cathedral plummeted to its doom, before entering the lighter and closing the ramp. He found Malik doubled over on the compartment floor.

'Sergeant Hasdrubal?' the former Night Lord said through pain-gritted teeth.

'No,' Occam said, shaking his helm slowly.

'Strike master,' Carcinus Quoda said across the compartment vox, bringing Occam from dark thoughts of shock and loss. The strike master hit the vox stud.

'Let's go,' Occam said finally.

'Where?' the sorcerer replied across the crackling channel. 'The Dark Apostle wasn't wrong. Where is there to go?'

'We continue as planned,' Occam the Untrue told him. 'A great deal has happened but nothing has changed.'

'How do we get off this wretched planet?' Quoda asked.

'It will take all of your talents, sorcerer,' the strike master said, 'but like all things the Alpha Legion put their mind to, it can be done.'

X

SNAKES ALIVE

The *Dissolutio Perpetua* held station over the tiny shrine world of Procul-Sanctus. Occam the Untrue stood motionless on the warped bridge of the Word Bearers daemon ship, staring out of the fanged maw of the forward lancet screen. It had been days since the Redacted had stolen a pilgrim lighter and escaped the havoc of Suspiria Proctor.

He looked down at the backwater shrine world and could only imagine the horror unfolding below.

'Dark Apostle,' Iaxor Phel said, addressing Occam. He leaned against Gorghastragar, his chin resting upon the skull-pommel of the daemon sword. 'You should really be down there, leading the daemon brotherhood of the Varga Rax in the slaughter. You should indulge yourself – especially after the betrayal of those faithless serpents.'

The entity trapped within the jagged blade of Gorghastragar glowed within the metal in both agreement and daemon hunger. Occam gave his First Acolyte a withering gaze. For several weeks now what remained of the

Redacted had been in command of the Word Bearers dae-mon ship. Pretending to be Goura Shengk and his two Word Bearers honour guard, the three Alpha Legionnaires had managed to escape Suspiria Proctor and rendezvous with the *Dissolutio Perpetua* under the premise that Occam the Untrue had betrayed them to the Angelbane. Using his potent psychic powers of manipulation, an exhausted Carcinus Quoda had managed to keep up the deception.

It had been tough going on all of them. Quoda had never had to maintain a manipulation for so long at such close quarters and the sorcerer looked haggard and drained. Vilnius Malik was recovering from his grievous wound at the hands of the Grey Knights. Occam had to do his part to present a realistic portrayal of the Dark Apostle to his own men.

Part of this had been achieved by occupying the Word Bearers of the Barbed Oath with dark service. With con-siderable Ecclesiarchy forces alerted to the presence of renegades at Suspiria Proctor and Occam unable to take the daemon ship back to Ghalmek, the strike master had unleashed Goura Shengk's Varga Rax upon several back-water shrine worlds in the outlying Tempora sub-sector.

First Acolyte Phel had been a constant irritation, press-ing his master to return to Ghalmek or avenge the Word Bearers by hunting down the Emperor's priests, opera-tives of the Inquisition or traitors of the Alpha Legion in equal measure. Occam knew ambition when he saw it. Blind ambition, at that. Phel, ignorant of the fate of Goura Shengk's former acolyte, thought that he could taste opportunity in the Dark Apostle's failure at Suspiria Proctor and ached to lead the daemon Space Marines of the Varga Rax. While the Barbed Oath boasted traitors whose flesh was still their own, Shengk's Varga Rax were daemon-afflicted to a man. For Occam, this meant deploying all of the Alpha Legion warband's skills and resources. The strike master had not just to maintain a deception that would convince rank and file Word Bearers but also the warp-sired entities that possessed them.

Occam found Host Captain Sor Vhorpall easier to work with, on account of the monstrous officer having little or no personality. The captain simply lived to lead the Varga Rax in slaughter and this Occam had indulged on Secratia IV, St Herod and now Procul-Sanctus. The shrine worlders were not indiscriminate victims of Occam's disappointment or Captain Vhorpall's rage. The strike master had spared Suspiria Proctor the wrath of Kar'Nash'gahar, Slayer of Worlds. The Ecclesiarchy still had to pay for costing Occam dearly, in their collusion with the Inquisition and the Angelbane – however unwitting.

'Clear the bridge,' Occam growled, dismissing First Acolyte Phel with an impassive sweep of his gauntlet. The strike master could feel Phel's eyes burning into his back. 'We are to be alone with our thoughts. Leave two guards.'

Phel left the bridge with the other daemon officers of the Varga Rax and a small army of cloaked cult minions manning the runebanks. Even the *Dissolutio's* sorcerer-astropath and possessed Navigator vacated the fang-lined command deck. Beyond Quoda and Vilnius Malik, only withered corpse-servitors remained, their mummified remains interfaced with their cradles and core system consoles.

'You think the xenos will come?' Quoda asked.

'He'll come,' Occam said, pulling the black cube of the Tesseraqt from his belt. 'We have what he wants. What the Lord Dominatus desires.'

'And he demands it now, fleshling,' came the ageless metallic voice of Omizhar Vohk.

Occam allowed himself a snarl of satisfaction as the skeletal metal monster stalked out from shadows in the corner of the command deck. Vohk seemed to use the depths of such darkness to move from one place and moment to the next.

'You took your time, xenos,' Malik spat as the hunched Vohk stomped out onto the bridge, his footfalls heavy on the deck, the wicked metal digits of a claw extended.

'The Tesseraqt,' the creature demanded.

Occam nodded and both Quoda and Malik brought their plasma guns up. They were not the fine specimens of alien engineering they had left behind on the *Iota-Æternus* but warped and unreliable weapons taken from the Word Bearers armoury. They glowed and pulsed with an unhealthy energy while their scorched muzzles opened wide like jaws in the morphed semblances of dog-like daemons. Their presentation was still enough to stop the alien in his tracks. His optic glowed intensely at the black cube in Occam's hand.

'We do not have time for games, fleshling,' Omizhar Vohk said.

'The Alpha Legion play the long game,' Occam told him. 'For us, there is always time.' He stepped forward angrily and landed a brutal kick on the alien. Stamping the sole of his armoured boot into the spindly thing's midriff, Occam broke Vohk's spine and sent the alien clattering back across a set of consoles. As the strike master moved forward, Vohk got back to his feet, his metal spine repairing itself before Occam's very eyes. The act was impressive and the strike master nodded his approval. The creature's optic blazed green with cold alien fury.

Malik and the sorcerer closed in with their humming plasma guns while Occam stormed on. Jumping down from the other side of the console bank he seized the skeletal menace and heaved the weight of his metal form off the deck, smashing him back into the runebanks lining the bridge wall. Occam brought the Tesseraqt back in his other fist.

'You want your precious artefact, do you, xenos? I don't think I'll ever be convinced that you didn't have something to do with the Angelbane reappearing at Suspiria Proctor.'

'I did not,' Omizhar Vohk told him.

'You serve your master well, xenos,' Occam said, 'and if he is who I think he is then telling me is more than your miserable existence would be worth.'

'You think that the Lord Dominatus is–' Vohk began.

'I know he is,' the strike master said.

'He is not.'

'Spoken like a true servant of the true Legion,' Occam said. 'I would expect no less of you. Of him.'

The gaping jaw-barrels of Malik's and the sorcerer's plasma guns moved in close to the alien's gaunt metal face as Occam held him against the wall.

'What do you want?' Omizhar Vohk said at the prospect of his skull being melted from his shoulders.

'I want you to take me to our leader,' Occam said, 'whereupon I shall turn over his prize personally.'

'Impossible,' Vohk told him. He flashed the green of his optic about the bridge of the *Dissolutio Perpetua* and specifically at the sorcerer Quoda. 'Just as I could not venture into the riftspace of the Maelstrom, this is a place you cannot go.'

'We'll risk it,' Occam the Untrue determined. He dropped the Tesseraqt on the deck and hovered an armoured boot over it. 'And so will you. We have all sacrificed so much for this cube and the Lord Dominatus' wishes that we might as well sacrifice a little more.'

'Don't,' Omizhar Vohk said in a metallic hiss.

'Make me, xenos.'

'Why is this so important to you?' Vohk asked.

'Because this is a test to be passed,' Occam told him. 'Because, like all in my Legion, I have questions that demand answers. Because if the Lord Dominatus is who I believe him to be, then he is the living answer to all such questions and like me, serves the God-Emperor still. Take your pick, xenos.'

With a clatter, Omizhar Vohk seemed to sag.

'Then however unadvised this course of action,' the alien said, his metallic hiss resigned, 'I shall honour our arrangement and take you to your Lord Dominatus.'

'Where is he?' Occam demanded.

Omizhar Vohk told him.

Releasing the alien, the strike master picked up the Tesseraqt and moved over to a bridge console. Quoda and Malik still kept their plasma guns on the xenos. Occam punched in a sequence of studs, opening a vox-channel.

'Send word to First Acolyte Phel,' Occam commanded. 'He is to return with Captain Vhorpall and the Varga Rax. We are done with the shrine world. Also, have the Navigator attend us on the bridge and set a course for the Galactic Core.'

It was like nowhere Occam had ever seen. The strike master had operated in the various segmentums of the

Imperium, across alien empires and even the riftspace of warp storms. The Galactic Core had a strangeness all of its own. Whereas the empires of galactic species had their own characters and the Maelstrom was perversity incarnate, the Core was like the end of the universe. It was where the void was lost and stars – impossibly ancient – went to die.

The *Dissolutio Perpetua* had entered the immaterium and had plunged on further towards the Core than the daemon ship's twisted Navigator had ever travelled. Further than the details of his bloodstained maps showed, into regions without names and zones unknown. When the daemon ship had gone as far as it possibly could, it dropped out of the warp without warning. When Occam, still masquerading as an imperious Goura Shengk, demanded an explanation, the Navigator had nothing for him but the insistence that the warp was fading, that it was no longer with them – that they had reached the shores of the Sea of Souls.

Pushing on, with the *Dissolutio*'s sub-light engines roaring through the ship, the daemon vessel entered a realm of light. Here the darkness of the void shrank away and crowded clusters of ancient stars stained everything with a glowing light. Everywhere, stars burned their last and fed upon one another. Dust and debris cloaked the Core while systems, old beyond reckoning and unvisited by all but the most enduring of races, were stellar carousels of primeval catastrophe. Planets were little more than shattered remnants, boasting but the ash and dust of long perished civilisations.

It was here, in this barren place of blinding desolation where time had run its course, that Omizhar Vohk insisted the Lord Dominatus could be found. So Occam pushed on. He pushed the Redacted on. He pushed the Word Bearers, enslaved to his deception, on, on and on.

Here they found worlds long dead. They encountered the ruins of once civilised worlds and the same structures over and over again. Rocky moons, radioactive ghost worlds and the cracked shells of planets that had suffered some ancient, apocalyptic fate – all boasting the same strange alien architecture. Colossal pylons, like bristling nests of needles reaching up from the surface of planets, seemed to afflict the worlds of the Core. The *Dissolutio Perpetua* found them everywhere as the daemon ship moved from system to system, working its way towards the sterile centre of the galaxy. Some were impossibly old, while others appeared to be fairly recent constructions amidst the dereliction of dead worlds.

Quoda, between periods of feverish malaise, had hypothesised that the pylons were of ancient alien origin and said he had seen them on the worlds of the Cadian Gate in the Eye of Terror. They appeared to have a calming effect on the warp but here in the Galactic Core and in such concentration, they nullified the warp entirely – making immaterial travel and astropathic communication impossible. When Occam questioned Vohk about the pylons the alien said little but that it was a project beyond human supremacy that had been started by ancient races long ago and continued even to this day. The strike master noted that corruption was being driven from the daemon Word Bearers and the sorcerer Quoda could barely call on a fraction of his powers.

All but Malik, Omizhar Vohk and the strike master suffered.

The warp was almost gone. It took all of Quoda's effort to maintain his manipulations and even the blurred semblance of the legionnaires' Word Bearers appearance. This didn't seem to matter. The Word Bearers themselves were changing. They suffered torments both physical and spiritual. All but cut off from the pollution of the warp, the warped brothers of the Varga Rax were driven from their daemons. Their bones untwisted, their daemon brawn shrank and their minds achieved an agonising clarity. Undergoing such dreadful torture and disorientation, Phel, Captain Vhorpall and the brotherhood of the Barbed Oath saw in Occam the Untrue what they expected to see: their Dark Apostle – strong, unswerving and intent upon oblivion.

The possessed cultists that manned the daemon ship went mad without the comfort of their polluting entities. This was nothing compared to the sufferings of the daemon ship itself. So far from the ritual nourishment of Unholy Ghalmek, the Maelstrom's boon or even Imperial space – where the warp was but a thin veil away – the *Dissolutio Perpetua* underwent a monstrous exorcism. Like the Word Bearers and its crew, it became largely separated from that which had corrupted it. The infernal beast that squirmed within its superstructure, roared through the ship's gunfire and warped the architecture to reflect its monstrous will, was now but a ghost of itself. A thing that whimpered in the static of voxmitters and haunted the darkness of the dungeon decks. It retracted the fangs that framed lancet screens, bulkheads and blast doors. It bled foul ichor that flooded the keel, frothed and rose periodically up through the lower deck mesh like a tidal misery.

'How much more do you think they can take?' Malik

asked his strike master on the bridge. They listened to the moaning of Word Bearers, the insanity of their cultist crew and the dread suffering of the daemon ship about them.

'Do we care?' Occam said, staring out into the blinding light of stellar death flooding in through the lancet screens.

'What about him?' Malik pressed, indicating the feverish Quoda, who sat on the deck, leaning his pauldron against the wall.

'He's Alpha Legion,' Occam said, his voice like steel. Omizhar Vohk gave a sneer of contempt from the shadows.

'You are flesh,' the alien told them, 'and you are weak.'

The strike master walked dangerously towards the xenos abomination as it skulked in the shadows.

'How long do you think you'll last if I shoot you from our torpedo tubes into one of these stars?' Occam put to him.

Omizhar Vohk moved into the brilliance flooding the bridge and became a silhouette against the lancet screens.

'My brothers grow tired and I am impatient, xenos,' Occam told him, backing the creature up to the armoured plas. 'How much further? Where is the Lord Dominatus?'

'He's been with us for a while,' the alien told him, tapping a metal knuckle against the glass. Occam peered out into the blinding light.

'Filters,' the strike master ordered. The warped servitors and cultist crew had become useless in the warpless intensity of the Core. Malik pulled one of them back from where it was lying wasted across a console and manually altered the screen filters. As the light was dialled back, Occam saw the hazy outline of a vessel some way distant but running parallel to their course. Occam looked at Omizhar Vohk. The alien pointed to starboard. Walking across the bridge, Occam joined Malik in staring out of the screen on the other side of the command deck. She was a light cruiser with distinctive lines and piratical augmentations.

'I know that ship,' Malik told him. 'I've been aboard her. Reznor even did some work on her. She's the *Sigma Sophistra*, flagship of The Chain Unbroken. That's Naetrix Krayt's ship. I'd bet my life on it.'

Occam turned back towards Omizhar Vohk.

'Your brothers come from far and wide to serve the Lord Dominatus,' the alien said in his metallic hiss. 'These vessels have been given instructions to escort us in.'

'In?' Occam said. 'Where?'

The alien gestured forward. Through the glare of several nearby stars, raging brilliantly in their death throes, Occam could make out the hazy outline of a planet.

'Filters,' he said again and Malik cycled further filters across the lancet screens. There, before the daemon ship and its Alpha Legion escorts, and almost invisible in the combined glare of three suns, was a planet. It roasted in radioactive glory and appeared urchin-like, its cracked and baked surface covered in needle-like pylons across its entire surface.

'Where are we?' Occam demanded.

'Royal Belphagar,' Omizhar Vohk told him. 'One of the earliest home worlds of my race. Once, my own home world. Now it is but a shell of ancient glories, used by your Lord Dominatus as a base for his operations. Come, he awaits both you and his prize. Your army brothers shall take us in.'

Krayt's pirate ships escorted the *Dissolutio Perpetua* towards a chasmic crack in the planet's surface about the equator. With ancient pylons rising up above them the daemon ship plunged slowly into the planet. Under Krayt's guns the daemon ship glided silently down through the abyssal crack with the rocky mantle of the planet passing on either side.

Quoda groaned as they passed within the planet and the intensified influence of the surface pylons. He could no longer exercise his powers of manipulation and the three members of the Redacted now appeared to all in the glory of their scaled plate and legionary colours. The deck servitors and cultist crew cared little for the change; they appeared barely aware of it.

Occam expected to find cavernous darkness within the planet but was surprised to see light ahead. Royal Belphagar was no ordinary planet. Incredibly old and adapted with the ancient and powerful technologies of some elder race, the world was full of surprises. As the daemon ship moved slowly inside the planet, Occam stared out of the lancet screens in silent wonder. It was a world of strange reversals. The planet was hollow. While its radiation-baked shell had been bare but for thousands of alien pylons, the interior of the hollow planet boasted cities, preserved in silent perfection. The ancient civilisation that made the planet interior their home were long gone, however, and the cityscape of alien monuments, black pyramids and grand architecture had the feeling of a planetary tomb buried deep below the ground.

Suspended in the centre of the hollow space raged the planet's metal core. It sat there like some kind of sun, held in place by gravitational technologies advanced and ancient. It swirled and rotated, glowing like an abandoned furnace that cast the xenos cityscape in the grim red light of a dying fire. Cast in silhouette against the core and holding station far above the cityscape, Occam saw a flotilla of vessels. They were all fast and stealthy specimens, frigates, armed freighters and light cruisers favoured by the Alpha Legion for their dread work. Some no doubt belonged to Captain Krayt's The Chain Unbroken, while others were pledged in service to other Alpha Legion warbands, units and harrowmasters.

Slowly, the Alpha Legion escorts brought the *Dissolutio Perpetua* in line with the flat top of a colossal black pyramid. It seemed clear from the slowing craft that the daemon ship was to hold station there.

'What now, xenos?' Occam said, but ominously the skeletal alien had gone – once more disappearing into the shadows and making use of his strange teleportation technology. Occam cursed under his breath before turning to Vilnius Malik. 'Phel? Captain Vhorpall? The Word Bearers?'

'The cultist crew are afflicted. I've secured the Word Bearers on their temple decks as ordered,' the former Night Lord told him. 'They are severely weakened by the effect of this alien technology and are indulging in their rancid rituals. They barely know where they are, let alone where we are.'

'I'm not sure even *we* know where we are,' Occam said, 'but let us do what we came here to do. Sorcerer, are you with us?'

'For the Emperor...' Carcinus Quoda managed, pushing himself up unsteadily from the deck.

'Aye,' Malik said, handing out Word Bearers plasma guns, wicked blades, melta bombs and daemon-sculpted bolt pistols to Quoda and the strike master.

'For the Emperor,' Occam echoed, nodding before leading what remained of the Redacted off the command deck and down to the main airlock.

ψ

THE REPTILIAN BRAIN

Stepping off the daemon ship and onto the flat plaza decorating the top of the pyramid, Occam became immediately aware of something strange in his environment. It wasn't the atmosphere or temperature, which his plate registered as within acceptable parameters. It was the gravity.

The pyramid was impossibly tall and commanded an incredible view of the ancient but empty cityscape that sprawled and curved across the interior of the globe. It was crafted of a type of black stone with which Occam was unfamiliar and was covered in green glowing lines in a pattern like some kind of alien circuit. It reminded the strike master of the Tesseraqt.

Moving was strange at first. Occam led Quoda and Malik across the plaza and down the pyramid side, where a set of black steps took them into the city and towards a grand ceremonial reception area. Ornamental pits flanked the steps, punctuating the Redacted's progress on either side. It seemed that everything had been reversed within the hollow planet. Cities clung to the planet interior rather than its outer shell, with towers and looming monuments pointing vertiginously up towards the suspended core. The core established a gravitational pull that was itself a reversal of what Occam expected. His steps did not have the reassuring thud of gravity dragging him down. He felt that if he slipped down one of the ornamental pits he would not fall far – no further than he could ordinarily jump in his powered plate. If he were to leap from the steps, however, he feared that he might not return to solid ground but instead fall upwards towards the glowing planetary core. It was disorientating in the extreme.

Further down the side of the pyramid, the exertion took its toll on Quoda and the sorcerer stumbled, forcing Malik to make a grab for him. Righting himself, Quoda pushed on, insisting that he was all right. As Malik and Occam exchanged glances, the legionnaire noticed something beyond and indicated to his strike master. The ancient city was silent and empty, but there was movement ahead, figures in plate working their way up the steps to meet them. Occam's gauntlets creaked as he held his plasma gun at the ready. Ready for anything. Ready for everything.

As the Redacted moved down to meet the oncomers, he saw that they were garbed in the colours of the Alpha Legion. This should have put Occam at ease, yet it didn't. With traitors like the Word Bearers back on the ship, Occam knew what he was getting. He understood their deviance. All traitors and renegades were predictable in their own ways. With the Alpha Legion, however, anything was possible.

The legionnaires didn't show any obvious signs of outward corruption. As Occam closed with them, they stood aside on the steps to create an armed escort. If the detail of their plate was anything to go by the group appeared to be made up of legionnaires from different warbands. An officer in black plate, the faint coils of serpentine patterning and a helm boasting a bulbous targeting optic, came forward.

'You are of the Legion but unknown to us,' the officer said in a thick accent. 'What is your business here?'

'I am Occam, strike master of the Redacted,' Occam returned. 'I seek an audience with the Lord Dominatus. I have travelled far to meet with him and have fought unknowingly in his service. I would fight knowingly, but for questions that remain unanswered.'

'And you would have the Lord Dominatus answer your questions?' the officer asked.

'I would have the Lord Dominatus act in accordance with his wisdom and conscience,' Occam said.

'You will not need your weapons,' the officer said, gesturing to the plasma gun pulled in close to Occam's midriff – its muzzle wavering unconsciously from one legionnaire to another. The armed escort stepped forth to take the plasma guns and slip bolt pistols from holsters but the Redacted suddenly stiffened, Occam and Malik bringing their plasma guns up level with their optics. While the strike master covered the officer and the front, Malik swept the muzzle of his weapon around the back. A fatigued Quoda tried to lift his weapon from where he loosely held it at his hip but failed.

The escort seemed unconcerned. The red dots of targeters drifted across the Redacted's plate from legionnaires hidden in surrounding structures.

'You are Alpha Legion, yes?' Occam put to the officer.

'As are you,' the legionnaire said, burning into the strike master with his bulbous targeter.

'Then, brother, you know that only a fool would give up his weapons right now,' Occam said, 'and none of us here are fools.'

The officer seemed to consider Occam's argument before nodding his helm at the flanking escort and turning to lead the Redacted down the side of the pyramid.

At the bottom of the structure, the escort peeled off and the officer led Occam and his legionnaires through the strange alien architecture and sculptures of a reception plaza. Ancient tombs and monuments reared up, framing the hollow sky with jagged black stone. Everything was saturated in a queasy red and green. Green circuits ran through the black stone, the illumination from which mixed horribly with the furnace-glow of the suspended molten core. The tops of alien temples burned with a green phosphorescence while towering monoliths of midnight stone projected stabilising beams of green energy.

Occam picked out the shapes of Alpha Legionnaires manning sentry posts and criss-crossing the reception plaza with the red beams of targets that never left the Redacted. It was difficult to estimate the numbers encamped here in the hollowed centre of a dead world. Gunships lifted off from dark quads and ran legionnaires, operatives and materiel between the stationed flotilla of Alpha Legion vessels and the camp. A smaller pyramid forming the rear of the reception plaza opened, bleeding green light into the open space. The towering black throne that formed the centrepiece of the reception plaza became framed in the alien luminescence and a procession of silhouettes proceeded from the opening. Occam thought that he could make out robed cultists, Alpha Legion renegades in powered plate and the freakish shapes of varied xenos operatives.

When they had left, another figure filled the opening, a towering black shape. His outline was suggestive of ornate plate while the nodes of his pack were crafted into a pair of serpents, facing and spitting at one another across a fanged helm. He walked towards the Redacted, half obscured by the throne. The legionary colours of his plate were so deep that Occam thought him lost in them and a luxurious cloak of glittering scale slithered behind him.

As the tall figure walked up and around the spiral steps of the elevated throne, the Alpha Legion officer went down on one knee. Legionnaires at sentry posts about the reception plaza did the same. Occam turned to Malik and nodded. The pair lowered their plasma guns and took a knee also. The withered Quoda needed little persuading to do the same.

As the figure sat in the looming throne, looking down on the plaza, the officer stood.

'My Lord Dominatus,' he proclaimed. 'Newcomers have arrived without clearance or invitation. Occam, strike master of the Redacted, begs you for an audience.'

'That is not strictly true, my lord,' Occam called, getting up off his knee. Malik and Quoda followed suit. 'We have been invited.'

'By who?' the Lord Dominatus called back, his commanding voice cutting through the alien architecture of the plaza like a blade. It carried the wisdom of age with the enthusiasm of relentless youth. 'For it was not me. You are one of few to have made it here without guidance.'

'I fought for the Angelbane,' Occam said, 'exterminating

the Emperor's servants about the borders of the Maelstrom in your name.'

'A worthy cause,' the Lord Dominatus said. 'And indeed I did set the one known as the Angelbane to such service. I know not those he recruited in turn. Where is the Angelbane now?'

'Dead, my lord,' Occam said, honestly. 'By my hand but with your mission accomplished.'

'Some might call that treachery...'

'And some necessary,' Occam returned. 'I fear he served himself as much as he did your interests, my lord.'

'And you killed him for me?' the Lord Dominatus said. 'Only a member of the Alpha Legion could claim to prove his loyalty by stabbing his brother in the back.'

'He was a serpent whose mind had been baked in the heat of battle, my lord,' Occam told him. 'Striking out at all around him, friend and foe. I killed him because I had to.'

'He was a tool I held at arm's length,' the Lord Dominatus said, 'where his talents were employed at their best. Now you have come here, uninvited and expect me to take you into my trust?'

'We fight for the same thing, Lord Dominatus,' Occam said. 'Something madmen like Quetzel Carthach and many of our fallen brothers could barely comprehend.'

'And what is that?' the Lord Dominatus asked, getting up out of his throne.

'We fight for the Emperor,' Occam said. 'I for always and you still. For his blood runs through your veins and you make his strength your own.'

'A bold claim for both of us,' the Lord Dominatus said, dropping off the elevated throne and landing with cat-like grace in his glorious plate. The black stone cracked about the impact of his boots. 'Who do you think I am?'

'I hope,' the strike master confessed, 'and I fear that you are father to an orphaned Legion. That you are the son of a god and humanity's last chance for survival.'

The Lord Dominatus approached slowly. He leant in to share a private confidence with Occam but the intensity of his presence made the strike master take a step back.

'I have lived long,' the Lord Dominatus told him, 'and I have heard many such stories in my time. I wish I was the one you speak of. For the good of the Emperor, his Legion and his people. But I am not.'

'You are the second son,' Occam insisted. 'You have to be. You are the Omega, and we the Alpha. The end and a new beginning. You can take us out of the shadows and into the light of the Emperor's mercy. You hide here in the dead heart of an empire that wants to live. We can watch it fall to the fires of oblivion or wither and rot on the vine, but if we act – together, as one Legion – we can save it. Through us it can bloom again and usher in a second Golden Age.'

'What you talk of cannot be done,' the Lord Dominatus said savagely.

'What is the alternative?' Occam demanded. 'Here you sit on your hollow throne, gathering idle sons and launching proxy wars through those who actually dare to believe in you. Make the Legion your own once more. Drag it back out from the darkness and give those who have lost their way direction. Unite us. Lead us, lord primarch.'

'He's right,' a voice proceeded from the shadows. 'What you speak of cannot be done. At least, not by the Lord Dominatus...'

ω

OUROBOROS

Occam recognised the voice.

Its metallic hiss belonged to Omizhar Vohk. Both Occam and the Lord Dominatus stared about the plaza.

'Xenos?' Occam said, but the alien was one with the darkness.

'Your hope does not reside in this living lie,' Vohk said. 'This thing exists only for death. It is oblivion incarnate. An end to all things, natural and otherwise.'

The Lord Dominatus peered about the plaza and then across at the legionnaires manning their posts.

'So, you come all this way to play games with me,' he told Occam, producing a scowl of confusion from the strike master. The Lord Dominatus gave a signal and the legionnaires fell in, searching the plaza and probing the shadows with their boltguns. 'You will regret that.'

'Lord primarch, no, I would–'

'This thing is not your galactic prince,' Vohk went on, his metallic voice coming from everywhere at once. 'No mere primarch stands before you. This creature strides the void. It feasts upon the stars, leaving the sky in deepest darkness. It lives deception as you breathe air. Transcendent. Timeless. Vampiric. The ghostly reflection of blinding doom in a shattered mirror.'

'Enough of this,' the Lord Dominatus roared, clearly infuriated at the accusations. 'Have your operative show yourself.'

'*My* operative?' Occam marvelled. 'But Omizhar Vohk works for you. He pledged us to your service and brought us to this dread place.'

'Omizhar Vohk…' the Lord Dominatus said, stomping about the plaza and looking for the xenos. As he did, more legionnaires poured out of the entrance of the small pyramid to join the search. 'Omizhar Vohk, I know that name.'

'As I know yours, star god,' Vohk said. 'Mephet'ran… the Deceiver.'

'I thought I had rid this world of your miserable kind,' the Lord Dominatus said.

'Not quite,' Omizhar Vohk said. 'I have returned, Deceiver. To ensure the survival of my dynasty and avenge the lifeless alloy of my kindred. To undo what has been done and bring this realm of lies crashing down into the dust.'

'Of course,' the Lord Dominatus said. 'Omizhar Vohk. The techno-sorcerer. You think you can imprison a god? I am shard-born. I am of the Deceiver. Did you think that I would not get free? That there wouldn't be consequences? I am no weapon to be wielded by the lesser races of the galaxy. How does it feel, techno-sorcerer, to have such a weapon turned back upon your people? They might have been obliterated by my hand but it was you,

Omizhar Vohk, who unleashed me upon the galaxy. Do not forget that. Never forget that.'

'I appeal to every mortal thing on this planet,' Omizhar Vohk said. 'Everything living and breathing. Of flesh loyal or polluted. This abomination will end us all. The havoc it has sown through manipulation of the renegade Legions is merely the beginning. It means to extend the ancient technologies of my race out beyond the Galactic Core and cut you off from your immaterial realm. The Sea of Souls will dry up, carrying no more your vessels or messages to distant worlds. Your gifted will no longer be able to draw upon their powers or the afflicted achieve communion with entities unclean. Indeed, the storms such beings called home will be swallowed by silence. Destroy this thing before the Deceiver feasts upon the souls of your people as he has done mine.'

Occam the Untrue stared up at the Lord Dominatus.

'Kill the interlopers!' the Lord Dominatus snarled to his own legionnaires.

Occam felt the hesitation. The Alpha Legion renegades, all pledged in service to the Lord Dominatus, had guarded his hollow planetary stronghold. They had operated out of the Galactic Core. They had helped him carry out his manipulations and puppetry far beyond. Listening to the voice of Omizhar Vohk, momentary doubt had crept into their hearts and minds. No less than his legionary brothers, Occam had to face the fact that he too had been caught up in the Deceiver's lies and Omizhar Vohk's machine vengeance.

'Down!' Occam called, pushing a feverish Quoda behind a sculpture just moments before a blasting stream of Alpha Legion boltfire tore across the plaza. Malik spun around and blazed several orbs of plasma back at the attacking legionnaires, turning one into bubbling slag and scorching a second.

'No,' Occam called to the former Night Lord. 'We must unmask that thing.'

Using the alien architecture for cover and with bolt-mangled black stone shredding all about him, the strike master fired upon the Lord Dominatus. Occam blasted sphere after raging sphere of superheated plasma at the figure in ornate plate. The Lord Dominatus roared in pain and fury. Occam pumped at the trigger, sending continual plasma shots at the Lord Dominatus, soon joined by Malik and Quoda. All the while architecture shattered about them as boltfire criss-crossed the plaza from Alpha Legion sentries.

The Lord Dominatus bellowed, holding out his gauntlets to deflect the plasma. Spheres of crackling energy blazed into his plate left and right, producing howls of monstrous anguish from the target. As his hands melted away and his cloak caught fire, the Lord Dominatus turned into a raging inferno. Occam's hydrogen flask ran dry and he dropped the plasma gun, instead snatching a melta bomb from his belt. Cranking the grenade, he let it fly, and it detonated as it struck the Lord Dominatus. Instead of vaporising, however, he blazed into brilliance, transforming into a tornado of white flame.

The shockwave knocked Occam back and put a swift end to the boltfire aimed his way. The column reached upwards, twining and turning in fury before crackling and raging in contact with the agitated surface of the planetary core.

Occam backed from the manifesting star god. Within the

tornado of raw elemental power, he could see a towering, spindly nightmare of glorious horn, claw and perfect limb. Like a thundering angel of destruction it whirled gracefully within the storm, its face a mask of alien ferocity.

The force of the star god's storm began to tear up the black stone of the floor about it. Ancient structures were demolished and sky-scraping monuments shattered to join a secondary storm of black rubble and chunks of debris that orbited the Deceiver.

Malik grabbed Occam and pulled him back out of the path of a smashed statue that had been ripped up next to him. Quoda was thrown aside by a stream of rubble that crumpled his plate but the sorcerer managed to get back to his feet and stumble through the storm back towards his strike master.

'We've got to go!' Malik called through the cyclone.

'No,' Occam roared. 'This thing has to be destroyed.'

Moving back across the plaza through the high winds and rattle of debris across their plate, the Redacted retreated. Occam adjusted his vox to an open channel.

'All legionnaires, all legionnaires,' Occam called across the channel. 'This is Strike Master Occam of the Redacted. We have been deceived. This alien entity has fooled us all, brothers. It has used us and made a mockery of our Legion's honourable name. But the Alpha Legion adapts. The hydra strikes with many heads. Let us turn the monstrous fury of our collective upon this heathen god. Hit it with everything you've got. For Alpharius! For the Emperor! For the Legion!'

As Occam stumbled back towards the steps of the colossal black pyramid, he passed the Alpha Legion officer and several renegades taking cover behind a fallen monument.

With the bulbous targeter of his helm trained upon the whirling storm, the officer and his legionnaires emptied their boltguns at the star god. Legionnaires in surrounding towers pumped Stalker rounds into the maelstrom before jumping down from their positions as the storm tore through their structures. Bright flashes bloomed about the star god as heavy weapons legionnaires fired their missile launchers into the swirling brilliance, but the storm of the Deceiver swallowed it all.

'Unleash the Word Bearers,' Occam called, slapping Malik on the pauldron.

'They'll want to kill us all,' the former Night Lord said.

'We're going to need their rage,' Occam told him, pushing Malik up the steps towards the *Dissolutio Perpetua*, which rocked in station above the pyramid in the swell of the storm. 'We need everyone.'

More blossoms of flame erupted about the star god's swirling havoc as heavy weapons legionnaires launched missile after missile into the alien entity. Occam launched another melta bomb at the storm, only to have the vaporising flash simply assimilated into its brilliance and fury. Surrounding the Deceiver, Alpha Legion renegades emerged from the cover of ancient tombs and techno-mausolea to unleash their weaponry upon the star god. The strike master could see the flash of barrels as legionnaires, unified in their abhorrence of the alien creature and their desire for vengeance, pumped bolt-round after bolt-round into the furious thing.

The star god's column of white fire began to swirl about like loosening rope. The destruction ploughed through the ancient structures of Royal Belphagar, tearing through temples, tombs and monuments. Above, the energy maelstrom crackled across the surface of the molten core, drawing some of the orb's own fury down into itself. Swirling around, the column cut through the flotilla of Alpha Legion vessels stationed there. Several frigates were sheared in two, while a light cruiser was plunged straight into the fiery core.

Other vessels were flung away, tumbling strangely through the gravitational reversals to crash and detonate spectacularly across the cityscape. One demolished one of the colossal temple nodes that projected a stabilising beam of green energy up into the planetary core. As the thick beam stuttered and died, the core began to tremble.

Gravitational reversals began to tear through the city-scape and Occam could feel the black pyramid shaking beneath his boots. It was as if the whole planet were shaking itself apart. Beyond the apocalyptic boom of ancient buildings collapsing, Occam could detect the distant thunder of a similar destruction on the planet surface. The quakes had set in motion a chain reaction of toppling pylons, the thin needles cracking and falling over – only to strike several more structures in the cluster.

Occam looked up the pyramid at the *Dissolutio Perpetua* and the Alpha Legion light cruiser flanking it.

'*Sigma Sophistra*,' he voxed across the open channel, 'this is Strike Master Occam on the ground. Concentrate your fire on the target – point blank. Legionnaires expendable, I repeat. Dump everything you have on that monstrosity.'

Occam pulled the sorcerer Quoda back up the steps of the pyramid.

'All legionnaires receiving,' the strike master called across the vox. 'Pull back. Fire incoming.'

The broadside came faster than any of them were

expecting. Naetrix Krayt had ordered his starboard gun crews level their cannon fire at the swirling brilliance carving a path of devastation through the city. The sound was ear-splitting, even within Occam's helm. When the cannonfire hit the city, it felt as if the world were ending. Massive explosions ripped through the buildings, blasting dust, darkness and debris outwards in a wave that took the strike master off his feet, further up the steps of the pyramid.

As the murk cleared, Occam could see that the devastation had knocked out the swirling tornado of brilliance. A tall figure stalked through the destruction. Lithe, otherworldly, lethal. It appeared to be some kind of alien angel. Uncaring and monstrously powerful. It had played its games, meddling in the affairs of mortals, drawing superhuman renegades of the Alpha Legion to do its bidding. Now it seemed to have grown tired of its manipulations and wished only to end the cold beauty of its masquerade. It desired obliteration for all that it had created.

Occam heard the bark of boltguns in the drifting dust. The Alpha Legion were bringing destruction to the xenos monstrosity that had fooled them. The thing that had pretended to be their galactic prince, their warlord, their genic sire. Missiles rocketed out from cover while the thick beams of lascannons cut through the obscurity. Boltguns flashed in a closing cordon.

'End it, brothers,' Occam ordered, getting back to his feet, drawing his bolt pistol and adding his fury to the onslaught. 'We are first among equals. We are the last thing our foes will see. We are the cure for the galaxy's many ills. Send this thing back to oblivion. It thinks that it is a god, but the blood of the one, true God runs through our veins. Let it not fail us in the face of enemies unnatural and ancient. For we were engineered to bring death to such monsters.'

The star god strode through the murk and havoc – impassive and untouched. It narrowed its alien eyes at the oncoming hail of bolt-rounds, blinking them into flaring trails of obliteration before they reached the alabaster brilliance of its unflesh. About the abomination, reality seemed to warp and wrinkle. It snarled at legionnaires shooting from cover, turning the ground beneath the renegades and the shattered sections of stone they hid behind into liquid unreality. As demolished buildings and toppled columns sank into the stone floor, legionnaires flailed and splashed below the surface. The star god walked on through the desolation, allowing the ground to solidify once more about the trapped renegades.

Waving the perfection of its alien claws at oncoming grenades it made them detonate harmlessly in the air. Fat beams of energy from lascannons threatened to cut the creature in two, but it phased in and out of reality, passing out of their path, allowing them on through the dust-laden air. Missiles surged away from heavy weapons legionnaires stepping out from cover. Holding its palm flat out before it, the star god arrested the progress of the missiles and forced the weapons back towards their launchers. Detonating as they re-entered their weapons, the missiles blew the legionnaires who had fired them to pieces.

Reaching out with its claws and grasping for open space, the star god seized Alpha Legionnaires from where they were taking cover and reloading. Snatching them one by one, the creature used its brutal powers of telekinesis to drag the renegades through the air towards itself. Some smashed through the derelict structures with a bloody splatter. Others were thrown into each other at sickening speed, their broken armoured forms then flung away.

A stamp of the star god's foot on the ground sent a ripple through reality, knocking the closing attackers out of cover. With a searing gaze of annihilation, the Deceiver turned legionnaire after legionnaire to clouds of ash that tore away to join the rising maelstrom that encircled the pyramid. Whatever the blinding brilliance of the creature's eyes fell upon died. Nothing could stop it. The whirling storm of shattered stone and dust became stained with blood and the ghostly stream of souls upon which the star god gorged.

'*Sigma Sophistra,*' Occam called across the vox as the legionnaires fighting below died in their droves. 'Fire again. Everything on our position.'

The star god had not forgotten about the vessel stationed above them. While a hurricane of shattered black stone, green crackling energies and dust encircled the colossal pyramid, it began to rain within the deathly calm at the storm's centre. All Occam could hear across the vox-channel were the screams of the afflicted. He ducked down as he realised what it was. The alien abomination had fixed its gaze upon the *Sigma Sophistra*. In the reality-bending sights of the star god the vessel was melting, turning rapidly into a deluge of liquid metal falling from the sky and hammering Occam to his knees.

Everything was unfolding obliteration. About the star god and the pyramid the unnatural storm raged. Beyond, enormous cracks felt their way through the cityscape. Buildings collapsed and monoliths toppled in vaulting clouds of dust. The planetary core, suspended far above

Occam's head, was losing stability. It raged and spat, while its wobbling rotation tore with gravitational insistence at the hollow planet. Sections of surface began to fall through, creating colossal holes and tears in Royal Belphagar. The towering pylons on the surface were toppling over and smashing, and those surrounding the opening chasms were falling through the openings.

Occam felt quakes through the pyramid superstructure. The star god had followed him. The strike master fell back on the crumbling steps and peered up through the last drizzle of the *Sigma Sophistra*. The star god stood above him, its face a sneering mask of absolute supremacy. Being so close to the thing made Occam's plate vibrate, his blood course and bones burn. He felt the absolute emptiness of the thing, its hunger for souls and the elemental untruth of its existence. *Deceiver*. It had deceived them all.

Occam's mind raced with the being's insatiable need. He felt the last, dark days of the galaxy come to pass. Pylons erected everywhere: bringing the nullifying deadness of the Galactic Core, like a growing blot, to all corners of the Imperium. The warp and its polluted riftspace of raging storms vanquished. The fragmentation of humanity – a single, vast empire plunged once more into isolated civilisations, each one cut off and destroyed by the Deceiver. Billions upon billions, human and alien alike, marched into the soul forges of the abomination. With their passing, the stars of the galaxy were extinguished one after another by the gluttonous star god. Then, nothing. An obliterated absence – for the thing could not deny its eternal desires.

The sorcerer Quoda had been experiencing much the same and threw himself at the star god. The creature reacted with revulsion at the psyker's furious approach and with a cruel splaying of a clawed hand, sent the sorcerer bouncing back across the stone steps of the black pyramid.

Occam yanked furiously on the trigger of his pistol, blasting bolt after bolt up into the thing. With every impact, the Deceiver changed. At once it was a ghostly apparition allowing the shell to rocket straight through. Then it became the black stone of its surroundings, a bolt ricocheting off its solid surface. A sudden silvery liquid of its form swallowed the next bolt while the returning brilliance of its perfect skin slowed another and another to spinning shells in front of the star god, which it flicked away with contempt.

Everything was the swirling boom of destruction, but about the Deceiver and Occam was only closing darkness. Occam knew he was about to die. Snatching his last melta bomb from his belt he primed it with a clunk. The star god opened its claw and the grenade flew from the strike master's gauntlets into the creature's enclosed fist. As the grenade detonated the Deceiver's hand glowed. It grew bright and then molten, streaming to the floor. Then it became a small inferno, a raging flame that swirled, resettled and resolidified into a cool, clenched fist once more.

Occam watched as the star god flinched. Several balls of plasma splattered, crackled and burned against the alabaster perfection of its chest. Occam looked up the steps to see that Vilnius Malik had returned. He was blasting his plasma gun at the abomination in an attempt to save his fallen strike master. The Deceiver hissed an ageless hatred at the legionnaire, turning him into smoking shadow smeared up the steps.

The legionnaire had not been alone, however. He had freed the Word Bearers and somehow convinced them that a far greater threat lay outside their ship than the Alpha Legion. Out of the darkness, the stuff of nightmares raged forth. The Varga Rax, led by Iaxor Phel and Captain Vhorpall, had regained some of their daemonic monstrosity. No longer the wasted specimens they had been on their journey across the nullified space surrounding the Galactic Core, the daemonic Word Bearers of the Varga Rax were blessed once more with incredible strength. Occam could only reason that with pylons collapsing across the surface of Royal Belphagar, both Quoda and the Word Bearers were regaining some revitalising connection with the warp.

Having seen the ineffectual nature of boltguns upon the star god, they rushed the monstrous creature with cursed blades and possessed weaponry. Storming the entity, the Word Bearers – red of warped muscle and plate – were like a swarm of attack dogs. The star god towered over the Traitor Space Marines, the same look of revulsion on its terrible face as it had reserved for the sorcerer Quoda.

As the melee swirled about Occam, it was all the strike master could do to back up the steps and feverishly reload his pistol. He heard a horrific shriek, a sound that caused his ears to bleed within his helm. It was the sound of a god in agony.

The Deceiver had knocked aside warped blades with telekinetic force and melted weaponry with a flash of its eyes. But rushed by so many Word Bearers, it had not been able to stop Phel's daemon sword Gorghastragar getting through. The blade opened the creature up across its thigh and the blinding light of a thousand suns blazed through from the gash. Even the filters cycling through Occam's optics couldn't shield him from the light.

The star god shrieked its alien rage, recognising the warp-channelling weapon as a real danger to itself. Silhouetted against its own brilliance, the creature's vengeance was swift and terrible. Knocking aside the vicious thrusts of Word Bearers weaponry and the slash of daemon claws, the star god laid its nullifying claw on the cursed plate of the daemon Word Bearers. The ceramite turned white hot to the touch, each suit turning into a raging furnace of purifying flame. The Varga Rax died one after another, spontaneously combusting and roasting in the flames of their own nullification.

Avenging his brethren, Captain Vhorpall slashed a monstrous talon at the creature's face. The star god drew back and glared down on Vhorpall with its eyes alight. The captain melted, drizzling away in a cloud of liquid ceramite and blood.

'Die, unnatural thing!' First Acolyte Phel roared, holding his daemon sword above his head with two hands. The star god reached out with a perfect white claw and laid it upon Phel's rune-encrusted breastplate. Seconds later, there was nothing left of the Word Bearer. Phel had simply exploded, his suit turned to shrapnel and his grotesque half-daemon body blazing away to nothing in a brief, blinding flash.

As the daemon sword clattered to the steps, the monstrous alien continued its rampage. Occam still lay before it. He grabbed something from his belt. The star god suddenly stopped and the strike master's head was filled with the excruciating sound of alien agony. The Deceiver stumbled. A blade was protruding from its midriff. The daemon blade Gorghastragar. Quoda had picked up the possessed weapon and plunged it into the star god's back.

The daemon writhed across the perfect flesh of the Deceiver, attempting to find some spiritual purchase but failing. The touch of the infernal beast was an anathema to the star god and for a moment the pair raged at each other.

Unable to seize upon a soul that simply wasn't present, Gorghastragar was forced to return to the cursed blade. The star god shrieked its pain and fury, causing the blade to melt and dribble down its brilliant white flesh. Turning with savage speed, the entity didn't even bother visiting its reality-bending powers on the sorcerer. It plunged a claw through the legionnaire's breastplate and tore his hearts from his chest.

As the dead sorcerer's body collapsed and tumbled down the steps of the pyramid, the star god turned back to Occam. The strike master was up on his feet.

'I have something for you, entity,' the strike master said. He pulled an object from his belt and threw it at the star god. The Deceiver caught the thing in its claw, believing the object to be another melta bomb. When the device failed to go off, the creature opened its claw. Inside sat the Tesseraqt, primed, opening, blazing with the green light of interdimensional incarceration.

An ageless snarl wrinkled the horrid perfection of the star god's face before being lost in the blaze of green light. Alien energies crackled and spat, arcing between the pyramid and the Deceiver, the sky and the storm. These grew to horrific intensity, as though the star god was fighting its imprisonment. Occam stumbled back, holding a gauntlet up before his optics.

A moment later, the star god was gone. The black cube containing its incarcerated form crackled with spidery green power and dropped to the ground. It bounced down the steps until it stopped at the foot of a figure advancing up the pyramid. The strike master realised that the hunched silhouette belonged to Omizhar Vohk. The alien machine picked up the Tesseraqt with a metal claw and approached Occam.

'You exceeded my expectations, strike master,' Vohk told him, the metallic hiss of his voice laden with an alien satisfaction. 'I would be sorry for the deceptions to which you have been subjected and the loss of your legionary kindred but for the fact that everything we achieved here today was absolutely necessary. That entity was a weapon that turned itself against my people. It would eventually have done to same to yours. Its lies would have destroyed us all.'

'And yet, it knew a great deal of the man I seek,' Occam said.

'Your galactic prince?' Omizhar Vohk said. 'Well, indeed. Are not the most effective lies laced with some element of truth?'

'Yes,' Occam said and completed loading his bolt pistol. Raising it, he coldly put two rounds through the metal skull of the alien techno-sorcerer. Like Quoda before him, Omizhar Vohk fell back and began to clatter down the steep steps of the pyramid.

Picking up the alien Tesseraqt, Occam made his way up towards the apex plaza where the *Dissolutio Perpetua* still remained in station. Bounding up the steps and with the hollow planet falling apart about him, the strike master opened a vox-channel with the bridge.

'Fire up the sub-light engines,' he ordered the command deck cultists. As he reached the top of the pyramid, he stepped through the airlock and into the ship. 'Reverse thrust. Back the way we came. There is only death to be found here. Even the world is dying. I have no intention of being buried here amongst these tombs.'

With satisfaction, Occam the Untrue noted the speed with which his order was obeyed. The *Dissolutio Perpetua* began backing towards the great opening in the planetary crust. The strike master watched Royal Belphagar tear itself apart from the inside. From the bridge of the Word Bearers vessel, he observed the ship's passage through the planet's surface and out above the ancient world of shattered pylons. The *Dissolutio Perpetua* was barely clear by the time the planet collapsed in on its unstable core.

'Course, master?' one of the cultists asked from the depths of its hood. The strike master didn't have an answer. He knew not where he was going or even what he was going to do when he got there. He held up the alien Tesseraqt. All he knew was that the black cube in his hand and the abominable entity within held such answers.

ABOUT THE AUTHOR

Rob Sanders is the author of *The Serpent Beneath*, a novella that appeared in the *New York Times* bestselling Horus Heresy anthology *The Primarchs*. His other Black Library credits include the The Beast Arises novels *Predator, Prey* and *Shadow of Ullanor*, the Warhammer 40,000 titles *Adeptus Mechanicus: Skitarius, Tech-Priest, Legion of the Damned, Atlas Infernal* and *Redemption Corps,* and the audio drama *The Path Forsaken*. He has also written the Warhammer Archaon duology, *Everchosen* and *Lord of Chaos* along with many short stories for The Horus Heresy and Warhammer 40,000. He lives in the city of Lincoln, UK.

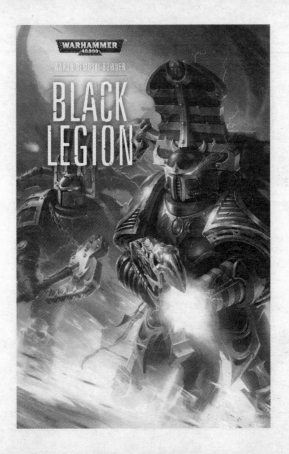

JOIN THE FIGHT AGAINST CHAOS
WITH THESE COMIC COLLECTIONS

WARHAMMER 40,000
VOL 1 / WILL OF IRON

GEORGE MANN
TAZIO BETTIN
ERICA ANGLIOLINI

WARHAMMER 40,000
VOL 2 / REVELATIONS

GEORGE MANN
TAZIO BETTIN
ERICA ANGLIOLINI

WARHAMMER 40,00
VOL 3 / FALLEN

GEORGE MANN
TAZIO BETTIN
ERICA ANGLIOLINI

WARHAMMER 40,000
DEATHWATCH

AARON DEMBSKI-BOWDEN
WAGNER REIS

BLOOD BOWL
MORE GUTS, MORE GLORY!

NICK KYME
JACK JADSON
FABRICIO GUERRA

DAWN OF WAR III
THE HUNT FOR GABRIEL ANGEL

RYAN O'SULLIVAN
DANIEL INDRO

7/18